SIGNATURE AFFAIR

LOVE, LIES and LIAISONS

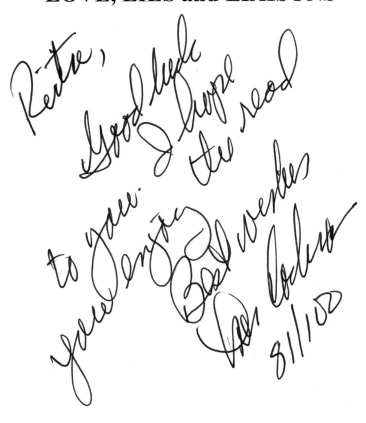

SIGNATURE AFFAIR

LOVE, LIES and LIAISONS

BY

LES COCHRAN

www.bookstandpublishing.com

Published by
Bookstand Publishing
Morgan Hill, CA 95037
3938_8

ISBN 978-1-61863-559-4

Library of Congress Control Number: 2013944128

First Edition

Printed in the United States of America

DEDICATION

To my mother, Dellcena Cochran, for her unwavering support and love. She never told me how to do anything; yet, I always did what needed to be done. Through her encouragement she motivated me to complete tasks and achieve goals that I thought were out of reach.

For most individuals that would suffice but not for her — she wrote the book. When she discovered in the fifth grade that I couldn't read, she took a part-time job at 40 cents an hour to pay for a tutor. She kept score at hundreds of my baseball games and charted shots at my basketball games. And when I arrived home four minutes late from a date, she glared from her favorite living-room chair.

She cheered when I won and hugged me when I lost. It didn't matter where I was, far or near, she pushed me to do more. Thanks, Mom, for always being there.

ACKNOWLEDGEMENTS

Special thanks to my wife, Lin, who encouraged me to write this book, and spent countless hours reading it and giving constructive criticism. And thanks, too, for reacting to the storyline, raising questions and editing it one more time.

I'm indebted to my editor Beth Rubin, whose knowledge of the craft of writing and perseverance pushed me to the brink — and sometimes beyond.

I am grateful, also, for the professional assistance of Dr. Francis R. Valenti and Eileen McBriarty who shared their professional expertise on addictive behavior.

My gratitude to the many friends who read and critiqued early drafts, especially Bill Abbott, Ginny Antonson, Barbara Bender, Tom Harte, Lauchette Low, Charlie McBriarty and Dick Reichow. Your efforts made a difference.

CHAPTER ONE

Fall, 1989: Drum rolls reverberated through the stadium. The crowd rose as former president Bill Thornton strutted down the red carpet. He held the university mace at a sixty-degree angle and directed it toward the stage.

The ovation echoed across campus as the procession of professors in their multi-colored hoods followed their outgoing leader.

Tall plants and vases of red and white flowers filled the stage for the inauguration of the president. Crews had worked for days to install a new sound system, add seating, and replace the goal posts with university banners.

A red carpet reached from the tunnel to the dais. After several years of Bill's Machiavellian planning, his protégé, Steve Schilling, would succeed him as president of Eastern Arkansas University. He congratulated himself on having single-handedly manipulated the system to achieve his goal.

The processional ended.

The board chairman stepped to the podium and acknowledged guests and dignitaries before delivering his laudatory introduction of the new president. His voice rose.

"Ladies and gentlemen, it is my distinct pleasure to present to you the ninth president of Eastern Arkansas University, Dr. Steven Schilling."

Steve rose and tipped his tam to the roaring crowd. "Thank you." He raised his head to acknowledge the faculty. "Thank you. Thanks, to all of you." He waved to the crowd and gestured for them to be seated.

After introductory comments, Steve moved to the talking points his mentor had crafted. He cited faculty, student and staff accomplishments then highlighted EAU's history.

1

Paying tribute to his mentor's twenty-five year career, particularly Bill's transformation of the small teacher's college into a major state university, he nodded to Bill in the first row. "Will President Emeritus Bill Thornton please rise?"

Bill got up. "We are gathered here today because of this giant of a man," he said. "In recognition of his leadership I am pleased to announce, on behalf of the Board of Trustees, that Old Main – the symbol of EAU – will now and forevermore be known as Thornton Hall."

Clapping and cheering, the crowd stood. Bill waved, tears flowing freely down his face. Steve wiped the perspiration from his brow and nodded to his mentor.

After proposing several new academic programs and heaping accolades on the faculty, Steve asked the faculty to rise. Smiling broadly, he unrolled a document.

"I am pleased to read the following proclamation. 'As Governor of the great State of Arkansas, I, William Jefferson Clinton, hereby authorize the establishment of the Governor's Scholars Program at Eastern Arkansas University. EAU will become the first state university to grant more academic full-ride scholarships than athletic scholarships.'"

Waving mortarboards filled the faculty section.

As Bill had instructed, Steve continued to bestow praise on distinguished individuals from the university hierarchy and the community. He singled out the Ruston girls' softball team which had recently won the state championship.

"In closing, I ask everyone to please rise." Steve paused while the sun-drenched crowd rose.

"On behalf of the University of Arkansas and Eastern Arkansas University, I am thrilled to announce that the state's two largest universities have agreed to a five-year football pact. In two years, the Rough Riders will play in Fayetteville, and seven years from today the Razorbacks will play right here in Howard Clark Stadium."

Thundering applause broke out.

The orchestra struck the Grand March. Bill rose and, carrying the mace high, led the recessional.

Knowing that he had nailed his speech, Steve absorbed the crowd's vocal support then spent the next hour acknowledging well-wishers before making his way to the reception center.

Bill hung his tam, hood and robe in the stadium's dressing room. The day had far exceeded his expectations. He had ensured his legacy, and he *knew* Steve would make an excellent president.

***

Bursting into his kitchen a few minutes later, Bill called out, "Sarah. Sarah, where are you?"

His housekeeper appeared from the utility room. "I'm here Bill."

"Stop what you're doing. Come have a drink with me."

"I'm finishing the laundry. And I need to start dinner."

"That can wait. I want to tell you about Steve's speech. He was spectacular."

"Okay, but your chicken and dumplings won't be ready until after seven."

"That's fine," he said. "Let's have a drink in the den."

After filling a glass with ice and gin he poured Sarah half a glass of Chardonnay. She had little tolerance for alcohol. "Here's to the successful presidency of Steve Schilling."

She smiled. "I'm so happy for you."

"I can see it now — all my dreams for the university coming true."

Bill took a long sip then joined Sarah on the sofa. "He had the audience in the palm of his hand. He spoke eloquently, and his delivery was flawless."

"I'm not surprised. He's very smooth. And he had an expert for a role model."

"He's signed a contract to play the Razorbacks. I never imagined …"

Sarah patted his hand. "Now Bill, slow down. Don't have a heart attack. Walk me through what happened, one step at a time. Tell me about carrying the mace. How did that go?"

"It was much tougher than I'd imagined. At first, fifteen pounds didn't seem like much. After a while I thought my arms would fall off. I hummed the fight song to keep my mind off the pain."

"Oh, my dear, would you like me to rub your arms?"

"No, they're fine now," he said, taking a sip. "We're going to have more academic full-rides than athletic scholarships. No other university in

3

the country spends more money on academic scholarships. The faculty ate it up."

"They should."

"And Old Main will be renamed Thornton Hall. Can you believe it?"

"That's wonderful, Bill." She leaned over and kissed him softly on the cheek. "You deserve it."

"I'm tuckered out from all the excitement. I'm going to take a nap before supper."

Reclining on the queen-size bed, he recalled how he'd begun his plan of deception, six years ago. He had hatched it the morning after being fêted on his 20th anniversary as university president. At the Ruston Country Club, Governor Clinton – dark hair slicked back, Hillary beside him – had presented him with an engraved plaque. "On behalf of the great state of Arkansas," Clinton began, "I am pleased to present this resolution for extraordinary leadership to Bill Thornton, the guru of higher education in our state."

Despite the barrage of backslaps and accolades, Bill's focus that night had remained on his wife, Virginia. He couldn't take his eyes off her. Her pale blue chiffon gown showed off her broad shoulders and décolletage. Though far from being the youngest woman in the room, her elegance drew every eye as Bill led her around the dance floor.

The next morning he'd glimpsed her without makeup, walking from the bedroom to the bathroom. She's still a natural beauty, he had thought. *The golden-haired girl I met and wooed in high school.*

"God, you're beautiful," he had said.

Long ago those words would have sent chills up her spine. But she failed to acknowledge the compliment — or his presence. He had betrayed her.

He deserved her fury but her rejection still stung.

He had walked over and kissed her gently on the forehead.

"Breakfast," she said coolly a few minutes later.

Over a western omelet with grits and toast, Bill chattered about the St. Louis Cardinal's poor spring record.

She said little.

He picked up the sports page, retreated to the den and sank into his favorite chair.

"Well, what's next?" Her abrupt entrance startled him.

He dropped the paper. "What's next about what?"

"The university. When you retire, who's going to succeed you? What are your plans? You just can't leave it up to the faculty. The place will fall apart."

Bill sat up and gave her his full attention.

"Will you work another five years then retire? I fear some outsider will come in, make a bunch of changes and undo all you've accomplished. It'd be a crime. Twenty-five years wasted."

"I hadn't thought of it that way," Bill fibbed. In fact, he thought of his retirement daily. Letting go would be the most difficult thing he'd ever done. Being in control drove him. Yet, he knew time was running out. He would have to step aside.

She stood over him. "What about Brian Anderson? Or, Ernie Minelli?"

"Mm, maybe."

Virginia raised her voice. "Well, if not them, who?"

"I've been thinking about Steve Schilling. He's inexperienced, but very smooth. He's articulate and everyone likes him. Some even say he's a lot like me."

"But Bill, you know he has a problem. Do you think he can keep his pants zipped?"

"I think he'll be okay. Suzanne is strong. She'll keep him in line."

"I'm not so sure. You can't put off a decision much longer." Virginia stormed out, her footsteps rat-tat-tatting on the parquet.

Bill picked up the paper then threw it down in disgust. Once again, she was right.

***

Ruminations over a possible successor stressed him. He had trouble sleeping; his appetite had gone south. Virginia's hounding chipped away at his usually calm demeanor. He could count on her daily assaults.

"Bill, have you made up your mind? What's your plan? Have you picked a successor?"

One morning, while pouring coffee, he caved. "I can't procrastinate any longer."

Virginia smiled for the first time in weeks. "It's been hanging over my head like Damocles' sword. I've made a decision."

She sat on the edge of the sofa. "Well, let's hear it."

"I've scrutinized everyone we've discussed. I even considered Ed Conley. None of them stacks up to Steve Schilling. He's stronger in every leadership category. It doesn't hurt that he played football here. Plus, he has Suzanne. Her political connections are considerable."

"True. And they seem to have a strong marriage. They share similar values and they're active in the church. I think they'd make a great team. But I still have misgivings about his behavior."

Virginia walked across the room then turned. "For now, I'm willing to set that aside until I learn more about his personal life. What would it take to groom him?"

Bill scanned his notes, buying time. He knew from experience that his wife was just warming up.

"He needs to work on four areas. We need to get him involved in the right social events from here to Little Rock. And ..."

Virginia interrupted. "I'll take care of that. I'll meet with Suzanne. In three years she'll have him prepped. Shoot, in five years she could have him running for governor."

"Slow down. He hasn't been named president yet. He has to be perceived as a leader on campus. Involvement in the community is a must." Bill stroked his chin.

"Next, he needs experience with athletics so the boy's downtown will support him. And, we'll have to beef up his fundraising credentials. If he appears credible against the other candidates, I can do what's necessary with the Board."

"How long will it take?"

Bill ran his fingers through his hair. "Normally, I'd say anywhere from ten to twelve years."

Virginia pursed her lips. "I knew we should have started sooner," she said adamantly. "Can you whittle it down?"

"Maybe we could do it in eight years. The toughest part is his lack of administrative experience. I can't control who's going to retire."

"I think we should aim for six. What's next?"

"Okay. But it's a long shot."

Bill grimaced. "I'll invite him over for a drink Monday afternoon. I can probably get through my agenda in two or three sessions. Maybe by

Christmas we'll be ready for the four of us to have a set-down meeting. You know … talk about the plan and make sure we're all on the same page."

***

Steve Schilling parked his red Mustang convertible in Bill's driveway. At thirty-six, he was in top-notch condition — the perennial college jock.

Owing to regular workouts, 200 pounds were equally distributed on his broad-shouldered, 6'2" frame. Square-jawed, he sported a five-o'clock shadow.

He wore his dark, wavy hair combed straight back from a widow's peak. Though not traditionally handsome, he attracted others (especially the ladies) with his warm brown eyes.

Virginia greeted him and led him to the sunroom before disappearing.

"Hi, Steve. Have a seat. How about a drink?"

"Sure. What are you having?"

"Tanqueray on the rocks with three jumbo olives."

"I'll have the same."

Bill poured the gin then set Steve's drink next to a dish of cashews. After rehashing a senate report on tenure, Bill asked, "What would you like to see happen in athletics over the next eight to ten years?"

Steve reached for some nuts. "Well …"

Bill sensed Steve's discomfort, seemingly preventing him from being candid. "Speak your mind, Steve. I want to know what you think."

Steve perked up. He spoke about the need for a football training facility and more stadium seating. "Games should be broadcast on TV in Memphis. We need to go Division I, and someday play the University of Arkansas."

Bill leaned forward. "Sounds like you've given a lot of thought to athletics."

"I have, but it's just one piece of the puzzle. Ten years from now EAU can be much bigger and better. You've done a fantastic job, don't get me wrong."

"No offense taken."

"We're good. But we can be great. I bet you had similar thoughts twenty years ago."

"Sure did." Bill glanced at his watch. "I can't believe it's after five. We'll have to end it for now." They got up and moved toward the door. "How about meeting in two weeks? Same place, same time?"

"Sure, I look forward to that."

Bill paused. "Don't do anything I wouldn't do."

Steve gave Bill a quizzical look then ambled to his car. Bill felt uneasy. Steve's words were politically correct, but his body language told a different story.

When Virginia came in from errands an hour later, Bill had already set the table. "How did the meeting go with your fair-haired boy?" she asked.

"More than ever, I feel he's the right person. He has a strong sense of direction. I'm thinking about naming him as the university NCAA faculty representative. What do you think?"

"Sounds like you've already made up your mind." She shrugged. "I suppose he'll do fine as the rep. But remember, that's only one step."

***

A week later, the men sat across from each other in Bill's office. "Steve, I was impressed with what you had to say the other day about athletics. We need fresh ideas around here. I'd like to appoint you as the NCAA faculty rep. What do you think?"

Steve wore a blank expression. "Well, of course, if that's what you want."

"Understanding athletics is fundamental to a president's success. Most people don't get it. Boosters rarely grasp the whole picture. They see sports as merely something exciting to rally around. They have no idea of the complexity or volatility. And then there's the faculty. They whine about the financial resources consumed by athletics. It's a dichotomy you need to understand."

"I know, Bill. And I admire how you've been able to balance it over the years."

Bill nodded. "We can talk more about that later. What's your vision for EAU? What do you see happening over the next ten years?"

Steve appeared flustered. "I don't have the foggiest notion."

"You must. Don't try to second guess me or figure out what's in my head. I want to know what you think."

8

Steve opened a small, black notebook and took a deep breath. "First and foremost, the campus needs a strong leader to continue your legacy. He must know the community, athletics, and have a big-picture plan for the future."

Steve paused to catch his breath then pressed on. "We need an academic plan. Ph.D. programs should be added along with undergraduate options in health care and computer science. We need to go high tech. Then, there's Memphis. We should be there every day, recruiting and fundraising. It's our future."

Steve laid his notebook down and swallowed hard. "What do you think?"

"That's quite a dream." Bill got up and topped off his drink.

"It's not a dream. I can make it happen."

Through the sunroom window Bill gazed at Old Main, silhouetted by the setting sun. "We'll have to stop. Virginia and I have a social obligation."

He extended his hand to Steve then, without knowing why, hugged him. "You're absolutely right. It can happen."

Bill visualized Steve in a navy blazer and gray slacks strolling across campus. The son he'd never had — his clone. He heard the garage door open and close.

Virginia breezed in with her arms full of groceries. He helped her put them away. "How did your meeting go?" she asked.

"He's the right guy. He wants to do the things I've only dreamed of."

"That sounds wonderful, Bill. But what about his philandering? I know I've been harping, but we need to learn the truth. If his reputation is half as bad as I think, it will be a deal-breaker."

"Jesus, Virginia. What do you want? Do you expect me to ask him, 'Are you screwing around?' Do you think he'd give me a straight answer, knowing I'm considering him as my successor?"

Her face reddened. "Yes, I do expect you to ask. I can't believe you'd ignore such a potential bombshell. You're so analytical and thorough about everything else. The last thing we need around here is someone else who can't keep his pants on."

Bill bit his lip and drew blood. He knew nothing could be gained by rehashing his indiscretion of twenty years ago. He licked his lip.

"Okay. What do you suggest?"

"Well, for starters, what about Kate Blanchard?" Virginia spoke with renewed verve. "They were an item in college."

His temples pulsated. "So what? Maybe they're just friends."

Virginia slammed her palm on the table. "Puhleeze. You can't be that naïve. He's been married for fifteen years."

"Okay, you win. I'll ask." He'd never struck her but he felt like doing so. He couldn't recall when she'd aroused his ire so much.

***

The two men had their next meeting a few days before Thanksgiving during a freak heat wave. Bill poured two iced teas and led Steve out the back door to the deck.

Steve paused to admire Bill's garden. "How do you find time to grow such perfect roses?"

"Like anything that's important, you make it a priority." Bill sat in a swivel-rocker shaded by the large green umbrella. They had settled into university small talk when Bill found the gumption to broach Virginia's concern. "Steve, Kate Blanchard's name has popped up. What can you tell me?"

He sputtered, his face reddened. Bill allowed him time to clear his throat and regain his composure.

His voice a whiny pitch, Steve answered. "Kate had it all. She was my dream girl. I almost married her. But it didn't work out."

"Steve, I have to be candid. It's difficult for me to ask this but I must. I can't retire then kick myself because I didn't ask the tough questions."

"I understand. It's your responsibility." Steve paused. "You know, I'm committed to the university, too." The afterthought rang hollow.

"Do you still see Kate?"

"Nah. I … I have to be honest with you." His head dropped to his chest. "I cheated on Suzanne when I was working on my Ph.D. in Knoxville. When I completed my degree and came home, I told Kate we were done as a couple. That was twelve years ago."

"And that's it?" Bill spoke slowly. He felt uncomfortable with Steve's fidgeting and lack of eye contact. "Your car has been spotted at her place several times."

Steve's voice rose. "Geez Bill, I told you. It's over. Kate had car problems. I lent her my second car. Loaned a car to my friend. That's all we are. Friends. You can check it out with Ruston Ford."

Bill glanced down at his Mister Lincolns. "Steve, I had to ask about Kate. I had to hear it from you."

"I know. I would have done the same. Bill, you've done a wonderful job at the university. I would never do anything to harm or jeopardize its reputation."

"I appreciate that." Bill sighed. "Thank you for your candor."

***

Bill and Virginia took their places at the table. She dished out a tuna casserole. "I had a good meeting with Steve. Asked him about Kate Blanchard."

Virginia took a bite of salad, but didn't look up.

"He told me the whole story," Bill continued. "They had an affair when he was in grad school. He had a plausible answer for every question."

Virginia glared. "Of course he did. What are you going to do?"

"I'm moving ahead. He's got the right stuff."

"What about my concern?"

"It's not a problem. He had an affair. It ended years ago. I told him that he has to be careful. He can't afford to be seen in what might be perceived as a compromising situation."

Virginia shook her head. "If he stayed home at night where he belongs, he wouldn't have to worry. He'd have nothing to hide."

"Well, you know what I mean."

Virginia's voice rose. "And you know what *I* mean. It's going to be a problem. You're out to lunch if you think otherwise."

Bill bristled. Hating confrontation, he said nothing.

"Well, what about his infidelity? You're going to ignore it?" The woman was a terrier.

Bill turned abruptly and spoke through clenched teeth. "Virginia, I told you I have made my decision."

Her lower lip quivered. She met his stare then blinked.

"Okay, if you insist. You're the president. I'll schedule a meeting with the Schillings during Christmas break."

Virginia, ever the gracious hostess, welcomed the Schillings two days after Christmas. Steve joined Bill at the dining room table while Virginia and Suzanne chatted in the foyer.

Suzanne had a pert, round face. Her dark-rimmed glasses complimented her short bob. Her bubbling personality served her well as EAU's Director of Public Relations. A spunky go-getter, she had long been one of Bill's favorite people.

When Virginia and Suzanne came into the dining room, Bill hugged Suzanne. "That's a lovely scent. What perfume are you wearing?"

"Trésor. Steve keeps me in Trésor."

"How thoughtful. I like it." He gave Steve thumbs-up then sat at the head of the table. Sounding like a strict disciplinarian, he said, "I'm sure this is unnecessary, but I'll say it anyway. Nothing said here today can ever be repeated. Ever."

Bill made eye contact with each one and waited for their affirmative nods. Droning on for an hour, he outlined each step that had to be completed before Steve's appointment.

Wrapping it up, he said, "No one can ever know what we've done to, um, facilitate the process. Everything must appear to be routine. I'll schedule quarterly meetings with Steve as the NCCA rep so we can talk. Suzanne and I will meet bimonthly to discuss PR. Any questions?"

Everyone kept silent. "Good, that settles it. Let's have a drink."

CHAPTER TWO

"You've done a great job publicizing the university, Suzanne."

"Thanks, Bill."

"You'll be a tremendous asset for Steve."

"I hope so."

Bill handed Suzanne the state government handbook.

"I'd like you to pick two or three committees — at least one that's sexy — where Steve would be a good fit. I'll push him from my end. My thinking is one appointment this year, one next."

"Will do. And I'll slip his name into the next press release to make him look like a mover and shaker."

"Perfect." Bill pushed his personal calendar toward her. "Use this as a guide for next year. Steve needs more exposure. It'll be a good template."

She ran a finger over January. "You sure have a lot of meetings."

"That's only the tip of the iceberg. Check the weekly schedule in the *Daily Gazette* and reserve key dates. Pick a couple of biggies. And throw in a social club or two."

***

On Valentine's Day Steve went to Bill's office for his first faculty rep meeting. Bill dispensed with the pleasantries in short order.

"I've given a lot of thought to your vision for athletics. You're right about playing Western Kentucky, UAB, and Louisiana Tech. But before we can recruit top players we have to upgrade our football training center."

Bill gazed out the window overlooking the quad. "And … I want to build a new football stadium. It will be the capstone of my career."

13

Steve dropped his pencil. "That'd take at least ten years."

Bill sat down then rocked back in his chair. "We're going to do it in five."

"Five?" Steve's eyebrows shot up. "I don't mean to be disrespectful, but …"

"I read an article recently about PERT. It's a planning system used by the Navy. They tackle various projects simultaneously. Their projects are running months ahead of schedule. We can do it, too, and shave off years."

Steve shook his head. "You lost me."

"Here's the plan. I'll set up a meeting with Howard Clark in Blytheville. He played tackle for Ole Miss. He must own fifty gas stations between St. Louis and Birmingham. I figure he'll spring for a million if we put his name on the training center. Martha Brown in the state office says it'll take $2 million. I can raise the other mil."

"Sounds like a super-ambitious strategy."

"That's only the beginning. I want you to call Martha. She knows everything about athletic facilities. Remember she's the tall redhead who set all the women's basketball records at Arkansas? Her picture was plastered everywhere when you were in college."

Steve nodded. "I remember. She was a knockout."

"Let her know you're going to be our point man. Once you've learned the state procedures we'll be off and running. Any questions?"

"No. I, um … I guess I understand."

Bill raised his voice. "Steve, I don't want to hear any of that 'I guess so.' There's no room for that kind of talk. You're going to be a leader. You have to take charge."

"But I can't keep up with your agenda — learning state procedures, raising money, building new facilities. I've never raised a red cent. How can I possibly oversee the construction of a training center?"

"One step at a time, my boy."

Steve saluted. "Yes, sir."

Steve reminded Bill of his younger self — wet behind the ears, yet passionate and driven.

***

After introducing himself to the receptionist, Steve thumbed through *Time*. At 10 o'clock the door opened. Smartly dressed in a form-fitting charcoal gray suit, the statuesque woman extended her hand.

"Hello, I'm Martha Brown. But, from now on it's Martha."

Tall, slender, and with a sprinkling of freckles, she had a youthful demeanor that Steve found charming. And sexy.

He followed her into the small, cramped office and sat down. "I understand you're interested in building a football training center. What size facility do you have in mind?" she asked.

"Nothing specific. We're still planning. I can give you an overview."

"I'd like that."

During his spiel, Martha nodded frequently. From the way she leaned forward and repeated his phrases, Steve deduced that he'd made a favorable impression. "Once we build the training center, upgrade our schedules and construct the stadium, we'll be able to take on the big guys."

"You're not wasting any time. Are you aiming for Division I?"

"We haven't addressed that question yet."

She fixed him with her gaze. "What do you know about training centers?"

"A lot." He puffed up. "I played football at EAU."

"Oh, I mean *building* training facilities. You know — building codes, square-foot allowances, equipment specs — that kind of thing."

Steve looked up sheepishly. His cheeks flushed. "I don't know much. But I'm a quick study."

"Don't worry. When I started I didn't know much either. What do you teach at EAU?"

"History." He sounded ashamed.

"No problem. I majored in social work. If I can learn this stuff, anyone can." She pulled two manuals from the shelf. "Sounds like we need to get you on a fast track. Ready to start?"

"Sure. You're the professor."

She grinned. "I like that. Okay, here's the plan."

***

While driving to Blytheville, Bill gave Steve a mini-course in fundraising — how to plan a request, make the ask and close the deal. When they arrived at the country club, Howard Clark was standing at the bar.

An imposing figure with thinning gray hair, he slapped Bill on the back. "How ya doing? Want a drink?"

"Sure do. But first, I want you to meet Steve Schilling. He's our new faculty rep."

"I read the story." Howard turned to Steve. "Hey, you look better than your picture."

"Thanks." Steve followed Bill and Howard to a corner table overlooking the golf course. "My daughter Christina and her husband Eric are still playing," Howard said. "I've asked them to join us when they're done. It's important for Christina to listen in. She'll be running the business in a couple years."

"Of course." Bill nodded.

"Good," Howard said. "Let's order. I'm starving."

The men were finishing their lunch when Christina and Eric arrived. One of the town's few female physicians, Christina headed the internal medicine group at Blytheville Memorial.

Her husband trailing, she was dressed in a designer golf outfit and showed no signs of fatigue — or exertion. Bill watched as Steve looked her over. *I'll have to speak with him.*

After introductions, the couple sat down.

"Well Bill, what's on your mind?" Howard asked.

"You may recall our conversation last year about building a football training facility. Well, it's time. In fact, it's probably past time."

"See, Christina, I told you he was after your money," Howard said.

She smiled in a forced way. Eric seemed preoccupied with a foursome on the 18th hole.

Bill sat upright. "Our football training center used to be an old dining hall. The ventilation system is awful. We need a state-of-the-art facility with the latest technology."

Steve chimed in. "That place was bad when I played."

"I'd like to build something better than Fayetteville's." Bill slowed, trying to read Howard.

"I need a $1 million matching gift from you. We'll call it the Howard Clark Football Training Center. What do you think?"

16

Howard glanced at Christina. Bill had instructed Steve to keep quiet. After the ask, the ball was in the donor's court. Steve swallowed, fidgeted with his pen then glanced at Bill whose gaze remained fixed on Howard.

Howard pressed his lips. "Bill, I love the sport. But I think we need to build a facility for more than football. Christina reminds me that things have changed. I never thought much about fair and equitable treatment, but she's right. Short answer, yes. We need to build a center for the entire athletic program. How much do you think something like that would cost?"

"Off the top of my head, I'd say $3 million."

Howard turned to his daughter. "What do you think, sweetie?"

"Done. We'll match the $1.5 million, one for one."

"Deal," Bill said. He leaned over to pump Howard's hand.

"I think we should call it the Christina Clark Athletic Training Center."

"Perfect," Bill agreed.

After a celebratory drink, the group parted.

As soon as Bill pulled onto the street, Steve began waving his arms frantically. "I can't believe it. I can't believe it. Did you see how casually she flipped out $1.5 million?"

"I saw it. I was wondering if you noticed anything other than her ass."

***

Steve heard Bill's raised voice and what sounded like a fist crashing on the table. A few minutes later two vice presidents filed out of Bill's office, heads low. Perhaps, they'd endured a tongue-lashing too. Bill waved Steve in and closed the door.

"Damn vice presidents. I've yet to meet one who could make a decision." He turned to Steve. In a gruff voice he asked, "What do you have to report?"

Steve hesitated. "I've been thinking ..."

"Well, that's good. Don't keep me in suspense. Speak up. I have a speech at noon. How's it going with Martha?"

"We're making great progress. When I first met her, she seemed naive, like a country bumpkin. Boy was I wrong. She's got a tiger in her tank. She guided me through the state procedures. Last month I went to Fayetteville. In January I'm meeting some national consultants at the NCAA convention. I think we're ready to name the advisory committee."

"Good. Draft me a statement outlining the committee's charge and give me a few campus names. I'll appoint you chair, then add Christina and a couple of the downtown boys."

Steve shifted. "You expect me to run the committee? I've never chaired a group like that." He sputtered. "I won't be able to answer any of their questions at the first meeting. I have no idea how big the center will be, what it will cost or where it'll be located."

Bill scowled. "Cool your jets. First, you know I'm committed to $3 million. That's the bottom line. Second, Martha has a cost-per-square-foot formula. Just divide the $3 million by the square-foot cost and you've got it. And remember, every chance you get, tell folks that no university dollars will be spent on the project. I don't need any asshole faculty on my case."

Bill paused to catch his breath. "Now, stop and think. Where's the most logical place to build it?"

Steve shrugged his shoulders. He spoke haltingly. "North of campus? Where the new student parking lots are being built?"

"Of course. Just north of there the hills form a natural bowl. I've paced it off." Bill laughed. "See, you had the answers in your head. You need to think before you spout off."

* * *

Bill sat down with a legal pad and pen to list Steve's tasks for the upcoming year. They'd be singing "Auld Lang Syne" at the country club in a few days.

Hearing footsteps in the hall, he looked up as Virginia passed by in her robe. He glanced at his watch: 10:20. It wasn't like her to sleep late.

He followed her to the kitchen and filled his mug. Out of the corner of his eye, he watched her move slowly to the sunroom and ease onto the sofa. "Are you okay?"

"A little tired. I guess I'm whipped from all of the holiday parties."

"You look pale. Maybe you should make a doctor's appointment."

"I'm okay. I'll stop by Dr. Peterson's later and get some vitamins. My annual physical is in six weeks. What have you been doing this morning?"

"I made a list of projects for Steve. He's off to a great start."

She folded the paper. "Really? Seems to me he's been following you around like a little puppy dog."

He gritted his teeth.

***

Bill waited in the kitchen for Virginia to return from her physical. He'd been worried sick about her. Taking more vitamins had done nothing. If anything, she had less energy. She often fell asleep after dinner. And during the day she complained of not feeling rested. He heard the garage door go up.

She came in the kitchen door and fell into his arms. "Virginia, what is it?"

She wriggled free. "I don't know yet. I've lost a couple of pounds. The doctor wants to run a few more tests." She hung up her jacket in the hall closet.

"What kind of tests?"

"Standard stuff. Cholesterol. CBC. Chest X-ray. I've scheduled them for after Easter."

She slipped off her shoes and stretched out on the sofa. "Be a dear and get the afghan off the bed." Her voice was weak.

"Sure, anything else? Want some hot tea?"

"No thanks."

Bill tucked the afghan around her. "Thank you," she said softly. "I didn't mean to scare you. I'm sure it's just a virus."

"I hope so."

"I've been thinking about doing something different for Easter. I'd like to invite Sarah over for dinner. Molly, too, if she's home. What do you think?"

Bill squirmed. He couldn't imagine the prospect of Virginia and Sarah fixing a meal together then eating at the same table.

Virginia had been cordial to Sarah for the twenty years she worked for them, but she'd kept her distance.

"Sure, if that's what you want, dear."

Virginia sat up. The color had returned to her cheeks. "Yes, that is what I want. I'll call Sarah tomorrow."

Gritting his teeth, Bill wondered, what's gotten into Virginia?

***

Following Easter services, Virginia and Sarah worked side by side like long-lost buddies — chopping, mixing and tasting. A slender black woman in her mid-fifties, Sarah had an aristocratic bearing and wore her hair in a sleek bun. She had always been deferential to Virginia; and Virginia had always treated her with respect. But this was something different.

Virginia began asking Sarah questions, as if she were interviewing her for a magazine feature. "What did you like to do when you were a girl? Where have you traveled? What TV programs do you watch? Where do you shop?"

While he watched TV with Sarah's nephew, Jimmy, Bill scratched his head and wondered, *What the hell is going on?* Sarah had raised Jimmy, her sister's son, since her sister's death two years after Sarah began working for them. Jimmy had been a fixture around the house since he was three.

At first, Virginia had been skeptical that Sarah would perform her duties fully with a youngster underfoot. But the child was well-behaved and entertained himself with crayons and coloring books. And he loved to read.

Bill bought Jimmy the latest children's books and sometimes played Double Solitaire with him. Before Jimmy could pronounce "President Thornton," he called him "Mr. Bill." The name had stuck.

Molly arrived and slid a bottle of champagne in the freezer. Her long, dark hair spring-curled over her light-skinned black shoulders — her figure more perfect than when she was a cheerleader in college.

After helping her aunt in the kitchen, Molly set the table. "Mr. President, could you open the champagne?" she called an hour later.

"Sure, Molly. We've known each other a long time. I'd prefer it if you'd call me Bill."

He filled the glasses and joined the women in the dining room. Raising his glass, he said, "Here's to the best cooks in the world."

Bill led the prayer, the same one his father and grandfather had recited. Jimmy piled his plate with ham, sweet potatoes, greens, biscuits and five-bean salad. Before the others had made a dent, the teenager dug in for seconds. Bill looked lovingly at Jimmy. He'd matured into a fine young man. "Hey Jimmy, want to watch the Celtics game?"

"Sure do. Is it okay?"

"Virginia, will you excuse us?" Bill asked.

Without meeting his gaze, she replied blandly, "Of course."

"We'll be back for some warm pecan pie," Bill said on his way to the den.

Virginia poured a splash of wine for each of the women then turned to Molly. "Now that you're a VP at FedEx, what's next in your future?"

Molly creased her napkin. "Every time I overcome a hurdle, two more surface. I've probably peaked in the organization."

"You need to continually better yourself," Virginia said. "Have you ever considered coming back to EAU?"

"Not really," Molly said. "Sometimes I think about getting out of the corporate rat race. If I went into higher education, I'd have to get a doctorate."

"Maybe so. But a Ph.D. would offer expanded opportunities," Virginia said. The two talked like mother and daughter. Virginia probed and offered suggestions. Molly smiled and nodded.

Bill woke early in the fourth quarter. "Damn." He had missed almost half the game. Jimmy was gone. He yawned, ran his fingers through his hair and went to the dining room. Like magpies, the women continued to chatter. Dirty dishes littered the table. He eyed a second empty wine bottle. "Hey, what happened to the pecan pie?"

***

Bill stood on his redwood deck gazing at the Ozark fieldstone path traversing his rose garden. He recalled that Easter, now four years ago. Soon after the gathering with Sarah and Molly, Virginia had been diagnosed with Stage IV, pancreatic cancer.

A second opinion at MD Anderson in Texas confirmed the diagnosis. They had spent Virginia's last weeks going through their photo albums, reminiscing about their courtship and marriage, and listening to their favorite recordings by Bing Crosby, Rosemary Clooney and Perry Como.

He thought of Virginia's twinkling blue eyes and how the wind blew her golden hair when he put the top down on his Chrysler Le Baron convertible. *God, she was beautiful.* A tear trickled down his cheek as he looked at Virginia's yellow Peace roses and his Mister Lincolns.

He would never forgive himself for inflicting such pain on her. His flings and affairs were unforgivable.

How many women had there been? He had lost count. As far as he knew, Virginia had been aware of only one.

He went inside to answer the ringing phone.

"Bill, this is Howard."

"Good to hear from you."

"How are things going?"

"Hmm, okay."

"You don't have to pretend with me. How are you really doing?"

"I'm still struggling."

"I understand. I remember what I went through when Millie died. With all due respect to Virginia, you need to move on. Start dating …"

Bill squirmed. "I have zero interest."

"Well then, get involved in something exciting."

"Like what?"

"Build that stadium you've always talked about."

Bill's mood brightened. "Sure. I'll run a campaign, raise $15 million, obtain in-kind commitments from local contractors and install the turf. Then I'll be the next Pope."

"You don't have to lay the turf. And frankly, I can't picture you in a miter and robe."

"Where would I find the stamina to take that on?"

"Stop right there. If Virginia were alive you'd be asking me for a $2 million naming gift. Right?"

"Well, maybe"

"No maybe about it. I'm certain. Let's cut to the chase. I'll give you the damn $2 million. You announce your campaign and name that Schilling fellow and me as co-chairs."

"Steve? He's not ready."

"Christina thinks he's a mover. With your help, he'll look ready."

"I can't do that. It'd be a sham."

"So? You're in the smoke-and-mirrors business. Your dream comes true. And Schilling will be groomed to replace you."

"Where did you hear that?"

Howard chuckled. "You just told me."

"Why don't you come over Saturday after the game? I'll do ribs and we'll talk more."

"Thanks, Howard. You're a lifesaver. I'll bring your German beer."

CHAPTER THREE

Steve smiled to himself, knowing he'd be with Kate in a few hours. Bill breezed in, out of breath.

"Sorry I'm late. I … I have some bad news — very bad news — from Howard Clark."

"What is it?"

"Eric was killed in a hunting accident. The sheriff in Missoula called Christina this morning."

"My God. What happened?"

"That's all I know. Howard said he'd call later."

Steve shook his head. "I'm in shock. Just last month Suzanne and I were Eric and Christina's guests at the Hospital Ball. They seemed like a close and fun-loving couple. I'll send a note, of course. Anything else I should do?"

"Hold off for now. I'll keep you posted."

"Sure. By the way, Christina is doing a superb job on the committee. She met with an equipment manufacturer at her expense. And last week she picked up the tab for the design group's trip to Dalton to pick out carpet."

Bill waved to the waitress. "Let's order. I have two meetings this afternoon."

"Poor Christina. She must be devastated."

They ordered eggplant Parmesan.

"Remember when we talked about PERT?" Bill asked.

"I do."

"We need to crank it up. I want to raise $15 million and get the stadium plans approved. Construction must begin within eighteen months."

"Why take so much time?" Steve jested.

"Check in with Martha. Make sure you're up to speed on architect selection and bidding procedures. We need to push hard on the silent phase of the campaign. I want to have at least $9 million in the bank before we announce."

"Nine million?"

"The success rate is much higher when you have 60% in hand before announcing."

"Should I get started on a campaign flyer?"

"No, no." Bill frowned. "Campaigns start at the top. I'll have Carol schedule you into my meetings with the big hitters. We need to get 80% of the campaign dollars from them. Once two or three donors are onboard, the rest will fall like dominos."

Steve clasped his hands together. "Sounds exciting."

"Well, enough of that. What's happening on your end?"

"The athletic director sent out a needs assessment. We had follow-up meetings with the coaches. If we do everything the coaches want, the training center will be bigger than the stadium."

"Welcome to administration," Bill said. "There's one more thing on my list."

Steve grinned. "I was hoping you'd have something to keep me busy."

"I want you to ask Howard Clark for a $2 million naming gift for the stadium."

Steve looked shell-shocked. "You gotta be shittin' me. I can't do that."

"Sure you can. Just follow my lead. After a few meetings, you'll be up to speed. You can start by making a couple of $100,000 asks, maybe one for $250,000."

"How about we start at $25,000?"

"That'd be a waste. Once you've nailed a few donations the amount doesn't matter. We'll double-team Howard. I'll describe the stadium. Then you can make the ask."

"Hmm, I don't know."

"Say whatever you want. Suggest he do it for me, for the good of the country. I don't care. Now go home and collect your thoughts. Practice with Suzanne."

***

Hands shaking, Steve flipped though his notes one more time. Bill took the Blytheville exit and drove to the country club. Pine boughs and wreaths decorated the exterior. He set the brake and turned to Steve.

"Ready?" Steve seemed paralyzed. "Steve? Wake up. It's show time. Give me your notebook."

Reluctantly, Steve handed over his bible. Bill ripped out the notes and returned the cardboard cover.

"Jesus, Steve, you're sweating like a hog." He handed Steve a pocket square. Steve mopped his face and straightened his tie.

"Just be yourself. This is between Howard and you."

Bill lagged behind. Steve's shoulders rose as he approached Howard's table. The men shook hands. "How's Christina doing?" Steve asked, softly. "I'm so sorry about Eric."

"Thank you. Christina is much better, thank you. It'll take time, but she's over the initial shock. She sends her regards, and says she'll be at the next committee meeting."

"Good. We've missed her." They picked up their menus. "What do you recommend?" Steve asked.

"The teed-off burger is excellent. I like the Reuben, too."

"Sounds good to me," Bill said to Howard.

Conversation centered on the upcoming football season. Bill spoke of his dream for a U-shaped, 20,000-seat stadium with corporate loges, a reception area, and a connecting walkway around the top.

He winked at Steve.

Steve took a deep breath. His posture straightened.

Making eye contact with Howard, he began his pitch. "Nothing on campus is more important than building a new stadium. A gift from you would be a tribute to Bill and a powerful statement that you believe in EAU's future. For $2 million we'd name it Howard Clark Stadium and locate the training center at the open end. It would be an extraordinary complex," he said without taking a breath. "The best in Arkansas."

Steve paused to let his words sink in. "Howard, would you honor us by making a $2 million naming gift?"

Bill read relief on Steve's face. He sat still and waited.

Howard gazed at the golf course. "I like that. Yes, I'll do it."

"Yahoo!" Steve exclaimed then covered his mouth. "Sorry," he said, rushing around the table to pump Howard's hand.

"Forget it. You just got $2 million."

Howard caught the bartender's eye and snapped his fingers. "We need a drink."

***

Steve kicked off his shoes and sank into the sofa. Suzanne laid her paperback aside. "I can't wait for spring break. We've been on a treadmill forever."

"Can't remember the last time we had a free evening. Between Bill and Martha Brown, I don't have time to think," he said.

She looked at him with tenderness and patted his arm. "I've been thinking, Steve. I'd like us to renew our vows. How do you feel about that?"

"I-I'd never thought about it. Well, maybe …"

She planted a kiss on his cheek. "Steve, I love you."

The phone rang before he could say more. He shuffled in the kitchen to pick it up.

"Steve, Dean Harte in performing arts called a few minutes ago," Bill said. "He has a problem. I volunteered you, said you'd be glad to help out."

"Sure," Steve said. Cradling the phone under his chin, he raised his hands in exasperation.

Suzanne frowned and mouthed, "Who is it?"

Steve rolled his eyes, and covered the mouth piece. "Bill."

Bill went on. "Harte is searching for a chairperson in music. He has to find someone before the end of the school year."

"Why the rush?"

"Professor Schultz broke his leg skiing and will be out six weeks. I told Dean Harte you'd be glad to fill in as the outside rep. It'll be good visibility for you with the arts faculty."

His reply was flat. "I'll call him in the morning."

***

"I can't thank you enough for helping us out," Joe Harte said. "This department has given me grief for years. We need some new blood." He handed Steve a stack of papers. "I've made copies of the candidate files. The committee is meeting next Wednesday."

After staying up half the night to review the files, knowing he couldn't squander his first opportunity, Steve willed himself through the committee meeting, and went home.

He was barely in the door when Dean Harte called. "Steve, I hate to impose on you, but I need you to meet with Sandra Whitehead. She's our first choice. Take her somewhere nice for lunch. Have a glass of wine. We need to make a good impression. And time is of the essence."

"How about Molino's?"

"Excellent choice. I'll drop her off at the restaurant around noon next Friday."

***

The dean's car pulled up. Steve stepped from the shade of the canopy and opened the passenger door.

"Thank you," Sandra purred as she took Steve's hand and stepped out. She was dressed for success in a dark pinstriped suit, her blonde hair in a chignon. His pants bulged.

The waiter guided them to a table next to the small fountain in the courtyard. "How lovely," she said. "It feels like we're on the Riviera."

"It's not the Côte d'Azur, but they have the best French food in town."

"I love French cuisine. I studied at the Conservatoire National in Paris."

"I know," he said, holding up her résumé.

"Yes, sorry," she said, burying her head in the menu.

Steve smiled.

***

Bill strolled toward his protégé, approaching from the direction of the rotunda. "Let's walk over to the stadium site. We can talk along the way." He didn't waste any time. "I liked the confidence you demonstrated last week. And, nothing wrong with receiving $100,000."

"Thanks. It felt good," Steve said. "Sometimes I'm flying by the seat of my pants and feel as though I'm about to crash. When the donor says yes, I'm on an extended high."

"That's normal. Each time it gets easier. Anything else we need to talk about?"

"Not much. Dean Harte hired Sandra Whitehead. She has a degree from Juilliard. She'll be a valuable addition. I especially like that she's not full of herself like the other candidates."

"I heard she was very talented."

Bill stopped at the top of the hill and gazed into the bowl carved by nature. "Can you imagine in two years the stadium will be there?"

***

In late July, with the thermometer threatening to shatter a 100-year record, Steve lugged boxes of display materials in prep for the summer trustees' meeting. He turned to get the perspective from the audience before stepping onto the dais.

After checking the placement of the trustee's chairs and making adjustments, he returned to his seat. Minutes later Christina took her place beside him.

The gallery filled with members of the community and the media.

Precisely at 4 o'clock, President Thornton and the trustees filed in. The chairman gaveled the meeting to order, fulfilled his perfunctory duties and announced, "The first item of business is the approval of the Christina Clark Athletic Training Center."

Bill nodded to Steve who rose and walked to the podium. "Dr. Schilling would you provide an overview of the project?"

"Yes, thank you, Mr. President."

Steve introduced the committee, presented a special resolution recognizing Christina and the Clark family, then co-presented the proposal with the architect.

The board quickly approved the plan.

Bill strutted like a peacock to the podium. "Mr. Chairman, on behalf of the Board of Trustees I'd like to read the following resolution commending Dr. Steven Schilling for his outstanding leadership." The crowd stood and applauded. The committee members congratulated each other as they left.

***

28

Christina and Steve chatted on their way to the parking lot. Fumbling for his keys, he said, "Let's celebrate. How about a drink?"

"Well, I ... Sure, why not?"

"Super. I'll meet you at the Holiday Inn in fifteen minutes."

Steve arrived first; went straight to the bar and eased into a booth. Minutes later Christina joined him. They ordered drinks and made small talk.

"You've been through so much. I can't imagine. How are things going?" he asked.

Tears stained her rouged cheeks. "Oh Steve ..." She pulled a tissue from her purse. "It's been awful. I still can't believe Eric is gone. After nine months the pain is still unbearable. And there's nobody I can talk to. Eric was my best friend. I told him everything."

"You can talk to me," Steve said, sliding his hand across the table and squeezing hers.

"Thank you," she said, blotting her cheek. "It was so unexpected. I had looked forward to doing so many things with Eric." She broke down.

"Let it out," he said, folding his hands on the table.

Christina pressed her fingers against the back of his hands. She rambled on about Eric, how they'd met and their marriage. After a second drink she began sharing details that would have been better left unsaid. She told how Eric had demanded sex, whether she was in the mood or not. As a husband, he said he was entitled to it — whenever and wherever.

Steve squirmed. Aside from Suzanne and Kate, he had never discussed intimate matters with anyone. He slid his hand on top of hers.

She withdrew her hand, placing it in her lap. "That's not a good idea," she said.

"I didn't mean to offend you."

She paused for what seemed like an eternity. "What do you think about Memphis?"

Steve swallowed. "I love it. I'd live there if I could."

"I go every fall, stay at the Peabody, shop and get my fill of barbecue. And my favorite French restaurant, La Table d'Or is there."

"Maybe we could have lunch on your next trip."

She smiled. "I'd like that."

***

Steve glanced at the paintings and fresh-cut flowers in the elegant restaurant.

"Bonjour Monsieur. Madame is waiting." The maître d' led him to a corner banquette.

Christina's shiny, dark hair caught the reflection from the crystal chandelier. Steve eyeballed the Belle Époque French décor. It was too rich for his taste — but he wouldn't dare admit it.

"What do you think?" she said.

His eyes landed on her décolletage spilling from the off-white, scoop-neck blouse. "I think you look wonderful."

She waved her hands. "I mean the restaurant."

Glancing at the impressionist paintings, he knew he was out of his league. "It's very pleasant."

He asked her to help translate the menu. "Everything sounds delicious. Why don't you select for both for us?"

"Fine." The bow-tied waiter returned. "For hors d'oeuvres we'll have pâté aux herbes."

"Excellent, Madame."

He filled their champagne flutes with a 1989 Veuve Clicquot Ponsardin. "Santé."

Steve felt like a king. And Christina, he thought, was classy but not ostentatious. She wore simple jewelry and light makeup.

The waiter refilled their glasses and presented the pâté. "Bon appétit."

Christina nodded. "For entrée we'll have sole amandine and salade verte."

After a pleasant lunch they sipped espresso and chatted like old friends. "There are several ladies' boutiques not far from here. Would you like to go with me?"

"Sure, I love to shop."

"You what?"

"Yes, unlike most men, I like to shop."

Steve followed her into a high-end boutique, applauding or giving a thumbs-up each time she appeared in a different outfit.

He filled her trunk with bags, boxes and dress bags then followed her to the Peabody in his car. They caught up in the Peabody's cavernous lobby and sank into overstuffed chairs.

The sound of gurgling water from a Romanesque fountain soothed. He gazed up at the oversized columns and crafted beams in the three-story atrium — a far cry from his stays in Holiday Inns and Ramada's.

Christina sipped an Absolut on ice; he, his gin with stuffed olives.

They talked about their travel experiences, food and sports. During a lull she smiled, inclined toward him and asked if he'd like a private fashion show.

Steve sprang up. "I'll get the check."

She licked her lower lip. "I've taken care of it."

They walked in silence to the elevators. She opened the double doors to the penthouse. He took in the chandeliers, period furnishings and damask-covered walls.

Christina opened the hallway closet and withdrew a blue satin dress. "I'm going to try on this one. The champagne should be chilled. Would you pour us some?"

Steve did as he was told then sat at the small table in the living room. The late afternoon sun streaked in.

The bathroom door opened.

"Showtime," she said.

"God, you're beautiful."

When Steve started to get up from the silk French provincial chair, she pushed him back with a gentle but firm touch.

She sipped champagne then turned to face him. His heart raced.

"Well, what do you think?" she whispered in his ear.

"Perfect. A 10 … The dress is nice too."

Laughing, she pulled him from the chair, ran her fingers through his hair and kissed him gently on the cheek. He kissed her hungrily then stepped back.

"You're a very special person," he said, pulling her to him.

He slid his hands around her waist; his fingers inched up her back. Her head relaxed on his shoulder and she moaned. Steve could feel her heart pounding.

Slowly, he unzipped her dress and let it fall to the floor.

CHAPTER FOUR

Autumn leaves crunching under his feet; Bill crossed the quad to Dean Browning's office. He walked in, grabbed a Krispy Kreme and sat down. "Well, Richard, the marathon is over."

"I have to hand it to you, Bill," his old friend said. "You took a small teacher's college and made it into a major university. Saturday's reception was a small token of the university's appreciation. The *Gazette* photo said it all — your hands joined with Steve's in solidarity."

Bill nodded. "Thank you. I'll remember the reception for the rest of my life. But you know me, I'm never satisfied. I've been thinking ..."

"I figured you didn't come here just for the donuts."

"You're right. I've been reviewing the presidential selection policy."

"I remember fifteen years ago how you insisted on adding 'highly qualified, open process, highest integrity.' Right?"

"Good memory." Bill paused, searching for the right words. "There's something else."

"What's that?"

"There's a potential flaw in the policy. We need to fix it."

The dean scowled. "A flaw in the policy approved by our expert? I can't imagine. What's the problem?"

"It doesn't spell out how the list of finalists should be submitted to the board. It gives the committee too much discretion. Hell, they could place the names in rank order or write narratives for each candidate reflecting their preferences. The board should have complete freedom to pick whomever they want."

"I agree."

"Richard, I've talked to Jack Bradley, the board chairman. He's going to make you chairman of the presidential search committee. A wise and experienced dean like you can clarify things. You know … make sure everything's kosher. There can be no strings attached to the names in the final group."

Dean Browning's stern look morphed into a smile. The men shook hands.

***

Browning greeted the committee members in the anteroom then followed the last straggler into the small conference room. After grabbing a glass of water, he took his place at the head of the table.

"Let's begin with brief introductions." He nodded to the man on his right. When the last person had spoken he passed around ten folders.

"There are a few points I'd like to emphasize. We all know that rumors spread like wildfire on campus. We can't afford any leaks. It's imperative that we maintain the highest level of confidentiality. Am I clear?"

He extracted a nod from each person.

"Second, there's a copy of the selection policy in your folder. Please read it later. Then read it again." He paused, smiling to himself. "There are three phrases I'd like to emphasize." He defined them and stressed their importance.

"And last, by May we need to provide the board with a list of three to five finalists. Each candidate must be acceptable to us. The names will be placed in alphabetical order so the media can't read anything into our recommendations. Any questions?"

Silence.

"Good, let's get started."

***

Bill heard a soft knock on his office door and looked up. "Come in and have a seat, Steve. I'll be with you in a minute."

Steve took his usual place and began fiddling with his fingers.

Bill signed a letter then gave Steve his full attention. "Thanks for coming by on such short notice."

Steve grinned.

"I've wanted to speak with you about the search committee meeting on Monday. We have to change our strategy."

Steve stopped fidgeting.

"We must stop meeting so frequently. We can't afford a hint of impropriety. During the selection process everyone will be looking at us through a microscope. We can't toss the faculty the tiniest crumb of doubt."

Steve nodded. "I understand."

Bill sat across from his protégé. "Good. Let's move on."

Steve took out his notebook.

"You'll be the only local candidate. As such, the media will phone you every time there's a hiccup on campus. You have to be vigilant. You can't say anything that might be misconstrued. Do you understand?"

"Yes, I got it."

"No driving infractions. No partying …" Bill's voice trailed off. "Don't let yourself be drawn into petty controversies. And always take the high road."

"Of course."

"In the final weeks rumors will fly. People may say nasty things about you. Don't take it personally. And, for heaven's sake, don't lose your cool. You could blow everything with a benign, off-the-cuff remark. You must act presidential. Am I clear?"

"Yes, sir. I have it."

***

Committee deliberations took five months, eating up most of the spring semester. Steve followed Bill's instructions to the letter.

No sparks ignited.

After the board received five names, legal counsel conducted background checks. Four days later the board went into executive session.

Suzanne and Steve waited at home for the results. Suzanne wiped the kitchen counters numerous times after dinner. Steve opened a second bottle of wine. A little after 9 o'clock the phone rang. Steve scrambled to pick it up. "Hello," he said, hesitantly.

"It's Bill." His voice a whisper. "You got the job."

"Oh my God." Steve gave Suzanne a thumbs-up. She ran over and hugged him.

"Steve, Steve, can you hear me?" Bill asked.

"Yes, I can. I'm in shock."

"Never mind that, just listen. I'm with the board chairman. He's already called the media. In twenty minutes the board will come out of executive session. They have to vote in public. The two of you need to hightail it over to the university center ASAP. Slip into the rear of the gallery. There's going to be a celebration."

***

Bill closed the door to his office. The two embraced. Bill placed his hands on Steve's shoulders. "Well son, how does it feel?"

"I'm numb."

"That's normal." Bill smirked. "Right now you're in dreamland. But you can't afford to linger. It's time to start thinking about your transition."

"Transition? I was just appointed yesterday."

"There is no time to waste. You must get started." Bill got up and paced. "First, Carol's the best. Down the road there'll be times when she'll be the only person you can trust. She'll protect you."

"Good, I like her — and she seems highly professional."

"Absolutely. She'll be unwavering in her commitment to you," Bill said. "Second, people will see you in a different light now that you're president. Friends may treat you differently. Remember, you're not different. You simply have a new job and title. So don't change. Once your friends see you as the same guy they've known for years, they'll support you all the way."

Steve nodded. "What else?"

Bill went to the window then did an about-face. "Today everyone is on your side. But with every decision you make, your list of detractors will grow. Regardless of your successes they'll be waiting, ready to pounce."

Steve frowned. "Why?"

"Trust me. They'll be laying in the weeds. You have to build a team to counteract the bastards. Start right away. Meet with the deans and vice presidents. Go to their offices. Reach out. You'll score major points."

While Steve rubbed his forehead, Bill pressed on. "In the fall do the same with all the directors and department chairpersons. Meet in their offices — on their turf. They'll eat it up."

"Bill with all of the meeting and greeting that could take all semester."

"Probably so. Get used to it. You need them on your side. And don't lose sight of that." Bill paused. "Remember, people will always be evaluating you, taking notes, checking on your comings and goings, who you talk to, and how you walk. They'll be watching what you eat and how much you drink." He chuckled. "It's strange. They want you to be successful; yet, they'll be looking for flaws — something, anything that might bring you down."

Bill glanced at his tattered chair and the chipped paint on the wall. "That reminds me. I've made noises about sprucing up this place for years. I've been remiss. I'll have Mary Ann Kellman in the interior design program make suggestions for getting this place in shape. When the samples and swatches are ready, I'll give you a call."

"Thanks, Bill, I appreciate that."

"And last, it's not too soon to start thinking about your inauguration speech. It's a leadership opportunity. People want to see you in action. Your comments should touch everyone — faculty, students, staff and people in the community."

"Thank you. I'll get on it." Steve stood. "Bill, there is something on my mind that's very important to me." He took a deep breath. "I want to continue our quarterly meetings. I'd be lost without your guidance."

"I appreciate that. But when I walk out of this office, I don't intend to stop by on a regular basis. Besides, it wouldn't look good. People need to see in charge."

"I understand. But I still need your advice. Could we meet at your house?"

"I don't know …"

"Please." He sounded like a teenager pleading for the keys to the Cadillac. "At least through the rest of the year. We're only talking about seven months."

Bill sighed. "Well … okay."

***

Summer rain pelted the window in Steve's den. For five long months he'd lived in a fish bowl, weathered jabs and deflected low blows. He thought it had been more grueling and exhausting than the six years of Bill's Gestapo training. The faculty seemed to delight in dropping innuendos about Kate. He wondered where they got their information.

Some friends — at least, those he had thought were friends — waffled or abandoned him to support another candidate. Suzanne fussed over him and seemed to derive pleasure in telling him he'd aged ten years.

Glancing at the *Daily Gazette* headlines plastered on the wall — SHILLING NAMED PRESIDENT — he laughed. "We outfoxed the bastards."

He'd never imagined such an outpouring of public support — hundreds of letters, an interview by an anchor for Memphis TV24, and numerous receptions hosted by faculty and friends.

Cards and notes covered his desk. Each required a response. His mother had always said, "Its common courtesy to thank someone who took the time to write." He signed and sealed one more thank-you note.

Suzanne cracked the door and poked her head in. "I'm going grocery shopping. Want anything?"

"No. I'm gonna have one of the cigars your daddy gave me, then get ready for poker."

"Good luck, dear. I hope you're a big winner."

Steve pulled a Balmoral Torpedo from his desk. Picking up a beer and a damp rag to wipe the patio furniture, he went outside. He kicked off his shoes, propped his feet on a chair, lit up and took a couple of drags.

Watching the smoke trail, his mind drifted to the women of his life. He had tried to end his affair with Kate when he and Suzanne got engaged. He tried again, and failed again, after their wedding. No breakup lasted more than a few weeks.

Over the last twenty years he had stopped questioning himself. His unconditional love for her outweighed any misgivings. He suffered no guilt when he was with Kate. And he loved Suzanne too. He needed both women. That was justification enough. He chugged his beer, snuffed out the cigar and changed for poker.

Heading toward the country club, he slowed at an intersection, turned down a side street and pulled into Kate's driveway. She flew out of the house, wrapped him in her arms and planted a big wet kiss on his cheek.

"Oh, darling, I'm so proud of you. I could kiss you all over."

"That can be arranged. I've missed you so much. It's been crazy."

She pulled him into the house and slammed the door. They kissed wildly on their way to the couch where he pulled her down beside him and caressed her.

Kate ran her fingers through his hair then straddled him. She loosened his belt and pulled out his shirttails as he pressed against her. She tore off her sweatshirt and undid her bra.

Steve massaged her back then pulled her closer. His tongue circled one nipple. He sucked the other. She moaned.

He clenched his teeth, willing himself not to come too soon.

Kate jumped up, and slipped off her jeans and panties. He pulled off his slacks and boxers. Back on top, she fondled his hairy chest.

He pushed into her then thrust deeper. Her hot body slammed against him. Steve gasped then found her rhythm. He grabbed her hips and pulled her closer then slowed.

Kate kissed his ear and teased, then shoved harder. Steve pushed against her again and again. Kate clawed his shoulder. They came together.

"I love you," he said.

"Love you too."

Steve ran his fingers around her lips. They snuggled and talked about what might be. "There are so many places I want us to go after we're married," Kate said. "It may be a cliché, but I'd like to see Niagara Falls."

"Your wish is my command." Steve kissed her on the forehead.

The corners of her mouth turned down. "Oh Steve, I wish you could stay all night."

"So do I. Be patient. Someday we'll be together forever."

"I can't wait."

***

Steve ducked into the men's room to freshen up and check his zipper before joining his friends for their bi-weekly game at the country club. They welcomed him with good-natured jabs about playing poker with the Prez.

"You guys will always be my friends as long as you stay regular." They laughed and joked. Steve pocketed $25. On the way out, he said, "If you turn into pompous Ph.D.'s you can kiss my ass goodbye." The group roared.

Lightening flashed in the distance. Steve pulled into the garage as the clouds opened up.

Walking into the kitchen, he filled an old-fashioned glass with ice and Amaretto. He stopped by to check on Suzanne. Seeing her asleep, he picked up his drink, walked into the study and flicked on the desk lamp.

Sipping on his Amaretto, he thought about Kate. He recalled the night they first did the deed; he'd caught the game-winning pass. She'd been the captain of the cheerleading squad. Every guy on campus wanted to get in her pants.

They'd connected at a victory party and drove twenty miles to a motel. Within minutes he was inside her. She was all over him. He gave her three — or was it four orgasms? *God, she was good.*

Steve smiled to himself then downed the Amaretto. He stretched out and dozing off, he saw Christina — running, waving and laughing. Before he could reach her, the clouds opened up, drenching him to the bone. She pulled off his soaked shirt and jeans. He felt her warm hands caressing him, her body sucking him in.

He saw her standing in the shower, her hands resting on the tiles, water dripping from her nipples. He eased behind her, massaged her shoulders and back before moving south … they rode toward the barn, and once inside, they rolled in the straw, laughing and kissing like teenagers. She unbuttoned his shirt, caressed his chest and loosened his pants. She fondled and teased.

Thunder crashed. Steve sat up, his shirt soaked. He wiped his face on his sleeve; his gaze landed on the photo of Christina and Howard taken at the ground-breaking for the training center.

Thinking back six months to Memphis, he couldn't imagine life without her. He'd become a regular at her estate — riding, walking through the meadow and sunning on the deck.

Her intelligence was an aphrodisiac. She had exciting ideas about things he'd never thought of. And he felt comfortable with her, as though he'd known her forever. He wanted to be with her night and day.

Feeling that familiar ache, he called out, "Christina, I love you."

CHAPTER FIVE

Kate threw her arms around Steve. "Darling, I've missed you so much. It seems like an eternity since we've been together."

"I know. And I've missed you desperately. My life has been nothing but work the past month. I had no idea what I was in for."

Wearing a petulant expression, she freed herself. "Sometimes I wonder where I rank on your to-do list."

"Kate? How can you say that? I adore you.?"

She pressed her fingers over his lips. "Let me finish. When you walked in the door I wanted to grab you and jump into bed. But Steve, I'm so frustrated. Now that you are the president there's no reason why things can't change. I don't want to spend the rest of my life as 'the other woman.'"

"Kate, you're everything to me."

She cut him off. "Hear me out. Have you ever thought about what my life is like when you're out and about, going to fine restaurants, doing exciting things ..."

"Kate, that's not fair. It's part of my job."

"I understand. And I know you're exhausted when you go home." Her tone changed. "To Suzanne."

He looked stricken. "You rarely call and say, 'Hi sweetie. How are you doing? I'm on the run. I just wanted to say I love you.'"

Steve lowered his head. "You're right. I've been so caught up in the transition ... I'm sorry."

"When you're out gallivanting, I'm home reading or watching a dumb TV show. I don't have a lot of friends. It's lonely. Yes, I date occasionally, but it means nothing. It's just something to fill in the time. I would never cheat on you."

"Kate, I know it's hard. Give me a chance to make things better. How about a trip to Chicago, just the two of us?"

"Chicago? Really?"

"I'm attending the North Central Association summer meeting in two weeks. Bill told me it's a must. He made a reservation for me at the Marriott on the Magnificent Mile. Please come with me. Think of it — Neiman-Marcus, Saks Fifth Avenue, the museums. We'll have a ball. And wait until you see the restaurant list Carol is putting together."

"But you'll be working."

"Only a couple of hours a day. You can go to the spa. The rest of the time we can have fun."

She hugged him. "That sounds fantastic. I'm sorry I was tough on you. I'd like to kiss you all over."

"Well ... I don't have to play poker."

Kate planted a kiss on his cheek, pulled him into her bedroom and tossed the bedspread on the floor.

***

Steve's thoughts ricocheted from Kate to his inauguration speech. He had less than three months to prepare. How would he find the time to do a decent job with his crazy schedule and also put a smile on Kate's face?

He heard Bill's words again, and again: "Son, your first speech will be the most important of your presidency."

Steve flew up the backstairs of Thornton Hall and burst into his office. Pausing at Carol's desk, he blurted, "Here's your first assignment."

His super-efficient assistant wore her hair in a bob with bangs that made her appear much younger than her fifty-nine years. "Okay. I'm all ears."

"I need a grabber for my inauguration speech, something that will get everyone's attention — students, faculty and the community. Do you have any ideas?"

"Sure," she said without hesitation. "The stadium. Everyone is talking about it."

"The stadium?" He scratched his head. "That's it?"

"Yes, that's it."

"Of course," he said, as if he'd known the answer all along.

42

Later, at home, he jotted STADIUM on a sheet from his legal pad. It landed in the round file. Then he drew a large U on a blank page. Around it he wrote: STUDENT, FACULTY, FRIENDS, COMMUNITY.

Unable to make a connection, he crumpled the paper and threw it at the wall. He closed his eyes and breathed slowly. Nothing came to him.

He scrawled: PEOPLE and STADIUM. The connection between fans and football is obvious, he thought. But what else? He stared at his empty iced-tea glass as if it held the answer.

Banging the desk with his fist, he shouted, "I've got it. Razorbacks. Play the Razorbacks."

Feeling proud of himself, he clasped behind his head and rocked back in his chair. *Could I pull off such a coup? How?*

On his notepad, he wrote, "Call Martha Brown."

The next morning he picked up the phone and called.

"Good morning, this is Steve Schilling at EAU."

"Yes, Mr. President ... congratulations," the receptionist said.

"Does Martha have any time this week? I need to see her. It's very important."

"She's booked solid and she'll be out of town next week."

He listened to dead air.

"Excuse me, could you hold for a moment? I see her coming down the hall."

"Sure," he said, perspiration dampening his forehead.

He waited.

"President Schilling, you're in luck. She said to pencil you in at 4 o'clock on Thursday. Can you make it?"

"Yes, I'll be there."

                                    ***

Steve arrived fifteen minutes early with a red rose for Martha's administrative assistant. Martha rushed in out of breath in gray slacks and a navy blazer. "Are we celebrating something?" she asked.

"President Schilling gave it to me — for scheduling an appointment with you."

"How thoughtful." Martha caught his eye. "Congratulations, Mr. President."

"It's Steve," he said, following her into her office. "Thanks for making time for me."

She sat on the edge of her chair and wasted no time with chitchat. "Okay, what's so urgent?"

"I want to talk about EAU playing the Razorbacks in football."

Martha rolled her eyes.

"Play Arkansas? Surely you jest." She shook her head. "Steve, you did a wonderful job on the training center and the stadium. But a game with the Razorbacks … that's out of the question."

"Not so fast. At least hear me out."

She nodded. "Okay, you have my full attention."

"Playing Arkansas is about more than football." He paused to let his words sink in. "It's about the university. Our programs are accredited just like theirs. They play out-of-state Division II schools. And, it's a big deal when they win. Why shouldn't they play us too?"

"Steve, you don't understand. Arkansas has nothing to gain and everything to lose."

He bristled. "Because they think they might lose against us?"

"That's not the point."

"What is the point?"

"Steve, let's revisit this sometime in the future. Not now."

He raised his voice. "Leadership is about timing. Leaders make the time right. They don't wait for things to happen. In a few months I'll give my inauguration speech. It'll be about the future. Martha, the future is now."

Her eyebrows shot up. "Now that's the most logical thing you've said." She glanced at her watch. "Look, it's almost 5 o'clock. We're not going to resolve this today."

"I have to drop a report at John Ferguson's by 6:30. I have over an hour free. Why don't we have a quick drink and wrap this up?"

"Steve, Arkansas is …"

He stood up. "An hour. One drink."

"Okay. I guess I can spare an hour. McCabe's Pub is three blocks away, at the corner of Capital and Slocum. Meet me there in ten minutes."

"Sure. I know where it is."

***

Peanut shells littered the floor. Beer signs, college banners and posters of Ireland covered the walls. The bartender called out, "Hey Martha, want a Killian's Red?"

She glanced at Steve. He nodded. "Make it two, Rick." She picked a corner booth then excused herself to go to the restroom.

On an adjacent wall hung a signed photo of Martha receiving an All-American plaque. Next to it were shots of her Olympic team and Martha shaking hands with Governor Clinton. *She was some looker. And she's still hot.*

The bartender brought the beers. Watching her ramrod posture as she approached, he wondered what it would take to loosen her up.

She sat down and they clinked bottles. "Here's to you, Mr. President." With a flirtatious smile, she said, "Okay, let's hear it. Why should the Hogs play the Rough Riders?"

He ticked off the reasons then came in for the kill. "It's about stature, recognition, enrollment and fundraising. Playing the Hogs validates EAU. It raises our image in the public eye."

The bartender brought two more beers. "It's on the house."

"Steve, Arkansas has no interest in validating EAU. Why would they? You're the new kid on the block. And you're competing for students and resources. It's not going to happen."

He tried a different tack. "Fine, let's drop it for now. Tell me about Martha Brown."

She looked surprised. "There's nothing much to tell. I grew up in a small town in Oklahoma. And always wanted to play Division I basketball. Our coach sent my video to a coach he knew at Arkansas. Next thing I knew I was on scholarship, playing for the Razorbacks. I worked hard — and here I am."

"Being an All-American and competing in the Olympics takes a lot more than hard work."

"Want another round?" the bartender asked.

Steve glanced at his watch. "It's 6:20. I have to go."

"I'm sorry. Sometimes I talk too much. You didn't get anything to eat."

"I'll grab something on my way home."

"Why don't you stop by my place? I'll cook a couple of steaks. You can have a quick bite and be gone."

45

"That sounds good. I'll phone you if I'm running late."

She jotted directions on the back of her business card.

***

Steve rang her bell an hour later. She answered the door. While still fluffing her hair, she said, "I returned a few phone calls. Time slipped away. I haven't even unwrapped the steaks."

"No problem," he said. "Where did you get that beautiful squash blossom necklace?"

"At a Navajo reservation outside of Albuquerque when we played the University of New Mexico."

"It's very distinctive. And the color matches your sweater."

"Thank you. I don't wear a V-neck often, but ..."

"You should. You look very sexy."

She blushed. He imagined her naked, writhing under his caresses. He held up a gift bag. "I picked up a bottle of wine. How about a glass before we eat?"

"Sure. But I'll start the steaks first," she said on her way to the kitchen.

"Slow down," he said, taking her hand and guiding her to the pass-through between the kitchen and dinette. "Sit down and relax. I'll pour the wine."

She eased onto a counter barstool. "The glasses are in the cabinet next to the refrigerator. There's a corkscrew in the drawer beneath it."

Steve opened the Merlot and filled their glasses. Raising his, he said, "Here's to the most professional businesswoman I've ever known."

Their eyes met. He felt a jolt pass between them.

"I left something outside," he said. "Just a minute. I'll be right back. Close your eyes."

Steve returned with a box from the florist which he placed before her. "Okay, you can look now. It's a little thank you for all you've done."

She untied the satin ribbon and opened the box. Leaning over the red roses, resting on a spray of baby's breath, she inhaled their fragrance.

"No one ever gave me roses," she said, her voice quavering. She picked up her glass. "Here's to you, Mr. President." She kissed him lightly on the cheek.

"Thank you," he said.

"I'll start dinner."

"Sure, let me help. Can I make a salad?"

"The fixings are in the crisper drawer."

Steve joined her in the galley kitchen. After putting together romaine, tomato, celery and green pepper in a wooden bowl, he rubbed against her hip on his way to the fridge for dressing.

He admired her curly red hair. *How long before I find out if she's a natural redhead?* he mused.

He knew better than to grab her. In their six-year association, she'd never given him a signal. At first, he thought she might be gay. Now, he seriously doubted it.

He leaned over to gently kiss the nape of her neck. Her broad shoulders twitched.

He backed off.

Martha took a deep breath, turned off the broiler and faced him. She kissed him softly on the cheek then moved to his lips.

Draping her arms over his shoulders, she pulled him tight against her and whispered in his ear. "This will not get you a game with the Hogs."

CHAPTER SIX

The early morning sun reflected off the dome. Perched on a ridge near the Mississippi, the campus overlooked Main Street's pizza parlors, bookstores, mom-and-pop shops, and an Art Deco movie theater

Staff stocked shelves at Woolworth's and Lowenstein's. At the corner pharmacy, Doc Peterson greeted customers by their first names, as he had for decades.

Pickups filled the lot outside Frank's Diner at the south end of Main Street. The small café had opened in 1964 and, except for the new roof added during Governor Clinton's first term, little had changed.

Customers squeezed past the counter stools to reach the scratched-up wooden tables and worn, red-vinyl booths. Near the entrance, the Wurlitzer flashed psychedelic colors and Kenny Rogers twanged, "Know when to hold 'em."

Some good ol' boys at a corner table shook their heads, pointed fingers, and jumped on each other's remarks. The topic didn't matter. If it had to do with change, they didn't like it.

Toting coffee mugs from home, they showed up early every Saturday and rarely left before eleven. They wailed about big government and welfare programs. Today's headline about the inauguration gave them something to chew on besides their Skoal.

A geezer with a flattop droned. "Can you believe it? After a national search and spending thousands of dollars, they chose a local history professor."

"Yeah," one bib-overalled farmer said. "And those are my tax dollars."

Across the table, a plaid, flannel shirt weighed in. "Hey, did you read about that sociology professor with tenure? He doesn't want to be evaluated. Thinks the world owes him a job for life."

"I don't understand how Bill Thornton put up with all that crap. He did a great job," said a clean-shaven gent who looked like the small-time accountant he was.

The tall fellow at the end of the table chimed in. "How about that football team? Looks like another championship. They should be playing the Razorbacks."

"Hell, the Razorbacks wouldn't play us. They think their shit don't stink."

***

Steve Schilling stepped out of his shiny, cobalt-blue Cadillac, straightened his red EAU tie, buttoned his jacket and, looking very presidential cruised into Thornton Hall.

Unlocking the office door, he whiffed fresh paint and newly laid carpet. He eased into the black leather chair and gazed across the cavernous room at Bill's favorite wing-back, reupholstered and trimmed with brass tacks. The upscale drapes and cornices added a touch of class, he thought.

He checked the events on his desktop blotter-calendar and looked over the pink message slips stacked neatly by the phone. The mail had been categorized into three piles — junk, correspondence and unopened personal — just as Bill had instructed.

He glanced at the large framed photo of Suzanne on the credenza then turned to his desk, and gazed at the smaller picture of his mother in a white dress, standing in front of their house. Behind her was the swing that hung from the old oak in their yard.

He felt wistful recalling his youth in eastern Kentucky. After his father died, his mother had sewed for the neighbors and taken in laundry to make ends meet. She often told Steve and his siblings — a sister and brother — "We're not poor. We just don't have any money."

Dad worked the coal mines. When he died, nothing much changed. The town had one less drunk.

Poor mom. The white dress had been a present she had received the day before Thanksgiving of his junior year in high school. A blaring car horn had drawn him to the front door.

"Mom, it's Uncle Freddie," he had shouted.

His father's younger brother had driven up from Corbin in a 1960 Oldsmobile. "Dottie, are you there?" Freddie called.

She dabbed some lipstick on her pale lips and arranged her hair to cover the thin spot on top, then welcomed her brother-in-law. She pecked him on the cheek and gave him a hug.

"I just robbed Kroger's," he blurted

"You what?" He popped the trunk. It was filled with groceries, a turkey wedged in the corner.

Her hand flew to her mouth. "Freddie, you shouldn't have."

"That's for me to decide. It's my pleasure." He withdrew a football. "Steve, this is for you. Go out for a long one." He tossed the ball to his nephew.

"Thanks Uncle Freddie."

"Good catch ... Dottie, I have a present for you too." He handed her a floral sleeve, stapled along the edge. She peeled the green tissue paper as if it held a fragile jewel then sniffed the red rose

"Freddie, it's beautiful. I'll put it in water right away."

The men unloaded the trunk. Freddie placed a large box on the kitchen table. "What's this?" she asked.

"It's for you. Something special."

She undid the ribbon, removed the wrapping and pulled out a white-lace sundress. Holding it up, she danced around the kitchen.

Steve had never seen his mother so ebullient.

"Let's have some champagne," Uncle Freddie shouted. He pulled a bottle from the refrigerator.

"Where'd that come from?" she gasped.

"I slipped it in when you weren't looking. Steve, get us three glasses."

Steve wrinkled his nose. "I don't want any. And I'm late. I'm going to Johnny's for dinner and to stay over. I want to watch the Lions play the Packers tomorrow on their new TV."

Steve placed two juice glasses on the table and headed for the door. "Is that okay, Mom?"

"I don't think so. We have a guest."

"Please?" Steve pleaded.

"Your uncle drove a long way to see us. It would be rude to leave now."

Freddie interceded. "Let the kid go. I'll be here all weekend. Steve and I will go fishing one day."

She caved. "Well, I suppose."

She turned to Steve. "But I want you home as soon as the game ends. I'm fixing a big Thanksgiving dinner. And there's nothing worse than dried-out turkey."

"Don't worry, Mom. I'll be here." He said his goodbyes and left.

Halfway to Johnny's Steve remembered he'd forgotten his kicking tee. He tried to hurry, but climbing the hill made it difficult.

The house was dark. He wondered if they'd had a power failure. Then he noticed a flickering light through the kitchen window.

He drew closer and peered in. There, bathed in candle glow, stood his mother with the front of her dress unbuttoned.

Her hair, usually pinned up, hung loose over her bare shoulders. His heart beating wildly, he ran all the way to Johnny's.

***

Back in his office, Steve shifted to the present. Why had his dad been so uncaring? He'd never bought her a thing, much less a dress. He never took her out for dinner or paid her a compliment — what a sonofabitch.

Steve glanced at the inauguration program lying on his desk. He felt like he was on top of the world. A poor kid from Kentucky had become a university president. He ached for his mom. How he wished she could have been at the inauguration.

He looked at his calendar for the coming two weeks — meetings from 8 to 5, and events every night. He buzzed Carol.

"Good morning, Mr. President."

"Carol, there are no breaks in my calendar, day or night. I told you I need to meet with the directors and department chairs. This schedule makes it impossible."

"It's standard procedure. I can start saying no if you want."

He sighed. "No, don't do that. I must make myself available. I just thought it would lighten up."

"Well, Mr. President, let me tell you what Bill Thornton may have not said. Based upon his appointment schedule over the last few years, here's what you can expect: You'll have eight to ten meetings a day, 200 off-campus meetings a year — at least one event every evening, some with Suzanne."

"Hooray. You mean I'll get to see my wife occasionally? Tell me this, when do I run the university?"

She laughed. "In the meetings."

***

Taking a deep breath of air freshened by a February shower, Steve congratulated himself on having met with every department head. Crossing the fine arts quad, he recognized Sandra about fifty yards ahead.

"Dr. Whitehead," he called. She stopped and turned. "Sandra, it's me, Steve."

He jogged toward her. "President Schilling, how are you?"

Steve paused to catch his breath. "I'm fine. Busy, as usual. Have you settled in?"

"Yes, we're still making changes in the department. I meant to call, but …"

"What's on your mind?"

She hesitated. "You mentioned that you like the Memphis Symphony."

"Yes. I have season tickets."

"I'd like to audition, but there's so much red tape. Do you have a contact there?"

"I'll see what I can do. Give me a few days."

"Thank you."

Steve returned to his office and phoned Harold Newman, executive director of the Memphis Symphony.

"Mr. Newman will be pleased to hear from you," his receptionist said. "He's always talking about your catch against Central Arkansas. He was in the marching band when the brass section stormed the field. I'll connect you now."

"President Schilling, what a pleasant surprise."

"Please, it's Steve, old 82."

"I read about the university all the time. You're doing a superb job."

"Thanks. I have a favor to ask. I'm hoping you can help me."

"I'll help any way I can."

"Dr. Sandra Whitehead, our new music chairperson is a very talented violinist. She has a degree from Juilliard. She's working night and day to improve our music program and would love to audition for the symphony. She's so busy here she doesn't have the time to jump through all the hoops. Can you facilitate?"

"I'd be glad to start the process. It'll take about six months."

"Six months? I had hoped for a week or two."

Harold laughed. "I wish. We have a limited staff and move at a snail's pace."

"Would two tickets for the homecoming game help? President's box?"

"Um ... how about four? I'll invite Earl Bernard, our maestro. He makes the final decisions."

"I can make that happen."

***

Six weeks later Steve followed Sandra to a table in the university deli. He tried not to stare at what had to be the biggest boobs he'd ever seen.

"Thank you again for arranging my audition. I've already signed a contract. I'm extremely grateful."

"The director was in the marching band when I played football," he puffed, then leaned closer. "When we're chatting like this I'd prefer you call me Steve."

"Certainly, Mr. President, I mean, Steve." She handed him the spring-summer concert schedule. "The performances mesh well with my university responsibilities."

Steve scanned the schedule and looked up. "It's very impressive. I may be able to attend May 7 or 8. I'll be attending our annual athletic conference meetings then in Memphis."

Sandra smiled and removed her horn-rimmed glasses. "That'd be very kind of you."

***

Steve raced across town from the conference meeting to make the matinée. He arrived in time to acknowledge a few friends before taking his seat. A glance at the program told him Sandra was performing second.

He leaned back and relaxed.

Striding center stage, she took his breath away. Her blonde hair cascaded to her shoulders; her luminous green eyes sparkled.

His eyes went straight to her breasts. She was a knockout.

Sandra and the conductor made eye contact. She looked scared, like a sparrow that had fallen from its nest, Steve thought. He wanted to pull her to him and comfort her.

The conductor raised his baton. Her bow struck the opening notes of the Brahms Violin Concerto in D Major.

Her performance was flawless.

Steve stood and clapped until his palms hurt.

After two curtain calls, he slipped backstage and watched from the wings. She freed herself from the crowd that had gathered and worked her way toward him. "What did you think?"

"You were fabulous. Your whole body moved with the music. You looked transported."

"Thank you. It happens whenever I play."

He moved closer. "You have lovely green eyes, Sandra."

She blushed. "Thank you."

"Have you had lunch?"

"No, I never eat before a concert. I tried it once and got sick in the wings."

"I haven't eaten either. There's a wonderful French restaurant nearby."

"You know my weakness for French food. Give me five minutes."

She changed.

He carried her violin case and dress bag toward the car. "Can we walk?" she asked. "I need to unwind."

"Of course, it's only four blocks."

Sandra placed her things in her car, then babbled about the conductor and the orchestra's affinity for Brahms. Steve kept quiet.

They entered La Table d'Or.

She stopped to take his arm. "Oh Steve, it's like Paris in the 1890's — I love the gas lamps and crystal sconces. It's spectacular."

The maître d' escorted them to a small alcove table. Sandra gushed as she surveyed the place. "I'm mad for the Impressionists. That's a Degas."

She nodded toward a large mural. "That's a Monet. He's my favorite."

With his knowledge of French limited to wine, Steve steered the conversation in another direction. "Would you like an appetizer?"

"No thanks. But I will have a glass of Chardonnay."

Steve motioned to the waiter. "We'll have a bottle of Côte des Blancs Chardonnay and an order of paté aux herbes."

She raised an eyebrow. "That's a delightful choice. What do you know about French wines?"

"A little. I'd like to learn more."

"Maybe I can help."

Relaxing in the restaurant, Sandra raved about Provence — its shops, markets and people. She spoke of her youth in New Paltz, New York, where she and her mother had performed duets in the civic orchestra.

Steve said little, choosing to give Sandra his full attention — and the stage. Her sophistication and classiness astounded him. They lingered, sipping espresso, until staff began setting up for dinner.

***

With June 24, Sandra's next performance, etched in his mind, Steve relaxed with Suzanne on the patio. A breeze ruffled.

"Have you made plans for us this summer?" he asked.

"No. But I've made reservations in October for our annual fall foliage getaway. How does Petit Jean State Park sound?"

"Wonderful. We haven't been there in years. I remember that romantic dinner we had last time. Any other plans?"

"No. Daddy called last night. He wants me to attend the State Democratic Convention with him on the 23 and 24. I'm thinking about it, but I don't know, I've been ..."

Steve cut her off. "You ought to go. You love politics. And it'd be a chance to see your Mom."

"Thank you, dear. That's very sweet. Are you sure you can do without me for two days?"

"It won't be easy, but I'll try."

***

The house lights dimmed. Steve watched as Sandra strode confidently across the stage in a form-fitting yellow gown. She threw herself into Dvorak's Romance in F min. Op.11 with abandon, tossing her hair and moving with the increasing tempo in a way that aroused him. He thought about jumping her right there. *God, what a lay!*

He anxiously waited for the concert to end.

Following three curtain calls, he drooled backstage waiting for the well-wishers to disperse before walking toward her dressing room.

Sandra intercepted him in the hallway and threw herself at him. "I didn't think you came."

Steve looked around before kissing her on the cheek. "Of course I came. You can count on me. I'll never let you down. You were wonderful. I've never seen — or heard — better."

Her eyes brightened and she squeezed his hand.

"How about a drink at the Peabody?" he asked.

***

Steve parked in the garage and met Sandra when she pulled in next to him. "Welcome to the Peabody, Madame," he said with a bow while opening her door.

She giggled and took his arm.

They found two seats in the lobby bar. "This feels like a dream," she said.

A shapely waitress in a black miniskirt placed a bowl of nuts and some cocktail napkins on the table. "What can I get you?" she asked, leaning over to give Steve an unobstructed view of her cleavage.

Steve looked away. "The lady will have …"

"A double scotch on the rocks," Sandra said.

"And I'll have a Tanqueray on the rocks with three olives."

Sandra paused. "Do you always drink Tanqueray?"

"Yes, mostly for the olives."

She laughed. "I'm so lucky sitting here in this beautiful hotel, having a drink with the university president. I can't imagine anything better."

"How about dinner at a four-star French restaurant? I'm staying here tonight."

Her gaze connected with his. "President Schilling, I mean Steve. I don't think that'd be proper. I mean, it wouldn't look right."

He shrugged. "No different than having a drink like we are right now. You've been on the go since you arrived in Ruston. You deserve a break."

"You're right about that. I haven't gone out much."

"That settles it. You can freshen up in my room. There are plenty of towels." She looked uneasy. "And you'll have privacy."

She frowned. "I don't ... Maybe we could just have hors d'oeuvres."

"Perfect," Steve said. He signaled the cocktail waitress.

"The appetizer plate looks nice," Sandra said.

He ordered it along with another round.

"Tell me about those changes you're making in the department."

"I'm so pleased. Everyone has rallied. They've bought into my ideas. A faculty member is talking about auditioning for the symphony."

"That would be wonderful." He eyed her. "You know, dinner would be a perfect way to cap-off today."

"It sounds lovely, but ..."

"I can smell the crepes." His eyes connected with hers. "Come on. I'll walk you to your car for your things. Then you can go up and change. I'll stay here."

She smiled then extended her hand.

Steve gave her the room key then spoke with the maître d' at Chez Philippe before returning to the bar. He wondered how long since she'd been with a man.

Moments later, Sandra stepped out of the elevator in a strapless, red cocktail dress. Heads turned as she sashayed from the elevator. His jaw dropped. "You look gorgeous."

She answered with a smile.

"Ready for dinner?"

"I'm starved." They crossed the lobby to the garden-like entrance. The maître d' greeted them then escorted them to the table Steve had chosen.

Sandra oohed over the crystal chandeliers, marble columns and rococo detail. She squeezed his hand. "Steve, it's so charming."

The maître d' pulled out her chair and opened her napkin with a snap of his wrist.

Steve slid his chair closer to hers. "How about a bottle of the Clos Pepe Pinot Noir? 1987 was a very good year." *I never spent $60 on wine before. Tonight better be worth it.*

"That sounds lovely." Her eyes glowed in the candlelight. "I'd like to suggest that we order the escargot and the crab soup. We can share."

"Perfect," she said.

Steve raised his glass of wine. "Here's to the best violinist in the world."

By the time his tenderloin arrived, dinner was the last thing on his mind. His hand grazed her leg then caressed it.

Sandra picked at her salmon. He leaned over and kissed her cheek, then whispered in her ear.

She glanced at him coyly.

He paid the check, leaving a generous tip, then took her hand.

Unlocking the door of his room, city lights flickered through the gauzy curtains. He sensed her uneasiness.

"Would you like to get comfortable? Maybe slip into a robe?"

She nodded.

He gestured to the bathroom. "The robe is hanging on a hook."

A few minutes later, wearing an uneasy expression and the Peabody's ultra-thick white terry robe, she left the bathroom.

He walked toward her and gently pulled her to him.

He could feel her arms shaking. "I love your eyes. You look lovely," he said.

She flashed a smile.

His fingertips circled her lips and he kissed her.

Moving his hands to her shoulders, he steered her to the side of the bed and loosened her robe. Gently, he pushed her onto the bed.

She pulled him on top of her.

When the morning sun streaked across their intertwined bodies she stirred. "Steve, you're my first ... I never ..."

His kiss silenced her. "You've said it all," he said, and pulled her on top of him.

CHAPTER SEVEN

After the July 4th break Steve rocked back in his office chair and gazed at his mother's picture. She would have been proud, knowing her son had completed his first year without a hitch. Faculty and staff members were enthusiastic about the school's prospects. An across-the-board salary increase bolstered everyone's morale, and the board had given him a $5,000 bonus.

Standing in the searing heat, Steve rang Bill's doorbell repeatedly. Despite the overwhelming success of his tenure, he still needed validation from his mentor. He glanced inside.

The lights were off.

He walked to the back of the house where Bill's old straw hat lay on the ground. "Hey Bill, how are the Lincolns?"

When no response came, Steve looked around. His eyes landed on Bill, crumpled over next to the gazebo.

Steve rushed to his side and knelt to find a pulse. "Bill, Bill, are you all right?"

No response.

Steve ran inside and called 911, grabbed a wet washcloth and scrambled down the steps.

Hearing sirens in the distance, sweat poured down his face soaking his shirt. "Hang on, Bill."

While reciting a prayer, Steve cradled Bill's head in his arms. He placed the damp washcloth on Bill's forehead.

Rocking Bill like a baby, Steve begged for a miracle.

The EMS truck pulled up and the paramedics rounded the house. "Over here," Steve shouted.

He watched the paramedics evaluate Bill's vitals, administer oxygen and strap his unconscious body on the stretcher. Steve's voice quivering, he asked. "Will he be alright?"

"It's hard to say. His right side maybe paralyzed. It could have been a stroke, or a heart attack. We'll know more after we get him to the ER and stabilize him."

Sirens blared as the truck pulled away.

Steve kicked a clump of grass then dashed inside to call.

"Sarah, its Steve. Bill's had a stroke. A heart attack. Maybe both. EMS is taking him to Ruston Memorial."

"Is he okay?" she gasped.

"I don't know. I hope so. I'll pick you up in five minutes."

***

Steve and Sarah waited outside the intensive care unit. She dabbed at her eyes and wet her handkerchief.

Steve made repeated trips to the coffee pot and paced. Occasionally he'd stop and stare out the window, weeping and whispering a prayer.

It was midnight when the head of surgery greeted them. Looking drawn and pale, he wore a half-smile.

"I think we're over the hump." The doctor removed his mask. "Bill had a severe ischemic stroke. That's a major blockage in the femoral artery. We couldn't determine how long he'd been unconscious so we did a mechanical thrombectomy."

The cardiologist stared at their blank faces. "I'm sorry, that's breaking up a clot as fast as possible to limit the loss of brain cells."

"That sounds awful," Sarah blurted.

"It's not as bad as it sounds. The main problem we're having is dealing with the paralysis. We moved quickly, but we can't assess the extent of damage. It'll be a while before we'll be able to fully determine his prognosis. I'm sorry. I wish I could be more definitive."

Sarah collapsed in Steve's arms. "We need to make arrangements so Sarah can stay with him all night," he said to the doctor.

"No problem. I'll take care of it."

***

Steve drove slowly down the side streets doing his best to navigate home. *What if Bill was unable to guide him?*

He arrived home in one piece, went inside and poured a glass of gin. Taking a slug, he flopped in the recliner.

Unable to hold together a moment longer, he broke down and bawled. Suzanne rushed to the family room.

"What is it, Steve?"

"Bill is paralyzed. He might have brain damage."

"Oh, no." Suzanne set his glass of gin aside and sat on Steve's lap. She stroked his hair. "Slow down. Tell me exactly what the doctor said."

Steve blubbered. She listened and soothed him.

"Steve, you need to relax. A lot of stroke victims recover fully. Don't think the worst. Remember, Dr. Bryant said it's going to take several days before he knows the extent of the damage."

"But what if ..."

Suzanne held him tight. "Steve, we have to wait and see. Bill is really a strong person. You need to get some rest."

***

For a week, Bill lay motionless, wired and plugged into monitors. Steve and Sarah took turns holding his hand, and waiting for test results.

Saturday morning Dr. Bryant called Steve and Sarah to a meeting in Bill's room. He spoke softly and deliberately.

"Bill is lucky to be alive. His right side is still paralyzed and he hasn't regained his speech. For most people I'd say full recovery was unlikely, but for Bill ... who knows?"

Sarah asked, "What do we need to do?"

"I'd like to have him admitted to a specialized stroke unit as quickly as possible."

"Where would you recommend?" she asked.

"Given the severity of his paralysis I recommend the Cleveland Clinic. I've checked them out. They can take him right away."

"Well, that's what we will do," Sarah said. "Will Bill understand when I tell him?"

"Yes, but he won't be able to respond."

***

Over the next six months Sarah lived in an apartment near the hospital. Bill made remarkable progress. She received weekly letters from Steve, touting his many campus successes. She wrote responses for Bill.

What Steve omitted from his letters to her was that he'd gained twenty pounds and was drinking too much. He allowed his frustration to overwhelm him at work, frequently losing his cool. More often than not, what was a normal conversation turned into a shouting match. By the end of the month he'd received three grievances from the staff association.

And there were rumblings in Little Rock that budget cuts were imminent.

***

A month later, shortly after Bill came home, Steve was delighted when Sarah invited him over.

She waved from the porch as Steve stepped out of his car. "It's nice to see you," she called. "Bill's been so anxious to see you. How have you been?"

"I'm fine. More important, how is he doing?"

"He's much better. The doctor's say it'll be another four months before he's back to full strength."

"When do they think he'll be ready to have our regular one-on-ones?"

"Not for some time. Visits are restricted to fifteen minutes for now. All he'll want to talk about is the game with Arkansas."

"I'll give him a brief update." Sarah noticed the buttons on Steve's shirt threatened to pop. His stomach hung over his alligator belt.

"Good, but don't let him get too excited." Sarah squeezed Steve's hand and they walked into the house together. "We've put his bed in the sunroom where he can see his roses and the dome. I'll give you a sign when it's time to go."

Steve followed her to Bill's bedside.

"It's good to see you, son," Bill said softly.

Steve stared at his frail mentor. "Am I glad to see you. It's wonderful that you're making such great progress."

"Bah. They have me tied down. What's happening on campus?"

"It's fine. Everyone wants to know how you're doing."

"Hogwash. They're talking about the game. Give me an update."

"I can only stay fifteen minutes. Sarah is keeping time." Bill frowned. "The media has started the hype. You'd think we were playing for the national championship. I'm getting half a dozen calls a week. Can't imagine what it will be like by fall."

"You'll be bombarded."

"The local media made a big deal about Arkansas paying us $200,000. Once I showed the reporters that was the going rate for playing a Division II school they got off it."

"They're always trying to make something out of nothing. What's happening with the students?"

"They're fired up."

"Wait until fall, it'll be wild."

Steve caught Sarah's wink. "That's enough for now. I'll give you another update next time."

Bill stirred. "Sarah, I need to know more. Schedule him for the same time next week."

"There will be plenty of time, Bill. You need to rest now."

***

The Monday before the game, the cabinet meeting ended early. Steve snapped at Carol when she handed him ten message slips from state media outlets.

By noon another twenty sat unanswered on his desk.

He worked through lunch.

At 5 o'clock he made his last call. Wiping the sweat from his brow, he closed the office door and leaned back.

Carol rapped on the door. "Mr. President, I'm leaving now."

"Fine, I'll see you in the morning," he said, pressing his fingertips into his temples. He buried his head in his hands. The walls seemed to be closing in. His head throbbed.

He needed to share his problems with someone he trusted. Steve raked his hair then reached for the phone.

"Directory assistance, what city please?" the operator asked.

"Fort Smith, Arkansas," he said. "John Deere Farm Equipment."

Steve dialed. A woman answered.

"I'd like to speak with Eddie Wilson."

"One moment, please."

"Hello, this is Eddie Wilson."

"Eddie, its Steve. You know Wilson to Schilling — the TD machine?"

"Jesus Christ, how are you? Oh … I'm sorry. I mean how are you doing, Mr. President?"

"None of that stuff. It'll always be Steve."

"Man, what's happening?"

"I need to talk like we did back in college."

"You okay?" Eddie asked.

"Yeah, I guess. Could we meet in Fayetteville on Thursday before the game?"

"Sure. How about dinner at the Holiday Inn at seven?"

"Super. I've got some heavy shit to share. I'll see you then."

***

As game day approached the fever spread throughout the community. The *Daily Gazette's* countdown fed the frenzy.

"BEAT HOGS" signs hung from Frank's Diner to the motel marquees along the freeway. Banners filled dorm windows. Students put down their books to paint signs and ready their trucks for the trek across state.

On Thursday Suzanne and Steve shared breakfast, a weekday rarity. She looked haggard, with dark under-eye circles.

"We have to find time for the two of us," she said. "When I schedule something with you, it seems important — then it falls by the wayside."

"Bill mentioned that he and Virginia used to have Saturday chats. Maybe we could try something like that. What do you think?"

She brightened. "I'd like that," she said. "I'm leaving early today so I can spend an extra day with my mother. I told her we'd stop by Saturday night after the game."

"Good. I'm having dinner with Eddie Wilson tonight."

"I miss talking to him. He has a lot of common sense. Give him my regards."

***

Steve stopped by the office to sign a couple of letters while Carol made some minor changes. He felt anxious and tight as a drum. He signed the letters, threw them on her desk and stalked out.

On the way to Fayetteville, he stopped in Little Rock to see Martha where he detailed every aspect of Bill's recovery as if she were his therapist. Her warmth and support helped him relax.

He chugged a second beer then dragged her into the bedroom. She didn't resist. He caressed her. They undressed quickly and he climbed on top.

"I can't get an erection," he said, pushing her away in embarrassment.

She snuggled against him. "Don't worry, you're stressed out. It happens."

"The damn thing is limp."

Martha held back a giggle. "Let me explain what's going on. Your body is reacting to extreme stress. It can't handle …"

***

A thousand questions raced through Steve's mind on the drive to Fayetteville: *What if he had a permanent problem? What if it happened again? What if?*

He blinked twice at the US 71 sign, north to Fayetteville. He couldn't recall last the 100 miles, passing through Conway and Clarksville. He stopped at a 7-Eleven, gassed up and bought a large coffee.

Driving north, he turned up the music and cracked open a window. The car slid onto the gravel and he jerked the steering wheel. Coffee spilled onto the passenger side.

"Damn," he said, pulling onto the shoulder.

He unlocked the glove compartment. Several envelopes fell on the floor. He tossed them on the seat and grabbed a handful of napkins to soak up the mess.

Back on the road he glanced at the envelopes. He recalled the first one he'd received. Kate had suggested it'd be smarter to write than drop by his office. For her next birthday he had given her lavender stationery with pre-addressed envelopes to him at Thornton Hall.

He liked the anonymity and felt sure that if Carol ever suspected something funny she'd remain loyal.

He blotted the coffee stains from a yellow envelope and held it to his chest, catching a trace of the Trésor perfume he had given Sandra. He picked up a blue envelope that matched Christina's eyes then glanced at the green envelopes from Martha.

North of Fayetteville he pulled in at the Holiday Inn. After locking the envelopes in the glove box, he lumbered into the lobby.

Eddie tossed a newspaper onto a glass-topped table, walked over and slapped him on the back. "How the hell are you?"

Steve turned.

Eddie stepped back. "Jesus Christ, you look like shit. When did you get so fat? Drop your suitcase in your room. I'll order us a couple of Buds."

Steve did as he was told and a few minutes later, he joined Eddie in a booth. Catching up on their old teammates, they had another round then ordered bacon-cheeseburgers, fries and onion rings.

"So what's this heavy shit all about?" Eddie asked.

Steve stroked his whiskers. "It's a very … very long story. I don't know where to start."

"Is Kate involved?"

"Yes, she's part of it."

"Why don't you start with her? I never understood why she picked you anyway."

Steve sighed. "Okay. I've been seeing her since college."

"You told me that at the class reunion. Big deal. So you're having an affair."

"It's not an affair. I love her just like Suzanne."

Eddie mashed his teeth. "Steve, you're married to Suzanne. She's your wife. Kate's someone you fuck."

"It's not like that. When I'm with Kate I love her completely. It's like we're married. There is no one else. Then, when I'm with Suzanne she's the only one. Does that make sense?"

"Yeah, sounds like you want to have your cake and eat it too."

"That's only part of the problem."

Eddie gulped his beer. "Are you seeing someone else?"

"Well, sort of."

"Sort of. Shit man, either you are or you're not."

68

"I'm seeing three others," he mumbled.

"Jesus Christ." Eddie tossed his napkin in the air. "You're in love with Suzanne and Kate and you're having three other affairs?"

"They're not affairs. I love each one of them."

"Sorry. So you're telling me that you're in love with five women." Eddie caught the eye of the bartender. "We need another round."

He turned to Steve. "Okay, let's start with Kate."

"I see her before poker twice a month and occasionally when I'm out of town. I've promised to marry her."

"Steve, you can't. You're married," he said, shaking his head. "Okay, who's next?"

"Christina, I guess. She's a physician, really a classy lady. I've been seeing her for four years. We play golf and go horseback riding, maybe twice a month. Once in a while we stay overnight in Memphis and go shopping."

"Don't tell me you're into dresses, too? Sorry, who's next?"

"Sandra. She's in our music department. She plays the violin with the Memphis Symphony. She has huge boobs. I've been seeing her since last summer."

Eddie shook his head. "Jesus, you're getting laid five or six times a month and we're still counting. You never scored that much in college." He took a breath. "Okay, let's hear about the last one."

"Martha. She's a tall redhead. Works in Little Rock. I see her once a month and at a national meeting or two. She played basketball for the Razorbacks when we were in school."

Eddie frowned. "You're having an affair with... I mean you're in love with Martha Brown?" Steve nodded. "God, I won't be able to sleep tonight."

"Want another beer?" Steve asked.

"No. Not now, I have to concentrate."

Eddie bolted from the booth, paced back and forth then slid back in across from Steve. "You've proposed to Kate. And you're in love with Christina, Sandra, and Martha. Did I get that right?"

"I guess so. Christina and I have talked about marriage too. That's part of the problem."

"Steve, that's not the problem. You're the problem."

"Eddie, you don't understand I just want to make them happy. Sometimes I write to them. They love getting my letters. It makes me feel better."

"Jesus Christ, you've put all of this in writing?" Eddie slid out of the booth. "I've gotta take a leak."

Five minutes later, Eddie slammed the *Yellow Pages* on the table. "Here, call a shrink."

"I tried that. I cancelled the appointment. I couldn't handle the thought of going through all that. Suzanne would divorce me if she found out. So what do you think?"

"I think you're fucking nuts. And you need professional help. Look, I'm an old quarterback who sells farm equipment. I know what I know."

"But Eddie, you always listened in college. You helped me deal with women."

"Crap. You were in college for God's sake. That was different. Now you're married. And you're fuckin' five women. Trust me, it's not normal."

Eddie threw his hands up.

"Shit, man. If you put them all together you'd have the perfect woman. One has big boobs, another great legs, one is rich, and one's a musician ..." Eddie's voice trailed off. "You play golf, go horseback riding and to the symphony. Damn, maybe I'm the crazy one."

"Eddie, it's not funny. I really love them all."

Eddie gazed at the empty bar. "How's it going with Suzanne?"

"She's wonderful. I love her. We're like you and Peg. Everything is fine."

"Everything is not fine. You've got big problems. You didn't listen to me in college. And you don't want to listen now. You've got to keep your God damn zipper up. Stop seeing them. Stop writing letters. Take care of Suzanne. See a shrink. Yesterday. If you don't, you're going to fuck yourself to death."

CHAPTER EIGHT

Steve woke up early feeling refreshed and invigorated. He wrote a note to Eddie, left it at the front desk then set off for interviews with newspaper and TV reporters, and meetings with alums and donors.

Seven hours later he trudged back to the Holiday Inn, in need of some shuteye. As he approached the elevator, a deafening roar assaulted him. "Beat Hogs! Beat Hogs!"

Squeezing by fans jammed in the hall outside the bar, he heard a booster call, "Hey, Prez. How about a drink?"

Another called, "Yeah, I'll buy."

Howard Clark waved from the bar and motioned to Steve. Taking the stool next to Howard, Steve greeted his friend. "Want a beer, Doc?"

"Sure do. I'll have a Bud Light."

Howard signaled the bartender and ordered. "Ready for the big one?"

Steve gave a thumbs up. "I've been waiting two years for this."

"It reminds me of the first time we played Alabama. But more exciting," Howard said, sucking down his beer. "Today, this old guy needs a nap. I'll see you at the reception tonight."

Steve rubbed his eyes and wished he was the one taking a break.

The reporter on the 6 o'clock news poked fun at the Rough Riders, projecting them as 40-point underdogs.

"That's enough," Steve said to the bartender. "I've had it." Turning to go, he felt a nudge in his back.

A woman said, "We'll have a couple of Tanqueray's on the rocks. Three olives, please."

Steve saw a tan-skinned woman in her early thirties slip onto the stool Howard had vacated.

"Ah … nice to see you, Marie," he said. Marie Cabrera supervised the university mailroom.

He had last seen her at her father's retirement party in July. While not particularly attractive, she had luxurious long dark hair that appealed to him.

"How did you know I like olives with my Tanqueray?" he asked.

"I pay attention to details. You'd be surprised what I see."

A frown creased Steve's forehead. "Like what?"

"There are yellow envelopes. Sometimes blue. Sometimes there's a lavender one."

Steve squirmed. "Tanqueray and colored envelopes. What are you talking about?"

"You know what I'm talking about. We need to talk, say 10 o'clock tonight in room 529."

He scowled. "Are you crazy?"

She eased off the bar stool and squeezed his arm. "See you at ten."

Steve peered in the mirror behind the bar and watched her sashay out. *How did she come up with the Tanqueray? And three olives? The envelopes?* He wondered, downing his gin.

***

Over 600 alums jammed the Kickoff Reception. Steve glad-handed and schmoozed everyone in sight. He didn't discriminate; undergraduates or distinguished alums, they all got the same treatment.

He checked his watch regularly then shortly before ten, said his goodbyes and slipped out.

He took the elevator to the fifth floor, walked to 529 and knocked.

The door cracked opened, and a slender arm reached for his hand, drawing him in. Incense filled the air.

Steve squinted, trying to adjust to the dim light. She wore a red blouse and tight jeans.

A bottle of champagne rested in an ice bucket next to a rose in a bud vase. Perspiration broke out on his forehead.

She gestured toward the ice bucket. "Would you pour me some champagne?" Steve stood rooted to the dark green carpet. "Mr. President," she purred. "I'll have some champagne."

Without speaking, he uncorked the bottle and filled her glass.

72

She snatched it from him, gulped it and tapped the empty flute. He refilled it while searching for something — anything — distinctive about her. She emptied the glass and held it out for another refill.

He obliged.

"Have a chair, Mr. President."

Steve did as he was told. He felt incapable of thought or speech.

She rose slowly and staggered toward him while shaking her index finger. "Mr. President, you've been a bad boy," she slurred. "You've been messin' where you shouldn't be messin.'"

His face reddened and he found his voice. "What are you talking about?"

"You're lucky I'm the only one who knows what's going on." She tossed a yellow envelope on the table. "Let's start with Sandra."

He was having trouble breathing. "Where did you find that?"

"In the mailroom, of course." She pulled the letter from the envelope.

"You can't read my mail. That's illegal," he sputtered.

Her right brow rose. "Mr. President, you're not in a position to talk about ethics. Tell me about her."

Steve shifted uncomfortably and loosened his tie, his shirt was soaked. "There's nothing to tell."

"Now, Mr. President, we don't want to read about the two of you in the *Gazette.*"

"Look, I'm not …"

Reaching across the table, she pressed her fingers to his lips. "Tell me about Sandra."

"There's nothing. I've seen her perform with the symphony. We had lunch. That's it."

"And what about dinner at Chez Philippe? She sounds pretty hot to me."

"Big deal. So I've seen her a few times." He stood up and straightened his tie.

"Not so fast, Mr. President. No. I think I prefer Steve. Let's talk about Christina."

"Christ, we served together on the training center committee. We've played golf a few times with her father and his friend. Honest to God, that's the truth."

"What about the time at the gazebo? And how about those hot steamy showers?"

"Look, I'm not going to take this. I'm leaving."

"Not so quick." She tossed another envelope on the table. "Why is Kate's lavender?"

"It's her favorite color," he said before berating himself.

"You've been with her a long time. Right?"

"Since college."

"Now that's more like it," she said. She slipped behind his chair and ran her fingers through his hair. "What do you like best about her?"

He pulled his head away. "Shit, what's wrong with you?"

"Maybe you like how she seduces you." Marie pushed her oversized breasts against the back of his head. Unbuttoning his shirt, she slid her hands over his hairy chest and caressed his pecks. "Is this what you like?"

He swallowed hard and licked his lips.

"You like that, huh?" She moved around to straddle him, and pushed against his bulging pants. Her hands held his face and she stuck her tongue in his mouth.

"Okay … okay, what do you want?"

"I thought you'd never ask," she said. "I want an arrangement."

"A what?"

"An arrangement. Like you have with the others. We could meet at away football and basketball games."

"Look, I'm sure you're a very nice person …"

She interrupted. "It's simple. I know what you like. And I know what I want," she said, before planting a wet kiss on him.

He pulled back and paused then looked her in the eye.

"We'd have to have ground rules."

"Like what?" she asked.

"You can't tell anyone. We can't be seen in public. And there'll be no fooling around with anyone else."

She smirked. "Will I have my own stationery?"

"Sure," he said. "Now can we go to bed?"

"Beats shaking hands for sealing the deal."

Steve stripped to his shorts and got in bed. He watched as she unbuttoned her jeans and crawled out of them. Her red-lace thong was barely visible between melon-like cheeks.

74

She took off her blouse and slid into bed beside him. She caressed his chest and fondled his tool, her kisses sliding down his chest.

She teased him then sucked him until he thought he'd pass out. Moving on top, she rode him as if he were a mechanical bull.

Seconds after he came she moaned and collapsed on his chest.

Twenty minutes later Steve returned to his room. He took a quick shower and slipped into bed. Suzanne turned. "I didn't see you in the bar when I checked in."

"Eddie and I went downtown. We had lots to catch up on. I'll tell you more about it in the morning." He pecked her on the cheek. "I love you, Suzanne."

***

Arriving late at the team breakfast, Steve took his place at the head table as the minister stood to deliver the blessing. His mind floated between Marie's proposition, the invocation and Marie's blow job.

He willed himself to make a few motivational remarks then left for the Family and Friends Reception. He ran into Marie near the bar and felt a surge of lust.

"Good morning, Mr. President," she cooed.

He tried to look away from her form-fitting workout top. "Morning. How are you doing?"

"Super, I'm really excited ..." Her voice trailed off as a young couple approached. "Good luck, Mr. President." She winked and walked away.

Steve met up with Suzanne at the reception, went through the motions of at the meet and greet then led the official delegation into the stadium. Seeing 70,000 red-clad Razorback fans took his breath away.

The Hogs were ahead 7 to 0 when he reached the president's box. At halftime EAU had inched ahead 17 to 14. But a fumble on the first play of the second half darkened his hopes for a win.

He had trouble focusing on anything but Marie. Suzanne whispered in his ear.

"Steve, put on your game face. You're an embarrassment. You look like you're attending your own funeral."

He gave a false laugh. "Sorry, I'd hoped we would do better."

"It's only a game. There are important people here. There's work to be done."

Steve faked it through the rest of the game; chatting and glad-handing while envisioning Marie.

Following the 42-17 loss, he kissed Suzanne on the cheek and walked her to her car. "When will you be home?" he asked.

"Around seven tomorrow. Mom has matinée tickets. I'll be home after the show."

"I'll fire up the grill and make burgers."

"Sounds delicious. I can't wait."

***

On his way to Martha's he replayed the previous night with Marie. By the time he pulled into Martha's he had a hour-long hard-on.

Turning off the ignition, he thought about Martha. She had become the stabilizing force in his life. He picked chrysanthemums from her garden on his way to the door.

She welcomed him, looking fetching in cutoffs that flattered her long sexy legs. He handed her the flowers. "Oh, Steve, you're so thoughtful. Come in."

"It was a long, lonely ride from the game. I can't remember when I've been so low."

"I'm sorry EAU lost." She took the flowers to the kitchen and put them in water then rejoined him in the living room.

"The game reminded me of when we played smaller schools. We'd racehorse up and down the court. The coach would clear the bench in the first half. By the second half their players were exhausted. Your coach has to learn that he can't win the game in the first half. The starters have to rest."

She sat on the sofa next to him. She seemed quieter than usual.

"You okay?" he asked.

"A little bummed-out by the game. But my thoughts were more with you. I know how exciting it can be in the president's box. I kept picturing you and Suzanne — the president and first lady, chatting with friends."

"It wasn't fun getting our ass kicked."

"That's not the point, Steve. It was the two of you. You had each other. You were the guests of honor, the celebrities. I sat here alone listening to the game and feeling sad. It's corny and trite, but I'm the other woman. No one knows me; no one cares. I cried through the second half."

"Geez, Martha. I'm sorry."

She raised her voice. He'd never seen her agitated before. "Steve, it's not fair. I can't take it anymore." She sobbed and ran to the kitchen for some tissues.

"I need to say what's on my mind. I can't go on like this."

"I told you, darling. I'm going to work it out. It'll take a little time. Be patient, then we'll be together forever."

"That's what you say and ... that's what I want. But I've heard it so many times — from you and from women at the office who are having affairs. It's just a line."

"Martha, it's not a line. I love you."

"I'm tired of waiting. I'm a player. I can't be a reserve, sitting on the bench. I've given this a lot of thought. I want it all or nothing."

"Sweetheart, I hate to hear you talk that way. We have so much in common. You're everything to me."

She bit her lip. "Steve, I've never known a man like you. You're kind, caring and great in bed. Do you have any idea how lonely it is for me? I can't stand to think of you out having a good time with Suzanne. Or, in bed. I can't live my life this way. It's eating me up."

"I'll make it better. I promise," he said, sliding closer to her. She pulled away when he tried to hug her and stood up.

"Stop it. I don't want to make a scene. I need space. I think you should go."

"Martha, I ..."

She cut him off. "I don't want to say anything I might regret."

Steve hesitated. "Can't we talk this out?"

"There is nothing to talk about. I can't — I won't — play second fiddle. Just go."

Steve shuffled toward his car. He couldn't imagine life without her. Martha made his life complete. He broke into a cold sweat and made it down a few steps before vomiting on her flowers.

Trembling, he got into his car, wiped the perspiration from his face and slowly regained his composure. He gassed up at the I-40 interchange, bought some Pepto-Bismol and a Coke before heading home.

Pulling into a rest area, chills seized him. He staggered from the car, fell on the grass and upchucked. Laying on his back, he stared at the sky and cried, "Martha, please don't leave me. I'll do whatever it takes to make you happy."

He laid there for the longest time reflecting on the good times they'd had, and the places they'd gone. He sat up, rinsed his mouth with Coke and got back on the road. *What would I say to Suzanne? How could I give Martha what she wanted?* For the first time since college he would have to choose.

Pulling into the parking lot a short time later, he walked purposefully into his office. Withdrawing a sheet of personalized stationery from the bottom drawer, he wrote:

Dear Martha:

The drive home today was agonizing. I've been so focused on my feeling for you that I forgot about you. I've behaved badly. You deserve better.

You're the most important person in my life. I can't go on without you. And I won't. I will prove my love for you. In the months ahead I'll make changes so we can be together. You'll see.

I want to spend the rest of my life with you — do all the things we've talked about.

Martha, I love you and I want to marry you.

Love always,

Steve

CHAPTER NINE

Steve flipped through the pink slips — twenty, at least, and all marked *Urgent, Stat* or *ASAP*. He tossed the slips in the air. They landed like confetti on the desktop and carpet.

Regaining his composure, he got down on his knees, picked up the papers, laid them back on the desk and dialed Bill.

Sarah answered. "Good morning, Thornton residence."

"Sarah, its Steve. How is Bill doing?"

"Very well. He's been flitting around the house all morning."

"That's amazing. How did he take the game? I was afraid he'd have a setback."

"He was excited in the first half. Disappointed with the outcome, of course. But he's already talking about next year."

"When can I meet with him?

"In two weeks he'll be ready. Why don't you come over October 23 around noon? I'll fix a light lunch."

***

Sarah adjusted the umbrella. Bill put three place mats, forks and napkins, and a bowl of German potato salad on the table. He hesitated. "It sounds like Steve just drove in."

A minute later, wearing a broad smile, Steve greeted his mentor. "Bill, you look terrific. How are you doing?"

The men shook hands.

"I feel fine. And ready to go to work. What's on our agenda?"

Sarah interrupted. "Slow down, Bill. We're going to have lunch first, with no business talk."

Over soup, chips and BLTs they chatted about Bill's recovery which included one hour a day, working and tending his roses. Bill tapped his fingers on the table.

"Thanks for lunch, Sarah. That really hit the spot," Steve said.

"You two take it easy," she said then got up and carried dishes into the kitchen.

"Let's get to work," Bill said. "What's on your agenda?"

"The weightiest issue is the state budget. I'm afraid we're in for big cuts. And I'm out of my league. Any suggestions?"

"As I've said before, whenever you see a negative coming, create a positive. Otherwise, the faculty will eat you up."

"How can I create something positive out of cutting the budget?"

"Divert their attention. Give them something else to think about. Have you considered conducting a campus-wide capital campaign?"

"I wouldn't know where to start."

"With a good consulting firm I bet you could raise $20 million."

"You really think so?"

"If you like, I could check out a couple of firms for you."

"I'd appreciate that."

"Let's meet again in two weeks."

"You sure that's not too soon? Maybe we should wait a month."

"We don't have time to waste. Two weeks will be fine. Since Sarah fusses over me, and I don't like to worry her, just say you happened to be in the neighborhood."

***

Steve handed Sarah a box of chocolates.

"Well, thank you," she said.

"It's nice to see you. I'll just be a moment. I want to drop off a report."

"Is that Steve?" Bill called from the sunroom. "Send him in."

Sarah rolled her eyes. "He's on his way."

"Come on in and fix yourself a drink."

"I'll pass. How do you feel? How did you do with the consultants?" Steve asked.

"Excellent on both counts. I talked to four consultants."

"What did they have to say?"

"They all concur that mounting a campaign is the right thing to do. And they think the community will step up to the plate."

"That sounds exciting. I know I can raise money. It's the managerial details that bother me."

"Not a problem. I've spoken with Ketchum and Associates. They'll do a community assessment and put people in place to run the campaign."

"That's a relief, but …"

"If you have a good chairman, you'll be in business."

"Who might that be?"

"Do you know Don Cagney? He's the CEO at First National Bank.

"No, but I see his name all over. He's on several boards."

"He's very well-connected. Chaired the United Way last year. I've invited the Cagney's over for Thanksgiving dinner. Want me to mention it?"

"Yes, I do. That'll give me time to follow up with the folks at Ketchum."

His arm around Steve, Bill walked his protégé to the front door. "I see Suzanne's name in the paper. How's she doing?"

"Outstanding. The governor is going to appoint her to a commission on tax reform. We've never been happier."

"Good for you. Everyone sees the two of you as the perfect couple. Keep those home fires burning."

"Don't worry. I will. Suzanne is the best."

***

Snow had dusted Ruston when Steve squeezed past the bar stools at Frank's Diner to reach Bill and Don Cagney. Fiftyish with gray sideburns, Don wore a blue paisley tie with a matching handkerchief in his breast pocket. Steve took a seat at the four-top. "Sorry I'm a little late."

"No problem. What's happening with that campaign Bill's been talking about?" Don asked.

"It's an exciting opportunity. Ketchum says we can raise $25 million. All we need is a good campaign chairman. Someone who's a strong leader and well-respected in the community. Would you do it?"

Don glanced at Bill. "This old guy tells me I don't have a choice. What's your plan?"

"I'm not quite there. Next week I'll meet with a representative from Ketchum. He'll walk me through their proposal. After that I'll give you a call."

"Sounds good to me."

***

Steve read the Ketchum plan and gasped. "I'll have to raise 50% of the goal during the silent phase. That's $13 million in eighteen months."

Knowing that he'd have to raise 80% of the money from the big hitters, he paced his office trying to determine how he'd manage his time. He figured he'd best structure his schedule around Sandra's performances. He couldn't allow anything to interfere with her March performance — a time to celebrate their first anniversary with dinner at Chez Philippe.

He glanced through the morning mail and spotted a yellow envelope. Tearing it open, he pulled out her letter. The fragrance of Trésor filled the room. He read the letter twice then answered it.

Sandra:

You're the most cherished person I've ever known. I love you more than you can imagine. I can hardly wait until we can spend the rest of lives together.

Love always,

Steve

***

On Sunday morning Sandra woke early, thinking about Steve's loving note from three weeks ago. She reread it several times since then.

A little before 9 o'clock, she put a vegetarian quiche in the oven. Peering at two sparrows in the single birdbath in her yard, she thought about her mother's myriad of birdbaths. She wished she could visualize her father in that scene but he had died when she was five.

From then Sandra and her mom had become closer than ever. The two shared a love of music and performed duets at community centers throughout the Hudson River Valley.

Her mother had always talked about the importance of waiting for the right man, one who was caring and thoughtful; a man who performed the niceties such as opening car doors and bringing flowers for no special reason. *I know Steve's the one. He's perfect, just like daddy was for mom.*

Sandra took a deep breath, picked up the phone and punched in her mother's number.

"Hello, Mother. How are you today?"

"I'm fantastic. The sun is out. The leaves are turning. It's a spectacular day. I was just thinking about your father. I still miss him. He was so sweet. He'd always hold my hand when we walked. Never raised his voice. He was so kind and gentle."

"Mom, remember when I told you I was taking a job in Ruston?"

"Yes, I had to look it up in the atlas."

"Mother, it isn't that bad. People are civilized and cultured too."

"I suppose. What's going on in your life?"

"Remember how I thought I'd never find that special person?"

"Yes, of course. I told you to be patient that someday he would come along."

"Mother, it's happened. I'm in love."

"Oh Sandra, I'm so happy for you. Tell me about him. Who is he? What is he like?"

"He's just like daddy, the man you described. He gives me flowers. Opens doors. He's perfect in every way."

"How sweet. How did you meet?"

"He was on the selection committee during my interview two years ago, but we didn't go out until last spring. He loves concerts. We had a drink after a performance."

"What does he do?"

"He's the president of the university."

"My, he must be very smart."

"He knows everything. Everybody. The faculty love him."

"Sweetheart, I'm so happy for you. I'm sorry to cut you off but my ride for church is here. Can we chat later?"

"Of course. Love you, Mom."

83

Waiting for Martha to come on the line, Steve looked out the office window at the flowers the grounds crew had recently planted.

She broke the silence. "Good morning. This is Martha Brown."

"Martha, its Steve."

"How are you doing?"

"Fine. And again, I want you to know that I'm going through with the divorce. It's going to happen."

"I know what you say, Steve. I just have to see action."

"I'm thinking about setting up a meeting with the Commissioner of the Southeastern Conference. I want to lay the groundwork. What do you think?"

"Makes sense. Down the road that'll make it easier to schedule games with the conference schools."

"My thoughts exactly. I have an idea. We could fly to Birmingham in the morning, have lunch with the commissioner, maybe mess around in the afternoon and have a nice dinner. You could be back at work by noon the next day."

He waited for her to digest his offer.

"I'm not sure, Steve. I have a lot of things to sort out. I don't want to get back into something that's going nowhere."

"I didn't mean it that way. This would be strictly work. I need your help to make the sell."

"Well, okay, as long as you understand, no fun and games."

***

Steve helped Martha out of a cab, through a wall of fire that's Birmingham in June and into the Wynfrey Hotel. She took in the lobby's oversized marble columns, crystal chandeliers, and French Provincial furnishings.

"This place is elegant, Steve."

A distinguished-looking man walked toward Steve. "Good afternoon. I'm Fred Stanton from the Southeastern Conference."

"Nice to meet you. I'm Steve Schilling and this is Martha Brown, the state official I mentioned on the phone."

Stanton glanced up at her. "Martha Brown. Now, I know why your name sounded so familiar. I saw you play in the Olympics."

She grinned.

Steve reached for Stanton's hand. "I appreciate your willingness to take time out of your busy schedule to meet with us."

"Hey, that's why they pay me." He steered them toward the dining room. "Let's chat over lunch. Those in the know say they serve the best food in Birmingham."

They ordered and Steve began his spiel. "We have a long-term contract to play Arkansas. We'd like to add a few other Division I schools."

"That's a good start. What's your long-term plan?" Stanton asked.

Steve outlined EAU's step-by-step plans to go Division I. Martha chimed in, praising Steve's leadership skills and emphasizing the state's commitment. Steve answered each question in specific terms.

"I like your plan," Stanton said. "You're moving forward in the right way. Too many schools try to make the jump before they're ready. I'll drop a line to our athletic directors so they'll know where you're headed."

* * *

That night the maître d' seated Martha and Steve at a small table in the Veranda restaurant. Steve ordered a bottle of wine. They chatted about the SEC and the schools he might target.

"Do you know what I like best about you?" he asked.

"I have no idea."

"You're sexy as hell in professional settings."

"Steve, I told you. This is all business."

"I know. And I'll respect your wishes. But I have to say it. I love you because you're so real. You're well informed, and you're so smart. You're affectionate, warm and understanding. And I'm totally relaxed when I'm with you."

"Don't look at me with those big puppy-dog brown eyes. You're not getting any tonight."

"Hey, who said anything about that?"

From a nearby table, Becky Mae Nelson watched Martha and Steve, then turned to her husband. "I'm telling you, Jed, that's Steve Schilling. And he's with some woman. That is not Suzanne. And there's nothing wrong with my eyesight."

"Now, Becky Mae, don't jump to conclusions. You don't know why he's here."

"I know what he's doing here. I can tell by the way he's looking at her."

"Forget about it. No need to start a rumor."

"It's not a rumor. I've heard he's been with a doctor at Blytheville Memorial. My girlfriend saw the two of them playing golf at the country club."

"Maybe he was fundraising."

"Jed, look, he's standing up. Tell me that's not him."

Jed glanced Steve's way. "Okay, so that's him."

"Wait until the girls hear about this."

"Maybe it's a business meeting or an interview," Jed sputtered.

"Interview my ass. He's interviewing her for a horizontal position. He's got the look of a hungry predator."

"Becky Mae, your imagination is working overtime."

"I can tell, Jed. A woman knows. What are you going to do about it?"

"Me? What are you talking about?

"You need to check it out."

"I do? I don't care."

"You don't care? He's the president. He shouldn't be messing around, especially in a big-city restaurant."

Jed shook his head and sighed. "Okay. What do you suggest?"

"Find out if he's having an affair."

"How? Hide under his bed? Hire a private investigator?"

"You could report it to the *Daily Gazette.* They have ways of finding out things."

"Becky Mae."

He avoided eye contact with his wife and sighed.

"Okay, you win. I'll talk to the editor next week. I'll tell him he had better get to the bottom of this, or you will. In the meantime, you must promise not to say a word to anyone. Deal?"

She scowled. "Jed, that's not fair."

"Look, you either want me to get the truth or you want to stir things up. Which is it? You can't have it both ways."

"Okay, but I'm not waiting forever."

***

Wednesday morning Gerry Coleman, editor of the *Daily Gazette* shook Jed's hand and closed the door. "It's been a long time, Jed."

"About two years ago when we played at the Blytheville member-guest outing."

"You're right," Gerry said, positioning himself behind his large oak desk. "So what's this sensitive topic you want to discuss?"

"Gerry, it's not me. Becky Mae has this thing … I'll be blunt. Last Thursday night we were in Birmingham. We saw President Schilling having dinner with a young woman. Becky Mae went into a tizzy. She's ready to spread the word."

"There could be lots of explanations."

"I know but you know how she is. I love her but … in a week she'll have everyone in Blytheville believing the story. And before the month is over all of Ruston will think Steve is having an affair. I know my wife. I told her that I'd speak with you."

"Jed, do you know how often I hear similar stories? Hell, your name has come up once or twice."

"Now Gerry, no need to go there. He's the president of the university. If you don't do something, Becky Mae will have him strung up by the balls. She could get him fired."

Gerry nodded. "You're probably right."

"There must be something you can do. Steve deserves a chance. You have to move quickly. I know Becky Mae. She will crucify him."

Gerry fidgeted in his chair. "Okay, I'll do something. But it might take a month or so."

CHAPTER TEN

Entering Thornton Hall on another insufferable August day, Gerry wiped his brow. He'd uncovered nothing to warrant a meeting with Steve and had considered canceling. But Jed and Becky Mae were not a couple you could brush off. He had to follow up or there'd be hell to pay.

Carol smiled, revealing perfectly white teeth. "I was hoping you might arrive early."

"Wouldn't miss an opportunity to see you. Even for a few minutes."

Steve stepped out of his office and shook Gerry's hand. "It's good to see you. C'mon in. Want some iced tea?"

"Sure do. It's hotter than blazes out there."

"What brings you to campus?"

"This is difficult for me. Err, it involves you."

"No problem. I deal with 400 Ph.D.'s. I know about uncomfortable conversations."

Carol set the tea on the table and closed the door. Gerry ran a finger under his collar.

"Gerry, we've known each other for years. It can't be that bad. Spill your guts."

"You know, the press has to follow up on all kinds of stuff."

"Hey, it goes with the turf. I understand. Speak your mind."

Gerry took a deep breath. "There's a rumor going around. I hate to bring it up but ..."

Steve cut him off. "I'm no stranger to rumors. What is it this time?"

"I've heard from a reliable source that you had dinner with a very attractive woman last Thursday night in Birmingham."

Steve didn't miss a beat. "I sure did. Had meetings all day in Birmingham. Even through dinner."

"Want to tell me about them?"

"Well, I'd rather not read it in the paper," Steve said, loosening his tie. "Just a second." He buzzed Carol. "Please bring me Fred Stanton's address and phone number. Martha Brown, too. And print a copy of my expense report for Birmingham last week."

"Gerry, here's the confidential part. This is off the record."

Gerry nodded. "Of course. I won't breathe a word."

Steve lowered his voice. "We're trying to schedule a couple of games with SEC schools."

"Wow. That's impressive."

"You bet. Last week I met with SEC commissioner Fred Stanton in Birmingham and Martha Brown, our state rep for athletics. We worked all afternoon. It got to be 6 o'clock and, to tell you the truth, my stomach was growling. Fred had a pressing engagement so Ms. Brown and I had dinner and finalized the game plan."

"That'd be something — Ole Miss or Tennessee on the schedule," Gerry said.

Carol came in and handed Steve a folder which he passed to Gerry. "Here are the details. Feel free to call them. No secrets here."

"You've given me everything I need. Steve, I'm sorry."

"You're only doing your job."

Gerry stood. "And Steve, no need for concern. I'll hold that football story."

***

Football practice started the following week. While the media hype from last year had diminished, it had not dampened the team's spirit. "BEAT HOGS" signs again blanketed Ruston. Steve continued to schmooze at civic clubs, meet with boosters and hype the students, all the while predicting an EAU victory. The day before the game he squeezed in one more meeting.

The Big Boy marquee lights guided Steve into the lot. He waved to Don Cagney, standing near the entrance. "Glad to see your alarm worked," Steve joked.

"I hit the snooze button twice. You better have good reason for dragging me out of bed."

Steve gloated. "Let's order before I show you the numbers."

They settled into a booth and Don signaled the waitress. "Good. I'm starved."

Steve cut into his waffle. "Remember when I told you we needed at least 50% of the goal in the bank before announcing the campaign?"

"Sure. You made a big deal about it. Sign up the heavy hitters during the silent phase."

"Right. Well, we've done it. There's $13 million in your bank. I'm ready to announce. What do you think?"

"That's amazing." Don reached over to pat Steve's arm. "I can't believe you did it in less than a year." He paused. "With another $2 million we could reach 60% of the target. That would sound even better on the nightly news. Maybe we should hold off."

"I like that. You never know what might happen. It'd be a perfect way to end the year."

***

Driving toward Fayetteville, Steve felt on top of his game. Raising $25 million would be a milestone — a feather in his cap, and one that Bill had never achieved.

The next day he parked and went into Hugo's in Fayetteville. Inside the popular college watering hole, a hefty waitress pointed to a well-dressed gentleman in the rear.

Steve nodded and, crunching peanut shells under his tasseled loafers, approached the nerdy-looking man.

Short and balding, the man stood up. "Mr. President, I'm Earl Edwards, associate legal counsel with Wal-Mart."

"The pleasure is mine," Steve responded as they shook hands.

"Would you like a beer?" Earl asked.

Steve nodded. "A Bud Light would be fine."

Earl ordered a couple of beers and then cleared his throat. "We're impressed with what we're hearing about your planned campaign."

"Thank you. This is our first comprehensive one."

"I know. We're talking about establishing an endowment at EAU."

Steve's spine straightened. "That'd be tremendous."

"I thought you'd like that. We've set aside $2 million for a Chair of Retail Management."

"That'd get everyone's attention." Steve hesitated. "It sounds super, but I'm a little confused."

"What's the issue?"

"I'm not following you. You're headquartered in Bentonville just twenty miles up the road. Ruston is 350 miles away. With the University of Arkansas nearby, why are you interested in us?"

Earl glanced around and leaned forward. "You didn't hear this from me. We're going to introduce a new concept, called superstores. They'll have everything a customer could desire. We plan to increase our market share."

"I've heard you're targeting K-Mart and Toys R Us."

"You didn't hear that from me. We're doing what's best for the customer."

"I suppose that means another nail in Woolworth's coffin and putting the squeeze on small chains like Lowenstein's. Pretty ambitious."

"We're Wal-Mart. We're going to revolutionize the retail industry. We're establishing four national test sites and want one in Ruston."

Steve's eyes widened. "Wow, that'd be something."

"We're building partnerships with leaders. You know — we give a little, you give a little."

"What would I need to do?"

"Nothing. Well, we'd like you to be on the dais when we announce the store location."

"That's something to chew on. Will one of the Walton's come to campus?"

"Of course. We'll pull out all of the PR stops. There'll be a big spread in the paper, a photo of the two of you shaking hands. So, what do you say?"

Steve raked his hair with his fingers. *Woolworth's and Lowenstein's are the heartbeat of downtown Ruston.* "$2 million is one thing but moving business to the freeway. I don't know. That'd kill downtown."

"Look, change is coming. If it's not Wal-Mart, it'll be someone else. You have an opportunity to make Ruston a model. Imagine downtown filled with boutiques and specialty shops. It'd be fantastic."

"I like that," Steve said. He stood and extended his hand. "You've got a deal." Earl squeezed the gold band on Steve's ring figure.

Steve could barely keep his feet on the ground. He'd have to restrain himself until he got to Marie's hotel room.

***

Steve put on his red fedora before sauntering into the banquet room for the team breakfast. He gave a brief rah-rah speech then left to chat with the alums pouring into the hotel.

Spotting Suzanne across the lobby, he walked over. She looked sporty in her EAU sweater and red hat.

"Guess what daddy told me," she gushed.

"I can't imagine."

"The governor is not running for reelection. The party is developing a short list, and daddy put your name on it. Two bigwigs want to interview you tonight. Isn't that great?"

"Yeah, it sure is," he said without gusto.

Suzanne scowled. "Aren't you excited?"

"You've always been better at politics than me."

"I'd die for something like that," she said. "How did it go yesterday?"

"Fine. I'll tell you more on the way to the stadium."

They settled into their seats in the president's box. Suzanne appeared dazed. "I can't believe that $2 million just fell into your lap. I'm so proud of you."

"Thanks, hon. With you by my side, I can do anything."

Working the crowd during the game Steve caught an occasional glimpse of the action. Suzanne chatted with the politicos and paid special attention to Fayetteville's mayor. Steve couldn't bear to watch the Rough Riders implode. By the fourth quarter they were down by 24.

Suzanne kissed him goodbye. "I'll see you at mom and dad's later."

Steve lingered until the bitter end then headed for his in-laws' house.

***

Harriet Hudson greeted him with a glass of gin. Still slender and pretty, she looked young enough to be Suzanne's sister. "I'm sorry about the game. Sounds like the boys ran out of gas."

"Steve, come into the den," Suzanne's dad called.

Frank Hudson rose, giving center stage to his beer gut. He greeted his son-in-law. "I just spoke with Clarence Smithton, state chairman of the Democratic Party, and a couple of big donors. They're on their way over."

"Anything I should know?" Steve asked.

"Nah. Just be yourself. You'll do fine. You can relax on the patio and have a beer."

Frank escorted the party officials outside. The chairman had slicked-back hair and an attitude. Smithton introduced the two distinguished-looking gentlemen then lit up a cigar.

They drilled Steve for three hours.

"What are your views on abortion? How do you feel about the planned housing project in Little Rock? What do you think about funding state pensions?"

Harriet spoke to Suzanne about the social aspects of public life. "Sweetie, I know you love politics, but you need to make sure this is what he wants."

"I know, Mom. It has to be his decision. We can talk more in the morning."

A little after eleven, Steve opened their bedroom door. Suzanne sat up and smoothed her hair. "What did they say? How did it go?"

"Very well. It was mostly exploratory. A lot of what-ifs." He leaned over to kiss her.

She recoiled. "You smell awful. Take a shower."

***

Before breakfast was finished Suzanne was planning Steve's election bid. Steve slept in.

"Well, what did you think?" Frank asked when Steve joined them at half past ten.

"It was exciting. How did I do?"

"They were very impressed. I could tell by their body language."

"Steve, this is the chance of a lifetime," Suzanne added.

"Maybe. But it's not my thing."

"You're missing the point," Suzanne said. "They're considering you."

"Doesn't matter," he said, pushing away from the table. "I'm leaving now. I need to catch up on the lawn work at home."

Frank talked with Steve on the way to the car.

Suzanne shook her head. "Mom, I just don't understand him. Sometimes he can be so wonderful then he's a shithead."

"Honey, he's a man," Harriet said as the two loaded the dishwasher. "How are things going at home?"

Suzanne paused then blurted, "Steve is having an affair."

Harriet dropped a dishtowel in the sink. "Oh my gosh, Suzanne."

"I wasn't going to say anything but I couldn't hold it in any longer."

"Want to talk about it?"

"I'm a failure. I don't know what I want to do." Suzanne broke down.

Harriet handed her a tissue. "Sweetie, I'll be glad to listen."

Suzanne took a deep breath. "It started in college. Miss Everything, Kate Blanchard, decided she wanted him. I know she slept with him."

"Was it an isolated thing?"

"No. For months they were the hot couple on campus."

Harriet poured tea. "Go on."

"They broke up, and we started dating again. Everything seemed fine. We got married. Down deep I had a funny feeling. I'm sure she met him in Knoxville when he was working on his Ph.D. I ignored it. I guess I went into denial. I know that was wrong, but I did it."

"Sweetie, you were in love. It's natural that you'd expected him to be equally committed. Betrayal is a terrible thing."

"I've been married to Steve Schilling for twenty years. Now, I'm the first lady. And she sleeps with him whenever she wants. It's awful, Mom."

"I'm sorry. I know how painful this must be. If you love him, and you don't want a divorce, you'll have to work through it."

"I'm bone weary from working through it. Friday night was the last straw. I called his room three times. He never answered. He comes home late at night. Maybe he's working. Maybe not. He has more overnight meetings than ever. And he's gone most Saturdays. Half the time I don't know where he is. I'm at my wits end."

"Dear, you're not the first woman who's had to deal with infidelity." Harriet paused. "I want to share something I've never told you."

Suzanne looked up. Her eyes were red and swollen.

"Years ago I was in your shoes."

"You were?"

"That's right. Your daddy had an affair. And to make matters worse, he had a chickie babe on the side. Two women at the same time. I thought I'd die of humiliation."

"What did you do?"

"I talked to your grandmother. She said, 'You made your bed, now sleep in it.' I told him the chickie had to go."

Suzanne took a sip of tea. "And then?"

"We argued for weeks. I told him that if he ever crossed that line again, I'd go to the press. Well, he still sleeps with the other woman."

"Oh, Mom. How do you live with that?"

"I don't know. I should have divorced him long ago." She shook her head. "Suzanne, you're smart and attractive. You're still young. You don't need to settle. I think you should dump him."

***

Three weeks later, Carol buzzed Steve. "Mr. President, Senator Hudson is on the phone."

"Put him through."

"Senator, how are you?"

"Fine. Can we talk?"

"Yes, I'm alone."

"Good. Harriet is terribly distraught. Last night she told me about a distressing conversation she had with Suzanne. Suzanne is convinced you're having an affair."

"That's ridiculous. I love Suzanne. Whatever give her that idea?"

"That's what I told Harriet. She went on about a Kate somebody."

"Jesus, Frank. That was twenty years ago. That's ancient history."

"I told Harriet it was probably something like that. But you know how women are."

"Do I? When Suzanne gets something in her craw she won't let go."

"She's just like her mother, Steve. You need to make amends. Take her out for dinner. Go on vacation. Do something special. And, for heaven's sakes, don't mention we've talked."

"No. Of course not. I need to spend more time with her. Show her how much I love her."

That night Steve took a bottle of wine and cheese and crackers to the patio. Suzanne poked her head out the screen door. "What's going on?"

"Just relaxing, thinking about you. How about a chilled glass of Chardonnay."

"I don't know …"

"C'mon. You're always saying we don't talk enough."

"Well … okay. Let me change first."

A few minutes later, after fortifying himself with a glass of wine, he spoke, "I've given a lot of thought to how I've treated you."

"Like what?"

"Everything. I've been caught up in my work. I should have been more considerate. I'm sorry."

"It's not all your fault. We both have let things slide."

Steve leaned over and kissed her. "I want it to be better." he said.

"Steve, not here, the neighbors might see us."

The next morning he slid into the shower behind her. He massaged Suzanne's neck and caressed her shoulders. "Steve, you're going to make me late for work."

He laughed. "I'll call the boss."

"Don't be funny. I have a project I need to finish this morning."

"Just relax."

***

Saturday morning while Steve played golf, Suzanne called her mother. "Maybe I overreacted."

"Overreacted? Suzanne he's been lying and cheating for years."

"He's been under a lot of pressure. I'm not sure I'm being fair. The game was a huge disappointment."

"Things don't change overnight. Keep your eyes and ears open."

"Mom, it'll be okay. I feel better."

"Take it slow, dear. I think you should step back for a while."

That afternoon, Steve called home. "Honey, I'm at the country club with a major donor. When I'm finished I'm going to stop by the County Line Tavern for a cold one with the guys."

"Fine, we're having lamb chops. I won't put them on until you get home."

"Sounds perfect," Steve said, hanging up. He turned to Christina. "Want a drink?"

"I need a shower. Go ahead and fix yours. There's a jar of olives in the fridge."

He took a long sip, stripped, and joined her in the shower.

***

Steve glanced at his watch. *Perfect. A stop at the tavern and he'd be home by 6:30.*

A dozen heads popped up when he walked into the bar. "Hey Prez, come join us," a gray-bearded geezer shouted. "We got some heavy shit to share with you."

Steve joined them and ordered a couple of pitchers.

The burly guy across from him said, "Prez, I don't understand how you get any work done up there. With all that stuff walking around I'd have a hard-on all day."

"It's hard," Steve jested. The guys roared.

The bearded one asked, "Doc, how about that stuff over there in the corner?"

Steve turned to see Marie chatting with two friends. Turning back, he gave a thumbs up.

Marie stood and paraded to the restroom, titties at attention. Every eye followed her. On the way back she flirted with the guy with a flat top, then flipped her hair on her way out.

"Well guys, I gotta go home to momma."

The guys howled.

Steve pointed his Caddy toward Ruston, drove a couple miles then turned up a sandy lane and parked behind Marie's house.

She flew out the back door and threw her arms around his neck. "I've missed you so much. I was hoping you'd stop by."

"Honey, I'm running late. I just wanted to say hi. I can't stay."

"Don't worry, darling," she said, tugging him inside. "I have a special treat for you."

***

After slaving all day, changing the sheets, hosing-down the patio and cleaning the house, Suzanne paused at six to take a break.

She took a relaxing shower, dabbed herself with Trésor and put on the sundress Steve loved. She poured a glass of Chardonnay and went to the patio where she reflected on the good times — canoeing on Cutoff Creek, walking through Blanchard Caverns and dining at Anthony's in St Louis. She refilled her glass.

Glancing at the clock an hour later, her mood plummeted. She emptied the bottle then hurled it onto the patio. Skirting the shattered bottle, she ripped the screen slider from its track and ran, sobbing, to the bedroom.

Steve stepped onto the patio then tiptoed over the broken glass. "Oh shit," he whispered under his breath. "Suzanne. Suzanne? Are you okay?" Reaching the bedroom, he jiggled the locked knob then pounded on the door. "Suzanne."

"Stay out you bastard," she shouted. "I'm done. I can't believe what you've done to me."

"What are you talking about? Are you crazy?"

"Crazy" fueled her fury. She unlocked the door and burst into the hall.

"Crazy?" she shouted, punching him in the chest. She shoved him again and again.

He staggered back and fell onto the sofa in the family room. She leaned down and pressed her finger against his forehead.

"Crazy? You're the one who's crazy. Three days ago you seduced me right here. And today you fucked her. Now tell me, who's the crazy one?"

"What are you talking about?"

"You screwed her in Knoxville. You spent an extra day in Nashville. You're always late after the symphony. You've lied to me for years. You've lied about your lies."

"It's not what you think."

"It's the same thing my mother has gone through."

"Your mother? What does she have to with this?"

Suzanne waved her finger in his face. "Don't play dumb. You know exactly what I am talking about. Kate Blanchard."

"That ended years ago. You're stressed out. You need to see a doctor."

"Stressed? You're the one who's always late. And all the time you've been screwing her."

"Can I say something?"

"Hell no. I'll tell you when you can talk." Suzanne paced, replaying episode after episode, spewing years of frustration.

An hour later she crumbled.

Steve reached for her. "Stop right there," she said. "Keep your ass on the sofa."

Steve leaned back. Meekness in his voice, he asked. "Can I explain now?"

Trembling, Suzanne looked away. "I don't care what the fuck you do."

Steve stood and stepped toward her. "Here's the truth. I played golf with Howard Clark this morning. We had lunch and he introduced me to one of his friends. I had a beer. I was running late so I called you. I stopped at the Tavern and had a couple beers with the guys."

Suzanne sneered. "God, you're really good. You make it sound like it happened just that way."

"It's the truth. Come on honey, let's go to bed. We can talk about it in the morning."

"Go to bed? Is that the only solution you know? I don't want to be in the same room."

"Honey."

"And I don't want to hear any more of that honey crap. You can call me Suzanne. And you can move your stuff to the guest bedroom."

"But ..."

"There'll be no buts. You can fuck Kate all you want. You're not going to touch me. And if you cross me again, I'll have you fired. Do you understand?"

Steve didn't budge. She looked down at him. "You're a sorry mess. Don't just sit there. Get your ass moving."

CHAPTER ELEVEN

Steve pulled a Bud from the fridge. Kicking over the wastebasket on the way to the study, he dropped onto the sofa and surfed for the Green Bay-Detroit game. He couldn't imagine that Suzanne had gone to her parents without saying a word.

He wondered if she'd lost her marbles. Helluva way to spend Thanksgiving, he thought, sucking down his third beer.

Squinting at the clock on his desk, twelve hours later, he wondered what had been bugging her. *Out-of-whack hormones?* Since she'd thrown him out six weeks ago, they rarely connected.

He was no closer to an answer than he had been the night she'd blown up. His heart raced. He had to talk to someone, someone he could trust.

Steve picked up the phone and dialed Rusty McGuiness, his old history department colleague. Rusty would understand.

"Rusty, how are you doing?"

"Steve? I just stepped out of the shower. It's 6 a.m. Are you okay?"

"I'm not sure. I need to talk. Can we meet for breakfast?"

"I guess. See you at Perkins at 7:00."

Fit and trim, with a buzz cut, Rusty fit the model for a CIA agent, not a professor. Seeing Steve, he said, "You look like hell. I can't believe Suzanne allowed you out looking like a skid-row bum."

"She's away."

Rusty cocked his head. "Everything alright?"

"Not really. She kicked me out of our bedroom. I don't know what's wrong. She has everything she could possibly want. She's on everyone's social list. Every woman in town would kill to be in her shoes."

"Slow down. You're not making sense," Rusty said.

"She flipped out. Cut me off for no reason. I'm working my ass off to provide for her."

"That doesn't sound like Suzanne. How is she handling the situation?"

"Suzanne? What about me? Does she think she could raise $25 million? Run a multi-million-dollar university? Or, deal with the faculty?"

"Don't BS me. Get a grip. Are you still seeing Kate?"

"No. But Suzanne thinks so. She's suspicious of everything. She never used to be that way. Every time I walk in the house I get the cold shoulder. Or an inquisition."

"Obviously, your strategy is not working."

"Strategy? I just want to get back in her good graces. And into my bedroom."

"She knows you like a book. You have to be different. Maybe lighten up, kid around."

"Ha. Have you ever tried kidding with a she-wolf?"

"Do something positive. She'll notice. They all do. There are only three weeks left in the semester. You need to soften her up. You'll have plenty of time to talk over the holidays."

***

Steve followed Rusty's directions, did everything he could to be positive and supportive. Suzanne seemed oblivious. On the last day of the fall semester he left the office early. On his way home he picked up two dozen roses. Suzanne's car was gone. On the kitchen table was a note.

Dear Steve:

The thought of being with you for ten days makes me anxious and sad. I need time alone to think. I'm spending the holidays with my parents. I'll be back on Jan 2.

Suzanne

"Damn." He threw the roses in the sink, walked outside and wondered how he'd manage for ten days without her. He considered calling Rusty for moral support then remembered he'd gone skiing in Colorado.

Martha was on a cruise with friends. Sandra was at her mother's in New York. He thought about Kate. He should have married her when he had the chance. Too late now. If he divorced Suzanne, he'd have to pay the price on campus. That is, if Bill didn't kill him first.

He grabbed a bag of pretzels and a bottle of gin on his way to the study. He drew the curtains and turned off the lights before stretching out on the sofa.

Between slugs, he thought about his early years in Kentucky. He grinned, recalling his first love, Mary Lou Kitchen. The summer they met, he was sixteen and she was fourteen.

They had walked along the riverbank almost every day. The first time he kissed her, she was the one.

A few days before the first football practice, they had walked home hand-in-hand on a narrow dirt road. In the distance he saw a pickup and a cloud of dust.

Before he knew it they were engulfed, barely able to see each other.

His dad's pickup slid to a stop. His father jumped out, ran around the truck, flung Steve against the door and slapped his face.

Mary Lou screamed. "Don't hurt him."

His dad smacked him again. "Please don't' hurt him," she cried.

"Dad, what's wrong?"

"You've been skinny-dipping with her, haven't you?" his dad slurred, and shoved Steve into the truck. Mary Lou pounded on the door.

"Dad. We were just walking along the river and talking. Nothing happened."

"You banged her, didn't you?"

"No. I didn't touch her."

"I can tell. You've been banging her all summer," his dad said and put the truck in gear.

"Dad, I didn't do anything," Steve said. He watched Mary Lou in the rearview mirror as she ran after the truck.

The truck screeched into the driveway. His father set the brake, ran to the passenger side and jerked Steve from the cab. Ripping off his belt, he caught Steve with a lash across the back as he ran inside.

Steve fell on the kitchen floor and covered his face. His dad continued to beat him.

A half-hour later, his mother returned from shopping to find Steve sprawled on the floor, his shirt shredded, blood oozing from the welts crisscrossing his back. She dropped the grocery bags. "Steve, are you okay?"

Steve had whispered, "Mom, don't touch me. Lock yourself in the bedroom." She turned away, but not before his dad's fist connected with her jaw, knocking her out.

Steve scrambled up. His dad's belt opened a wound on his shoulder. Another blow flattened him. "Serves you both right," his dad shouted, stumbling toward the bedroom.

Steve pressed his hands against his face, recalling just one of his dad's many drunken rages. He had felt so humiliated, so diminished.

His mother had endured so much pain. He wondered why she stayed. And why his father had been such a bastard.

Why couldn't his dad have been more like Uncle Freddie?

Steve awoke with a stare, unsure if he'd been asleep for minutes or hours. A glance at the wall clock and he realized that Suzanne would be home in a few hours.

"Christ," he muttered. He had to clean the house — and himself — and put on a show, as if everything was hunky-dory. He took his first shower in a week and lathered up. He could feel Christina's hands stroking him.

"God, I love you, Christina," he sighed.

He never heard Suzanne come in.

The next morning he saw her half-empty mug in the sink. He phoned Carol to say he'd be in by ten.

He dragged himself in the office around eleven and left early that afternoon. Over the next few weeks he missed meetings, lost his temper over minutiae and swore at staff members.

***

On a gray day in late February Steve marched past Carol, tossed his briefcase on his desk then did an about face. "I'm going across campus," he said. "It's too damn stuffy in here."

Head low, he tripped, leaving the building and banged his knee. Breaking his pledge never to talk to Sandra on campus, he pulled his collar up against the rain and walked toward her office.

Near the front door of the music building, he bumped into her assistant nearly knocking her down.

"Good morning, Mr. President," she said. "I'm going to pick up Sandra at Ruston Ford."

"Tell her 'Hi' for me," he mumbled, before returning to his office.

Carol gave him a quizzical look as he lumbered past her and stuffed his briefcase with papers. "I'm coming down with a cold," he barked. "Taking the rest of the week off. Don't call me unless the building is on fire."

He opened his umbrella and walked to his car. A familiar voice stopped him cold.

"Slipping out early, Mr. President?" Marie asked.

"It's been a bitch of a week," he said, opening the car door. "I've got to get out of here."

"Want to come by for a drink?"

His frown turned to a smile. "Sure. I'll see you in twenty minutes."

***

Steve grabbed for the ringing phone, knocking an empty gin bottle to the floor.

"Yeah, what do you want?"

"It's Rusty. We have to talk. Now. Meet me at Perkins in twenty minutes."

"Rusty, its spring break."

"You heard me. Get your ass over here."

"O-okay," Steve stammered. "I'll be over as soon as I shave and shower."

Rusty unloaded before Steve had removed his jacket. "What's wrong with you?"

"I'm stressed. Suzanne won't talk to me."

"Suzanne? Don't give me that crap. You're not prepared for meetings. You've been canceling appointments. Everyone is talking. What's gotten into you?

"Nothing, I'm okay."

"Bullshit." Heads turned. Rusty lowered his voice. "You're not okay. What's going on?"

Steve shrugged.

Rusty pulled a slip of paper from his pocket and tossed it across the table. "Here are nineteen incidents I've heard about in the last six weeks. The shit is ready to hit the fan."

"What?" He wore his hang-dog expression. "That's not possible, I'm doing the best I can."

"Baloney. You've been a no-show several times. Your assistant has covered receptions — three that I know of. Worst of all, you sent Ed O'Connell to run the budget hearings. Christ, you know what the faculty thinks of him. You might as well have sent the devil."

"Geez, he's the financial VP. Who else would I send?"

"You should have been there yourself. People are calling me. I don't have time to cover your ass. Everyone wants to know what's happening. You'd better get control of yourself. Do you understand?"

Rusty and Steve had shared an office for eight years. Rusty did not wait for an answer and left in a huff.

Steve stared at his empty cup. *We've never disagreed before. How could Rusty be so critical?*

Steve acknowledged that he'd asked Carol to rearrange a few meetings. Did the faculty expect him to ignore a state senator? Hell that could have cost the university millions.

He walked to his car and drove slowly toward home before making an abrupt U-turn and speeding toward Marie's. He knocked.

She parted the curtains then unlocked the door.

Steve grabbed her and held her tight. "Sweetie, I need you."

"What's wrong?"

"I couldn't sleep. Things are a mess."

"Come in. I'll make some coffee." She hugged him. "Don't worry. We can work it out."

***

Crossing the family room after being with Marie for two days, Steve caught Suzanne's sneer. "You bastard. You've been with her, haven't you?"

It was not a question. "I can't stand being around you. I'm going to my parents. I can't take it anymore."

"Good. Maybe your mother can talk some sense into you," he shouted.

"Sense? You've got a lot of nerve. You're the one with no sense."

106

***

On Wednesday Steve stopped by Kate's before poker. She watched him shuffle up the steps. "Are you okay?" she asked. "I've never seen you look so bad, or move so slowly."

"Everything is fucked up."

"What are you talking about?"

"I'm doing my best. No one appreciates how hard I work. Even Rusty McGuiness blasted me. He said I'm 'in deep-shit city.' He's never treated me that way."

"Maybe you are trying to do too much," she said, sliding her arms around his waist.

Steve pushed her away. "When Rusty speaks I need to listen."

"That's fine." She brushed the hair from his eyes. "Darling, you need to listen to me, too. I can smell booze on your breath. You're disheveled. People notice things like that. You've got to get back to being your old self."

"I can't relax. I'm having trouble sleeping."

"Steve, you're rationalizing. Making excuses. That's not like you."

"I'm okay. I'm going to play poker," he said.

***

By mid-summer, a hair away from stepping down, Steve pulled into Bill's driveway and waited for the thunderstorm to subside. When the rain slowed, he made a beeline for the porch.

Water gushed from the gutter, soaking him. "Damn, I get dumped on everywhere I go."

Once inside, Bill tossed him a towel. "Here, I'll fix you a drink."

"Make it a double," Steve said. "You look good, Bill."

"Thanks, I'm doing fine. I played golf with Don. It sounds like the campaign is in full swing."

Steve perked up. "Yeah, we've exceeded $22 million. Don and I met with a couple of his friends. They had their checkbooks out before I finished my pitch."

"There's no one better than Don Cagney. Anything else happening?"

Steve fixed another double. "I feel like I'm pushing the locomotive, not driving it. How did you deal with the pressure?"

Bill leaned back in his recliner. "It's tough. There's no magic formula. You learn to cope. Pace yourself. Virginia helped me a lot. She listened. I could vent to her without judgment." He paused. "Are things okay between Suzanne and you?"

"Couldn't be better."

"Good. I've seen stress destroy a lot of guys. It creeps up on them. Some drink too much. Others have a fling or two. Then an affair. It makes them feel pumped up for a while, then they lose their drive for work. Next they have personal problems. They start to cover one lie with another. Pretty soon sex becomes the problem. It drags them down. That's why it's so important to keep those home fires burning."

"I hear you. No problem there."

***

A couple days before the season opener with Arkansas, Steve stormed out of his office. "Christ, Carol, can't you do anything right? I gave you a simple letter to type."

"Mr. President, your handwriting was difficult to read. I'm sorry."

"Difficult? I've been writing that way all of my life."

"I understand, but …"

"Don't talk back to me."

"Yes, sir."

"And don't give me any of that condescending 'Yes, sir' stuff."

Her eyes filled. "I'll make the changes right away."

Steve turned, slammed his door and dialed Eddie.

"Are you coming to Fayetteville again for the game?" Steve asked.

"Yeah, I'll call you for dinner when I arrive Thursday nights."

***

Friday morning Steve answered the phone.

"Steve, its Eddie. I ate alone last night. Where the hell were you?"

"I got in late. Went straight to bed."

"You're full of crap. I'm in the restaurant. Get your ass down here."

"What the fuck is wrong with you?"

"You know. Get down here."

108

Steve moseyed into the dining room a few minutes later. "You look like shit. Where the hell were you last night? I called your room every fifteen minutes until after ten."

"I-I got tied up."

"You mean you got laid. Did you stop in Little Rock?"

Steve lowered his eyes. "I was with Marie all night."

"Marie? Who the hell is she? Don't tell me you're screwing someone else."

"It's not like that."

"Oh, excuse me. You're in love. Shit man, you're crazier than hell."

"I'm not crazy. I'm physically exhausted."

"And now you're a psychologist."

"I can only relax when I'm with one of them."

"You're worse than before." Eddie rolled his eyes. "Okay, let's hear about Marie."

"You wouldn't believe her. She gives the best blow jobs. Fucks all night. I love her."

"I suppose you write to her, too. What color is her stationery?"

"Rose. I gave it to her last year."

"Last year? Man, you're sicker than I thought."

"I'm not. I'm worn out."

"Here we go again. We're talking in circles. How's Suzanne?"

"She's cut me off. She has all these damn rules. I don't know what she wants."

"Steve, look at me. I told you to take care of her. Are you still doing the others?"

"Yeah, but I have it all worked out."

"I know. They're on a schedule. What about Suzanne?"

"She thinks Kate is the only one."

"That's a consolation."

"Look, Steve, I have a doctor friend in Ft. Smith. He's a good guy. I've described your situation. I'm very worried about you. He'd be glad to meet with you. No one will know. Will you see him?"

"I'll think about it."

"Think about it? You've got to do more than think about it. You're going down the toilet. You'll lose your job. Suzanne. Everything."

***

Steve replayed Eddie's words then suffered through the fumbles and miscues that dominated the Rough Riders 38-24 loss, then left the stadium and joined the traffic jam.

Exiting the freeway in Little Rock, he headed for Martha's. He rang her doorbell and waited. Martha opened the door and stepped back. "It's been months. Why are you here?"

"I should have called but I wanted to surprise you."

"I hope your surprise is better than the game."

"Wasn't that awful? And to think, all week I predicted we'd win."

"So what's the surprise?"

"Remember my telling you about Eddie Wilson?"

"Sure, he's your old quarterback. Easy to talk to."

"Right. We discussed Suzanne's behavior. I told him how I feel about you."

"Steve, I can't ..."

"Wait, that's why I'm here." Steve sat next to her on the couch and took a deep breath. "I've moved my stuff to the guest bedroom. It's going to happen for us, darling. I love you, Martha."

Her eyes glistened. "Steve, are you sure?"

"I'm positive. Eddie said it could be messy. He thinks I need professional help. You know someone to help me deal with the situation and all the shit she'll throw at me."

"I agree. You can't deal with campus issues and her at the same time. Darling, I can't believe it. Are you sure you have no doubts?"

"None, I've never been surer of anything in my life. I love you."

***

Monday morning Steve scanned the physician's section in the *Yellow Pages* then paused at David Gordon, MD. He circled his golfing partner's office number and dialed.

David greeted Steve at the door the next morning. Tall and lanky, he sported a salt-and-pepper goatee. "Thanks for coming in early," Steve said.

"Hey, what are friends for? Had any chest pains?"

"No, I'm zapped. Zero energy."

110

"I'm not surprised. Your job is highly stressful. What's bothering you?"

"I can't sleep. I'm anxious. Can't relax. Drink too much. And I've gained twenty-five pounds."

"Well, you're five for five on the stress-o-meter. I'm going to schedule an EKG. Normally, I'd tell a patient to slow down, but I know you won't. Here's a prescription to help you relax. And I want you to lose fifteen to twenty pounds."

"Is that it?"

"Has Suzanne mentioned any changes in your behavior?"

Steve looked at the floor. "We're not talking. She's pissed."

"Probably for good reason. She's reacting to you, to your behavior. Have you considered getting professional help? I hear Reverend Scanlon is a really good listener."

***

The doorbell rang and Bill shuffled to the front room for his fall meeting with Steve. He opened the door and gasped.

Steve's eyes were rheumy. His matted hair curled on his neck, and his stomach hung over his belt. "Button your shirt," Bill scolded.

"I can't take any more."

Bill gave him a hug. "It's not easy, son. I'm having an iced tea on the deck. Want some?"

"No. I'll fix a gin and catch up."

They sat across from each other at the glass-topped table.

"What truck ran over you?"

"I'm a little down from the game."

"A little down? I'm hearing grumbling on campus. Nasty rumors."

Steve straightened up. "Damn, what do they want from me? Enrollment is up. We're building an education building. We've completed our $25 million campaign. What more do they want?"

"They want you to be in charge. Not missing meetings or asking Carol to reassign things."

"Bill, I'm working my ass off."

"Have you talked to Suzanne about this?"

"What are you a marriage counselor?" Steve snapped and stormed out.

CHAPTER TWELVE

Steve peeled out of Bill's driveway. At a red light several blocks away, he slammed on the brakes. The car rocked, missing an Audi by inches.

He grimaced, fearing he'd offended Bill. A honk from behind startled him. Steve glanced in the rearview mirror, thought about flipping the SOB the bird then floored his Caddy.

Turning down the next street, he pulled over. He thought of returning to Bill's to apologize then slammed the car in gear and drove to Rusty's.

"What are you doing here?" Rusty asked.

"I just made a fool of myself."

"Again?" Rusty laughed. "C'mon in."

"I lost my temper with Bill. We were talking about Suzanne and I blew a fuse. He was trying to help. Maybe I should go back and apologize."

"It can't be that bad. Bill likes you. And he's a forgiving sort. Write him a note and thank him for his advice."

"Good idea. I'll do it as soon as I get home."

"Anything else?"

Steve scratched his forehead. "Things are messed up. I'm in deep shit. I don't know what to do."

"Steve, I can't tell you what to do. Nobody can. You have to decide what you want."

"I want to be president of EAU."

"No, no. I'm talking about your personal life. Do you want to be with Suzanne? Or, would you rather be with Kate? You can't have your cake and eat it too."

"Why would you even ask?"

"Because I'm your friend. You can't have it both ways. It's dragging you down."

"Rusty, I ..."

Rusty cut him off. "Look, everyone is watching you. This is a small town. Sooner or later someone will spill the beans. If you want Suzanne, I'll help. If not, you're on your own."

"Of course I want Suzanne to be the first lady."

Rusty glared. "Okay, but if you stray I'm outta here."

Steve stood tall. "You can depend on me. I'll follow your lead."

"This is going to take some time."

While Rusty lectured, Steve kept silent and nodded occasionally. "Remember," he concluded, "you can't deviate. Do you understand?"

"I'll do whatever it takes," Steve said.

"We'll start by meeting at my place on the first and third Saturday of every month."

***

Steve strolled into the office wearing a pressed shirt and new tie. He looked like he was showing up for a job interview. Carol glanced up. "Who's this handsome man?"

Steve placed a bouquet of multicolored tulips on her desk. "I want you to know how much I appreciate you. I'm sorry for the way I acted. I'll do better."

"That's nice of you. Thank you for the flowers. I know you're under a lot of pressure. If there is any way I can help, please let me know. I'm a good listener."

Later in the week, Steve parked and walked up to his friend's door. Rusty opened it before Steve had a chance to knock.

"You clean up real nice. Looks like you're off to a good start," he said. "How does it feel?"

"Super. I feel great. Until I get home. Suzanne hasn't changed."

"What did you expect? You haven't done anything to change her mind."

"I thought she'd at least be civil."

"Be patient. You have to take it one step at a time."

"I know, but ..."

"Follow my advice. Keep everything under control in the office. No spouting off. And show up on time for meetings. Stay the course."

"What about Suzanne?"

"She's long-term. It's going to take several months."

"Months?"

"Steve, people don't change overnight. You have to modify your habits. When Suzanne hears good things about you and notices that you're more attentive, it will help your cause. You can deliver later."

"Deliver what?"

"Court her, like when you were dating. Give her flowers. Open the car door. Fix things around the house that bug her. Take her out for dinner — not too fancy. Be thoughtful. And make sure there's nothing physical. A smile — that's it. No kissing. And for heaven's sake don't make any suggestive comments."

"It'll take forever to win her back."

"It may take six months or more. You need to convince her that you truly want her back. That you're committed."

"How do I do that?"

"You'll figure it out. And when the time comes, you have to be ready."

"Ready for what?"

"Think about how you can please her. It'll come to you."

***

"How's it going, Rusty?" Steve shook the snow from his overcoat and hung it on the coat tree by Rusty's front door.

"Fine. Looks like you're off to a good start this year."

"I'm on a roll."

"I can tell. There's a good buzz about you on campus."

"Oh?"

"I'm thinking, maybe it's time to take the next step with Suzanne."

"Which is? I don't want to offend her."

"Steve, I'm not talking about jumping into bed. Make use of your natural skills — your charm, like you do on campus."

Steve gave Rusty a blank look. "I ..."

"Do I have to script it for you?"

"No, but I …"

"Come on, Steve. Heads turn when you walk into a room. People like you. They want to be around you. Be charismatic with her."

"I don't know if I can do it. When I see her I want to grab her."

"Forget about sex. Act like you've never been with her before."

"I'm not that good."

"Stop right there. I've heard women talk about you. They'd wet their pants if you even looked at them. They talk about your eyes. How you look at them. Your sincerity. Shit, I bet half of them would trade-in their husbands if you blinked. You know what I mean?"

"Well, maybe."

"Valentine's Day will soon be here. Do you remember what you gave Suzanne for your first Valentine's Day together?"

"Sure. A heart-shaped box of chocolates and a dozen roses."

"That's a little much. Let's start with the flowers. We'll add the chocolates later."

***

Steve carried two bunches of daffodils he'd picked up at the town florist on his way home from work. At the front door, he eyed the blooming crocuses in the yard and felt hopeful.

Suzanne gave him a peck on the cheek when he handed her the bouquet. "Steve, the flowers are lovely. You didn't need to do that."

"Yes I did. You deserve them." His eyes swept the room. "Everything looks great. You sure know how to make a place warm and inviting."

He started to reach for her just as the phone rang.

"I'll get it," Suzanne said, and went to the kitchen.

Steve moseyed into the family room. Fixing a drink, he heard her exclaim. "Daddy, thank you. That's wonderful. We'll talk later." She joined Steve in the family room, looking like a little girl on Christmas morning.

"What was that all about?" he asked.

"The governor just appointed me the Regional Representative for Economic Development. Can you believe it?"

Steve got up. Forgetting the script, he went to her and they hugged. "That's wonderful. I'm so proud of you."

She held him tight. "Pour us some wine. I want to tell you everything."

"And I want to hear every detail."

"This is one of the best days in a very long time," she said, raising her glass.

"Good for you," Steve said, topping off her Chardonnay. "I have something to share too."

"What is it?"

"I've been meeting with Doc Gordon. He's given me a lot of sound advice and suggestions on how we can work out our differences."

Suzanne frowned. "Steve, I've told you."

"Please, just hear me out."

"There is nothing to talk about. Don't spoil my day."

"Suzanne, I don't want to mess up anything. But I need you to listen. Have I ever admitted that I lied, told you that I was wrong or said I was willing to meet with our minister?"

"No ... you've never said any of that."

"People change. I want to make our marriage work."

She bit her lip. "Okay, I'll listen."

"When you kicked me out of the bedroom, I was really in bad shape. At first I was pissed. Then I realized you should have kicked me out long ago."

Suzanne's lower lip quivered.

"I told the doctor about my lies. He gave me some straight talk. Said I had to deal with my problems before we could make any progress as a couple."

"Well, I agree with that."

"He suggested that I meet with Reverend Lucas Scanlon and tell him everything — how badly I've treated you and how much I want you back."

"You'd do that?"

"I'd do anything. He suggested that I see the reverend alone at first. Then you can meet with him. And when the time is right, the two of us can see him together."

"Steve, so much has happened ..."

"Is it okay for me to call the minister?"

"I want to say yes. But, I'm scared. I can't take another roller-coaster ride."

"Don't worry, darling. I won't let you down. Please say yes."

"I'll think about it." Suzanne sighed.

"Thank you. That's all I could ask." He glanced at his watch. "I've gotta cleanup for poker."

***

On Saturday morning, Suzanne and her mother were wrapping up their weekly gabfest.

"How are things at home?" her mother asked.

"Steve and I are trying to work things out."

Dead air.

"Mom, did you hear me?"

"You never mentioned anything about working it out. Are you sure?"

"Yes. I've given it a lot of thought. And we've talked a lot. He's changed."

"Suzanne, I've heard that before. Be careful."

"Mom, it's different. I can tell. He's on top of his game. I'm hearing good things from people on campus. He's changed."

"Has he tried anything?"

"Mom, he's been a perfect gentleman. He said he knows that he has to earn my respect. You wouldn't believe how kind and thoughtful he's been. It almost makes me want to …"

"Watch your step." Her tone sharpened. "You don't know what he's planning."

"Mom, he doesn't have a plan. I can tell. He's for real."

"Men don't change overnight."

"It's not like I'm going to jump in bed with him," she said with exasperation. "We're just trying to reconnect."

"I want you to be happy, dear. But, I don't trust him as far as I could throw him."

***

Steve parked behind the church and walked in. Reverend Scanlon looked up. "Good to see you, Steve. Want a cup of coffee?"

"Sure, black would be fine."

"Have a chair." The reverend placed Steve's coffee on the small table between them. After some chit-chat, he asked, "What's all of this personal stuff you wanted to discuss?"

"I'm a little embarrassed."

"There is no reason to be. Everyone has issues, challenges. Relax. And please call me Lucas."

Steve spoke slowly and chose his words carefully. "Suzanne and I are having problems."

"I'm sorry to hear that. What's happening?"

"In college I dated a girl. And I had a brief fling with her when I was in grad school, after Suzanne and I got married. I've seen her a few times since. There is nothing between us. I've confessed everything to Suzanne."

Lucas glanced up from his notes. "Sounds like you've taken a big step."

"I thought so, but Suzanne is still hung up. She's suspicious about everything. When I come home at night, she gives me the look. When I have a meeting out of town and have to stay overnight, I get the cold shoulder. Sometimes she doesn't speak to me at all. Other times she blows up. I never know what to expect. It's like I'm walking on eggshells."

"Steve, trust is hard to rebuild."

"We haven't slept together in ages."

"Sounds like this will take a lot of work from both of you."

"I know. We've agreed to try. We decided that I'd chat with you first. Then Suzanne can share her feelings. When you think we're ready, we'll come in together."

"That'll work." Lucas nodded. "Admitting there's a problem and agreeing to work on it is half the challenge. Want to start today?"

"Next week would be better. I'm leaving for Little Rock in an hour."

***

Rusty and Steve met at the end of the semester. "How's it going with Reverend Scanlon?" Rusty asked.

"Perfect. I can't believe how much he knows about people. I've told him everything. He hasn't been judgmental. He listens and makes suggestions. I feel like a new person."

"Good for you. And how's it going with Suzanne?"

"Pretty well. We're talking more. We started doing things together — watching TV, going to movies."

"That sounds like progress."

"She's finishing her sessions with Reverend Scanlon after the Christmas holidays. Things are a lot better at home. The other night I got the feeling she was ready for sex. I was a good boy, didn't make a move."

"Good. Keep doing what you're doing. She'll come around."

***

Suzanne got home after her final session with Reverend Scanlon and called her mother. "Mom, I feel like a new woman. I've thought about things I'd never considered before. I understand Steve. I can't wait until the three of us meet."

"Suzanne. I don't want to sound like a stick in the mud. But …"

"I know, Mom."

"It's none of my business, but has Steve tried anything yet?"

"No. He told me to take all the time I need. He isn't pushing me."

"That's good. I don't want you to get hurt again."

"Try not to worry. I know what I'm doing."

***

After a half dozen joint meetings with Dr. Scanlon, Suzanne clasped Steve's hand. "Dr. Scanlon, I want to thank you for helping us find ourselves — and each other," she said.

"I'll second that. You've helped us to sort things out," Steve said. "I'm eternally grateful."

The old minister smiled. "It's always gratifying when things work out. You've both worked hard. It's nice to see a happy ending. God bless you my children."

They shook hands and hugged each other.

Suzanne chattered all the way home. Pulling into the garage, Steve grabbed a box of chocolates from the back seat and followed her to the kitchen. He gave her a peck on the cheek and handed her the box.

"I love you, darling."

"You're so sweet."

120

She reached for him and pressed against him. "Reverend Scanlon was so empathetic. He seemed to know exactly how I felt."

"I know. He said things that made me appreciate how wonderful you are. How much I love you. And how much I appreciate all the things you've done for me. For us."

"I want tonight to be special," she said, loosening her blouse. "I'm going to change. Would you open a bottle of wine?"

"How about champagne?"

"Even better," she said.

Steve flipped the switch on the gas fireplace and put on the Kenny G's CD, "Don't Make Me Wait for Love." Feeling pleased with himself, he opened the champagne and stretched out on the sofa.

A few minutes later Suzanne appeared in an ankle-length black peignoir.

He eyed her and nearly spilled the champagne. "Here's to the most wonderful woman in the world."

"Oh, Steve, thank you for your commitment to restore our marriage. I'm so proud of you. I love you," she said, placing her glass on the table.

She pulled him to her and gave him a French kiss. "I want to make love to you all night." She took his hand and led him to their bedroom.

CHAPTER THIRTEEN

Gerald Coleman strolled into the *Daily Gazette* wearing his signature bowtie. Following in his dad's footsteps, he'd been editor of the paper for eighteen years. A town father, he was known for his high ethical standards.

Unloading a stack of papers from his briefcase, he glanced at his desktop calendar. May 15th was circled in red, reminding him that in six weeks, Steve Schilling would complete his fifth year as EAU president.

He recalled the feature he had written for Bill Thornton's retirement. It was his best work, but who'd remember?

This time he wanted Karen Holmes, his top reporter, to write the feature. In her four years with the *Gazette*, she'd paid her dues and, at 33, was the daily's rising star.

With a master's degree from the University of Missouri, she had already won three honorable mentions in state competitions.

Gerry walked through the newsroom and paused to read the note tacked to the partition marking her cubicle. At Ruston High. Returning at ten. Karen.

On her desk he left a reply to stop by his office at 10:30.

Karen tapped on his window.

He waved her in and gestured for her to sit down. "How's the high school science project going?" he asked.

"Wonderful. The kids will fire the rockets next week."

"You've done a splendid job on that. I have something for you to sink your teeth into. We're doing a feature on President Schilling's fifth anniversary."

"That's good. He deserves it."

"I want you to do a four-part series."

"But ... I've never done a major feature."

"You have to start somewhere. You're up to the task. Anne Mitchell will help you."

"Good. She's a real pro."

"I'm looking for a different hook. Most people don't have a clue what a college president does or what makes him tick. I'm hoping you can uncover something unique, maybe a life-changing event in his early life."

Karen worked through lunch. By 6:00 crumpled notes littered her normally pristine space.

Gerry popped in on his way home. "Are you done yet?"

She jumped. "You scared the crap out of me."

He laughed. "I'm just kidding. I wouldn't expect you to write it in one day. Let it percolate for a few days. We'll talk next week."

Karen straightened her office and went home. She tossed a salad and carried it with a plate of Triscuit's to the table. She thought about growing up in New Orleans. *How had that affected her career? Had she ever had a life-changing event?* She shrugged her shoulders. Not yet, she decided.

***

Looking stylish in her blue blazer and charcoal-gray skirt, Karen mounted a stool at the layout table. Anne sat across from her, a heavyset woman whose smudged glasses dangled from a silver chain. She finger-combed her salt-and-pepper hair.

"Where do we start?" Anne asked.

"I'm not sure. Gerry said he wants something different. I'm embarrassed to say that I didn't come up with much over the weekend."

"Did he give you any guidelines?"

"He told me to answer four questions."

"What were they?"

Karen flipped through her notebook. "How did growing up in rural Kentucky affect your life? When you were in college, did you ever think that one day you'd be a university president? What activities and events prepared you to become president? What's the toughest part of being a president?"

"Sounds like you're on target."

"Have any ideas?"

"Nah, you're the journalist. Just put the meat on the bones."

***

Gerry waved Karen in. She handed him the outline and sat down. He spent maybe ten seconds reading it. "It's good, Karen. But it could be better."

"Better?"

"You have the facts. People want to know more. What drives him? What are his beliefs?"

"You mean I have to start over?" she asked, her voice cracking.

"Just change the emphasis. Humanize him."

The following day, Karen parked her Camaro in the visitors' lot and followed the Victorian-style street lamps up the hill to Thornton Hall. She adjusted the skirt of her cream-colored suit and announced herself to the president's receptionist.

"May I help you?"

"Thank you. I'm Karen Holmes from the *Gazette*. I'm doing a feature on President Schilling and I'd like to make an appointment to interview him." She said it without taking a breath.

The woman opened a leather-bound calendar. "How about lunch next Friday at noon? That's June 1st."

"Lunch? That'd be fine."

"I'll call you that morning to confirm the location."

***

Stepping inside the Red Pepper Deli ten minutes early, Karen removed her sunglasses and looked at the classic décor — red and white checkered tablecloths and pictures of the Italian countryside adorned the walls.

A waving hand caught her eye. She headed toward her assignment. He stood. "Hi, I'm Steve Schilling."

"I'm Karen Holmes," she said, tripping over a chair leg and falling against him. He caught her arm and smiled. "It's nice to meet you."

"It's a pleasure to meet you," she said, regaining her composure.

"Would you like a drink?"

"Ah, yes. I mean no," she stammered. "I'll have iced tea."

"Are you sure? I'm having a glass of Chianti."

"Unsweetened tea will be fine," she said, forcing a smile.

"What does Gerry have in mind?" Steve asked.

125

"He wants me to focus on what motivates you." She sipped water to moisten her cotton mouth.

"I like that. But first, tell me a little about yourself."

As she opened her napkin, her fork dropped to the floor. "There's not much to say," she said, her head level with the table top.

Steve signaled for a clean fork. "Where did you grow up?"

Twenty minutes later she glanced at her watch.

"I'm sorry. I talk too much sometimes. What was it like growing up in eastern Kentucky?"

"Pretty dull," he said.

"Tell me about your parents."

"Dad was a coal miner. Drunk most of the time. Mom did everything — cleaned houses, took in laundry and sewed. She never complained. After dad died, mom insisted I go to college. She'd stuff a five-dollar bill in every letter. That was a real sacrifice for her."

"It must have been tough."

"I only saw her happy one time." His tongue loosened by the second glass of wine, he rambled. "A couple of years after my dad died, his brother Fred — my Uncle Freddie — came for Thanksgiving. He brought mom a red rose and a new dress. You'd have thought he gave her a diamond necklace. She danced around the kitchen. I'd never seen her do that." Steve shook his head. "My dad was an ogre. Kept her down." He glanced up, glassy-eyed. "I guess I got carried away. Maybe that shouldn't be in the story."

"No problem. I'd like to meet again in a couple of weeks."

"Sure. Let's make it here at noon on the 15th."

***

Karen strolled back to the *Gazette*, feeling foolish for having told him her life story. His easygoing manner invited conversation. He would have made a good journalist. She stopped by Gerry's office to check in.

"How'd the interview go?" he asked.

"Okay, I guess."

"What's your assessment?" The phone rang. "Excuse me a second while I get this."

The conversation was brief. "Thanks, Steve. I'm glad it went well." Gerry hung up and turned his attention to Karen.

"That was the president. He praised your professionalism and said he thinks you're a cute young reporter."

"Cute?"

"Forget it. Go home and enjoy the weekend. We'll meet next week."

Karen grabbed her briefcase and stormed out of the building. "Cute," she snarled. "He thinks I'm cute."

That night Steve nursed a drink on his patio. He smirked, knowing he'd have to work hard to continue fooling Suzanne. No problem, he thought. He'd pulled the wool over her eyes before, just as he fooled his dad in high school about skinny-dipping with Mary Lou.

He smiled, remembering the dimple just to the left of her mouth. *Karen had one there too. She could pass for Mary Lou's sister.* How he longed for Mary Lou.

***

Karen couldn't make up her mind what to wear. Settling on a pink blouse and black vest and slacks, she drove to the office. She flipped through her notes and practiced her questions. At 11:45 she smiled in the mirror, undid the top button of her blouse and left for the deli.

She adjusted her pearl necklace and strolled in as if she owned the place. Spotting him, she went to the table — the same one as last time. A glass of white wine sat at her place.

Steve raised his glass to her. "Here's to a most successful interview."

"Thank you," she said, unwrapping her napkin. This time she didn't drop her fork.

They ordered. Karen pressed forward. "Tell me about playing football in college."

"I was an average player, in the right place at the right time. In my senior year I caught the winning pass in the championship game. From then on, people thought I was an All-American."

"Well, you must have been pretty good." Karen pulled a handful of photos from her purse. "It looks like you're laying out the yearbook here."

"Actually, we were working on *The Rough Rider*, the college paper. Suzanne — my wife — is on the right."

Karen passed him another picture. "Are these your cheerleaders?"

"Yes, that's Molly Green in the center. She was the best — the first black student on campus."

"She's very attractive. Did you date her?"

"No. Molly was a good friend, someone I could talk with."

"Who's the blonde on the left?"

"That's Kate Blanchard. We dated in college. Off and on."

"What happened?"

He shrugged. "It didn't work out."

Karen spread the remaining photos on the table. "Anything else you'd like to mention?"

Steve sifted through the photos. "No, I think you've covered it all."

"Good. I'll be able to wrap this up in one more session."

***

Steve left the house early for a meeting with Rosemary Frye in Helena, about two hours away. He followed the Mississippi south for a spell, headed west toward Marianna then south again.

Near Helena, he stopped at a white bungalow with green shutters and a picket fence. Baskets of geraniums hung from the porch. He scanned her file, noting she had graduated cum laude as music major in the '40s. For many years she had been a member of the president's advisory committee.

The front door opened and a tall, stately woman in her late sixties stepped out. Her long dark hair blew in the breeze as she waved from the porch. "Hello, Mr. President," she called.

"Good morning, Ms. Frye."

"Please come in. I've made a pot of coffee," she said, holding the door open for him.

"I can smell it."

"It's nice to meet you," she said, shaking his hand. "Please call me Rosemary. Bill Thornton told me you'd come if I called."

"Do you know President Thornton well?"

"Oh yes, Bill and I have worked on several projects. We spoke last night. He said raisin pie is your favorite. I just took one out of the oven."

"Nothing better."

"Good, let's talk in the kitchen. How do you like your coffee?"

"Black, thank you."

"I bet you're wondering why I asked you to come," she said, slicing the pie.

"I must admit I'm curious."

"I have a story I'd like to share."

"Okay."

"About twenty-five years ago, Samuel Warfield willed his farm to the Helena Community Association. When he died, the farm was sold and the money was placed in an endowment to fund the Warfield Concert Series. It's free to the public, you know."

"Yes. The number of national performers who make guest appearances is quite impressive."

"Over the years people have contributed to the fund. For the last ten years we've had a single goal."

"What are you shooting for?"

"We want to name the music building at EAU after our town's favorite son."

Steve put his fork down.

"Bill said it'd take $1 million. Well, this spring we were $50,000 short."

"You have $950,000?"

"Hold on, you're getting ahead of my story. After seeing your Dr. Whitehead perform with the Memphis Symphony, I came up with an idea."

"You did?"

"I asked her if she'd play in a fiddling duel against Charlie Daniels. She said she'd never played country and western in public but would play if Charlie agreed. I challenged one of the good ol' boys to come up with the $50,000 if she won."

"And?"

"She won. Want another piece of pie before I make my proposal?"

***

Karen arrived a few minutes before the noontime rush and glanced at the empty table. A waitress appeared. "Are you Karen Holmes?"

"Yes."

"President Schilling just called. He's running late. He's ordered you a glass of wine which I put on that corner table."

"Thank you."

Karen took a sip and looked over the luncheon specials.

Steve joined her a few minutes later. "Sorry I'm late. I just got back from Helena."

"No problem."

"I went to meet with Rosemary Frye, an alum, about establishing a scholarship in music. She proposed a $1 million naming gift for the music building."

"Wow, that's exciting. What happened?"

"Well, I shouldn't discuss it." He stroked his chin. "It'd have to be off the record."

"Of course."

"Last spring they were a little short of their goal. Mrs. Frye challenged one of our alums to ante up the shortfall if an EAU faculty member could outplay Charlie Daniels in 'The Devil Went Down to Georgia.'"

"You mean like a duel?"

"Exactly. Instead of Charlie playing both parts — his and the devil's — they split it."

"Did she win?"

"Did she win? She did a Celtic dance step of rapid leg and foot movements while she played, had Charlie tied up in knots, sweating like a hog. Long story short, they have a million bucks in the bank."

"Who are they going to name the building after?"

"That's the best part. Close your eyes and listen."

Steve cleared his throat, and crooned, "Hello, darlin.'"

"Conway Twitty!" she shouted, then covered her mouth. "You made it up. It's not true."

"So help me God, its true. Conway Twitty is the favorite son of Helena, Arkansas."

"What did you do?"

"I walked her through the naming process. I'll give you the full scoop when it happens."

"Thanks." Karen hesitated. "I guess my questions are insignificant compared to that."

"Not at all. Don't put yourself down. What's on your list?"

Karen took a deep breath. "When you were in college did you ever think you'd be a college president?"

130

"Heck no. I wondered if I'd even graduate. Too many extra-curricular activities."

"Oh?"

"I think that's a topic for another time."

"Okay. Let's go back to athletics. When you joined the faculty at EAU, how did you maintain your interest in athletics?"

"I went to games, met with coaches. When President Thornton appointed me as the faculty rep. I began to understand the complexities of intercollegiate athletics."

"Like what?"

"Athletics are like a window to the university. People watch the games and form impressions about sports and their relation to the university. On Saturday boosters give it the rah-rah. Students get fired up. Someone like Howard Clark gives millions. And problems arise."

"How so?"

"Some push the envelope, don't play according to the rules." He shook his head. "Then there are the faculty. Some support athletics. Others see the program as a financial sinkhole. Sometimes I wonder, what is the purpose? We're supposed to be an academic institution. Our priorities are screwed up."

"Thank you for opening my eyes. I never considered the complexities. Anything else you want to share?"

"I don't think so." Steve touched her hand. "Karen, I want you to know how much I've enjoyed our meetings."

She shivered. "Thank you. I've enjoyed them, too."

CHAPTER FOURTEEN

Grabbing a chair at a high-top by the bar, Anne ordered two beers. "Thanks for bringing me here tonight. I don't get invited out very often."

"No need for thanks." Karen grinned. "We're a team."

"It's amazing how many kudos you've gotten from the series."

Karen shook her head. "I never thought my writing would garner a TV segment."

"You deserved it."

Karen ordered another around. "My mother read an AP version in *The Times-Picayune*. Can you believe it? My phone has been ringing off the hook."

After dinner, Karen dropped off Anne then stopped to pick up a few groceries. Fishing for her keys while balancing the bags, Karen nearly fell over a package from Ruston Flowers and Gifts. *Who could have sent her flowers? Her mother? Gerry? Her best friend, Sharon? Next thing you know I'll be a celebrity on a talk show.*

After sliding a frozen pizza into the oven she opened the box and withdrew a bud vase holding a crimson rose. She sniffed the bloom and read the card.

Congratulations. The series in the *Gazette* was terrific. So are you. I look forward to getting together again.

Always, Steve

Karen poured a glass of Merlot and thought about him. The smell of something burning brought her back to her senses. "Oh, shit."

The next morning Karen rolled over as the sun heated her bed. She made a pot of coffee and eyed the rose. *Get a grip, girl. A married man sent you a rose. Big deal.*

She filled her mug and unwrapped the *Gazette.* A photo of the stadium took up the top half of the front page of the sports section.

She scanned the story about the Rough Riders upcoming game, then dialed Sharon Black.

Model-thin and the PR director for the First National Bank, she was a master of the one-liner.

"Sharon, Gerry gave me two tickets to the home opener."

"For EAU?

"Yes."

"You're not even a fan."

"I am now. Want to go?"

"I'd love to. Did you hit your head?"

"Very funny. I need to branch out. Try new stuff."

"Hey, I've been telling you that for years. All work and no play ..."

"Okay, okay. I hear you. Let's wear our EAU sweatshirts."

"Anything else would be a travesty."

Saturday the women joined the hordes entering the stadium. Sharon babbled as the stragglers filed in. The cannon fired and the Rough Riders stormed onto the field.

The place went wild.

By halftime EAU had a 24-point lead.

Karen pointed at the press box. "Isn't that President Schilling in the red fedora?"

"So?"

"He looks pretty dapper."

"He's all over the sports pages. Students think he's cool. He looks good to me. For an old guy, that is."

"Sharon, he's married."

"Geez, I can still look, can't I?"

                    ***

After picking up the Sunday *Memphis Daily News,* Karen spent a lazy day at home. She spotted an ad for a weekend special at the Peabody Hotel.

Five minutes later she jotted down her confirmation number.

By the end of the week she was on her way to Memphis for a shopping extravaganza. *What could be better? Two days of shopping and two nights at the Peabody. Maybe someone will ask me for my autograph.* She laughed.

Lugging a dress bag slung over her arm, Karen thought she heard someone call her name. She paused and looked around the Peabody lobby.

"Hello, darlin.'"

"I haven't heard that in three months," she said.

Steve Schilling strolled toward her. "What a nice surprise. Do you come here often?"

"First time. How about you?"

"I just got back from Florence. We lost to North Alabama, 28 to 24. I'm having a drink before I meet with a donor. Want to join me?"

"I can't. I have a 7:30 reservation at Chez Philippe. I'm going upstairs to relax and change."

"Why don't you freshen up and come down for a drink?"

"Uh … I'm …"

"Come on. I won't take no for an answer. What would you like?"

"A Manhattan, straight up."

Karen took a quick shower and slipped on a dress she'd had for years. Wrinkling her nose, she took it off in favor of the form-fitting, black knit she'd picked up on a whim earlier in the day. Not bad, she thought, glancing in the full-length mirror.

Her heels tapped across the marble floor. Heads turned. Steve's eyes moved up her slender body to her cleavage then extended his arms.

"My, my look at you. You look terrific."

"Thank you. Tell me about the game." She let him talk, hadn't met the man who could resist talking about himself. And sports.

"Would you like another drink?"

She glanced at her watch. "I really can't. I'm late." She got up to go.

"Great running into you, Karen. Have a nice evening."

"Thank you. This was fun," she said, turning toward the restaurant.

"My pleasure."

Steve sucked the gin from the last olive, paid the tab and cruised by the restaurant. He was shocked to see her sitting alone. "What a waste," he said under his breath on the way to the elevator.

He got off at the 7th floor and knocked on 783.

The door cracked open. "You're a little late, sweetheart."

"Sorry, Kate. I ran into a donor. You know how it is."

***

While Karen waited in line at the Peabody coffee shop the next morning, a woman tapped her on the shoulder. "I was wondering, are you from EAU?"

"No, why do you ask?"

"I'm sorry. The sweatshirt ... I thought you were a fan and might like to share a table."

"Let's. Otherwise, we'll be here all day. I'm Karen Holmes. I work at the *Daily Gazette*."

"It's nice to meet you. I'm Marie Cabrera. I'm the mailroom supervisor at the university."

"Is there an alumni meeting here today?" Karen asked.

"No, TV24 is holding a press conference at ten. They're announcing a five-year deal to televise our home football games, and for North Alabama and EAU to top it off with our year-end matchup."

"Sounds exciting."

"It's wonderful. Do you go to many games?" Marie asked.

"I just started this year. They're really good."

"Things turned around when President Schilling took over. Now everyone dresses in red and he's seldom without his fedora."

"It looks like EAU has hit the big time."

***

Karen slipped into the large meeting room where Schilling and the North Alabama president flanked the station manager. She saw Ted Stevens, the sports reporter, and went over.

"What are you doing here?" he asked.

"I'm staying at the Peabody. A weekend gift to myself."

Catching Steve's eye, she waved. He winked.

The press conference reminded her of a tennis match. The North Alabama president made a statement. The boosters voiced their approval.

President Schilling made a comment; the EAU contingent applauded.

Posing for photos between the two, the station manager ended the match. Steve made his way toward Karen.

"What did you think?"

She felt her cheeks flush. "You were great."

"Thanks. But I was referring to the TV agreement."

"I don't understand what all the hoopla is about."

"The boosters got a little carried away. It's a big deal for EAU. It raises our visibility, affects recruitment and draws dollars. Having this push in Memphis gives us regional exposure."

They left the room together. Fans mobbed Steve in the corridor. "We're number one. We're number one," rang out.

Marie stepped from the crowd. "Good luck at the game next week, Mr. President."

Steve tipped his hat. "Thanks, we'll need it. Playing at Arkansas Tech is always a challenge." He turned to Karen. "Are you covering the press conference?"

"No. Just hanging out."

"What are you doing this afternoon?"

"Nothing much. I need to get my mother a birthday present then I'm heading home."

"Have you ever visited Mud Island?"

She shook her head. "I've heard the river walk is spectacular."

"You must see it. Why don't we go?"

"I don't want to impose."

"It's no imposition. I'm free until the symphony tonight."

"I should probably be on my way."

"C'mon," he said, giving her hand a tug. "I'll pick you up in a half hour. We can grab a bite to eat on the island."

"Could you make it closer to noon? I want to see the ducks at 11 o'clock."

***

The elevator doors opened and the Peabody ducks arrived from their penthouse home as they had for the last forty years.

Cameras flashed. Kids pushed against the roped-off area. The ducks waddled down the red carpet and plopped, one by one, into the lobby fountain.

Karen snapped a few photos then worked her way through the crowd lobby to the elevator down the hall.

After changing, she returned to the lobby.

Steve looked up from his newspaper, smiled, and gestured for her to turn around. She pivoted like a model. "You look fantastic."

"Thank you."

"The car is waiting. You'll love the river walk. It's a replica of the Mississippi River from its confluence with the Ohio at Cairo, Illinois, all the way to New Orleans."

"Wow. I can't imagine that."

"Just wait. There are twenty cities laid out along the way. It's like getting an aerial view of Memphis, Vicksburg and New Orleans. And then there are the museum galleries. By the end of the day you feel like you've flown over the Mississippi."

"I can hardly wait."

"First stop, we need to get a couple of the best hot dogs in the world."

***

Mid-afternoon they stopped for frozen orange drinks. Karen sipped hers while taking in the New Orleans mock-up. "You're right. I feel like I've been in a plane for the past two hours."

"I told you it was realistic. Let's head for the museum."

Later, in the parking lot, Steve took her hand. She squeezed his. "Let's go to the hotel and have a drink," he said.

"I'd like that."

Karen leaned back in a plush lounger and gazed at the stained-glass in the three-story atrium above. *What could be better? I feel like a queen.*

"What a day. I had breakfast with one of your employees …"

Steve interrupted. "Who was that?"

"Marie Cabrera. She's very pleasant. We chatted about the university. She spoke highly of you."

"Marie is one of our top employees, a very dedicated professional."

A server appeared. "It's happy hour until 6:30," she said. "Half off on the second round. We have nachos, chicken fingers and spicy meatballs."

"I'll have Tanqueray on the rocks, three olives. And nachos with extra cheese." He turned to Karen. "What would you like?"

"I'll have a Manhattan, straight up and … spicy meatballs."

"What did you like best about Mud Island?"

"It's hard to say. I liked it all. Thanks for taking me."

"The pleasure was all mine."

"That display of the 1811 and 1812 earthquakes was amazing. Do you think the Mississippi actually flowed backward?"

"That's what witnesses reported. The four quakes averaged over 7.5 on the Richter scale. They rattled dishes in Cleveland. Tremors were felt in Washington, D.C. You're standing right on an epicenter."

"Really?"

"Everyone talks about the earthquake in San Francisco. The New Madrid quakes were stronger and covered an area three times larger."

Karen paused, took a deep breath. "Something has been bothering me since I first interviewed you. May I ask you a personal question?"

Steve looked surprised. "Sure. Go ahead. I'm an open book."

"I've been wondering about your dad, and how different you are. Like polar opposites. Is that a fair assumption?"

"Yes. I think about that all the time. I'm lucky I didn't end up like him. Mom was my biggest influence."

"You didn't say much about your brother and sister, except they were younger."

"Stan was two years younger than me. He became a coal miner, kind of quiet. Dad gave him a hard time. He died of black lung when he was only 39."

"I'm sorry to hear that."

"I miss him. But it was a blessing. He was so sick."

"And your sister?"

Steve fidgeted and looked away.

"Sally's like Mom. She's a sweetie. Married with two kids, works in a daycare center. She was dad's favorite. He …"

Steve hugged his gut. The color left his face. He got up. "Excuse me," he said and bolted for the bathroom.

Minutes later he returned, patting his brow with a paper towel. "Sorry. Where were we?"

"We were talking about your sister."

"Oh yes. Do you have any brothers and sisters?"

"No, I don't. Let's get back to your sister."

"I have nothing to add. She's a wonderful person."

Karen grabbed her purse. "I need to go."

Steve touched her arm. "Karen, I've had a wonderful time."

"Oh, Steve …" She squeezed her purse. "Thank you for everything."

"Don't thank me." He caressed her hand. "You made my day."

***

Steve was reading the program when the house lights dimmed. He concentrated on Sandra's flawless performance, then joined the standing ovation.

He watched from the wings as Sandra and her colleagues exchanged compliments and replayed the performance. She gave him a quick hello then went to her dressing room and reappeared a few minutes later.

He took her violin case and dress bag, and they walked arm-in-arm to her car. Once inside they fell into each other's arms.

"Steve, seeing you from the stage, I wanted to reach out and touch you," she said between kisses. "I can't wait until we're together forever."

"Me too. I love you so much."

Back at the Peabody, he ordered dinner from room service, slipped into a robe and opened a bottle of wine. Sipping on his favorite red, he admired the high French Provincial headboard and the cluster of crimson and golden pillows below. *If mom could have only slept in a bed like this. Just one time.*

Sandra opened the bathroom door and stepped toward him, her robe loosely tied. "I love you, Steve." She planted a wet kiss on him and pulled on his belt, loosening his robe. "I want you."

"Not yet, dear. I have a special treat."

He draped a white hand towel over his arm. "Dinner is served, Madame." He escorted her to the table, removed the silver lids from the plates and bowed. "Bon appétit."

Halfway through dinner she loosened her robe. "I'm ready for dessert."

Steve smiled.

CHAPTER FIFTEEN

After tapping the snow from her shoes, Karen chatted with her newsroom colleagues on the way to her office. Feeling refreshed for the first time in months, she hung her coat and snatched the note from her desk. "Hmm, I wonder what Gerry wants to talk about."

Karen knocked once before entering her boss's office. "Do anything special this weekend?" he asked.

"Not really. I took it easy."

"Good. I want you rested because I have a big assignment for you. On athletics."

"Athletics? I know more about basket weaving."

"It's time you learned. You're going to New Orleans to cover the NCAA convention next month."

"Really? That's my hometown."

"Stay an extra day or two if you like. Consider it a perk."

"What about Ted?"

"He's going too. He'll cover EAU's move to Division I from a sports angle. I want you to focus on the bigger picture."

"Alright."

"People need more info about what's happening on campus. Being a Division I team takes in more than football. For starters, ask Steve Schilling about the Memphis press conference. What are the implications?"

"I was there."

His eyes widened. "You were there?"

"Yep. I was at the Peabody the day of the press conference."

"Good. You have a head start. Did you meet anyone you might interview?"

"Yes. I met a woman who works on campus."

"Perfect. Pick her brain. I want this story to run before Christmas."

***

Karen parked in the campus visitor's lot and made her way to the mailroom. Marie waved her into her office.

"I'm glad you could see me on such short notice," Karen said.

"No problem. How can I help?"

"I'd like to hear your thoughts on Division I."

"I'm a booster and probably biased. That aside, it's a big deal."

"How so?"

"Changes are taking place across campus."

"Changes?"

"We're receiving double the number of applications and sending out more mass mailings. Many more than last year."

"Did you hire more staff?"

"We have several new part-timers and purchased some automated mailing equipment."

"What about the faculty?"

"We've added fifty positions. And we're short of space. Sometimes two or three people have to share an office. Take a look at *The Rider*, our weekly newsletter, for more. Our instructors are researching more, presenting more national papers and getting more grants."

"What's the overall faculty response?"

"Most welcome the changes," Marie said. "But some are grousing."

"What about?"

"Same old, same old. Some prefer the status quo to taking on more work and responsibility. They preach about change, but they're still using the same old, yellowed notes. They're a bunch of sticks-in-the-mud, if you ask me."

"I had a couple of professors like that. Anything else?"

"Not that I can think of. Meanwhile, campus is abuzz."

***

"Nice to see you, again," Carol said. "Your series on the president was terrific."

"Thanks Carol."

"How can I help you?"

"We're doing a story on Division I. I'd like to arrange an interview with the president."

"I'll see if I can arrange something before Christmas."

"Christmas?" Karen's voice softened. "I was hoping for something within the week."

Steve stepped out of his office. "Nice to see you."

"Mr. President, this young lady wants to meet with you, ASAP," Carol said. "I told her your schedule was extremely tight."

"It is, but I'm sure we can squeeze her in."

Carol turned the calendar toward Steve. He ran his fingers down the week's schedule.

"How about meeting here next Tuesday at 12:45? I can give you a half hour."

"I'll be here. See you then."

***

Karen put down the list of questions she'd rehearsed all weekend. Glancing at the rose Steve had given her, she thought about the note he'd sent and wondered what he was like under the college-president façade. Did he really think she was terrific? Or was that part of his act?

She took her time dressing for work Tuesday. During the drive to campus, she fantasized about being in bed with him.

"Get real," she whispered under her breath. "He's married. What's wrong with you?"

Walking toward Thornton Hall, she saw him coming her way. Her cheeks flushed. "It's nice to see you, again," she said.

They shook hands.

"Looks like we're headed for the same place," he said.

She pulled her shoulders back. *Would he like my jonquil yellow jacket? Would he notice my tight black sweater? Would he even care?*

"You look very professional," he said as they entered the building. He gestured for her to sit down. "Would you like coffee or a soda?"

"A Diet Coke would be nice."

Steve buzzed Carol with the request. "It's great to see you, again."

"Thanks," she said. Butterflies stirred.

"What kind of story are you planning?"

"There'll be two. First, I'll cover the events leading up to the Division I decision. Then I'll do a follow-up on the NCAA convention."

"Smart. Too bad more of our faculty don't get it."

"I'm counting on you to help me bridge the gap."

"I'll try."

"Good." Karen flipped open her notebook.

"To start with, the upgrading of an athletic program is about more than football. Division I status will affect our image, stature, visibility, and how we're perceived."

"How so?"

"People will associate us with larger, well-known institutions. Recruitment will be easier. Applications will soar. Fundraising will increase. It's similar to the process of accrediting an academic program."

"Accreditation … now I get it."

Steve paced as he spoke.

She glanced at the blank page and jotted a couple of key phrases.

"Am I being helpful?"

"Yes, very," she said. "I hope I can convey this to our readers."

"I'm certain you will. You're an excellent reporter."

"Thank you. Gerry's sending me to New Orleans for the NCAA convention. May I interview you after the decision?"

"Of course," he said. "I'll see you there."

"Thanks for squeezing me in," she said. She picked up her untouched soda and left.

***

On the day before Christmas break, Martha answered the ringing phone. "Steve, it's so good to hear your voice. I can hardly wait until New Orleans."

"Me too. I get to spend three nights with you."

"I'm sorry to disappoint you. My boss needs me back in the office that Thursday. I'll only be able to stay one night."

"That's a shame. We can still have a nice dinner Tuesday. I reserved a table at Commander's Palace."

"Super. When are we meeting with the SEC athletic directors?"

"Tuesday at 4 o'clock. I'll pick you up at the airport at ten. Then the two of us can have lunch."

Martha hesitated. "Steve ... how are things going at home?"

"It's over."

"Thank God. Sometimes I think we'll never be together."

"That's ridiculous. I love you."

***

Two weeks later, Steve walked the few blocks from the Hotel Monteleone to the Royal Sonesta. Martha met him in the lobby and they strolled across the courtyard to the restaurant.

A waitress showed them to a table.

"It's good to see you, sweetheart." Martha sipped a mint julep.

"I can't wait until tonight," Steve said.

"Keep talking like that and I'll attack you right now."

"Promises, promises." He laughed. "So what's our plan for this afternoon?"

"We need a one game commitment from each of the athletic directors. That'll make it easier to land a game with Kentucky, maybe Tennessee."

"I'd love to play Kentucky. It would be like a homecoming."

"Steve, you have to understand these guys. They love two things: boobs and booze — in that order."

"They do?"

"They'll order bourbon. You can order gin for us."

"Can you drink and talk shop?"

"I'll fake it. Sit close to me so I can nudge you when to weigh in."

"Okay. Is that all?"

"I'll wear a push-up bra."

"Why? I don't ..."

"Don't worry. I'll let them fantasize a little. It's standard operating procedure."

"I don't know."

"I'll lean across the table and they'll be hooked. Then you can reel them in."

Steve frowned. "Are you certain?"

"Of course. And, it'll be good practice for tonight." She winked.

"Okay, but it makes me uncomfortable."

***

At 4 o'clock, two balding men in their mid-fifties joined Martha and Steve, seated hip to hip.

After 45 minutes and two rounds of drinks, Martha loosened her top button as Steve outlined EAU's plans.

"As the state rep," Martha began, "I want you to know we're very supportive of EAU's move. They have a long-term football contract with Arkansas and we'd like to see them have the same with you folks."

She leaned over the table. Four eyes zeroed on her décolletage.

"Sweetie," the shorter man said. "You're going to cost me a lot of money." He stared at her breasts for a second.

"Nothing you couldn't afford," she said.

He cleared his throat. "We'll pay EAU $250,000 for the season openers in '96, '97, and '99."

Steve sat up as if to speak. Martha elbowed him. "I think you can do better than that."

She squeezed the gawker's hand. "I'm sure you could add another $50,000 per year," she purred.

He stole another glance at her cleavage and turned to Steve. "That's quite a woman you have Mr. President. We'll do $250,000, $300,000, and $350,000 for the final year."

Martha nudged Steve. "Deal."

She turned her attention to the taller one. "We have open dates in '97 and '98. We'll pay $350,000 per year."

"Agreed."

Within minutes Steve had signed contracts in hand and the good ol' boys were gone.

Martha slid closer to him. "How's that for a day's work?"

"You were terrific."

"Another day at the office," she said, raising her half-full glass. "I don't remember a thing after the first round."

"You missed the whole show."

"Everything's a blur."

"I thought their chins would hit the table when you leaned over."

"You're putting me on."

"Come on, let's go upstairs."

"I thought you'd never ask."

Martha grabbed her purse and staggered toward the elevator. Pushing 3, she fumbled for her key.

Steve grabbed the key, jammed it into the lock and pulled her into the room. "Come in, Ms. Hot Stuff."

***

The next day Suzanne arrived at Steve's office. She wore an ear-to-ear grin. A graduate assistant welcomed her. "Good morning Mrs. Schilling. How are you today?"

"I'm fine, thank you. Is Carol in?"

"She'll be back in a minute. May I help you?"

"I'll wait."

Suzanne took a seat and watched a student worker drop off the mail before zipping out.

Suzanne gazed at a rose-colored envelope addressed to President Steve Schilling, Thornton Hall, Eastern Arkansas University, Ruston, AR.

She picked it up. Underneath it was a blue envelope with a Blytheville postmark. She felt sick inside.

Carol breezed in. "Hi, Mrs. Schilling. How are you?"

Suzanne's voice was pinched. "Good morning, Carol."

"Nice to see you. What can I do for you?"

"I'd like to hold some dates on Steve's spring calendar."

"The master calendar is in the backroom. I'll be right back."

Suzanne picked up the envelopes, caught a hint of Trésor from the blue one. She leafed through the other mail. On a promotional flier, she read:

BUY YOUR SECOND SET OF STATIONERY —
RECEIVE ANOTHER FREE.

Suzanne slid the flier into her folder as Carol returned with a large leather-bound binder. "Did you have a nice holiday break?"

"Yes, Steve and I went to St. Louis for the weekend. How about you?"

"I saw *Forrest Gump*. Tom Hanks was terrific." Carol opened the master schedule.

"It's a good thing you came by today. Half the days are already booked."

"I'd like a couple of weekends in April and May."

Suzanne thanked Carol and hurried down the hallway to the women's restroom. She entered a stall and locked the door. "Slow down, think rationally," she mumbled. "Don't do anything rash."

She took a deep breath then headed for her office. Tossing her coat aside, she scribbled down what she had seen.

- Two envelopes addressed in same font
- Rose envelope—Ruston
- Blue envelope—Blytheville
- Blue envelope—Trésor
- BUY YOUR SECOND SET

Maybe the envelopes held RSVPs. She checked the list of upcoming university events — nothing required a reservation.

Could they be thank-you notes? With postmarks from Blytheville and Ruston? And Trésor on one? "I don't think so," she said. *Why would he order stationery and not tell me? Did he buy it long ago for Kate? Why would she use it now? And why mail it from two different locations?*

Suzanne caught herself before her imagination raged further. "He's changed. He says he loves me. We've made mad, passionate love all weekend."

Hot tears filled her eyes. "Oh God."

CHAPTER SIXTEEN

Karen's parents met her at Louis Armstrong International. Her father snapped several pictures of Karen with her mother. "I thought you were only staying a few days," he said as he crammed her bags in the trunk of his 1988 Volvo.

Karen planted a kiss on his cheek. "I couldn't decide what to bring."

"I've shared your clippings with our friends," her mother chimed in. "It must be exciting to interview someone important. Is President Schilling tall, dark and handsome?"

"Mom, he's married."

"Well, he sounds very nice."

"He's kind and friendly. Everyone on campus loves him."

"And your boss, Mr. Coleman? That was generous of him to send you down here."

"He's the best. I've learned more from him than I did from all of my professors."

"Is he married?"

Karen rolled her eyes. "Mom, he's dad's age."

"Are there many Jewish boys up there?"

"I'm busy working. I don't have much time for socializing."

***

More than 500 university officials assembled in the Grand Ballroom of the New Orleans Marriott for the review of Division I football petitions. Banner-draped tables framed the podium where a huge NCAA logo hung.

Eleven university presidents waited for their institution's names to be called. Karen sat in the media section near the rear of the auditorium. She felt totally removed from the action before her.

Perusing the agenda, she noted EAU was seventh.

The first three applicants were denied in the opening two hours. The fourth applicant gained approval by a 10-vote margin. Five and six were dismissed without comment.

The NCCA president stepped to the podium and announced. "Eastern Arkansas University."

Steve approached the lectern and paused. "Mr. President and NCAA delegates." Conversation stopped.

A minute into Steve's description of EAU's Division I transition plan, a delegate rose. "Point of order, Mr. Chairman, point of order," the short, balding man said.

The NCAA president gaveled. "Order, I ask the delegates for order." He held the gavel high and waited for silence before proceeding. "The chair recognizes the representative from the Southeastern Conference."

"Mr. Chairman, the members of the SEC move and second that Eastern Arkansas University be accepted as a Division I football member."

"Objection." a representative wailed from the center section.

"Order. Order, I ask for order," the president said. He wielded the gravel, until the buzz stopped.

"We have a motion before the house to accept Eastern Arkansas University. Are there additional comments?" he asked, and without pausing, said, "Hearing none, I call the question. All those in favor of the motion, say, Aye."

Steve watched as the raised paddles were counted. "Those opposed?"

A man waving his paddle shouted, "Nay."

The gavel hit the rostrum. "Motion passes 82 to 1."

***

A publicist guided Steve to an adjacent room where at least fifteen sportswriters waited.

"How does that vote feel, Mr. President?" Ted asked.

"It's unbelievable."

"Did you expect someone to call the question that soon?"

"Not at all." Steve put on his jovial face. "I'll have to phone him. Maybe they'll play us."

Karen watched the reporters peppered him with questions. He replied with great self-assurance.

After an hour, the NCAA representative approached the podium. "Are there any more questions for the president?"

He looked around. "Good, that ends the press conference."

Ted flew to the platform and repeated each question that had already been asked. Steve responded cordially, as if hearing them for the first time. "I'm looking forward to reading your story, Ted, " Steve concluded.

"Thank you Mr. President."

Steve made his way past the empty chairs toward Karen. "What did you think?" he asked.

"That was quite a performance, Mr. President."

"Thanks," he said. "Remember, it's Steve."

Their eyes locked. "Sure, Steve."

"I've been looking forward to today for years."

"Where did that SEC guy come from?"

"Who knows?" Steve wiped his brow. "How about interviewing me over lunch? I haven't eaten all day."

"Sure, that'd be fine."

"I hear there's a nice restaurant in the Royal Sonesta."

"You must mean Begue's. It's only a few blocks from here. We can walk."

"Perfect." He took Karen's arm.

They strolled down Bourbon Street then stepped inside.

"It's just as I remembered," she said. "The columns and French-style courtyard. A perfect blend of European flair and Southern charm."

"Table for two, somewhere private, please," Steve asked the hostess.

She glanced at Karen then smirked. "Of course, sir." She led them to the same cozy booth he'd occupied with Martha the day before.

Steve loosened his tie. "How about a drink?"

"I don't drink at lunch."

"Come on, it's happy hour all day. Mint Juleps are two for one. I hear they're wonderful."

"You've twisted my arm. Why not?"

Steve ordered a gin then a second before his jambalaya arrived. He tore into it.

It was after 2 o'clock when the conversation slowed.

"Well, Mr. President. I'm sorry, Steve. Tomorrow you'll be featured in the sports section. Ted will quote every word you uttered and describe the scene, including the negative vote from the University of Arkansas."

"I can hardly wait. How will you handle your story?"

"I'm percolating. I need you to fill in the blanks."

"Go ahead."

"Six weeks ago the boosters went nuts in Memphis. And just before Christmas you gave me the importance of moving up. How does it all fit with the university's primary purpose?"

"Good question. It's not as complex as it may seem."

She smiled. "I'm all ears."

As a history professor, I'd love to see a section of the paper devoted to history. That will never happen. Every professor thinks his or her discipline is the most important one. As president, I have to step back and look at the university as a whole — a microcosm of our society. Whether you like sports or not, they're a big part of our culture. And, we need to be well represented in the media."

"Makes sense. How does today's decision impact our community?"

"Well Miss Holmes, here's your scoop. Remember when I told you that athletics was a window to the university?"

"Yes."

"That's the starting point."

Karen watched and listened, scrawling in her unique shorthand for almost an hour. Her hand ached.

Munching the last piece of crusty French bread, Steve asked, "Have any more questions?"

She shook her head. "Now I understand why Gerry wanted the story."

Their eyes met. "How about dinner tonight?"

"Dinner? I could never have dinner."

"Never? That's a long time."

"I didn't mean it that way."

"How did you mean it?"

"I need to write the story."

"Your story isn't running until Sunday. You have plenty of time."

"My parents expect me home tonight. And, I have nothing to wear. I'm sorry, I can't."

"Your parents are certainly welcome to join us." He laughed. "And nothing to wear? I bet if you dug deep in one of your suitcases you'd find something to wear to Commander's Palace."

"That's my favorite place."

"That settles it. We're having dinner together."

"It's not that simple."

"Seems simple enough to me. A glass of wine and something to eat at a fine restaurant. What's the problem?"

She searched for the right words. "You're the president. You're married. What if someone saw us?"

"So what? You're a reporter doing your job. What's the difference if we're here or having dinner?"

"There's a difference to me. I can't walk out of my parents' house with a dinner dress on."

"Big deal. Put it in the car. You can change in my room. I'll wait in the lobby."

Karen's right leg was a metronome under the table. She touched her knee to quiet it.

"Look, I'll meet you in the Monteleone lobby at 7 o'clock. Bring your dress. After you change, we'll celebrate the decision. This is a big day."

Karen pursed her lips then sighed. "Okay, I'll meet you at seven."

***

Steve put down *The Times-Picayune* and glanced at his watch. *Damn, it's after eight. Maybe she changed her mind.*

A few minutes later Karen ran toward him — her hair a mess. She looked like she'd been in a wreck.

"Slow down. Are you okay?" he asked.

She gasped for air. "I'm sorry," she said. "You won't believe what happened."

"You weren't in an accident, were you?"

"No."

"Thank goodness. Take it easy. I changed our reservation to 9:30."

153

"Everything took longer than I had planned. Mom had a thousand questions. Traffic was backed up."

"Relax," he said, handing her the key. "My room is 812."

Steve zeroed in on Karen's firm body as she walked toward him.

"Nothing to wear?" He shook his head. "You look gorgeous."

"Thank you."

Steve opened the door and helped her in the cab. On the way to the restaurant Karen played tour guide, pointing out important sights, including the street leading to her parent's home in the Garden District. And she reminisced about growing up in the city.

Steve tipped the driver and held the door for her. Karen took in the elegant décor, fresh flowers on every table and well-dressed clientele.

"This place is classic New Orleans. I just love it, don't you?"

"Nothing better."

The waiter showed them to a corner table. Her heart raced. She took a deep breath. "Steve, it's perfect. Let's take our time."

"Sure, we have the entire evening. I'm so pleased to share this with you. Not in my wildest dreams did I imagine a scene like today."

"And I'm very happy to be here with you," she said. *Shoot. Maybe I shouldn't have said that.*

The waiter served their entrées.

Karen touched Steve's hand. "Thanks for a great day."

"Me? You did the interview."

"You've been so generous with your time. And transparent. I admire that quality. It makes my job easier."

"What you see is what you get," Steve said, pushing his plate, with the last of the sugarcane-grilled pork chops aside.

He placed his hand on hers and caressed it. His knee brushed her thigh. She felt lightheaded. And damp.

"Would you like dessert?"

***

Leaving the restaurant, she felt tipsy and leaned against him. Steve pulled her tight. "This has been a wonderful evening."

Karen kissed him on the cheek. "Thank you so much."

154

Waiting for the taxi, Steve ran his fingers down her back and pulled her closer. He pressed against her.

"Mm," she purred.

"You're the most attractive woman I've ever met." He kissed her on the forehead and opened the door.

Traveling down St. Charles, Steve held her face with his hands. "Karen, I've never had a more delightful evening. Thank you for sharing it with me."

He kissed her on the lips.

Karen hesitated. Then she wrapped her arms around his neck and pulled him to her. She kissed him hard.

He tongued her. She pushed back then leaned against the seat. He kissed the tip of her nose. "You're perfect."

Karen rested her head on his chest, caught a glimpse of the sign for her parent's street. She recalled her mother's rules — never go to bed with a married man and never go to bed with a man you wouldn't marry.

She had followed those standards all her life. Until tonight.

***

She gazed at the city lights from the picture window in his room. "Don't you just love the city? It's so beautiful."

"So are you," he said, sliding his hands around her waist. They embraced and locked lips. She tried to catch her breath.

"Would you like some champagne?" he asked.

"Yes, but first I'd like to freshen up."

Steve gave her space and filled their champagne glasses.

Karen undressed in the bathroom and slipped on a white terry robe, appliquéd with the hotel's insignia. She left the belt loose and opened the door.

"What do you think about this?" she said, parading toward him.

"I like what's under it," he said. "My turn." He retreated to the bathroom.

Sipping the last of her champagne, she noticed a rose in a bud vase next to the ice bucket. How romantic she thought. Gazing out the picture window, she recognized her high school football stadium in the distance, recalled when she had played the flute in the marching band.

His hands encircled her waist. "I'd like more champagne, please."

"My pleasure."

Like a panther on the prowl, she moved toward him. She inched her robe off one shoulder then the other and stood before him in her lacy, low-cut bra and panties.

Steve's body hardened.

She turned slowly from one side to the other, her hands sliding over her firm curvatures. She could feel her heart pounding, her desires craving him.

She released her robe letting it coil at her feet.

Steve reached for her. "I want you, Karen."

She took a step toward him and froze.

"I want you too, Steve, but sex means more to me than lust. I'm sorry. I can't do it," she sobbed, and ran to the bathroom.

CHAPTER SEVENTEEN

Karen sat down with *The Times-Picayune.*

Her dad read the paper at the other end of the dining room table, covered in her grandmother's crocheted cloth. Her mother breezed in with fresh-baked muffins.

Karen rubbed her eyes, still burning from yesterday's smoked-filled rooms. Her father looked up from the business section.

"Good morning, Karen. Where did you go last night?"

"Commander's Palace."

He raised his eyebrows.

"Kind of fancy," her mother said. "Who'd you go with?"

"An old friend."

"Was he nice looking?"

"Kind of."

"I heard you come in after 2:00. Where did you go after dinner?" Her mother shot her a disapproving look.

"We walked around the French Quarter. Mom, I'm 33, you know."

***

Karen gave her dad a goodbye hug and dragged her suitcases to the airline check-in counter. She replayed her date with Steve as she walked to the gate. She felt him pressing against her, grabbing her ass.

She'd never been that brazenly sexual before. She cringed recalling how she'd run to the bathroom in her lacy underwear, like a scared teenager.

Her friends would be shocked to know that she was still a virgin. She dreaded her next meeting with Steve, if there was one. The thought turned her cheeks to crimson.

***

At the gate in Memphis Karen waved to Sharon who bombarded her with questions on the way to the baggage carousel. "Tell me everything. I want to hear it all."

"It was exciting. Hundreds packed the auditorium."

"No, I mean him. How did your interview go? What did he say?"

"It went fine. No big deal."

"No big deal? What was he like? Where did you meet?"

"We went to Begue's for lunch. And the interview."

"Begue's? That's a fancy place."

"Well, we couldn't talk at McDonald's, could we?"

"Very funny. Did you have drinks?"

"A couple of mint juleps."

"If I'd been there I would have had more."

"Well, you weren't." Thank God, Karen thought.

"Did he give you the eye?"

"Sharon, leave it alone."

"Come on. Did he make a move on you?"

"What? Why would you even ask?"

"I've heard stories about him, his wandering eye, his ..."

"Not Steve. I don't believe it. He's very sincere."

"Steve? Oh ... tell me about Steve. Or is it Stevie now?"

"It's not like that."

"Then how is it?"

"He asked me to call him Steve because Mr. President is too formal. What's the big deal?"

"And you fell for that?"

"Fell for what?"

"Come on little Karen. Relax, have a drink, dinner, maybe champagne in his room. Bingo!"

"C'mon. I finished the interview and left. That's it. Sorry to disappoint you."

158

"You sound defensive to me."

"Sharon, he's married."

"Married? So? He's a man. He would have jumped at the opportunity to bed you."

"I don't think so."

"I'll tell you what I would have done."

"Okay, let's hear it from the expert."

"Compared to you, I am."

"Alright, woman of the world. What would have you done?"

"I would have put on that sexy bra you bought last month at Victoria's Secret and your black dress with the cutout back. And flashed a little skin. Hell, I'd have him wrapped around my finger before dessert. After a little champagne I would have slipped into a robe, but left it open. Wham. I'd have banged him all night."

"Sharon, I can't believe you're talking like this."

"And I can't believe you didn't do it. You're such a prude. Who are you saving it for?"

"Thanks for the vote of confidence." Karen unlocked the door and lugged her bags in.

After her friend left, Karen wondered. *Maybe she was right. Who am I saving it for? Maybe I should have jumped his bones.*

***

The icy grass glistened in the morning sun. Suzanne could see her breath as she ran down the driveway and snatched the Sunday *Daily Gazette* from the paper sleeve.

She unrolled it. EAU GOOD FOR THE COMMUNITY spilled across the front page. Hurrying back to the house, she closed the door and skimmed the story. It'd be good fodder if Steve ran for governor.

She stared at the quarter-page photo of Steve in front of the stadium and ached with love for him. Thank heavens he'd changed, given up his wanton ways.

Her smile turned to a frown. There had to be a reasonable explanation for the pastel envelopes.

Bursting with excitement, she dialed her mother.

"Mom, Steve's all over the front page. He looks like a national hero."

"What's the story about?"

"The NCAA and going Division I. It's full of accolades for him."

"That's terrific. Has he seen it yet?"

"No. He got home late last night and went straight to bed."

"Are things okay?" Her mother spoke hesitantly.

"Wonderful. We went to St. Louis over the holidays. It was like a second honeymoon. We played tennis, dined in the finest restaurants, danced. He's been fantastic."

"I'm so pleased."

"We talk every night after dinner, over a glass of Amaretto or Bailey's."

"You drink after dinner?"

"Mom, it's not like that. We have a cordial. It helps him relax." Suzanne's voice trailed off. "Mom, are you there?"

"I was just wondering. All of this seems a little much. Are you sure he's for real?"

"I'm positive. He's rarely away overnight. We go to lots of events together."

"That's good, dear."

"Mom, I'll call you later in the week. I have to wake Steve for his golf match." Suzanne took off her pajamas and slipped on a negligée.

***

"Hey, man, it's good to see you," Steve said to Eddie. "I'm glad you could stop by. How long can you stay?"

"A couple of hours. I have a meeting in Nashville tomorrow. How have you been?"

"Fabulous. The place as gone bananas since New Orleans."

"All of the *Gazette* stories were in our paper. The Arkansas athletic director lost it."

"You should have seen him. He acted like a madman — ranting and raving."

"I had no idea it was such a tough process."

"There's a lot more to it than most people realize. And very political."

"Obviously. How did you convince the SEC guy to carry the ball?"

Steve laughed. "Sometimes it's better to be lucky than good."

"You're riding high, getting more press than the governor." Eddie leaned back. "Why the urgent call?"

"It's personal. Very personal."

Eddie leaned forward. "Suzanne okay?"

"She's fine." Steve hesitated. "I met someone else."

"Crap, not another one." Eddie shook his head. "Tell me about this one."

"It started in the fall. The clincher came in New Orleans."

"In New Orleans? You were shacking up while I was reading your success stories?"

"No, I didn't get laid. That's the problem."

"Hell, I've had that problem for years."

"Come on, Eddie. I'm serious."

"Okay. Okay."

"It started when she interviewed me. Fast forward to her being in my hotel room."

"The reporter was in your bedroom?"

"She slipped on this robe, ran her fingers through my hair. Then she dropped the robe. God, she was hot."

Eddie's eyes bugged. "And ..."

"Shit, whataya think? I made a move."

"What happened?"

"She stopped cold, said she couldn't do it. Then she bolted."

"Did you talk to her?"

"I didn't have a chance."

"Maybe she was a bimbo just playing around?"

"Not her. Eddie, I need your help."

"Jesus, I need time to think about this."

"Can you stop by after your meeting?"

"I suppose so."

"Good, I'll meet you at Johnny's, Thursday around 4:00."

***

Eddie grabbed a stool at Johnny's Sports Bar; his college hangout had seen better days.

Steve looked up. "Well, what do you think?"

"I'd like to order first."

Steve pushed a bowl toward Eddie. "Here, have some peanuts."

Eddie grabbed a handful then chugged half a cold one. "I'm gonna be straight. You're acting like a kid in a candy store. You see this. You want her. You see that. You want her. Next thing you'll be telling me this woman is the love of your life."

"Geez, how'd you know? She's the spitting image of Mary Lou Kitchen. Remember her? She was my first high school sweetheart."

Eddie threw his arms up. "God damn, Steve. Grow up. How long ago was that? Thirty years? You spent last year working things out with Suzanne. You've straightened out your life. The university is on the move. What more could you want?"

"You don't understand. I've got to see her."

"Jesus Christ." Eddie shook his head. "You can't blow everything over some broad."

"She's not a broad. She's ..."

"Whatever. You have to focus."

"That's why I'm here."

"I'm glad we got that figured out. Look we can talk all day, but it comes down to one thing. When your head is screwed on straight, things are fine. When you're screwing around, things go to pot."

"I don't know if I can give her up."

"Don't give me that 'I-don't-know' bullshit, Steve. Read my lips: No more crap about Miss whatever-her-name is."

"Eddie, I can't."

"Can't, won't cut it. Put her out of your mind. You're a damn good president, Steve. Do you want to jeopardize that? Focus. With Suzanne in your corner, you can do it."

"Okay." Steve sighed. "I'll try."

***

Suzanne sat in the family room reading when Steve joined her. "Did you have a nice visit with Eddie?" she asked.

"Sure did. He tells it the way it is."

"I like Peggy, too. We ought to have them over some weekend."

"I'd like that."

"What did you talk about?"

"Division I and the university. We spent a lot of time talking about you."

"Me? I doubt that. What's his take on Division I?"

"He's been onboard all the way. After hearing about what happened at the convention, he said my stock had gone up 100%."

She shook her head. "Isn't that something? The faculty piss and moan about athletics. But when you take the program to the next level they think you walk on water."

"A bunch of assholes, if you ask me. It's like someone turned on the switch. They finally connected the dots between Division I and the university's status."

"How can a bunch of Ph.D.'s be so dense?"

"Damned if I know."

"Did Eddie talk about anything else?"

"He said people across the state love you. And that we're the perfect team."

"What do you think?"

"Suzanne, you're the best. I couldn't have come this far without you. I love you so much."

"You're such a dear."

"One more thing. He said I was receiving more coverage than the governor. Even people in his hometown of Ft. Smith are hyped up. Things are cooking all over Arkansas."

"That reminds me. Mom called today. They're coming for Easter. She said daddy has some important news to share with you."

"Did she say what it was?"

"He wants to tell you himself."

"C'mon. Tell me. I'll act surprised."

"You promise?"

"Of course."

"Mom said it's hush-hush in Little Rock. The political wheels are turning. The party has narrowed the list of candidates for governor down to three. And you're one of them. Isn't that exciting?"

"Spectacular."

"You're not just saying that, are you?"

"No. When you first mentioned the idea, I was cool. But I've thought about it. A lot. I'm ready to rock and roll."

"Daddy has a group that will do the leg work, beat the drums and take care of the backroom stuff. All you have to do is stay the course. Before you know it, he'll have party officials standing in line begging you to run. And when you announce, it'll be a done deal."

"Terrific. The timing couldn't be better. I'm ready for a new challenge. That is, if you're up to it."

"Me? Of course, I'm ready. I love you." She hugged him. "Living in the mansion in Little Rock, what could be better?"

"Better? I can think of only one thing."

She smiled.

He grabbed her arm. "Let's go to bed and I'll show you."

CHAPTER EIGHTEEN

Steve knotted his tie and slicked back his hair. Suzanne called him for breakfast. Nearing the kitchen, he stopped cold when a vision of Karen appeared.

Licking her lips, she vamped in a skin-tight dress as strobe lights flashed around her. Steve stumbled over a throw rug and banged into the wall.

"You okay, dear?" Suzanne asked.

"Cobwebs in my head. The game wasn't over until after midnight."

She ignored the comment. "Patricia called. She's bringing a German chocolate cake for your birthday tomorrow."

"Her cakes are the best. I'm looking forward to seeing her and Rusty. We haven't talked in weeks."

"What's your schedule like today?"

"Three meetings with donors, then off to the concert at 3:00. How about you?"

"I'm speaking at the Garden Club. Then I'm going to the white sale at Penney's. Gotta pick up a few groceries, too. Want anything special for dinner?"

"How about veal chops?"

"Sounds good. What time will you be home?"

"I'd say 6:30 or 7:00."

***

That afternoon Sandra checked into the Peabody. She arranged for room service to deliver dinner at 6:00 then picked up birthday balloons which she tied to a chair back.

On a parson's table, she placed a red rose in a vase, a sentimental birthday card and Steve's favorite chocolates. She primped for an hour, dabbed Trésor behind her ears and in her cleavage, and then left for the concert.

Steve arrived as the stage lights dimmed. He waved to Sandra and settled into his seat. She smiled his way.

The way her body moved in sync with the music aroused him and made him feel as if she was performing just for him. After the performance and several curtain calls, he made his way backstage.

Sandra lingered by the stage door. "Aren't you going to change?" he asked.

"I wanted to surprise you, darling. I got us a room at the Peabody."

"Tonight?" He began to perspire. "Sweetie, we agreed to wait until next weekend."

"It's special," she purred. "I want to be with you both times."

"Oh, sweetheart, I ..."

"I love you," she said, pressing into him. "I've already ordered dinner."

"I love you, too."

***

Suzanne made the bed with the red silk sheets she'd picked up that afternoon. She pressed a damask tablecloth that had been her grandmother's and set the table with the good silverware and crystal, fresh flowers.

She took a moment to count her blessings. *I have a wonderful husband who loves me. I'm crazy about him. His work is going well. And we're back to being a team.*

She pinched herself to make sure she wasn't dreaming.

She turned on the evening news at 6:00 and waited for Steve. At 8:00 she made herself a sandwich. The candles flickered and died. Old memories — and doubts — crept in. She put away the dishes and got ready for bed.

***

Slightly after 10 p.m., Suzanne heard the garage door open. She caught a glimpse of Steve stripping to his shorts.

"Asleep, dear?" he asked as he eased next to her.

She bit her tongue. "I must have dozed off. Are you okay?"

"I had a flat tire. Had to hike two miles to a gas station. It took another hour to find someone to repair it. I'm sorry I'm late."

She turned to kiss him and caught a whiff of Trésor. Suzanne froze. *My God, he's lying. Again. I haven't worn Trésor all week.*

Steve spooned her. "I'm a little tired, darling," she said. "Can we talk in the morning?"

Suzanne curled into a fetal position and didn't budge all night.

When she heard the garage door close, she jumped out of bed, threw on sweats and raced to the office.

Ripping open the promotional flier, she stared at the words, trying to make sense of them.

Was it just an example of slick advertising? A coincidence? Had Steve bought stationery? Why? Had he been writing to Kate? Did that mean he was still seeing her?

She threw the flier on the floor, and shouted, "Liar. Liar."

Suzanne paced, her anger blocking her tears. *How could you have done this? You betrayed me. Deceived Dr. Scanlon. And lied to Bill.* She had to confirm her suspicions.

At 8 o'clock on Monday morning she took a deep breath and dialed.

"Southern Stationery, your custom specialists."

Suzanne cleared her throat. "Six weeks ago we received a letter from Edwin Long, your marketing manager."

"Yes, that was sent to our preferred customers."

"May I speak to him?"

"Of course. I'll transfer you." Suzanne held her breath.

"Good morning, this is Edwin Long."

"I'm interested in ordering some stationery."

"Excellent. Do you have your account number?"

"Sorry, it's not handy."

"No problem. I can verify everything with your phone number, name and address."

Suzanne gave him Steve's office number. "It's Schilling. Steve Schilling at Thornton Hall, Eastern Arkansas University in Ruston."

"Just a moment." Perspiration moistened her under arms. "Yes, Mrs. Schilling, how may I help you?"

"I've misplaced our records. Do you have a list of our past orders?"

"I have your file right here. Do you have a pencil?"

"Yes, I'm ready."

"Good. Over the last five years we've sent six sets of lavender stationery, three sets of light blue, two mint green, two rose, and four sets of sunrise yellow. Did you get that?"

"Yes, thank you."

"Do you need anything else?"

"No, I have more than I need." Her voice trailed off. "I'll get back to you." Suzanne's stomach churned. She slammed the receiver, ran to the bathroom and vomited.

***

Suzanne pulled into the garage, hands trembling, cut the engine and gazed at the blank wall.

"Why? Why?" she shouted then pounded the steering wheel. "Bastard. You bastard. Why did you do this to me?"

She marched into the house and fell onto a dining room chair. She looked at her notes. The colors jumped at her. Lavender. Blue. Green. Rose. Yellow.

Slow down, she thought. *You've got to work your way through this. Could there be more women than Kate? There can't be ... Five? It's not possible.*

She recalled the envelopes in the tray. *Rose was from Ruston, blue from Blytheville. That left lavender, green and yellow. Maybe he bought them in different colors. But why?*

Something about lavender gnawed at her. *Kate always wore lavender. It was her favorite color. Maybe there are three women.* Her heart sunk. *Maybe five?*

Seeing their framed wedding portrait on the mantel, she grabbed it then snatched two more pictures from the bookcase and crammed them into a drawer.

She broke into a cold sweat and covered herself with an afghan on the sofa. Her mind raced. *How could there be 17 boxes? When did he find time to*

168

write? What did he say? Had anyone seen the envelopes? Did Carol know? God, was Carol one of the women? Who else knew?

She pressed her fingers into her temples and recalled her mother's words. "Are you sure you can trust him?"

Two days ago she had sung his praises. "How humiliating."

She gave herself permission to cry, then pulled herself together and called her mother.

"Good morning, this is Harriet Hudson," her mother chirped.

"Mom." Suzanne broke down.

"Suzanne? Suzanne? What's wrong?"

"It's Steve. He's been lying for years."

"Oh baby, I was afraid this might happen. I'm sorry. Come home."

"I can't, Mom. I have too much work."

"The work can wait. You need to get out of there — and away from him. Please come home."

"I have to sort things out. I'll be there Friday."

***

Steve knocked softly on the bedroom door. He'd been in Little Rock overnight. "Are you asleep, sweetie?"

"No," she shouted.

"You okay?"

"Go away, you shithead."

"Suzanne, what's wrong?" He tried the door knob. "Let me in."

"I don't want to see you."

"Suzanne, I love you."

"I bet that's what you say to all of them."

"To all of them? What are you talking about?"

"I'm talking about you. And your lies."

"Lies? Suzanne, please unlock the door. I love you."

"Love? You don't know what the word means. I hate you."

"Honey, please open the door. Let's talk about what is bothering you."

"You're what's bothering me. Go away. I'm going to my mother's."

***

Sitting on the front porch rocker, Harriet saw approaching headlights. She pulled her cardigan tight across her chest and ran to the car. "Come in, Sweetie. I've made hot chocolate."

"Mom, it's awful."

"We can talk inside." She hugged her daughter. "It'll be okay. You're in shock."

"He didn't change. You were right. I'm so embarrassed. I don't know what to say."

"You don't have to say anything."

"You can't imagine what he's done. I couldn't stay in that house a minute longer."

"You did the right thing, Suzanne."

"I hate the bastard." Harriet squeezed Suzanne's hand as the two walked into the kitchen.

"Mom, he's lied and cheated all these years. And all the time I thought Kate was the only one. Mom, there are others."

"Others? Are you sure?"

"He's ordered stationery in five different colors. One for every woman he's seeing."

"Sweetie, you don't know for sure. It can't be that bad."

"Maybe there's a dozen. Who knows?" Suzanne laid her head on the table and wept.

"Let it all out, dear."

She rubbed Suzanne's shoulders.

***

The next morning, in their robes, the two sipped coffee. "You're right, Mom. I should have got a divorce long ago. I can't believe I was so blind."

"You weren't blind. You loved him. You expected him to share the same commitment. That's how I felt about your daddy."

"How did you ever deal with his philandering?"

"Sometimes I wonder."

"It must have been terrible."

"I pledged to live my own life. You'll have to do the same."

"Mom, we work together. I see him all the time. What will people say?"

"Don't worry about what people say. Do what is right for you."

"Our lives are so interwoven. He's the president, for God's sake. There's the university. And the community. I don't know where to start."

"Suzanne, nothing worth doing is easy."

"I'll have to make a public statement."

"Don't try to fix everything at once. Deal with one thing at a time. I'll be here for you."

"Thank you. I don't know what I'd do without you."

Harriet pursed her lips. "You need someone in Ruston, too. Someone you can talk with anytime of the day. Someone who'll listen and give you advice."

"There's Edwin Bennett, our lawyer. I trust him."

"Besides your lawyer."

"I don't know, maybe Reverend Scanlon?"

"Think about it. We're going out for lunch and have a glass of wine."

"Wine?"

"I may have two."

***

Harriet struggled to keep her eyes open. "Want a nightcap?"

"I'll get it," Suzanne said, opening the refrigerator door.

"Have you thought of someone in Ruston you can trust?"

"My best friend is Alice Porter. But she talks too much. I've narrowed it down to Bill Thornton and Gerry Coleman."

"President Thornton is a lovely man."

"He's wonderful. But he and Steve are very close. I'm angry, but I don't want to compromise their friendship."

"Who's this Mr. Coleman?"

"The editor of the *Daily Gazette.*"

"The editor? I don't know about that."

"We play bridge every month. I can count on him. He's a good friend, and he knows everyone in town."

"Sounds like you've already decided."

"Yes, I'm calling him."

***

Gerry waved Suzanne into his office. "How have you been?" he asked. He closed the door and moseyed to his desk.

"I've lost ten pounds, and on my way to losing another ten."

"Anything else?"

She grinned. "I have contacts."

"Very flattering. So what's on your mind?"

"I'm counting on you. This can go no further."

"Of course."

Suzanne sat straight and looked him in the eye. "I'm divorcing Steve."

"No." His smile disappeared. "What happened?"

"Steve's having an affair. No, he's having several affairs."

"Affairs? Are you sure?"

"At least 90 percent."

"Have you mentioned this to anyone?"

"My mother."

"Want to talk about it?"

Suzanne sighed and began spilling her guts, sharing what she knew about Steve's past episodes, describing their reconciliation, and telling Gerry about the multicolored envelopes.

"It's hard to fathom. Maybe one or two but five? I can't comprehend that," he said.

"I don't know what to do. It's so complicated."

"It's a mess. Kate is one thing. But others? We're talking about a major sex scandal. If this hits the national news, it'll spread like wildfire — *USA Today, Washington Post, New York Times*. They'll be like flies on ..."

"We can't let that happen," Suzanne said.

"Slow down. We have to work our way through this. First we must determine if any students are involved."

"Students? Oh my God, I never thought of that."

"It was my first thought."

"Do you think it's possible?"

"He wouldn't be the first. Or the last."

"I'd die."

"We've got to crank up an investigation."

"Like hire a private investigator?" Suzanne's voice rose. "That'd cost a bundle."

"I'm not ready for that. But ... I could justify devoting some company resources to it."

"What would you do?"

"A little fact-finding. If this blows we have to stay ahead of the fallout."

"I'd appreciate whatever you can do."

"Suzanne, I have to be candid. If it goes public, I'll have to print it."

"I know, Gerry. That's your job."

"And once I start, it's newspaper business. That's how it has to be."

"I understand."

"What's next?"

"I'm gonna assign the project to Karen Holmes. She's my best reporter."

"Holmes? Karen Holmes." She frowned. "Is she the one who wrote the Division I story?"

"And the feature on Steve last summer."

Suzanne pursed her lips. "She knows a lot about him. Maybe she's one of his women."

"Karen? No way."

"Don't be so sure. Anything is possible."

"What do you want me to do?"

"Give me a week or so. I'd like to talk to her.

"What will you say?"

"I'll say that I'm giving her a heads-up on the centennial plans we talked about last month."

"That'd be good. I was going to assign that piece to her anyway."

"I want to follow up on my intuition."

"Fine. I won't do anything until I hear from you."

CHAPTER NINETEEN

Steve staggered to the kitchen for the third — or was it the fourth morning in a row? He made a pot of coffee and tiptoed down the hallway.

Cracking open the bedroom door, he peeked in. Suzanne had made the bed. *Damn, we haven't talked in a week, and now she's gone to her mother's to sing the blues. What's wrong? I've done everything Rusty told me to do. And I even took care of Suzanne's honey-do list.*

Steve's coffee grew cold as he searched under a pile of rubble before finding Eddie's phone number.

"Wilson's," Eddie answered.

"How the hell are you?" Steve asked.

"Hey man, what's happening?"

"Nothing good. I haven't gone to work all week."

"What's wrong?"

"Things are worse."

"I told you to put that woman out of your mind."

"It's not just her. Suzanne is pissed. You gotta help me. I need to see you."

"Steve, I have to be honest. I've talked to Peg. I'll meet with you under one condition."

"Anything you say."

"You have to see a doctor."

"A doctor? I don't need a doctor."

"Listen to me, Steve. You're going off the deep end. I took the liberty of talking to my golf buddy, Fred Jones. He's a top psychologist. He said he'd be glad to see you. He's very discreet. No one will know. Will you do it?"

"I ..."

"Forget it. I'm tired of this game. I'm going to work."

"No, no, wait. I'll do it."

"Okay. I'll set up an appointment for Thursday afternoon when he's off. You and I can chat afterwards."

***

"Hi, I'm Fred Jones." The tall Brit peered through his horn-rimmed glasses. "You must be Steve Schilling."

"Nice to meet you," Steve mumbled.

"C'mon back. Want a Coke or something?"

"I'm fine." Steve settled into a tan leather chair.

"Eddie gave me some background. I'd like to know what brings you here. In your own words. Okay?"

"Sure, you're the doctor."

An hour later, the kindly shrink said, "Based on my 27 years of practice, I'd say, you're lucky to be alive. Running a university is a tough enough. A fling or two, maybe, but five affairs? Concurrently?"

Steve appeared stricken. "They're not affairs. I love them all."

Dr. Jones laid his notebook aside and shook his head. "So, you're involved with five women and pursuing another."

Steve felt ill. "Can you help me?"

"Steve, you're a Ph.D. This is not like fixing a car. It'll take two or three visits — maybe more — just to complete an assessment."

"Could you give me an idea of how long?"

"I'll do my best as we move forward. For now, I'd like to talk about your childhood. What were your parents like?"

"Mom was wonderful. A perfect mother to my brother, sister and me. She took in laundry, cleaned houses, did ironing, everything."

Dr. Jones nodded. "It sounds like you admired your mother, had a close relationship. And what about your father?"

Steve's voice rose. His right leg began to jiggle.

"You seem to have strong feelings about him."

"You would, too, if you endured the number of beatings I did."

"Want to tell me about them?"

"It was ghastly, horrible. I'd start shaking, felt nauseated if he came within twenty feet of me. I hated him. Still do."

"Have you ever thought about how you treat women?"

"No, I do what comes naturally. You know, try to please them, make them happy."

"How do you do that?"

"I write them letters, take them shopping and out to eat, give them flowers. Whatever it takes to please them."

"Sounds like you want to make them feel special."

"I suppose."

"How do you feel when you're having sex?"

Steve squirmed. "Geez, I don't know."

"What do you think about?"

"Making her have an orgasm."

"And after sex?"

"I think about the next time. Is that unusual?"

"For most men, yes. They usually think about themselves first. Their own pleasure. You know the old saying — wham, bam, thank you ma'am."

"That was my dad. He never did anything for mom. I felt sorry for her. She deserved better. I just try to give women what they should have."

"That's natural, Steve. But not five women at the same time. You're married. Your wife deserves your full affection."

"Dr. Jones, what are you saying?"

"Steve, you're exhibiting compulsive sexual behavior. It's also known as hyper sexuality or sex addiction."

"How does that work?"

"It means your sex drive overpowers your brain." He paused to let the notion sink in. "When you leave a woman, Steve, what do you think about?"

The patient shrugged. "That it was good."

"How do you feel about the woman after you leave her?"

"Hmm, I don't think about her."

"Not at all?"

"Well, maybe a little. I think about how I turned her on."

"That's it?"

"Sometimes I think about what I'll do next time."

"You don't have any feelings about her as a person?"

"Sure, I love her," Steve said with assurance. Then his voice softened to a whisper. "Doc, I really do."

"It seems that it's just about sex."

"No. I love them."

Doc shook his head. "I would guess that you have trouble maintaining an intimate relationship."

"Why do you say that?"

"Because there is nothing to sustain your relationships. Most people express their feelings about the person they love in several ways. They talk about personal attachments, their partner's personality, what pleases them. When most people say they are in love, their feelings are the connectors. You talk only about sex, and how it drives you."

"But I love them."

"Steve, sex and love are not synonymous. They're connected but they're not the same."

"They are to me."

"When you're having sex, does everything feel good?"

"Yeah."

"And when the woman is gone, do you feel empty? Do you start looking forward to sex again?"

"That's right. How'd you know?"

"That's the point. Sex is your connector. If you were in love, your feelings about her would be pulling you back, and help to nurture and sustain your relationship. What pulls you back is the thought of having sex again."

"Is that why I get a hard-on when I watch Sandra play the violin at the symphony?"

"Absolutely. You view her as a sex object. You don't see her for the person she is, her inside beauty, her attractive qualities, or how you feel about her. You're addicted to sex. When you're engaged in the chase and having sex, you're on a high. When you're not, reality sets in and you're back on the prowl."

"I guess I'm messed up, huh?"

"Maybe. Steve, having a strong sex drive is normal. And desirable. But your sex drive is out of control. It's the same for an alcoholic or a compulsive gambler."

"I can't believe you figured this out in less than an hour. Can you help me? I'm miserable."

"I can't promise. Compulsive behavior is very difficult to change. Even in the best case scenario, it takes a long while."

"There must be something you can do."

"I can give you a few suggestions. But compulsive sexual behavior is only part of your problem."

"Don't tell me there's more."

"I suspect you have a narcissistic personality disorder."

"What's that?"

"It's having an inflated sense of self-importance, believing that rules and standards of morality apply to others, but not you. Like President Nixon. He thought he was above the law."

"I hope I'm not like him."

"Sex is how you mask your low self-esteem. It probably goes back to your dad — how he treated you and your mother."

"What an asshole."

"Sex makes you feel like you are in control."

"Control? I don't want to control anyone."

"It's not something you do intentionally. But your sexual desire far exceeds your concern or feelings for others."

"That can't be."

"Steve, your words don't match your actions."

"What do you mean? It's not like I've done something wrong."

"Yes, you have. You've told women that you want to marry them, right?"

"Yeah."

"That's not realistic. You can't marry all of them. Eventually, you'll hurt someone. You probably already have. Have you ever thought about that?"

Steve looked dumbfounded. "I just try to please them."

"You're not being honest with yourself. You're rationalizing your behavior."

"I went out with a lot of girls in college. No one got hurt."

"How do you know? You have no way of knowing how they felt. Maybe you got one pregnant. And you don't even know it."

"I never meant to hurt anyone."

"As you matured, things got more complicated. As you've moved up the ladder professionally, you've used sex to compensate for your personality shortcomings."

"I don't understand."

"It's not simple. It'll take months to unravel all of this. And, as I said before, I can't promise that things will change."

"You make sex sound awful. What should I do?"

"Compulsive behavior isn't something you can just stop doing. Like flipping a light switch. Or giving up a food you're allergic to. You'll have to change behavior that probably started when you were a kid, maybe with a high school sweetheart."

"This sounds like a huge challenge."

"It will be. You'll have to learn to live in the real world, not the one you've painted. You'll have to recognize and work on your issues. About one percent of the adult population, mostly men, have narcissistic issues. We can take steps together. I can assist you, but I can't do it for you."

"I'll have to think about it, Doc." Steve stood up.

"Of course. Take your time. Just remember, nothing will change if you don't change."

***

Steve drove toward the country club in a fog. He found Eddie in the bar. Eddie gave him a firm hug. "How'd it go, man? Whaddaya think of Doc?"

"He really knows his stuff. He laid out my situation in no time."

"I told you he was good. Let's have a beer. You can give me an update."

Steve sucked down a couple of frosty mugs while answering Eddie's questions. "So what's next?" Eddie asked.

"I told him I'll have to think about it."

"Think about it? Steve, you have to take action. You can't continue this way."

"I'll look at my schedule. Maybe I can fit in some therapy sessions this summer."

"Maybe? You need to commit. It's show time."

***

On the drive home Steve wondered how, with such a busy schedule and so many things on his mind, he'd find time for appointments with Dr. Jones. *Don't I have enough going on with the university and the asshole faculty? And Suzanne? What about Martha, Sandra ... Kate? What if the word got out? Forget about living in the governor's mansion.*

Walking into the den, he glanced at the article tacked to the wall — EAU GOOD FOR THE COMMUNITY. His thoughts ricocheted to Karen. He imagined caressing her firm body.

He felt a familiar bulge in his pants and grabbed himself. "I love you, Karen," he gasped and fell like a rag doll onto the couch.

***

Steve opened the package from Southern Stationery, stopped at the florist then went home and called Karen.

"Good evening, this is Karen Holmes," she said.

"Karen, its Steve."

"How have you been?"

"Fine. More important, how are you?"

"Busy, busy, lots of paper work."

"I've wanted us to chat. In New Orleans you ran out before ..."

"I'm so embarrassed," she interrupted. "That was childish. I'm sorry."

"No, no, I was wrong. I shouldn't have put you in that situation. I feel bad."

"That's nice of you to say."

"There's so much I want to tell you. Could I stop by?"

"I don't think so."

"Please give me a chance to explain."

"I don't think it's a good idea."

"I'll stay just a few minutes."

"Steve, I ..."

"C'mon. You can kick me out after a half hour. I promise to behave. What do you say?"

"Okay, but ..."

***

Karen opened the door. Steve handed her a red rose. "Steve, I …"

"You didn't say I couldn't bring you a flower. I promise I'll be gone by 8:30."

"I'm holding you to that," Karen said, turning for the kitchen. Steve took a box from behind his back and slipped it on the seat of a chair.

She filled a bud vase, plopped the rose in it and joined him at the small table by the front window. "You have 29 minutes."

"I want to be honest. I've never done anything like that before. You were absolutely right to leave. Being involved with someone is much more than a physical thing. It has to come from the heart."

"Yes, it does. I'm glad you feel that way."

"Things are changing between Suzanne and me. I can't say more. It's important that you know that I'd never do anything to put you in harm's way. He placed a box of stationery on the table.

"In the weeks ahead I thought we might correspond. As friends."

Karen looked at the pale gray box. "I'm flattered. I don't know what to say."

"Just say what you feel. And I'll write back."

"I'm not very good at writing about myself."

He ran his fingers across the back of her hand. "Would you think about it?" he asked.

She smiled. "Sure."

"That's all I ask," he said on his way to the door. "See, it's only 8:28."

***

A few days later Sharon arrived with a salad and dessert. "You said you'd made lasagna so I figured you wanted to talk."

"What made you think that?" Karen asked.

"You always cook when you're antsy about something."

"Think you're so smart, don't you?"

"I've been around. What's on your mind?"

"Remember when you called me a prude?"

Sharon sat up. "You did do something in New Orleans, didn't you?"

"It's not what you think."

"I knew it," she said, rubbing her hands together.

"I had a couple of drinks with an old friend."

182

"Now we're getting somewhere."

"He called yesterday."

Sharon jumped up. "You gonna meet him?"

"We talked. He wants us to write to each other, as friends, like pen pals."

"Big deal." Sharon eased back on the sofa.

"He's married," Karen said.

"Oh?"

"Does that mean you don't approve? You're the one who called me a prude for not sleeping with Steve. And now you're not sure I should write to a male friend because he is married?"

"Writing can lead to things. It sounds innocent. You write about nothing, feel comfortable, safe. Then you put things on paper that you might not say in person. Next thing you know, you're in bed together."

"What?"

"It happened to me. We began as platonic friends. Then our letters got intimate. It wasn't long before I couldn't wait for the next one. Then we started meeting."

"Wow. You never told me."

"All I'm saying is you have to ask yourself, where is this going?"

***

Karen played back her messages. "Good morning, Miss Holmes, this is Suzanne Schilling. I'd like to speak with you about a special project. Please give me a call at the university."

Karen stared at the phone as if it was a coiled snake. *What does she want? Does she know something? Did she see Steve's car in front of my place?*

She agonized for hours before returning the call.

"Office of Communications," the receptionist answered.

"This is Karen Holmes at the *Daily Gazette*. I'm returning Mrs. Schilling's call."

"Yes, Mrs. Schilling asked me to interrupt her if you called. She'll be right with you."

"This is Suzanne Schilling. How are you, Miss Holmes?"

"Fine."

"That was a wonderful feature you wrote on Steve last summer."

"Thank you. It took a lot of research."

"I bet." Karen frowned at Suzanne's tone. "Last week I talked to Gerry about university plans for our centennial. He said he planned to assign the story to you so I thought we might chat."

"That's very thoughtful."

"How about lunch this Friday at the Red Pepper? Is noon okay?"

"I'd like that. Noon will be fine." Karen hung up. *Centennial? I don't think so.*

***

That night Karen counted eight times she'd been with Steve, including lunch and dinner in New Orleans. Her heart sank. *Did Suzanne know something? Had she and Steve been followed?*

Karen spent Friday morning dressing for lunch with Suzanne. She made a final appraisal in the mirror and headed for the deli.

Arriving early at the Red Pepper, she saw Suzanne waving from Steve's table. Dressed in her best business suit and polished pumps, Karen extended her hand.

"It's nice to meet you," Suzanne said. "Your stories about Steve have been terrific."

"Thank you, Mrs. Schilling."

"Have you worked at the *Gazette* long?"

"I'm finishing my fifth year."

"Where are you from?"

"New Orleans."

"That's Steve's favorite city. I like the personal touches you added to the stories."

"The credit goes to Gerry. He guided me all the way."

"That's a stunning suit," Suzanne said.

"Thank you. I got it in Memphis. I go there frequently to shop." Suzanne's eyebrows shot up to her hairline.

"Do you come here often?" Karen asked.

"Steve and I used to. Now we're so busy, we hardly have time to talk."

"I can imagine." Karen visualized their conversation as a chess match. She wondered how she was doing.

"What made you focus on Steve's childhood in Kentucky?" Suzanne asked.

Karen laughed for the first time. "That was Gerry's idea. My first draft was full of facts. He told me to humanize the story. So I took a different approach."

"Sounds like Gerry." Suzanne smiled. "Let me tell you about our centennial plans."

***

Suzanne called Gerry. "I talked with Karen."

"How did it go?"

"She's highly professional and very bright. And cute as hell."

"She's very professional. She reminds me of you at that age."

"A little naïve. And maybe a little infatuated with Steve, but she's not sleeping with him."

"That sounds definitive."

"Call it woman's intuition. Go ahead; she'll be fine on the project."

"I hate to sound like a broken record, Suzanne. If this goes public I'll have to print it. Are you sure you want to proceed?"

"Yes, I have no choice."

CHAPTER TWENTY

Over the weekend Karen replayed the conversation with Suzanne. *What did she know? What was she looking for?*

Suzanne had winced when Karen mentioned Memphis. Karen prayed that someone hadn't seen her with Steve and told Suzanne. She berated herself for her naïveté in spending so much public time with Steve. That had been foolish.

Monday morning Karen breezed into work. A note from Gerry requested her presence at 9 a.m. in his office.

She had a few minutes to collect herself. Her imagination shifted into overdrive. *Suzanne must have called him. I might as well pack up. I'll never be able to explain this to mom.*

Gerry motioned her in and closed the door. Karen sat in the electric chair. Her skin crawled.

"I've talked to Suzanne Schilling. We have a problem." Karen held her breath. *Fire me. I'll be gone by noon.*

"Suzanne thinks the president is having multiple affairs."

"Affairs?" Karen mumbled. *Not me. I didn't go to bed with him. Honest. I can explain.*

"What are you talking about?"

"Pull out your notepad." Karen's heart raced. "This may be your biggest assignment ever."

"Assignment? I ..."

"You've done investigative research?"

"Not much, Gerry."

"Review your old course notes, and I'll see you tomorrow at nine."

She packed her briefcase and trudged to her Camaro. Two days ago she'd fantasized about being in bed with him. Two hours ago she thought she'd lost her job. And now, she'd be investigating him.

***

Karen took her customary seat the next morning. "I don't have a clue where I should start," she told Gerry.

"I've already asked Anne Mitchell to assist you. She's savvy and knows the community."

"Good. I'll need all the help I can get."

"I've been giving this a lot of thought," Gerry said. "Steve's name started popping up four or five years before he became president. See what you can find out."

"Right away." Karen popped up and headed for the door.

"Wait." Gerry handed her a 3 x 5 card. "Here are three individuals who reported seeing the president's car parked at Kate Blanchard's. Check them out."

"You got it."

"One more thing. Last night I contacted Carol Beck, the president's secretary. She knows everything, and I mean everything, that has happened on the hill for the last thirty years. She has breakfast at Frank's every Saturday. Give her a call. See what she has to say."

***

Anne was rinsing her mug when Karen arrived. "Gerry told me. How about coffee at Frank's?"

"Sounds good."

The women jumped in Karen's car and were there in a flash.

They ordered, and when the waitress disappeared, Anne opened up. "Can you imagine? He's doing these women while Suzanne is working her ass off? I bet he expects her to put out too. What a son-of-a-bitch."

"Cool down, Anne."

"Who the fuck does he think he is? He's supposed to be a great leader. And he can't even keep his pants on. They ought to hang him by the balls."

"Anne!"

188

"Sorry, I had to say it."

"How long will it take to collect everything we have on him?"

"If Gerry asked, I'd say a week. For you, Monday."

"Good. I've already called Carol Beck. We're having breakfast on Saturday."

Anne beamed. "You know Gerry's been doing her for years. After his wife died last year, I figured they'd be married by now."

Karen rolled her eyes.

"What do you know about Kate Blanchard?"

"Miss Hot Stuff? Rumor has it she's been screwing the president for years. She's at the County Line Tavern every Friday night. She's probably caused four or five divorces."

"Gerry gave me three names. They've seen Steve's car at her place. Do you know anything about Mary Lou Redmond?"

"Damn, there's a credible witness. She was a cheerleader with Kate. I hear she dated Steve in college until Kate took over. She gets whoever she wants."

"How about Billy Joe McCoy?"

"BJ? He's a real stud — blond, six-five, square-shouldered. A 10 if I ever saw one. He played basketball for EAU several years ago. I've heard he and Mary Lou are an item."

"Know anything about Edna Willis?"

"Never heard of her."

"Good, I'll start with her."

***

Monday morning Karen walked into the photo lab. Anne gave her a big smile. "I did it." she proclaimed, pointing to the pix and stories covering the layout table.

"How many items are there?"

Anne shrugged. "Probably 140. What's next?"

"Put them in chronological order. And make a duplicate set. We'll probably need extras."

Karen walked back to her office and dialed Edna Willis. No answer. She called Tuesday. Still no answer. Wednesday and Thursday were the same.

A few minutes before 3 p.m. on Friday, Karen dialed again.

"Hello," an elderly woman whispered.

"Is this Edna Willis?"

"Yes it is, sweetie."

"I'm Karen Holmes from the *Gazette*. I'm following up on your letter."

"That's nice of you. The girls at the club said no one would ever call. I told them that if that Mr. Coleman didn't call soon I was going down there and give him a piece of my mind."

"Well, Mr. Coleman is quite interested. Could I stop by?"

"My shows are on. They'll be over at 4:30. Why don't you come by then?"

***

Karen knocked on the door. A petite woman in her seventies, wearing a flowery housedress, peered through the screen door. "Are you Miss Holmes?"

"Yes, I am."

"Please come in, sweetie."

Karen stepped into the living room. A large cross hung over the buffet in the dining room and family pictures covered the walls. "The tea is steeping. I made ginger snaps, too."

"Thank you. That's very nice of you."

"I know you're busy, so I'll get right to the point. This woman lives on the next street, behind the fence." She pointed to a five-foot-high wooden fence. "Her gentleman friend has been coming over for years. I never thought much about it, figured it was none of my business. One Sunday I was upstairs, sewing — I wasn't snooping. Her friend was grilling steaks. He had a red hat on. I said to myself, that's the university president."

"Yes, I've seen him in his fedora."

"I thought, 'That's not right. He's supposed to be a role model. And he has such a lovely wife. She speaks at the garden club every year.'"

"I've met her. Yes, she's delightful."

"I knew no one would believe me, so when he came over the following week I snapped a couple of pictures and started keeping a list."

190

Edna opened a manila folder. "Here are the pictures and my list covering the last 18 months. He visited 42 times. Shame on him."

Karen sorted through the photos. "You're absolutely right. May I borrow the folder?"

"Yes, I have a copy in my box at the bank."

Karen thanked Edna and headed for the office, her thoughts a jumble. *How could he do that? He seemed so sincere. I can't believe I fell for him.*

***

Karen's alarm blared. She had a headache from all the wine she'd downed after her meeting with Mrs. Willis.

She showered, slipped on a sweatshirt and jeans and drove to Frank's. Carol Beck had already settled into a booth.

Karen was struck by Carol's youthful appearance. Maybe it was the dark bangs and absence of wrinkles that made Carol look much younger than her years.

"Thanks for meeting me on your day off," Karen said.

"Sure. Happy to help — if I can."

Karen opened her notepad and tossed out a trial balloon. "What do you think about this mess?"

"I knew it would come unglued someday. You can't keep up that pace without slipping up. It's too bad."

"I have several questions."

"Remember, I can't say anything about matters that might be construed as confidential. I have a special allegiance to the office."

"I understand. Can you tell me about the envelopes?"

Carol nodded. "They started shortly after he became president. Like President Thornton, he opened all of his own personal mail. He knew I'd never say a word after the confidentially pledge I made on his first day. People on campus are always trying to undercut the president. I never could understand why Ph.D.'s are so conniving. Maybe they can't stand to see one of their own get ahead."

"Do you know who the letters are from?"

"I have some hunches. I prefer to stick to the facts. No surprise, the lavender ones are from Kate Blanchard. During his first month in office the two of them talked on the phone daily. Once in a while she'd stop by. One time they were in his office with the door closed. When she came out her hair was a mess, lipstick smeared. That's when the letters started."

"What about the light blue stationery?"

"Code blue?" Carol laughed. "I figure she works in a medical office. Her letters have a Blytheville postmark. They'd arrive once a week. Now it's every couple of months. She adds a touch of Trésor, the same perfume he gives Suzanne every year for her birthday. Sick, if you ask me."

"Why would a man do that?"

"Who knows? None of this is normal."

"What about the pale green?"

"There's something special about her. Most of her letters come from Little Rock. Occasionally, one is from Atlanta or Nashville." Carol paused. "How we doing?"

Karen shook her head. "If you wrote a book no one would believe it."

"You're right. The yellow letters come from someone on campus. I'm sure. I'd say three or four envelopes a week, then a month will go by with none. Most of the yellow ones carry a local postmark. One was from Memphis. Miss Yellow loads up on the Trésor."

"What about the rose-colored envelopes?"

"She's the latest. I think I know who she is, but can't say for sure. If she's the one I've pegged, she works on campus. Once in a while she sends him a letter from out of town. I haven't figured that out."

"I'm worn out. Anything else you want to share?"

Carol looked around. The next booth was empty. "This'll have to be off the record."

"Of course," Karen said, putting down her notepad.

"It's something I've never told anyone, not even Gerry. It might help you. But you have to promise never to mention me as the source."

"You have my word." Karen listened for another fifteen minutes then walked to her car. *This sounds like Peyton Place. There must be something in the water. I guess I was flattered by his attention and a little infatuated too. Thank God, I didn't end up as another notch on his belt.*

***

Karen zipped through the lab. "What's wrong with you?" Anne asked.

"I'm on a mission. Want to know what I've learned in the last few days?"

Anne looked up. "Go ahead. I was in the lab all weekend."

"Who do you want to hear about first — Carol Beck or Edna Willis?"

"Who cares? Give me Edna."

Karen gave a brief summation then opened her folder. "And here are the photos, all dated. He visited Edna's neighbor 42 times."

"Holy shit!" Anne slipped off her stool. "The little old lady in tennis shoes got the bastard. Let's tell Gerry right away. We'll haul the president's ass out of here."

"Slow down. This takes care of Kate. Four to go."

"We've got him. We don't need any more."

"Anne, our job is to uncover all the facts."

She wrinkled her nose. "I suppose."

"Do you want to hear what Carol Beck had to say?"

"Yeah, sure."

Karen shared her findings. "What do you think?"

"The plot thickens."

"Did you come up with anything in the lab?"

"Not compared to you. I made copies and put them in order. Now what?"

"Let's do the photos first."

At noon Karen looked up. "Who are these cheerleaders?"

"I know most of them," Anne said. "There's Kate and that's Mary Lou. The black one is Molly Green. She's an exec at Fed Ex in Memphis.

The tall, attractive one in the corner died some time ago. I think she committed suicide. I lost track of the other two.

"I'm following up with Molly," Karen said. "That'll give me a reason to do a little shopping. You start on the one who died and the other two."

* * *

The following Friday, Karen checked in at the FedEx security gate. Tall and slender, well-turned out in a dark suit, not a hair out of place, Molly Green greeted Karen at the door of her suite. "Would you like a soda?" she asked.

"No thank you." Karen looked around. "What a beautiful office. I love your tropical garden. There must be 25 plant varieties."

"Actually, there are 32." Molly smiled. "Have a chair."

Karen eased into a soft leather chair.

"What's the focus of your story on Steve?"

"We're looking at his college years."

"That should be interesting."

"What can you tell me about him?"

"Not much. Steve and I were good friends. Being the first black on campus, I thought I had to be perfect. Steve enjoyed campus life. The girls loved him — with his big smile and dreamy eyes. He's hard to pin down. I've always said Steve Schilling is Steve Schilling."

Karen lifted her pencil. "Interesting. Why do you say that?"

"He's the same today as he was then."

"Have you seen him lately?"

"No. We talked briefly at the class reunion last year. He never says a negative word about anyone. Never confronts anyone. It seems he just wants everyone to be happy. I used to wonder what made him tick. He seemed devoid of emotion. Almost robotic."

"Did you ever go out with him?"

Molly smiled. "No. We'd meet for a Coke in the university center and talk. Nothing more."

"What'd you talk about?"

"Nothing substantial. Our courses, sports, what he was doing."

"Sounds like he had it tough as a kid. I know his dad used to beat him. He liked his uncle. He told me about the Thanksgiving when his uncle visited and gave his mother a pretty dress."

Molly looked surprised. "You know about that?"

"He mentioned it one time when we were talking."

"Well, then you know Steve Schilling."

Karen placed her notepad in her purse. "What are your plans for the future?"

"That's hard to say. Right now, I'm dealing with today's corporate reality …"

Karen interrupted. "Like what?"

"Do you have any idea how many corporate CEO's are women? And how many are black?"

194

"I know there are few women at the top, and probably none of them is black. You have a Ph.D. Doesn't that count for something?"

"In universities it does. Not here."

"Have you ever thought about a job in higher education?"

"Funny you should ask. About ten years ago my Aunt Sarah — she worked for the Thornton's — and I were invited to dinner. It was the first time she'd been a guest in their home.

After dinner, Virginia, Bill's wife, told Aunt Sarah that the Board had extended her contract beyond Bill's retirement. That meant that she'd have steady employment for as long as he lived."

"That sounds odd. Then what happened?"

"Virginia asked a hundred questions. She wanted to know if I ever thought about returning to EAU. She suggested I pursue a Ph.D. By the time she finished I was ready to move back."

"Why didn't you?"

"I wanted to excel in the corporate world. Thought I'd be the example for black women and show the world that I could make it."

"What's next?" Karen asked.

"I think about EAU once in a while. I wouldn't make a good professor. And, I don't want to sound condescending, but I want to do more."

"What about being president?"

"President of EAU?" Molly shook her head. "No way. Steve will be there forever."

"Suppose he left?"

"Steve leave EAU? They'd have to drag him out kicking and screaming."

***

After checking into the Peabody Karen freshened up and headed for the lobby. She ordered a Manhattan. *What an interesting and accomplished woman Molly is. She could be anything she set her mind to. I bet she'd make a great college president.*

"What a wonderful surprise." Karen opened her eyes and took a double take.

"Steve?"

"How have you been?" he asked.

She hesitated. "Ah … busy."

"I'm going to the symphony tonight. Want a drink?"

"I don't …"

"Waitress," he called. "This young lady will have a Manhattan, straight up. And I'll have a Tanqueray on the rocks with three olives."

"Steve …"

"Don't worry about it. Are you shopping or working today?"

"A little of both."

"What are you working on?"

"A human interest story."

"What's it about?"

Karen took a sip. "I'm just getting started. There's not much to say right now."

"I look forward to hearing more."

Karen downed her drink and made a graceful exit.

***

Later that night Karen rolled over. Neon flashed 9:52 from the digital clock radio. She stumbled to the bathroom, splashed her face with cold water, combed her hair then headed for the deli downstairs.

After paying for pastrami on rye, two bags of chips and a large Coke, she left. Out of the corner of her eye she glimpsed Steve entering the lobby.

She blinked her eyes and looked again. A buxom blonde hung onto his arm. As they approached, Karen eased behind a magazine rack and held her breath.

She watched them stroll by. *Might she be the Memphis connection?*

CHAPTER TWENTY-ONE

Karen walked into the photo lab Monday, her head spinning. She had spent the weekend going over her notes. Nothing connected.

Anne greeted her. "How's our star reporter?"

"Okay. What'd you do over the weekend?"

"I laid around and watched TV. How'd your meeting with Molly go?"

"Quite well. She's very bright and very professional. I liked her."

Anne yawned. "Learn anything new?

"I'm not sure. She said something I'm still chewing on."

"What's that?"

"When I asked about Steve, she said 'Steve Schilling is Steve Schilling. He's just like he always was.'"

"I wonder what she knows. Maybe she meant he was screwing around then and he still is."

"Could be."

"How was the rest of your weekend?"

"I saw Steve on Saturday night."

"President Schilling?" Anne spun around. "You what? Where?"

"In the Peabody lobby. He was with a gorgeous blonde. She had two of the biggest knockers I've ever seen."

"What were they doing?"

"Walking toward the elevator, arm in arm. I ducked behind a magazine rack. They came within twenty feet of me."

"Geez, you're a regular Mata Hari. How do we find out who she is?"

"I scoured my notes looking for a clue. Carol Beck said she thought the woman worked on campus. Before I call Carol, I have an assignment for you. We need to organize everything."

"How?"

"By subject: Blytheville, Memphis, athletics and anything else you feel is relevant. Sort the photos and stories. If something belongs under more than one heading, make copies. Got it?"

"I think so."

"Good. I'll stop back after I talk to Carol."

***

"How are things going?" Carol asked.

"They're going. Can we talk?"

"Sure. What do you need?"

"You mentioned a possible connection with Memphis."

"Yes, I'm certain."

"I'd like to pursue that."

"How can I help?"

"I need to know more about the faculty. Where did they speak in the last year or so? What kind of activities were they engaged in? Can you get me that information?"

"Yep, I'd start with *The Rider.* Then I'd look at the annual calendar of events and move on to the annual faculty and staff directory. It lists all employees, their positions, phone numbers, campus and home addresses."

"Super." Karen felt flushed. She could barely contain her excitement.

"*The Rider,* our weekly newsletter, covers faculty and staff activities. You're sure to find Memphis mentioned there."

"Do you have archives?"

"How far back do you want?"

"Maybe …"

Carol interrupted. "How about eight or nine years?"

"Fantastic. Let me know when I can pick them up."

***

A week later Karen received two large boxes.

She opened the first and unpacked several hundred issues of *The Rider,* which she sorted by year on her dinette table. Starting with the oldest issues, she flipped through, searching for references to Steve and Memphis.

She found two entries in 1987, several more in 1988. On 3x5 cards she jotted info about Steve's appointments to the music selection committee, his rise to history department chairperson and role as NCAA Faculty Rep.

Working evenings for a week, she recorded over 200 entries for Steve, another 100 for Memphis.

Friday night, seeking relief, Karen poured a glass of wine and tossed a pizza into the oven, then attacked the week's mail. Underneath a pile of bills and the September issue of *Vogue,* she came upon a small box.

A shampoo sample, she thought as she slit the tape. She reached into the package and withdrew a bottle of Trésor. Her face flushed.

Karen:

It was wonderful to see you again. I hope you'll enjoy the Trésor as much as I've enjoyed the times we've shared. Looking forward to hearing from you.

Always, Steve

Her stomach churned. "Damn, he's sick. The jerk actually thinks I'm number six."

Her face reddened. "I'll find you, Ms. Memphis, if it's the last thing I do," she muttered.

Karen wolfed the pizza and made another pass through the index cards. Two hours flew by. Nothing connected.

She turned the cards over and tried again. Dead end.

What am I missing? Karen tossed the cards aside. *What do I know about Steve and Memphis? Where have I seen him? Where was he coming from? Where was he going?*

She scratched her head.

The first time was Florence. He was going to ... meet a donor. She grabbed the cards for Memphis and checked for donations, gifts, grants.

Nothing.

The next time she'd seen him, they'd gone to Mud Island after the press conference. *He had to leave. Damn, where was he going? Two weeks ago at the Peabody, he had plans. What plans?*

She paced. Maybe physical activity would stimulate her memory. She started her jumping-jack routine.

"To the symphony," she shouted. *He was coming back from the symphony.*

Karen shuffled through the cards. *Bingo.* "Schilling appointed to music chairperson selection committee." *Music — the symphony — that's it.*

She grabbed the faculty directory and ran her finger down the list of names until she found what she'd been looking for. On the last page she paused — Whitehead, Sandra, Chairperson, Department of Music.

Karen reached for the cards and counted the Whitehead entries. "Nineteen," she exclaimed. "Damn, she was here all the time."

In the morning Karen called Carol. "Does the university maintain a photo file?"

"Most faculty members share their ID picture. Who do you want?"

"Sandra Whitehead."

Silence.

"Carol, are you there?"

"Yes. I was taken back. I have her picture. Do you want to come by?"

"I'll be right up."

Carol smiled when Karen entered less than five minutes later. "Were you parked outside?"

"I move fast when I have to. This is important."

Carol handed Karen an envelope.

She tore it open and pulled out the photo. "Yes, that's her."

***

"Have a seat," Gerry said. Karen joined him at the conference table. "I hear you've made some progress."

"I have three things."

"Fire away."

"First, here's my draft on relationship number one."

"Good, I've been looking forward to reading it. I'll give you a call when I'm finished. What's next?"

"I've completed my work on relationship number two. That's Ms. Memphis. She's a faculty member at EAU."

"Who is she?"

"Sandra Whitehead. She's the chair of the music department."

"Yes, I've seen her perform. A real looker. What do you have?"

Karen shared her findings. "So, whaddaya think?"

"I'll tell you what I think."

The tone of his voice made Karen wince.

"You need a helluva lot more than that," he bellowed.

"But Mr. Coleman ... she's the one."

"Listen here, young lady. You're questioning the morality and ethics of a university president. You're talking about the careers of two highly respected individuals. Can you prove it?"

"I think so."

"You think so. I'll tell you what I think. You have a distraught wife who thinks her husband gave different-colored stationery to several women. How nice. You saw him in a hotel lobby with one of the alleged women. That's a biggie."

The wind went out of Karen's sail. "You have some circumstantial evidence. That's hearsay, not hard-hitting evidence. Do you expect me to write an editorial calling for his resignation? Give me a break."

"Mr. Coleman, it's not that way."

"I know," he said, softening. "But that's how his supporters will portray it. We need evidence — pictures, a confession. Times, dates and places. What you have on Kate is fine. That's a long-term affair that goes back to college. You'll have to play hardball with the others."

"Hardball?"

"You have to lay the cards on the table. Be brutal. Tell Ms. Whitehead that he's going down. Say to her, 'It's your life, your career, your family. Is he worth it?'"

"Ouch. Do I have to be that blunt?"

"Absolutely. You have to hammer her, take her to the brink. When she's ready to crack, then can you lighten up. Tell her she has a choice."

"A choice?"

"Tell her that we'll protect her, if she talks. We'll remove her name and photos from our files if she admits everything. Look her in the eye and say, 'It's your call.'"

Karen took a deep breath. "That's it? That's what you want?"

"That's it. Now, what was the third point you wanted to discuss?"

"Gosh, I forgot."

***

Steve breezed through a cabinet meeting, returned half a dozen calls and left for a luncheon speech. As usual, he snowed his audience. After a standing ovation, he stopped by the drugstore to pick up cashews and drove to Bill's.

His mentor gave him a warm hello. "What's happened to you?"

"You kicked me in the butt. And it worked. I got the message. I'm a new man. How about a drink?"

"Sounds good." Bill poured then led the way to the sunroom.

"I'm fired up, Bill. We have several programs in the hopper. I'd like your advice on a physical therapy proposal. It'll be our first healthcare submission."

"Go ahead."

"The deans have prepared a fine proposal but there's something missing. It's too academic, not very compelling. Any suggestions?"

Bill took a sip. "You have to neutralize the power base of the University of Arkansas. You're taking on their monopoly. The good ol' boys will come out swinging."

"That's what I'm worried about."

"Find two or three consultants from outside the state. Maybe one from Mizzou and an expert from Oklahoma or Tennessee. They can't take them all on."

Steve nodded. "Makes sense."

Bill paced. "You have to demonstrate there's a shortage of physical therapists on this side of the state. Rather than saying it, find a couple of local practitioners to carry the load. Ask for a letter from Howard Clark's daughter at Blytheville Memorial." He scratched his head. "What's her name?"

"Christina."

"Yeah, she's the one. Add the CEO from Ruston General and a bigwig from one of the Memphis hospitals. That'll show strong regional support."

"Gee whiz, Bill, you rattled off the whole game plan. How'd you do that?"

"Common sense. You have to think like those making the decisions," Bill said. "Steve, I have to ask again. What brought about these sudden changes in you?"

"Your words made me think about Suzanne, the university. How risky my behavior was. Bottom line, Ms. K is out of my life. Suzanne is the only woman for me. We're back on track," he lied.

"That's wonderful. Take it from an old psychologist, a lot of guys never figure out what's really important."

***

Karen poked her head into the photo lab. "Anne, I want to share something with you."

Anne covered the phone with her hand. She mouthed. "Shush."

Karen tiptoed in and sat down.

Anne hung up and took a deep breath. "You'll never believe this."

"What?"

"Remember when you asked me to follow up on the cheerleaders?"

"Yes."

"The two I didn't know are non-players. One moved with her parents to California. The other lives in Chicago."

"What about the one you thought committed suicide?"

"Rhonda Williams. What a tragic story."

"What happened?"

"I found her obituary in a weekly outside of Tulsa. There were three lines devoted to a Sam Appleton. I figured he was her significant other so I called him."

"Was he?

"Yes. He's an engineer at a flight simulator company there. He met Rhonda right after she graduated from college. She was pregnant and alone. He helped her get back on her feet."

"What happened?"

"She had lots of problems. Sam said she had dated a big EAU football star in college. When the jock found out she was pregnant he dumped her. She couldn't tell her parents, so she took off, ended up in Broken Arrow, Oklahoma."

"Did she have the baby?"

"A little girl. Stephanie. Sam said he'd asked Rhonda to marry him several times. She wouldn't. She was still hung up on the heartthrob. She told Sam that she'd never love anyone like that again. Poor guy. He choked up during our conversation."

"I guess we never know how lucky we are."

"Sam wanted to adopt Stephanie. He said he'd take care of Rhonda and Stephanie; give them the best. It didn't matter. Her depression worsened and she overdosed."

"That's tragic. What happened to Stephanie?"

"Sam adopted her."

"Well, maybe there's a happy ending for her."

"There's more."

"What?"

"Stephanie Appleton is a cheerleader at EAU."

"You gotta be kidding me."

"I made a copy of her picture in the yearbook. Want to see it?"

"Sure." Anne handed Karen the photo. "Geez, she looks just like Steve."

CHAPTER TWENTY-TWO

Karen answered the pounding. It sounded like someone was trying to break in. "Hold your horses. I'm coming," she said as she opened the door.

"Dr. Watson, reporting for duty," Sharon blurted. "Where's the wine you promised?"

"Follow me." Karen pointed to the Chardonnay chilling in a tarnished sliver ice bucket. "I'm glad you were free tonight. I need your help."

"I'm always free, unfortunately. What's going on?"

Karen handed her friend a full glass of wine. "Let's sit in the living room. I'll fill you in."

"Whatever you say, Sherlock."

"Enough of that, Sharon. This is serious." The women sat catty-corner. "Remember when you asked about the project I'm working on?"

"Sure."

"You can't tell anyone about this."

"I won't. You've known me how long? You can trust me."

"I do. But I had to say it."

"So, what's with all of the intrigue?"

"Well, I'm checking out President Schilling."

"Schilling? What for?"

"His extra-curricular activities."

"You mean those rumors are true?"

Karen nodded. Sharon kept quiet as Karen described Steve's affairs with Kate and Sandra.

"This is unreal," Sharon said. "Any more juicy gossip?"

"Are you sure you can handle it?"

"Bring it on."

"Take a look." Karen slid a folder across the coffee table. "Kate's neighbor took these. Mrs. Willis is a busybody with too much time on her hands. Thank heavens."

Sharon shuffled through the photos. She held one up to Karen.

"Look at this, his hands are grabbing her butt. And this one. It looks like they're doing it in the grass."

"They were together 42 times that we know of," Karen said.

"All recorded for posterity by a nosy old woman," Sharon said. "He's a dead duck. What's next?"

"I thought you'd never ask. I need help."

"Help?"

"With pictures, evidence. Anything that will connect the president to Sandra."

"That could be difficult."

"I'm hoping to catch them off guard. He'll be staying at the Peabody Saturday night. I'm sure. We'll start there."

"What do you want me to do?"

"Stake out the lobby. Photograph him checking in."

"Do you have a good camera?"

"Anne has a small one without a flash. I'm sure she'll let me use it."

"Perfect."

"You'll have to take the pictures, then change quickly for the concert. If you can photograph them at the symphony and afterward at the hotel, I'll do the rest."

***

Karen tapped her foot while waiting for Gerry to finish reading her report. "Nice job," he said. "In fact, it's damn good. I like Mrs. Willis. She'd make a great character witness. I can picture her on the stand."

"She's a jewel. Reminds me of my grandmother."

"Anything else we need to discuss?"

"I remembered the third point."

"The third point?" He frowned.

"The last time we met, I froze."

"Right. You were stuck on 'that's a biggie.'"

"Don't remind me. I'm researching Blytheville. Do you know any muckety-mucks up there? Anyone on the country club or hospital boards? And who's Howard Clark? And Christina Clark?"

"I've played golf with Howard. He's a heavy hitter, has fifty or so gas stations from here south. Christina is his daughter. She's a doctor, and a mover and shaker. She's chaired the hospital ball for the last five years."

"Can you get me the names on the country club board?"

"Piece of cake."

"How about the donors to the stadium and capital campaign?"

"No problem. Do you want all of them or just those from Blytheville?"

"Blytheville for now."

"I'm sure Carol can come up with that."

"I need old minutes for the athletic training committee."

"Carol can get that too."

"Super. That'll save a lot of time."

***

"My favorite restaurant is not far from here," Karen said as they unloaded their bags at the Peabody. "Let's review the plan over lunch."

"I feel like pizza and beer," Sharon said.

"Forget it. I know an upscale French place that you'll like. Gerry is picking up the tab."

"I love a free meal."

Karen parked around the corner from La Table d'Or. "The neighborhood seems a little seedy," Sharon said as they walked to the restaurant. "Are we almost there?"

"We're here," Karen said, opening the door.

"How did you ever find this place?"

"A friend told me about it. It oozes atmosphere."

"Sure is dark in here. See that alcove table? If President Schilling was here with one of his chickies, he'd be in her pants before the entrée arrived."

"Sharon, that's not funny."

"I'm dead serious."

***

At 5 o'clock Sharon patrolled the lobby. She stayed close to the deli to keep an eye on the entrance from the garage. He showed up around 6:30. She took several pictures as he checked in.

When he was out of sight, Sharon went upstairs. "He's here, Karen. And I got him."

"That's super. We'll talk in the car. Go change. We haven't a minute to spare."

"Okie dokie." Sharon disappeared into the bathroom.

Karen called the valet then shouted to Sharon. "Are you ready? The car will be out front by the time we get downstairs."

"Let's go. I'll put my lipstick on in the elevator. He could come down anytime. We sure don't want to run into him."

"Good point."

Karen gave the valet a 10 and sped to the concert hall. Traffic stopped them two blocks from the entrance. Sharon jumped out.

"I'll pick you up out front after the concert," Karen said.

She parked three blocks away and walked to a coffee shop across the street. Over several cups of tea, she wondered about Steve's modus operandi. How did he juggle so many women simultaneously? Keeping them apart must be a full-time job, she mused.

When she saw the first concert-goers leaving the hall, Karen retrieved the car and joined the traffic parade. Circling a third time, she stopped and flashed a smile at the policeman directing traffic. "May I please double-park until my friend comes out? She's recuperating from surgery."

He pointed to a loading zone. "Park there and keep your motor running."

Karen spotted Sharon and flashed her hazard lights. Sharon ran over and got in.

"I did it. I took some great pictures backstage," she gasped. "Sandra was hanging all over him. And he planted a big smack on her mouth. Maybe I'll win a Pulitzer."

***

From behind a potted palm, Sharon watched Sandra and Steve stroll through the lobby to the elevator. She slipped in just before the doors closed.

Sharon slid to the back where she had an unobstructed view of Sandra pressing her hip into Steve and running her fingers through his hair.

The doors opened. "Is there a vending machine on this floor?" Sharon asked.

"It's at the end of the hallway," Steve said, without turning.

She lagged behind, squeezing off shots every few seconds. Taking the stairs down two floors, she knocked softly and whispered, "It's me."

Karen opened the door. "Did you get them?"

"Unbelievable. I took one of them in a body lock, kissing in front of his room."

"You're the best."

"I'm famished. Can we order burgers and fries?"

"Anything you want. Grab a beer from the fridge and we can rehash everything."

As soon as she got home the next afternoon, Karen telephoned Anne.

"Were you successful?" Anne asked.

"We sure were."

"Let's meet at the office in ten minutes."

"I'll be there."

Later that afternoon Karen grabbed the fat envelope from Anne. "Have you met Sharon?" she asked her.

"No. I saw the two of you together at the mall once."

"She's my best friend. She's the PR director at First National."

"It's nice to meet you," Anne said. "You're a crackerjack photographer. These are fantastic. Where did you learn to take pictures?"

Sharon shrugged. "In the Girl Scouts. I earned a photography badge."

"You did a great job. Most people can't take a decent picture of someone standing still."

Karen emptied the envelope onto the counter. "Let's go over these, one at a time. Sharon, walk us through. Anne, you take notes."

Anne grinned. "Wait until Gerry sees these. He'll go bananas."

***

Karen and Anne flanked Gerry in the conference room.

He rubbed his hands together. "Let's see what you have."

Karen placed the first set in front of him. "Here is Steve checking into the Peabody."

Gerry went through them, selecting his favorites and handing them to Anne. "Hang on to the others. We may need them."

Karen handed him a second stack. "This is Steve entering the symphony hall.

"These are fine," he said, pushing three photos toward Anne. "I hope they get more interesting," he quipped.

"Don't worry. Here they are backstage." Gerry's smile broadened. "I like this one of them kissing."

"Here, they're returning to the hotel. And strolling through the lobby. This one's the closer."

Gerry's jaw dropped. "I'll say. Where did you take this?"

"In front of his room," Karen said.

Anne chimed in. "He's a goner."

"Terrific work," Gerry said. "Is that it for today?"

"Not quite," Karen said. "Did you find out more on Blytheville?"

"I've made three or four calls. Christina Clark's name keeps appearing. She's very classy and involved in lots of community projects."

"Including Steve Schilling?" Anne asked.

Gerry frowned. "Why would you say that?"

"Her name keeps popping up. She's a big-time donor. Active on the training center committee. She sounds like a perfect fit for him."

"I can't imagine that," Gerry said. "But, I'll check her out with Don Cagney. He plays golf up there, too, knows everything that's happening."

***

Karen and Anne walked toward the photo lab. "I could use some coffee," Karen said.

Anne flipped the switch to ON. "What do you think about Steve and Christina Clark?"

"Who knows?" Karen shrugged. "Not much surprises me lately."

Gerry poked his head in. "I just got off the phone with Don Cagney. There's a possibility that Christina Clark is number three."

"No kidding," Karen said.

"She's slacked off on her civic commitments. Don said he didn't think much about it. He thought she might be depressed over her husband's death. She shows up at the club only on Saturday mornings to play golf with her dad and his lady friend — and Steve Schilling."

"Wow," the two women said in unison.

"Wait. There's more. Christina told a friend she was teaching horseback riding to ..."

"Steve Schilling," the women crooned.

"I bet he was riding bareback," Anne blurted, then covered her mouth.

Gerry gave her a thumbs up.

***

"Are you okay?" Anne asked. "You look tired." Karen and Anne sat across from each other at the layout table.

Karen yawned. "I hardly slept all weekend. I keep thinking about Sandra, wondering how to play hardball with her."

"What do you mean?"

"Gerry wants me to pressure her into spilling the beans."

"How will you do that?"

"I'm not sure. Gerry said I need to hammer her."

"Geez, I could never do that. What does he expect?"

"He wants me to prod her to confess, admit everything and sign a form."

"What kind of form?"

"If she confesses and signs it, we'll remove her name from all records of her meeting with Steve. It gives her a way out. She'll get off scot-free. I'm meeting with Gerry and Kenneth Upton about that next Wednesday."

"Isn't Kenneth the nice-looking lawyer you dated?"

"We went out a couple of times. No spark. It's history."

"Guess there's no use dragging Sandra through the mud. He's the bastard we want."

"Anne, don't you think that's a little harsh?"

"Maybe. But, how would you feel if you'd been intimate with him, and then found out that you were number six?"

CHAPTER TWENTY-THREE

"Hi. I hope I'm not interrupting anything." Karen walked into the conference room where the men were deep in conversation. Kenneth and Gerry looked up.

Kenneth smiled. "Not at all. We're done."

"I just brought Kenneth up to speed," Gerry said. "Your timing is impeccable."

The young attorney grinned. "It's nice to see you, again, Karen. How have you been?"

"On overload."

"I can imagine on this high-stress assignment."

"It is. And the worst is yet to come. I don't know how I'll get through confronting his lovers. Gerry's training me in guerrilla warfare."

"I bet you'll do fine."

"Thanks."

"Kenneth, would you summarize the draft for us?" Gerry asked.

"Sure. Do you want a quick overview or point by point?"

"How long is it?"

"A little over six pages, I ..."

Gerry interrupted. "Stop right there. We want people to help us. We don't want to scare them off."

"I appreciate that, but we must include certain citations."

"To hell with the legalese. Give me four or five paragraphs and a signature line. One page max. Got it?"

"Yes." Kenny paused. "Anything else?"

"Nope. That's it. I want it on my desk by 10 a.m. tomorrow."

***

Karen walked back to her office, kicked off her shoes and took a deep breath. She knew she couldn't postpone the inevitable any longer. She had to play hardball. *I don't think I can. What if she clams up? What if she breaks down and cries? What if?*

Karen bit her lip and called.

"Good morning, this is Sandra Whitehead," came the whispery voice.

Karen's mouth went dry. "This is Karen Holmes with the *Gazette.* I'd like to schedule an appointment with you."

"For what purpose?"

"I'm researching some behind-the-scenes activities on campus."

"I don't think I can help you. I'm not involved in campus politics. I suggest you contact someone in the senate."

"I'm not covering the political angle. I'd like to speak with *you.*"

"I'm sorry. This is a bad time. I have a class in fifteen minutes. I have to review my notes"

Karen raised her voice. "Dr. Whitehead, it's very important."

"I can't talk now. My classes always come first."

"It's about President Schilling and the Peabody Hotel."

Sandra hesitated. "I don't know what that has to do with me. I really must go."

"It's imperative that we talk."

"Imperative? Young lady, I have a class to teach."

"I appreciate that. And, I know you'll want to hear what I have to say. When can we meet?"

Karen heard Sandra sigh. "Alright, I'll meet you for lunch at the Pasta House."

"I'd be glad to stop by your office, if you prefer."

"I'll meet you at the Pasta House at noon on the 17th."

***

Steve strolled into Johnny's Sports Bar. "Steve, how's it going?" the bartender asked.

"Fine. I'm meeting Eddie at six. I'll have a cold one while I wait."

"It's on the house. What'll it be?"

214

"Michelob and a bucket of nuts."

"You got it."

Steve shot the breeze with two sports fans. When they left, the bartender leaned over. "Don't look now, but there's a young lady in your favorite booth. She's been asking about you."

"Thanks, I'll check her out."

Steve nodded and smiled on his way to the men's room. She looked to be in her early twenties. Very attractive in an athletic, wholesome way. She met his gaze without blinking.

When he returned, he asked the bartender, "Does she always look that glum?"

"I've never seen her smile. While you were gone she said she wanted to talk to you."

"What about?"

"Something about her mother."

"Geez, can't I have a beer without someone bitching?"

"That's why they pay you the big bucks."

Steve chuckled. "I guess. Do you know anything about her?"

"She said she's an EAU student. She's stopped in every night for the last few months."

"Does anyone come with her?"

"Nah. She's always alone. Once in a while someone hits on her. She ignores it."

"Well, here goes."

Steve walked over to her booth. "I understand you'd like to see me."

"Yes, I would."

"How can I help you?"

"You can't. It's too late."

"Beg your pardon? Too late? For what?"

"I'm Rhonda Williams' daughter."

"It's nice to meet you," he said, extending his hand. "I'm Steve Schilling."

His hand hung in mid-air like a flipper. "I know who you are."

"I haven't seen Rhonda in ages. How's she doing?"

"She died 12 years ago."

"I'm sorry to hear that."

"I bet you are."

"Of course, I am. She was a cheerleader for our football team. We were good friends."

"Friends? Is that all?"

"Sure. Is something wrong with that?"

"You dated her, didn't you?"

He shrugged. "A few times. No big deal."

"No big deal?"

"Okay, we went out several times. So what?"

"So what? You got her pregnant, didn't you?"

"I barely knew her."

"How can you say that?" Stephanie tossed a bundle of envelopes on the table. "Twenty-three love letters. That's your signature, isn't it? 'Love always, Steve.'"

"Where'd you get those?"

"From my mom. She used to read them all the time."

"You really are her daughter, aren't you?"

"Of course. My name is Stephanie. And you're my dad."

"Your dad? You gotta be crazy."

"Me crazy? You're the one who dumped her and turned your back."

"I did no such thing."

"You did. I've read your letters. You told her how much you loved her. How beautiful she was. You said you wanted to marry her. You're a two-faced bastard."

The color left his face. "I didn't know she was pregnant. Honest."

"Don't lie to me."

"I'm not. I haven't heard from Rhonda since college."

"And what about the letters?"

"I wrote them when we were both in school."

"You're lying. You broke her heart."

"Stephanie ..."

She shouted over him. "You never called, didn't give a damn. Never sent a dollar. You son of a bitch. How could you be so cruel?"

"I didn't know. You have to believe me."

"You knew. She told me. You married someone else so you wouldn't have to marry her."

"That's not true."

"And to think I've waited all of these years. I should have never come back," she said, as she slid out of the booth.

"Wait, I want to talk."

"Talk — that's all you are. I hate you, you asshole."

***

Karen spotted Sandra at a corner table, sipping on what looked like a gimlet. She pinched herself. *Well here goes.*

"Hi, I'm Karen Holmes," she said in her best business voice.

"I'm Sandra Whitehead. Nice to meet you."

The waitress took their orders; Sandra ordered a second vodka gimlet. "Where are you from?" Karen asked to break the ice.

"I grew up in New Paltz, New York. It's a small town south of Albany on the Hudson River. Across from Poughkeepsie. My mother still lives there."

"How did you get into music?"

"I was a child protégé, performed all over the state, sometimes with my mother. I went to college in New Paltz and majored in music and theater."

"That's impressive."

"I earned a scholarship to Juilliard, and after graduation had several professional offers."

"What happened?"

"The bright lights of New York weren't for me so I went back to school, got a Ph.D."

"Interesting. How does a small-town girl from New Paltz end up in Ruston, Arkansas?"

"I've wondered that myself. I felt comfortable here. Department chairs don't come along very often. I decided to go for it."

"How did you meet President Schilling?"

"He was the chairperson in history. The dean named him to the music department chairperson search committee as the outside representative. That's a procedure President Thornton used in filling leadership positions when he was at the helm. He wanted to motivate departments to look beyond their parochial boundaries."

"Then what happened?"

"Happened?"

"What happened between the two of you?"

Sandra shrugged. "I was named the department of music chairperson. And he became university president."

"Maybe I should be more specific. How did the Memphis connection begin?"

Sandra shifted uneasily. "Memphis? I don't understand." She gulped her drink.

"You perform in the symphony, right?"

"Oh, yes, that's my Memphis connection. I never thought of it that way."

"But you don't just play in the symphony. What about the two of you?"

Sandra glared. "How dare you imply ..."

Karen interrupted. "What happens after performances?"

"I'm sorry, Ms. Holmes." Sandra stood. "I don't know what kind of a story you're trying to write, but I won't be a part of it."

"I have pictures." Karen pulled an envelope from her purse.

"Pictures of me at the symphony? So what?"

Karen spread several photos in front of Sandra. She singled out the one of them kissing outside Steve's room. "Please, Dr. Whitehead, sit down."

Sandra's mouth quivered. She ran into the restroom.

The lunch crowd had thinned. And Karen was sipping her iced tea when Sandra returned looking distraught, her mascara smeared. "I've never done anything wrong." Her voice cracked.

"What's going to happen to me?"

"It won't be pretty. The story will hit the wire services and fly across the country. Sex scandals sell. *USA Today, The National Enquirer, People,* every daily, TV talk shows."

Sandra's spine straightened. "Sex scandals?"

Karen looked her in the eye. "You're not the only one."

"No, that's not possible," Sandra snapped. "I love him. We're going to be married."

"You'll have to stand in line. There are others."

"Can't be. You're lying."

"I have proof."

"Proof? You're making this up." Sandra downed the rest of her gimlet. "Newspapers? All over the country? Including New Paltz?"

"*Every* paper."

"That'd kill my mom."

"I'm just saying that's what could happen."

"There must be another way."

Karen paused. "There is. It's up to you."

"Up to me? How?"

"President Schilling is going down …"

Sandra cut her off. "Oh, no. He's done so much for the university. Everyone loves him."

"None of that matters now. He's violated the public's trust."

"I can't believe this is happening."

"There's nothing you can do to save him. You have to think about yourself."

"There must be a way to help him. He's such a wonderful man."

"Dr. Whitehead, you're not listening. You're the only one with a choice."

"Choice?" She gave Karen a questioning look.

"Do you want to destroy your career? Have your pictures plastered across the tabloids?"

"No. Of course not."

"There's a very simple solution. If you admit you've had an affair with him, you can end it right here and now."

"No press?"

"Right." Karen handed her the form. "All you have to do is sign this. In exchange for your confession we'll remove all references to you from our files."

"Why would you do that?"

"We're after him, not you. Read it for yourself."

Sandra scanned the form. "Let me get this straight. If I agree that I've had an affair with him for the last five years, everything goes away?"

"That's it, plain and simple."

Sandra pursed her lips. "How do I know it's binding?"

"Our lawyers prepared it. You can take it to your own attorney, if you wish. We want to protect you."

"I'd like to read it again."

"Of course, take your time."

With a shaky hand, Sandra placed the form on the table. "What do you want to know?"

"Just the facts. Where did you meet? How did you stay in touch? What did you do?"

"You mean like sex?"

"No, just stick to the nature of your relationship. If I need anything else, I'll let you know."

Sandra rambled for twenty minutes while downing her third gimlet. "That's it. Need anything else?"

"Only your signature."

***

Steve stretched out on the sofa in his den and closed his eyes. *Shit. If it isn't one thing it's another. I have to deal with the piss ants on campus. Then it's Suzanne. People only care about themselves. And now, there's Stephanie. I've got to talk with Eddie.*

He grabbed the phone and called.

"Eddie Wilson, your John Deere State Rep."

"Eddie, its Steve."

"Hey, man, how ya' doin'?"

"Will you be on my side of the state anytime soon?"

"I'll be in Blytheville next Thursday."

"Could you stop by?"

"What for? I thought you were on the straight and narrow."

"I am. Something else came up."

"I'll meet you at Johnny's next Thursday between 5:30 and 6:00."

***

Eddie pulled up a barstool. The men exchanged pleasantries.

"She's here," Steve said.

"Who's here?"

"Rhonda Williams' daughter, Stephanie. She's in our old booth."

Eddie glanced at her. "Christ, she just fingered me. What kind of a broad is she?"

"She popped up a couple of months ago."

"What are you talking about?"

"Stephanie, she's …"

"Come on, Steve. Don't dance around. What's happening?"

"I'm telling you the truth."

"The truth about what?"

"Rhonda and me."

"One thing at a time. Who's Stephanie?"

Steve sucked down his beer. "I talked to her last week. She told me about Rhonda, then dropped a bomb, said I was her dad."

"You're Stephanie's dad? Get outta here. Is that true?"

"I didn't even know Rhonda was pregnant."

"No, I mean, are you the father?"

"Christ, I don't know."

"Is it possible?"

"Shit, anything is possible. We were in college."

"God damn, she looks a lot like you. How long did you date Rhonda?"

"Off and on for a couple of years."

"I couldn't get to first base with her. I remember she had a big-time crush on you."

"She was hot, gave me a blow job when I was driving across the Mississippi Bridge."

"I remember. Rhonda got smashed and spilled the beans to Suzanne. I thought Suzanne was going to kill you."

"Me too. She cut me off, didn't talk to me for weeks. And no sex for months."

"Did you write to Rhonda?"

"Two or three times a week." Steve ran his fingers through his hair. "What should I do about the kid?"

"Christ, I don't know."

Stephanie tapped Steve on the shoulder. "Here, you bastard," she said, handing him her tab. "The least you can do is pay for my drink."

Stephanie stormed out. "She has her mother's personality," Eddie said.

"I don't know what to do. You have to help me."

"Shit, I don't know. I've gotta talk to Peg about this."

***

A bedraggled Karen handed the report to Gerry's secretary and went to the photo lab.

Anne rushed to her. "What happened? Did you get number two?"

"Yes," Karen said. "It was awful."

"How did the meeting go?"

"Tough going. Maybe the most difficult thing I've ever done."

"I would imagine. Mind if I change the subject?"

"Please do. Anything to get Sandra off my mind."

"I think I can help you out."

"How?"

"I have an idea. I know a lot of people in Blytheville. I could snoop around the country club, like a private investigator. No one would suspect a thing. If anyone asks, I'm part of the grounds crew."

"What would you do?"

"Follow Steve and Christina around the course with my telescopic lens. I can get a good photo from a hundred yards."

"Really?"

"You bet. I read the scandal sheets. I know what to do." Anne winked.

"Hmm, I don't know."

"I'll be careful. I won't do anything dumb."

"If you screw up, Gerry will kill me."

"I won't. Please?"

Karen fixed Anne in her crosshairs. "Alright, Anne. But if there's one slipup, it's over."

***

Karen reached for the ringing phone and glanced at her alarm clock. *Who the hell calls at 6:05?* "Hello," she croaked.

"Karen, it's Anne. I'm sorry to wake you. But I thought you'd want to know. Stephanie Appleton committed suicide last night."

"What?"

"It's today's headline — COLLEGE STUDENT PLUNGES TO DEATH. Her picture is on the front page."

"What happened?"

"She left her car at the base of the bridge and walked the highest point. The coroner thinks she jumped between 1:30 and 2 a.m."

222

"That's tragic."

"They found her purse near the railing. In it was the last page of a letter. It was signed: 'Love always, Steve.' Do you think that could be Steve Schilling?"

"Could be."

"Below the signature someone had scrawled: 'What a bunch of bullshit. You lying bastard.'"

"She might have written that about Steve."

"That's the first thing that came to my mind."

"The police speculate that the letter came from Stephanie's boyfriend. They think the couple might have had a lovers' spat. What should I do?"

"Nothing. Sit tight. I'm on my way."

CHAPTER TWENTY-FOUR

Steve threw the *Gazette* on the floor. "Why? Why wouldn't Stephanie talk to me? We could have worked things out," he said, stumbling through the house.

Thoughts of Rhonda resurfaced. He had driven Rusty's old Buick to Gulfport over spring break of their senior year. He remembered Rhonda's fingers teasing him as she unzipped his pants, felt her mouth enveloping him. The entire week, they rarely left the bedroom except to shower or pick up fast food.

Wiping the perspiration from his brow, he recalled that Dr. Jones said he could hurt someone, maybe already had. "No, not Rhonda," he blubbered. "I loved her more than anyone."

***

Reverend Scanlon dragged his chair closer to Steve. "You sounded harried on the phone. Are things alright with Suzanne and you?"

"We're fine," he fibbed. "Working hard. It's not easy."

"Most people give up. They're unwilling to make the kind of a commitment the two of you have."

"I replay your advice every day."

"That's good, son. What's on your mind?"

"Something strange happened the other day."

"Tell me about it."

"It began two weeks ago. I was speaking with one of our students," Steve said. "She claimed to be my daughter."

"That must have been a shock. Is she your daughter?"

"Yes, I'm sure."

"And you had no idea?"

"It came out of left field. I didn't have a clue. She's the girl who jumped off the bridge last night."

"My goodness, Steve, that's terrible."

"I'm sick about it. And I don't know what to do."

"I can understand why. Finding out that you had a daughter, then losing her before you had a chance to know her or to reconcile. What a traumatic experience."

"I never wanted to hurt anyone."

"Usually, people don't intend to hurt someone else. But things happen. Circumstances …"

"I can't sleep. I can't …"

"You have to give yourself some time to work through this."

"I think I'm losing my mind."

The minister placed his hand on Steve's shoulder. "Would you like to set up a time to talk?"

"I'm snowed with work. I can't."

"This is a heavy burden, Steve. You should look to others for support."

"I feel better since I told you."

"That's temporary relief. It won't last. Do you have a good friend you can talk with?"

"Rusty, I suppose. Maybe Eddie. He was the quarterback on our college team."

"You need to speak with someone. Sooner rather than later. Don't keep this bottled up. Have you ever seen a psychologist?"

"No, but I'll give it some thought."

"It's important. I'm always available. And whatever you tell me will go no further."

"Thank you. I appreciate your offer."

***

"Suzanne, it's Gerry here," he said.

"Thank goodness. I'm a wreck. Have you found out anything?"

"Yes, I have." He heard sniffing on the other end.

"There's more than one woman, right?"

"At least two."

"Do you think there are others?" she asked.

"Probably so."

"What can you tell me?"

"We've done a lot of digging, and uncovered quite a bit. I hate to do this over the phone. Can you stop by my office around noon?"

"Sure, I'll see you then."

Gerry greeted Suzanne and closed the door. "Are you okay?" he asked.

"I guess. I'm not sure which is worse, speculating about what he's done or learning the truth."

"Neither sounds appealing to me."

"Don't want you to beat around the bush, Gerry. I need to know the facts."

"I'll do my best."

"And I'm not looking for sympathy. I've been preparing for this for a long time."

"I'll be straight with you, Suzanne."

She took a deep breath. "I'm ready."

"You know about Kate. We have an eyewitness who gave us photos of Steve and her together."

"How did you find out?"

"A witness came forward."

"I can't believe it. After all of these years, someone finally talked?"

"She did more than talk. She has the goods on him, saw them together many times."

"Where?"

"At Kate's house. That's all I can say."

"What's the nature of the photos? Can you tell me that?"

"There's one of him barbecuing in her backyard. Another of them kissing. And several of them fooling around on the lawn."

Suzanne gasped.

"Do you want me to stop?"

Suzanne wiped a tear from her cheek. "No. I just needed to catch my breath. Go ahead."

"We have times and dates when they were together over the last 18 months."

"How many times?"

"Forty-two."

"I can't believe it," she sobbed.

Gerry leaned back. "It's true. Just relax. We don't have to rush through this. Tell me if you want me to go on."

Suzanne collected herself and nodded. "Does it get worse?"

"Not worse, but there's another woman."

Suzanne nodded. "I'm ready."

"We call the second one, Ms. Memphis. We have several photos of the two of them. Here's one of them kissing backstage at the symphony hall in Memphis."

"My gosh, in public? Has he no respect for me?"

"This one was taken outside his hotel room."

"He always did like blondes. Is she attractive?"

"Very. And also very well-endowed."

Suzanne gnashed her teeth. "Thank you, Gerry, for sharing what you've found."

"I'm sorry, Suzanne. I never expected we'd find anything like this."

"I guess I always knew about Kate, but the others? I just can't …"

Gerry interrupted. "I'm surprised no one came forward earlier."

She shook her head. "I don't understand it. Not one friend said a word to me, in all these years."

"It's like he's Teflon."

"I agree. People have created this superhero image of him. When I confided my concern about him having lunch with another woman, my best friend said, 'Wasn't that nice of him to take time from his busy schedule?'"

"I've heard the same," Gerry said.

"I heard a rumor that he played golf with another," Suzanne lamented. "You know what the person said? 'He's so considerate to play golf with a grieving widow.' That's bullshit. It's like he's a saint riding around town with that damn red fedora on."

"I sure as hell can't explain it."

Suzanne took Gerry's hand and squeezed it. "I know this isn't easy for you either. Thanks for being such a good friend."

***

228

Suzanne sped across town, slammed on the brakes and made a U-turn. Pulling into the church parking lot, she stormed past the receptionist and knocked on Dr. Scanlon's door.

"I'll be right out," he called.

A few seconds later the door opened. "Suzanne, how nice to see you."

"Do you have a minute?" she asked.

"Of course my dear. I always have time for you. Come in. What is it?"

"It's Steve. He's been cheating on me all of this time."

"That can't be. I saw him the other day. Everything seemed fine."

"Everything always seems fine with him. That's part of the problem. He's a phony. He wants people to think he's a saint. He's not."

"I'm sorry to hear this."

"He's treated me like a dog. Has no respect for me. I believed him when he confessed about Kate. I just found out there are others."

"Others?"

"He's just like he was in college. He hasn't changed one iota."

"Are you sure?"

"Positive. A dear friend showed me photos, and he has documented dates and times."

"I'm so sorry, Suzanne."

"I'm filing for divorce. There's no turning back. I should have done it long ago. How could he humiliate me like this? And for so many years? He cares only about himself."

"His actions are of a selfish man. It doesn't make sense."

"I've given up trying to figure him out."

"Suzanne, you can't dwell on him. You need to focus on yourself and move on."

"That sounds like a plan. But it's not easy after twenty years. I don't know if I can move on."

"You're strong, Suzanne. You can't take on his problems — or solve them. You've done everything humanly possible. You have to do what is best for you."

"Thank you, Reverend. I needed that."

***

Suzanne walked into Edmond Bennett's office a month later. Dressed in a blue pinstripe suit, he had told Suzanne long ago that he would be glad to represent her. Now she knew why. "How's it going?" he asked.

"I'm okay."

"You look great."

"I've lost twenty pounds. I didn't think you'd notice."

"I did. New contacts, too."

"You're such a dear, Edmond."

"Should I go over the papers again?"

"Is there anything new?"

"Not really, I rearranged a few things."

"Let's get on with it."

"I'll go through it as quickly as possible."

"I appreciate that. You've been so patient. I can't thank you enough."

"That's what good friends are for." He smiled. "There's no way he'll contest this."

"I only wish I'd done it sooner."

"That's water over the dam." He pushed the papers toward her. "Please sign by each X."

She paused. "Edmond, there's something else."

"What's that?"

"I don't want to talk to him during the proceedings. He has a way of twisting things."

"I'll take care of that."

"Tell him this is it. There'll be no turning back, no compromises."

"I'll make that clear to his lawyer."

"And I don't want any dirt in the press. There's no reason to rip the community apart."

"Of course." Edmond hesitated. "Suzanne, I want to alert you to a challenge you may face."

"Another one?"

"Rumors are going to fly. People will say things about you that are not true."

"About me? I haven't done anything wrong."

"Trust me. It happens. When some couples split, their friends take sides. I've seen it too many times. One member of the couple will support you. The other will make you out to be the villain."

"Me?"

"We know you're not. I'm just sharing what I've observed."

"I've never taken sides."

"Not everyone is as high-minded as you. Divorces create unusual situations. Remember, always take the high road." Edmond walked around his desk and gave her a gentle hug. "Suzanne, I'll always be here for you."

"Thank you, Edmond. Having you in my corner has made this bearable."

"There's one more thing," he said. "You'll have to decide about living in your home. Since Steve receives a housing allowance from the university, he's expected to live there."

"I've thought about that. I'm not moving out. I'll be the first lady until the divorce is final."

Suzanne said goodbye and walked to the car, knowing it was time to call upon Bill Thornton.

***

"It's good to see you, Suzanne. It's been a long time."

"It has. I enjoyed your article about your Mr. Lincolns in the *Gazette*."

"I've always been partial to red roses. But let's talk about you."

"Thanks for seeing me."

"It's not every day that a young, attractive woman pays me a visit. I'm honored." He stepped back and looked her over. "There's something different."

"I've lost some weight."

"There's something else."

"I knew you'd notice. No more glasses. I have contacts."

"You look ten years younger."

"You big flirt. You better be careful."

He laughed. "Will you join me in a drink?"

"Yes. A light vodka and tonic sounds perfect."

"There are some cashews in the sunroom. Make yourself comfortable, I'll join you in a minute."

Bill brought the drinks then eased into his recliner. She toasted him, "Here's to the most respected man I know."

"I still can't get over how good you look."

"Thank you. Bill, I've made the most difficult decision of my life."

He leaned forward. "What is it?"

"I want you to hear this from me and before anyone else knows." Suzanne paused. "I'm divorcing Steve."

"Suzanne, no." Bill sat forward and rested his forearms on his knees. "Are you sure? Is there no other recourse?"

Her hands trembled. "I've weighed my decision long and hard."

"Suzanne …"

"Please Bill, let me finish. I want you to know the full story."

"Thank you for trusting me."

"Steve will tell you his side, I'm sure. And it will be packed with lies."

"I'm so sorry."

"He's lied to you, to me, and who knows how many others? Sometimes, I don't think he knows what the truth is."

Bill kept silent while Suzanne vented. She shared Gerry's findings then picked up the last broken cashew. "I don't know what to say."

"You don't have to say anything. I just need you as a friend."

"You have that. I'll be here whenever you call."

Suzanne paused. "There's one last thing."

"What is it?"

"Whatever happens, I will protect the university."

"Thank you. You've always been so considerate. Remember, I'm only a phone call away."

"You're such a dear. I love you," she said, a tear trickling down her cheek.

Bill walked her to the door and gave her a fatherly hug. "Let the tears flow. They cleanse the soul."

CHAPTER TWENTY-FIVE

Steve parked in the rundown river area, walked into the Tugboat and sat on a stool. He noticed the worn diving helmet that he'd rubbed before each game.

Except for the gray beard, the bartender looked familiar. "Steve Schilling, haven't seen you in a month of Sundays. It must be fifteen years or more. You've done a great job on the hill, going Division I and playing the big guys."

"Thanks Jess."

Jess looked up from polishing a highball glass. "Too bad about that girl, eh?"

"A tragedy. It's cast a pall on the campus."

"I wonder what made her do it. You'd think a young girl like that had everything to live for. Hell, she could have been your kid."

Steve kept silent.

"How about that boyfriend of hers? If he had any balls he'd come forward. People forget to think about how their actions affect others."

"You're right about that."

Steve ordered and Jess set a frosted mug in front of him. "Seen Eddie lately?"

"We talk once in a while."

"Funny thing, I always thought he'd end up being the top dog."

"Me too."

"What brings you here?"

"Memories, I guess."

"You're not the first. Let me know when you're ready for another."

The rumble of the garage door woke him. He sat up and finger-combed his hair.

Suzanne walked in. "You've been drinking again, haven't you?"

"I stopped at Tug's for a cold one."

"Tug's? What were you doing there?"

"Reminiscing. Suzanne, can we talk?"

"No. We're done talking."

"But I love you. Please give me another chance."

"Save your breath. We're done. I signed the divorce papers today."

Steve jumped up. "You what? We never talked about getting a divorce."

"There's nothing to talk about. I've had enough."

"What about the good times?"

"The good times were a lifetime ago."

"Suzanne, please."

She walked over to him until their noses were nearly touching. "Steve, I signed the papers in Edmond's office. Do you understand?"

"Edmond? Our lawyer?"

"He's my lawyer now. You'll have to find your own."

"How could you do that to me?"

"Ha. Do that to you? You're the one who's been sleeping around."

"What are you saying?"

"Here we go again. Don't play dumb. I know about Kate. And that chesty blonde in Memphis."

Steve covered his heart with his hand. "Suzanne, I told you it was over with Kate long ago. And Memphis? I don't have a clue what you're talking about. Where'd you get that notion?"

"Notion? I've seen pictures of you."

"Pictures?"

"Yes, Kate Blanchard pushing her tits in your face."

"That's not possible."

"Don't tell me what's possible. I saw her. And I also saw you kissing a blonde backstage at the symphony. Obviously you have no respect for me."

"But, Suzanne ..."

234

She stepped on his words. "No buts. I'm done talking to you. Get an attorney. All future conversations will be between Edmond and him — or her, if you prefer female representation. Good night," she shouted, slamming the bedroom door.

***

Steve barged into Edmond's office. "Where is he?"

"Mr. Bennett is in court today. Do you want to make an appointment?" the receptionist asked.

"When will he be back?" Steve barked.

"Tomorrow."

"Fine. I'll be here at 9 a.m."

The next morning, after nearly ripping the door off its hinges, Steve came face to face with Edmond.

"Stop, right there," Edmond said. "Apologize to this young lady."

Steve sneered. "I'm sorry."

"You can do better than that."

Steve turned to face her. "I'm sorry for the way I spoke to you yesterday."

"That's better. You have ten minutes." Edmond moved to his desk.

"How could you turn your back on me?" Steve blurted.

"How dare you speak to me in that tone? If you can't act civilized, you can leave."

"What do you mean?"

"You're in my office. I expect you to behave like a normal human being. And if you don't like it, you can leave."

"Not yet. I have something to say."

"You've said — and done — it all. You've been whoring around all these years."

Steve lunged across the desk. "What I do is none of your fuckin' business."

"Yes it is. I represent Suzanne. What do you want?"

"I want you — need you — to work this out for me."

"You must be kidding. Why would I do that?"

"I love her."

"You don't love her. You don't know what the word means."

"What makes you such an expert?"

"I know how you've treated her. You're despicable. She could have thrown the book at you, taken you to the cleaners for adultery."

"Adultery? She's had it pretty good."

"You think so? You must be in la-la land. You're the lucky bastard."

"Lucky bastard?"

"Watch it, Steve. I'm a baby step away from filling assault charges."

***

Steve rolled down his window as he whipped into Rusty's driveway. "Got a minute?"

Rusty stepped from the garage. "Sure, what's happening?"

"Suzanne's filed for a divorce."

"Oh, shit."

"You have to stop her, Rusty. I love her."

"Stop Suzanne? I don't think so."

"I haven't seen her this angry since after Gulfport when she heard about a conversation between Rhonda and Molly. She's gone wacko."

"Suzanne? Wacko? She's one of the most even-tempered, rational people I know. What triggered this?"

"She claims she saw photos of Kate and me."

"What kind of photos?"

"She said Kate was pushing her tits in my face."

"That'll do it."

"Hell, it's an old picture."

"Where was it taken?"

Steve shrugged. "I don't know. Suzanne said Kate was lying on top of me."

"Christ, you don't know where?"

"Maybe Kate's backyard lounger."

"Were you screwing?"

"No, we were just fooling around."

"Thank goodness for little favors. When was that?"

"Not sure. Maybe last April."

"How can you not know? How many times were you there?"

"Two or three. So, I made a little mistake. Big deal. I can explain it."

"It doesn't sound like you're doing a very good job. How'd Suzanne find out?"

"Someone took pictures of Kate and …"

Rusty scowled. "Is there another one?"

"Sandra Whitehead."

"The boobs in music? Christ, are you sleeping with her too?"

"It's not like that."

"I know you're in love. Try telling that to the faculty senate. Your ass will be in a sling."

"Suzanne told Edmond she won't say anything negative about me."

"You'd better hope so."

"What should I do?"

Rusty shook his head. "How well do you crawl?"

"What?"

"Get down on your hands and knees and beg."

***

The light blinked on Steve's private line. He grabbed the receiver. "Hello."

"I got your message, darling," Martha said. "Yes, I'd love to see you this weekend but I have to leave early Saturday for Atlanta."

"How about Friday night?"

"Sure, I'll be home around 7:00."

"That's fine. I'll have dinner ready."

"My fridge is bare. Will you pick up salad fixings?"

"Sure," he said, and hung up.

Carol poked her head in. "Bill's on the line. Did you forget about your meeting with him?"

"Crap. Tell him I'm on the way."

***

Bill stood in the driveway, arms folded across his chest. "Suzanne told me she's filed for a divorce. What's going on?"

"I think she's having an affair."

Bill raised an eyebrow. "Suzanne, having an affair? I don't think so."

"She must be. She's lost weight, got contacts. She hasn't looked this good in years."

"Maybe she's competing, or trying to show you what you're losing."

"Competing? Hell, she kicked me out of the bedroom."

"Marriage is about much more than sex — building a relationship and trust."

"I've given her everything she ever wanted."

"All she wanted was you."

"We're married, for God's sake."

"And she's had to share you. That's not a marriage. She has proof that you've been seeing Kate. You told me you broke that off long ago. You lied to me too."

Steve adopted his aw-shucks posture. "Kate had car problems last year. I gave her a ride home from the dealer. She asked me in for a beer. Next thing I knew she was ripping off my shirt. But it was just one time."

"And what's this Memphis thing?"

Steve paused. "It's nothing."

Bill's face reddened. "Suzanne said she's seen a photo of you with a blonde."

"Okay, here's the truth."

"Well, I'm glad we're finally getting to that."

"Last fall the director of the symphony invited me to a concert featuring one of our faculty. Suzanne had other plans, so I went. What's the big deal?"

"The lawyers will have a field day with that."

"It's the truth, Bill. After the performance I went backstage to congratulate her."

"Who is she?"

"Sandra Whitehead."

"Jesus, I can see her on the stand. With those world-class jugs, you're guilty before she opens her mouth."

"Bill, it wasn't like that."

"Oh? How was it?"

"She asked me to have a drink. I wanted to be gracious so I agreed. Next thing I know, she's pulling me onto the elevator."

Bill laughed. "I'm supposed to believe that this 120-pound woman dragged you kicking and screaming to her room? Get real, Steve. What planet are you living on?"

"It's true. She went into the bathroom and came out in a long black negligée. I'm only human. What would you do?"

"I wouldn't be there. How much does Suzanne know?"

"Nothing. No one knows anything."

"How about the people backstage?"

"What?"

"Suzanne saw a picture of you kissing a blonde. How many witnessed it?"

"Fifteen or twenty. They're all regulars. They won't say anything."

"Who saw you in the hall outside your hotel room?"

"No one."

"Are you sure?"

"Someone asked about the location of the vending machines."

"So, you're not positive."

"Suzanne made up the whole thing."

"We need to get into damage control," Bill said. "Have the board's lawyer prepare a positive statement on your behalf so the chairman can cover for you. We'll release it if we need to. That'll buy us some time."

***

Friday afternoon Steve arranged a half-dozen candles in Martha's living room. When he saw her car approaching, he lit them and turned on the oven.

She opened the door and gasped. "Steve, what have you done? It's beautiful."

"So are you, darling," he said, kissing her cheek.

"What do I smell?"

"Brie. Why don't you freshen up? I'll pop the champagne."

"Champagne?"

"Yes, we're celebrating. I bought a couple of steaks."

"Steaks?" She winced and palmed her neck.

"How about a massage?"

"I'm okay."

"Dinner can wait," he said, caressing her shoulders. Take a shower and I'll give you a back rub."

Martha rolled over. "You're a wonderful lover."

"I love to make you happy. Ready for the champagne?"

"Sure. But what are we celebrating?" She ran her fingers across his hairy chest.

"I want to marry you."

Martha pulled back. "Steve, that's not funny. You agreed that we wouldn't discuss marriage until your situation changed."

He pulled her to him. "Martha Brown, will you marry me?"

Her brow wrinkled. "Steve, be serious."

"I've filed for a divorce," he said. "Will you marry me?"

"Oh, yes." she exclaimed. "Yes. I love you."

CHAPTER TWENTY-SIX

Carol's buzz interrupted Steve's reverie. He couldn't imagine anything better than being with Martha forever. Finally, he thought, I'll be with the love of my life.

"Mr. President, Sam Appleton is here. He says it's very important."

"Tell him I'll be out in a moment." Perspiration dampened his upper lip. *Jesus Christ, what does he want?*

Steve took a deep breath and opened the door. He tried to sound cheerful. "Good morning, Mr. Appleton."

The visitor sneered. "You son of a bitch. You're the one, aren't you?"

"Come in, Mr. Appleton." Steve closed the door. "Please have a seat. What can I do for you?"

"You can't do anything for me. What kind of a man are you? Don't you have any remorse?"

"What are you talking about?"

"Don't give me any of that bullshit. I saw your picture in Rhonda's yearbook — the letters you wrote. You knew all along she was pregnant."

"I didn't know."

"You knew. You sent two floral arrangements to Stephanie's funeral. You signed one, Steve, and the other, President Schilling. You're her father."

"I didn't know until a few days ago. Honest. I just found out."

"You bastard. You got engaged as soon as Rhonda told you she was pregnant. You tossed her aside like a rag doll."

"No, it wasn't like that at all. I loved her. I didn't know what to do."

"Didn't know what to do? You insult my intelligence. Did it ever occur to you to do the right thing? Obviously not."

"I tried. I ..."

"You might as well have plunged a dagger into Rhonda's heart. I was there when she phoned Molly Green. I know Molly spoke to you, urged you to stand by Rhonda. You turned your back."

"I couldn't do it."

"Couldn't? More like you wouldn't. You didn't have the balls." Sam shook his head in disgust. "I can't stand looking at you. I came to pick up Stephanie's belongings but ... I couldn't leave without telling you what a despicable human being you are. I hope you rot in hell."

"Wait, I can explain."

"Explain? You can't explain. You destroyed their lives — two wonderful women." He slammed the door on his way out.

Slouched in his chair, Steve tried to sort through his feelings. *Why didn't Stephanie give me a chance to explain? Why?* His thoughts shifted to Rhonda. *What was I afraid of? Why didn't I marry her like I'd promised? I loved her more than anyone.*

***

Charles Bergmann, the senate chairman, stood when Steve walked in.

"Good morning, Charles. How are you today?"

"Fine," he said flatly.

"Mr. President, Dr. Bergmann asked if I could squeeze him in for a few minutes," Carol said. "I told him your schedule was extremely tight."

"No problem. I always have time for Charles," Steve said. "How is everything?"

"Classes are going well, but I don't like what I'm hearing on campus."

"About what?"

"There are rumblings about you."

"What kind of rumblings?"

"Steve, can I be candid?"

"Of course."

"We've been at odds over the years. But when I became senate chairman, I pledged that I'd keep my personal views separate from university business."

"I appreciate that, Charles."

"First of all, this has to be off the record. As far as I'm concerned this meeting never happened. Do you understand?"

"You have my word."

"Good. Since Suzanne filed for divorce, our office has been inundated with calls. They run the gamut from your missing meetings to you being seen with other women."

"I can't imagine. Can you be more specific?"

"I have reports of you having luncheon dates downtown and at the county club. Playing golf in Blytheville. The list goes on and on."

"That's a bunch of bull, Charles. I'm out raising money, selling the university. You know I can't do my job in an isolation booth."

"Yesterday, an alum called from Little Rock. She saw you at the airport two weeks ago, kissing a redhead. She said the woman was obviously not your sister."

"Two weeks ago?" Steve hesitated. "She must be mistaken. I haven't been in Little Rock in over a month."

"Are you sure? I read that you testified about the state tuition bill."

"That's right. It must have slipped my mind."

"It seems like you've been forgetting a lot lately."

"Not true, Charles. There's a lot going on. I can't recall everything."

"I know you're busy, but this is beyond busy. It's …"

Steve cut him off. "I'm sorry you've had to deal with this crap. If someone asks to meet with me, I can't say, 'It may look bad so we can't meet.'"

"You need to do something different. People are looking for a smoking gun."

"Rest assured, Charles. There's no smoking gun."

"Mr. President, I just wanted to alert you. I hope we don't have to deal with this on the senate floor."

"Don't worry. There'll be no need for that," Steve said.

***

Rusty watched Steve cross the restaurant parking lot, his head on his chest. "What's so urgent that I have to be here at 6:30 on a Saturday morning?" Rusty asked as he got out of his car.

"I can't take it anymore. I'm resigning."

"Resigning? You can't resign. You think you're the first president to go through a divorce?"

"The divorce is only part of it."

"Don't tell me you're in love again." Rusty snapped.

"No, it's not like that. Everything is screwed up. The university has run amok. I can't think straight. I can't get Rhonda and Stephanie off my mind."

"Rhonda and Stephanie? Who the hell are they?"

"You remember Rhonda Williams. She was one of our cheerleaders."

"Who wouldn't remember? What a knockout."

"We had a thing."

"Shit, you had a thing with everyone."

"No, she was different. She was the best."

"Steve that was twenty years ago. What's the big deal?"

"She had a kid. Stephanie. I found out recently that the girl was my daughter."

"Your daughter. You never said anything."

"I just found out."

"I'm confused."

"Stephanie Appleton, the girl who jumped off the bridge, was my daughter."

"God damn."

Rusty paused. "You wrote the letter they found in her purse."

"No. I wrote that letter to Rhonda in college."

Rusty tugged Steve's arm. "Let's go inside. This is going to take a while."

***

Steve paced his office. "What the fuck is wrong with everyone around here? Bergmann is out of his mind. Rusty doesn't understand. I've gotta get outta here," he said. "There's gotta be a rational way to deal with all of this."

He spotted a yellow envelope in the mail stacked on his desk. He picked it up and sniffed. Not a hint of Trésor.

Slicing open the envelope, he skimmed the first page. "I won't be able to see you Friday night. I've cancelled my performance. I'm going to my mother's in New York."

Steve's stomach turned. *What happened? Was there an emergency? Why didn't she call?*

He picked up the phone and called. When there was no answer at Sandra's house he tore over to the music building.

Stepping into the foyer, Steve saw the lights were off in her office. He shot out the side door.

***

Sandra crept down the stairs of her mother's New Paltz home. Looking drawn and bedraggled, she entered the kitchen. Her mother gave her a comforting hug. "May I fix you a piece of toast?"

"I'm not hungry, Mom. Maybe later."

"I'm here for you, baby."

"I know, Mom."

"Take your time, sweetie. We can talk whenever you like." She slipped on a jacket. "I'm going out to pick up the mail."

Sandra returned to her room.

A few minutes later Sandra's mother called up the stairs. "Sandra, you have a letter."

Sandra cracked her door. "Did you call?" She wiped her swollen eyes.

"You have a letter from Steve."

Sandra retrieved the envelope, walked slowly back to her room and sat in her grandmother's rocking chair.

Sandra,

I love you more than ever. I've filed for a divorce. I can hardly wait for your return so we can be together forever. I hope the situation you're dealing with works out for the best. I'm here for you. Please call as soon as you can.

Love always,

Steve

Sandra's hand went limp. The note slid to the floor. Tears streamed down her cheeks.

***

Steve gave Bill a perfunctory handshake. "Got an extra sheet of paper?"

"Here." Bill glared. "I hope you have something to write with."

Steve held up a pen. "I'm ready for work."

"It's about time, from what I hear."

"You can't believe all the crap you hear from the faculty."

"No, but sometimes they're right." Bill picked up his legal pad. "I have a long list for you."

"What for?"

"Damn it, Steve, think for a change. You're the president who's going through a divorce. People are talking, scrutinizing everything you do."

"What else is new?"

"Will you listen to me? People are voicing displeasure over things they overlooked in the past. When they see you with a woman, they're pairing you up. Do you understand?"

"Sure, but ..."

Bill cut him off. "I'm serious. We don't need a bunch of rumors flying around."

"Okay, I'll handle it."

"Handle it? I'm not saying this for my health. I'm telling you for your own good."

"Is it okay if I play golf with Howard, his lady friend, and Christina on Saturday?"

Bill slammed his pad on the table. "Damn it, Steve. What did I just say?"

"Alright, I won't play."

"Let's talk about Suzanne."

"Suzanne? What about her?"

"You have to treat her with dignity and respect. If not, you'll piss off every woman in town. Remember, they're looking to fix blame."

"Suzanne didn't do anything wrong."

"See, that's what I mean. If Suzanne didn't do anything wrong, you did."

"I didn't mean it that way."

"Well, that's what you said. You have to be careful what you imply."

"You make it sound like I'm a nitwit."

Bill raised an eyebrow. "I'll pass on that one. Let's discuss playing the affair card."

"Affair?"

"I told you people are looking to fault someone. It's either you or Suzanne."

"No, not Suzanne. I'm not pointing a finger at her."

"It doesn't matter what you want. We have to be prepared."

"For what?"

"Jesus, Steve. For the worst-case scenario."

"I'm not going there."

"Forget that. We have to think ahead. Now, who's she been with lately?"

"I don't know."

"Think about it. Who?"

"Reverend Scanlon, Gerry Coleman, Edmond Bennett, John ..."

Bill interrupted. "Edmond Bennett. Perfect. He's had a hard-on for her for years."

"For Suzanne?"

"Where have you been? You can't be that blind?"

"You think they're messing around?"

"Nah, she'd never do that. But, I'll tell you, if he thought he had a chance, he'd ..."

"I'd punch the bastard in the mouth if he touched her."

***

Carol buzzed Steve. "What do you want?" he snarled.

"There's a Samantha Whitehead on the line. She said it's urgent."

"Samantha? Yes, put her through."

"Good morning, Mrs. Whitehead," he said. "What a pleasant surprise."

"Mr. President ... may I call you Steve?"

"Yes, of course."

"I have very bad news." Her voice cracked.

"What is it?"

"Sandra died yesterday," she sobbed.

"My God. No. What happened?"

"She fell from a cliff at the Gunk's."

"The Gunk's?"

"I'm sorry. That's short for the Shawangunk Cliffs. They're at Minnewaska State Park just west of here. They're over a thousand feet high and very steep."

"How did it happen?"

"Authorities aren't sure. They think she must have gotten too close to the edge and slipped."

"That's awful. I can't believe it."

"I can't understand it." She paused, wiping a sniffle. "She'd been there hundreds of times. It was her favorite place, so tranquil."

"I'm so sorry, Mrs. Whitehead. Is there anything I can do?"

"Not really. She had a letter in her hand addressed to you. I'll put it in the box when I mail her Trésor to you. It was her special scent."

"She was the most wonderful woman I've ever met. Everyone on campus loved her. I'll get a flight out tomorrow."

"Oh, Steve, that'd be wonderful. Sandra said you were the most thoughtful man in the world. Thank you."

***

Steve drove through the open gate and parked in the garage. Christina greeted him with a Bloody Mary. "I'm glad you called off the golf match this morning. I had an exhausting week."

"Me too. The trip to New York wore me out."

"That was nice of you to fly up for the funeral."

"It seemed like the least I could do."

"She was a beautiful woman."

"Not as beautiful as you, my darling."

"Steve, you're the best. I love you."

"I love you too. So, what's for breakfast?" he asked.

"I thought you might like a welcome-back treat first."

Stepping out of the shower, Steve asked, "Want another Bloody Mary?"

"Sure, I'll join you in the sunroom as soon as I dry my hair."

Forty minutes later he put down the newspaper and glanced up. "There's a story about the Institut Pasteur. Anything new?"

"I received the fellowship. They called last night."

248

"That's terrific. Why didn't you say something sooner?"

"I had other things on my mind. And, I'm in a quandary."

"What's there to think about?"

"Now that you are legally separated, I want to be with you as much as I can."

Steve slid closer to her. "Don't worry about me. You have a once-in-a-lifetime opportunity. We can work it out, meet in New York or Paris."

"But you'll be alone at night. I want to be here for you."

"I want to be with you too. But, it's better right now if we're apart. You know how people like to talk."

***

Leaning over the porch handrail the next morning, Steve gazed at the gazebo. Christina slipped up behind him. "What do you want for breakfast?"

"I don't know."

"You okay, dear?"

"A little down."

"I can turn down the fellowship."

"No, it's not that."

Christina pulled him to her. "What is it? You can tell me."

"Remember when I told you about the cheerleaders?"

"Sure, Kate, Molly Green and a tall girl."

"Rhonda."

"There is something else, isn't there?"

"I just learned that Rhonda had my baby, a daughter."

"Oh, sweetheart, sit down. Please tell me all about it. I want to know everything."

"I don't want to bore you with my problems."

"It's not a bore, darling. I want us to share everything."

"College was a big step for me. I was more interested in chasing girls than going to classes or studying. I felt like a kid in a candy shop."

"Nothing unusual about that. You were a healthy, attractive male with raging hormones. No need to feel embarrassed."

***

Steve took the back roads and detoured at the sign for Bluff County Park. Pulling into the parking lot, he cut the engine.

He wondered, what's going on in my life? *Why are these terrible things happening? Suzanne is divorcing me. I could have had Rhonda. Why didn't I marry her?*

He stumbled from the car and staggered to the railing, grabbing the cold metal to steady himself. In the distance he could hear a tugboat. He saw its beacon searching the shoreline of the Mississippi below.

Where does it end? Rhonda is dead. Stephanie committed suicide. Sandra is gone. Christina is leaving for the year. I can't go on.

The engines groaned louder. Stephanie appeared before him, standing on the bridge. She flipped him the bird. "What's wrong?" he asked.

"You lying bastard. I hate you!"

"Don't jump. Please," he called as her body disappeared into the night.

Rubbing his eyes, he saw Sandra's hair blowing in the beacon's flash. He caught a scent of Trésor. "Sandra. Please, don't," he shouted.

She blew him a farewell kiss. "No, no. Don't," he called as she stepped off the cliff.

"I can't take any more," Steve cried as he fell to his knees. "Help me. Someone, please."

CHAPTER TWENTY-SEVEN

Looking forlorn, Karen plopped on a stool opposite Anne. "Want a cup of coffee?" Anne asked.

Karen was mute.

"I'll get it," Anne said and got up.

"Thanks," Karen murmured.

"How was your weekend?" Anne set the mug on the light table.

"Pretty pathetic. I searched my notes twice and didn't find a thing." She raised her head and did a double-take. "Did you have your hair done? It looks fabulous."

Anne fluffed her new do. "You like it?"

"You look ten years younger."

"Thanks."

"It's very becoming. How was the rest of your weekend?"

"Terrific. You won't believe what I discovered."

Karen shrugged. "An outfit to go with your hair?"

"No, silly. I was in Blytheville. And I have plenty to tell you."

"Okay, let's hear it."

"I checked out the country club a couple of times. Very fancy."

"I've heard its pretty snobbish. Did you talk to anyone?"

"Nah, I just walked around and tried to blend in."

"Weren't you nervous?"

"Nope. I kept saying to myself, 'Act like Karen and don't screw up.'"

"Don't keep me hanging."

"The place crawls with young studs. College guys in uniforms."

"Uniforms?"

"Most were in khakis and brown Polo shirts. Some were loading bags and cleaning clubs. Several were zipping around in golf carts. I tried to drive one but couldn't get it into reverse."

"There's a lever under the seat."

"So I discovered. A cute guy from the pro shop gave me a lesson. I had fun tooling around the parking lot."

"Then what?"

"I drove to Christina's. What a place. Three stories with a veranda and huge, white columns."

"Sounds like Tara."

"Yep. Stables, a gazebo and a huge meadow out back. The Mississippi flows along one side of the estate. A forest of pines — as far as the eye can see — on the other side."

"What did you do?"

"I went home and developed a plan, like you'd do. Later, I went back to the club and saw Christina and the Prez teeing off. I drove to the second hole."

"Did you take any pictures?"

"Sure did." Anne tossed a handful on the table and picked up one. "Here they're on the third hole. You'll notice that his hand is on her butt."

Karen's jaw went slack.

"I took this one between the sixth and seventh holes."

"Rather cavalier to be kissing in the golf cart in broad daylight," Karen said.

"I'll say," Anne handed over another photo. "On the 10th he pinned her against a tree."

"Slow down," Karen said. "I'm still on the seventh."

"Here they're locking lips." Anne handed another one to Karen. "Check it out. He's got his putter right up in there."

"How did you take these close-ups?"

"I used a telescopic lens."

"These are incredible."

"Then they went into the clubhouse. When I saw them order drinks I made a beeline to her place where I parked about fifty yards down the road. By the time I got back I saw them heading for the barn."

"That was lucky."

"I prefer to think I have impeccable timing. Here's Steve saddling her horse. In this one he's lying on the gazebo floor, shirt unbuttoned, hands tied to a post. Look at how she's caressing him. Pretty hot, huh?"

"I'll say."

"Wait. It gets better."

Karen pulled her stool closer to Anne. "His pants are half off. Look at that bulge in his shorts."

"Don't tell me you saw him in the altogether."

Anne leered.

"Come on, show me."

"I left those at home."

"Why?"

"I thought you might be embarrassed."

"Embarrassed? I'm not as naïve as you might think. Did you, um, see it?"

Anne laughed. "I did. And it's a humdinger."

"Ha."

Anne handed Karen another shot. "I got so carried away I almost forgot to snap the shutter."

"I can't believe these."

"Here, she's on top, banging the hell out of him."

"Holy …"

The lab door creaked and Gerry walked in. "Did I interrupt something?"

Karen blushed. "We were just finishing," she said.

He handed her a folder. "Here's the report on Sandra. Good job." He glanced at the photos. "What are these?"

Karen covered them with her arms. "Top secret."

"Top secret?" Gerry wrested the pictures from Karen's feeble attempt at censorship. "What do we have here?" he asked.

Gerry sorted through the photos while Anne provided the narration. "What do you think?"

"Three are missing."

"How'd you know that?" Anne asked.

"Because they're numbered. She's fondling him in nine, is on top of him in thirteen. Where are ten through twelve?"

"Would you believe I lost them?"

"You have pictures of him in his birthday suit, don't you?"

Anne laughed. "That's privileged information."

***

Karen reached Christina late in the afternoon. After congratulating her on being a national finalist, Karen hesitated. "There's something else I'd like to ask."

"Of course."

"I have some questions about you and your relationship with President Schilling."

"Relationship?"

"Yes. How well do you know him?"

Christina brushed her cheek. "I've worked with him on a couple of projects."

"You've been seen playing golf with him."

"Oh that. I filled in a few times when my dad and his friend needed a fourth."

"And you taught him to ride a horse."

"Yes, but …" Christina paused. "Ms. Holmes, I don't want to be discourteous but I have patients waiting."

"I have pictures of the two of you. I'm sure you wouldn't want me to send them to Paris."

"I'm sorry, I really must go."

"It'll only take five minutes."

Christina hesitated. "Well, I suppose I could spare five minutes. I'm off Thursday afternoon. Come by my home around 3 o'clock."

***

Karen used the brass door-knocker. Christina appeared in a white, lace sundress, lightly freckled arms exposed.

"Good afternoon, it's nice to meet you," she said without sincerity.

"The pleasure is mine." Karen peered at the immense crystal chandelier in the foyer. "What a lovely home."

"My father built it for my mother. It's very comfortable."

As Christina led the way to the sunroom, Karen glanced through an uncovered window at the gazebo and thought of the racy photos.

"Would you like some iced tea?" Christina asked.

"Yes, unsweetened, please."

"I hope I wasn't short on the phone," Christina said as she placed the pitcher on the glass-topped table. "We get calls from nuts all the time."

"Not at all. We get plenty ourselves."

Christina handed Karen a glass of tea. "Tell me about these photos."

Karen took a long sip. "I have pictures of you and President Schilling."

"I can't imagine. Where were they taken?"

Karen handed her a small envelope. "See for yourself."

Christina flipped through the pictures. The color left her face. "How much do you want?"

"I don't want your money."

"I'm sure. I want the negatives too. How much?"

"Dr. Clark, we're not interested in you."

"I'll give you $5,000. Cash. No one will ever know."

"That's very generous, but you don't understand."

"Let's make it $10,000."

"It's not about the money. President Schilling violated the public's trust."

"Public trust?"

"We have pictures of him with other women too."

Christina scowled. "I doubt that."

"I'm sure it's difficult for you to process, but there are others."

"You're lying. We're getting married next summer."

"I'm afraid you'll have to stand in line."

Christina covered her mouth. "What do you mean?"

"He's proposed to other women as well."

Christina went to the picture window overlooking the meadow then pivoted to face Karen. "You're telling the truth, aren't you?"

"Yes, I am."

"What do you want from me?"

"An admission that you've had an affair with him."

"And?"

"That's it. In exchange we'll remove everything from our files."

"The photos?"

"Yes. Everything. Would you like to see the release?" Karen pulled one from her briefcase and handed it to Christina.

Christina read the form. "Let me see if I have this right. I admit to having an affair with him. You remove my name and the photos from your files. Otherwise, everything goes public. Is that it?"

"Yes. You have nothing to lose and everything to gain."

"What do you want to know?"

"Just the facts. When and where. Things like that."

***

Karen swaggered into the lab. "I did it," she said.

"Did she confess?" Anne asked.

"Yes, but it was different this time."

"How so?"

"She was analytical, cool, as if she was taking it in stride."

"How can you take something like that in stride?"

"Maybe it's her medical training. Doctors learn to be poker-faced. She was a model of calmness."

Anne shook her head. "I don't get it. How does he win them over? They're all classy, professional women. And good looking, like you. And they all want to marry him."

"It's crazy. I wonder how he keeps track of them. He had seen Kate for more than twenty years. Sandra for five or so; Christina for eight."

"He must keep a scorecard."

"He's scoring alright," Karen laughed.

"I think he's only interested in fucking them. Pardon my French," Anne said. "Suppose it was you. What do you think his M.O. would be?"

Karen wore a quizzical expression.

"I think I figured him out," Anne said. "He'd take you to a fancy restaurant, order champagne and wine. He'd nudge your leg, caress your hand and look at you with those puppy-dog brown eyes. Pretty soon you're a goner."

"You're in dreamland, Anne."

"Hey, I know how these guys work. They play it cool until they get what they want."

"I think there's more to it."

"Okay, you're so smart. What do you think motivates him?"

"I don't think it's all about sex."

"You don't? Then what the hell is it about?"

"Sex is part of it. But I think he believes he's in love with each one."

"In love? With five at the same time?"

"To him it's not five at the same time. It's one at a time. Whoever he's with at the moment."

"No one is capable of that."

"I think his feelings turn on and off in an instant. Because he exudes sincerity, the women give him their unconditional love."

"What kind of a guy could do that?"

"One who compartmentalizes. Whomever he's with becomes the only one. Until he sees the next one."

"He must be crazy as a loon."

"Well, at least we agree on that."

CHAPTER TWENTY-EIGHT

Karen worked through the weekend on her report. Agonizing over every sentence, she empathized with Christina and wondered how a woman of such intelligence and standing got mixed up with someone like Steve. Not for the first time she asked herself, what drives him? She put the finishing touches on the report and met with Anne in the photo lab.

"Phew, I'm glad that's over."

Anne looked up. "You must be drained."

"I feel like a wet noodle."

"I would imagine. What's next?"

"Number four. I don't know where to start."

"Start?" Anne laughed. "This is your lucky day. I spent Sunday going through the Little Rock materials. I found her."

"You did? Who is she?"

"Martha Brown, State Director of Athletic Facilities. She was an All-American basketball star at the University of Arkansas."

"No kidding. What else?"

"Plenty. Here's a four-page spread. Take a look." Anne slid the collage across the table.

"She's stunning."

"Damn right. Look at those legs. Like you, she has what drives men wild."

Karen blushed. "Everyone has appealing qualities."

Anne glanced down at her broad hips. "I guess mine are well-hidden." She laughed. "Now what?"

"I need to double-check what you've done. You might as well start on number five."

"What shall I focus on?"

"Athletics at EAU. That's the only lead we have."

***

"This is Karen Holmes from the *Daily Gazette* in Ruston."

"How may I help you?"

"I'd like to arrange an interview with Ms. Brown."

"What is this in reference to?"

"I'd like to speak to her about President Schilling."

"Fine. I'm sure she'll be glad to meet with you. She thinks he's wonderful."

"Does she have time this week?"

"Four o'clock on Thursday is the only available slot."

"Fine, I'll be there."

Martha waltzed in the reception area, wavy red hair trailing. "Hi, I'm Martha Brown. Please, come in."

Karen followed her into the cramped office and sat down.

"I understand you're doing a story on President Schilling. What's your angle?"

"It's personal. Can we talk in private?"

"Of course." Martha closed the door and eased into her chair. "How may I help you?"

Karen spoke softly. "I have some personal questions."

"Have at it."

"I have good reason to believe that you're having an affair with President Schilling."

Martha's spine straightened. "Steve and me?" She licked her lips and struggled to regain her composure. "That's a good one."

"I've talked to the other women …"

"Other women?" Martha cut her off. "What are you talking about?"

"I have signed confessions."

"Confessions? About what?"

"About their affairs with him."

Martha frowned. "I think you must be mistaken."

"Ms. Brown, I know you are one of five."

"Five? No way."

260

"I have photos of him with each and every one." She drew out the words.

"That's not possible." Martha leaned forward. "What makes you think I'm one of them?"

"Let's start with the green stationery."

Martha shifted uncomfortably. "I don't understand."

"Maybe this will help." Karen told her about Steve's affair with Sandra.

Martha's face flushed. "My God, he really did have an affair with her."

"Several, I'm sorry to say. Do you want to talk about it?"

Martha bit her lip. "Look, I'm getting ready to leave for the day. How about we chat over a beer?"

"Sounds good to me."

***

Martha led the way into the small, packed pub. The bartender held up two mugs. Martha nodded and continued to a corner booth. "What do you want?"

"It's simple. You fill in the details, sign an acknowledgement that you've had an affair, and everything goes away."

Martha scowled. "May I see the agreement?"

"Of course." Karen handed her a copy. "Our goal is to protect you."

"What happened when the others signed?"

"We purged their files."

"You promise? No news stories?"

"That's right."

Martha signaled for another round. Her eyes misted over and she sighed. "This is not easy."

"I'm sure it isn't. Take your time."

Martha took a deep breath, and asked, "What do you want to know?"

"When did you meet? How often were you together? Where?"

She glanced at her photo as an All-American on the wall behind Karen. "Good-bye seven years," she said, pulling a pen from her purse.

"Want another beer?" Karen asked.

"Shit, I need a case." Martha held two fingers over her head. "I might as well get this over with," she said, tossing her luscious hair over her shoulder. "Where do you want me to start?"

"It's up to you."

"I can't believe this is happening. I thought I was a good judge of character. He was so damn sincere. Christ, I could have had anyone — pro athletes, big-name entertainers, politicians, even the governor. And to think, I ended up with a married lunatic with a sexual addiction."

"How did it start?"

Martha shook her head. "Innocently enough. We had a meeting that ran late. He suggested we have a drink. In fact, we sat right here."

"Did he make a move?"

"No, that's the thing. He was always a perfect gentleman. He didn't do anything inappropriate. I talked most of the time then I noticed he hadn't eaten. I invited him over for a bite before he left for Ruston. Next thing I know, I'm in bed with him. I fell hard. And here I am."

"It must be tough to talk about it."

"Tough? You don't know the half of it," she sobbed. "You can't understand Steve unless you've been with him. He makes you feel like you're the most important person in the world. What a sleaze bag." Martha signaled for another beer.

"Listen to this," she slurred. "Two weeks ago he was at my place. My back was killing me. Most guys would rub your back for five minutes and want to jump your bones, right?"

Karen nodded.

"Not Steve Schilling. He warmed my skin moisturizer between his hands and took his time massaging every knot out of my back. He caressed me for a long while.

I was lying naked, in a lather, trying not to come. Can you imagine?"

Karen's eyebrows shot up.

"In January, I was in New Orleans for the NCAA Convention. He took me to Commander's Palace. You've probably heard of it. Very upscale with great food and service."

"Yes, I've been there."

"He ordered champagne. We had wine with dinner. I was sipping a Baileys after dessert. Next thing I know, his hand is halfway up my thigh."

Karen swallowed.

"When we got to his room I put on a robe. We had champagne. He'd placed a red rose on the table. I could have fucked him all night."

***

The next morning Karen felt like she'd been hit by a Mack truck. *How could Steve be with Martha one night and me the next?* She took a couple of aspirins and a cold shower. Neither provided much relief. She called the office and took a half day off.

Slightly before noon she waited for the traffic to clear. Steve's black Caddy flew by. She switched lanes and gunned it.

Squealing to a stop at a red light, she watched his car turn down a country road marked by an old billboard: COUNTY LINE TAVERN 7 MILES AHEAD.

Peeling away, she turned down Mill Creek Road until she reached the tavern and cased the parking lot. No sign of him.

***

On Saturday Carol's warm smile greeted Karen at the diner. "Thanks for agreeing to meet me on your day off."

"No problem," Carol said. "How's your investigation going?"

"We're on the fifth woman. You said she's involved with athletics."

"Yes, I'm positive."

Karen slapped her forehead. "Season tickets. Why didn't I think of that before? I need a list of basketball and football ticket holders."

"I'll have Gerry drop them off next week."

"You said that she probably works on campus. Anything else?"

Carol pressed her lips. "Check out the County Line Tavern."

"For what?"

"Just go and observe. Take a friend. It'll be safer."

"Safer?"

"Guys figure if you're there, you're available."

"Thanks." Karen closed her notepad and paused. "I'd like to go back to our conversation about St. Louis. Do you have a minute?"

***

After watching *Fatal Attraction*, Karen updated Sharon. "I need for you to come with me to the County Line Tavern," she told her friend.

"Why?"

"It's a rough place. There's safety in numbers. Besides, four eyes are better than two."

"What are we looking for?"

"I'm not sure."

***

A Dolly Parton sound-alike blared out the front door. The women dodged dancing couples to a small table. Sharon took a seat facing the rear wall. "I can't see anything."

"Cool your jets. I'll trade with you later."

A braless waitress, past her prime, leaned over the table. "Whaddaya want?"

"We'll have a pitcher of beer," Sharon replied.

Karen surveyed the place. "Those NASCAR posters have seen better days."

"What a dump," Sharon said. "I can't believe this place is packed."

"I don't' know why Carol said to come here."

They were nursing their suds when the waitress bought a second pitcher.

"We didn't order this," Karen said.

"It's from BJ McCoy.

"BJ? Who's that?"

"Don't worry. You'll meet him soon enough," the waitress said. She'd been ridden hard and put up wet, Karen thought.

Sharon glanced across the room and winced. "Shit, that's my boss, Don Cagney. He's in that booth." She gestured.

"He's with a brunette floozy with big tits. I can't let him see me. Pay the bill. I'll meet you in the car." She ran toward the door.

While Karen searched her wallet, a curly-haired guy with deep-blue eyes slid next to her, pinning her to the wall.

He placed a beefy arm around her shoulder. "Hi, I'm BJ McCoy. You new in town?"

"Kind of. Listen, my girlfriend is waiting in the car."

"Girlfriend?" He pulled back. "You one of those lesbians?" He bolted for the bar like he'd been stung by a bee.

His friends roared when he pointed to Karen.

Karen paid the bill and hurried outside. She asked Sharon, "Why the hasty exit?"

"I panicked. Mr. Cagney has been the CEO for fifteen years. He has a wonderful wife. I never thought I'd see him with someone else."

***

Steve heard his sister's pleas for help. "No. No, Dad. Don't do it again. Leave me alone. Somebody help me, please."

Sobbing, Steve sat up, his pajamas and sheets soaked. "Leave her alone," he screamed. "She's a little girl. What's wrong with you?"

He woke himself up and swung his legs over the side of the bed. He'd had the same nightmare for years.

At first, it interrupted his sleep occasionally. Recently, once or twice a week. Again, he cursed his father and saw his sister's sad dark eyes. He pounded his fist on the bedside table. "I hate you, you bastard."

***

Steve stuck the *Gazette* under his arm and gathered the mail. He felt relief that the week was over. *Only three weeks before Commencement. Thank God, the malcontents will be gone. What a bunch of piss ants. Finally, I'll get some peace and quiet.*

He skimmed through the first section of the *Gazette* and tossed it aside. "Same old crap. Who gives a shit?" he grumbled.

A column on the last page caught his attention. DIVORCES. When he saw his name listed under the bold-faced head, he balled the paper and went into the kitchen.

Flopping down on chair, he spotted a hand-addressed envelope postmarked Little Rock. His frown turned into a broad smile. *The love of my life. How lucky can a guy be?* Opening the letter, he read:

Steve:

Words can't convey my feelings for you. I'll never forget last Friday night, and the many times we were together in Atlanta, New Orleans, Dallas and at my place. You treated me like a queen.

That said I am moving on. I've accepted a job with Global Sports in Charlotte. They've been after me for the last two years and made an offer I couldn't resist. I've resigned my position and am moving to North Carolina immediately.

I'm sorry.

Martha

CHAPTER TWENTY-NINE

"Good morning, Anne."

"And good morning to you. I've been jumpy as a cat. Quick, spill the beans. What happened Friday night?"

"What a dive. One couple was moments away from doing it on the dance floor. And some cowboy tried to make a move on me. I scared him off when I said I had to meet my girlfriend."

Anne snickered. "Sounds familiar. I guess the County Line Tavern hasn't changed. While you were having fun, I cross-referenced the season-ticket holders and whittled the list down to nine women."

"Great. What do we have?"

"Names, phone numbers, addresses and how much they contributed to the campaign."

"Read me the names. Let's see what clicks."

When Anne had finished, Karen shrugged her shoulders. "Maria Cabrera is the only name I recognized. I met her at the press conference in Memphis. Let's hear the names with their addresses."

Anne did as she was told.

Karen stopped her mid-list. "Hold it. Once more."

"Marie Cabrera, 38281 Mill Creek Road."

"That's interesting. The County Line Tavern is on Mill Creek."

"So?"

"We may be onto something."

"What do you mean?"

"Last week Steve's car passed me when I was stuck in traffic. I followed him out Mill Creek Road and lost him. Maybe he stopped at her place."

"You mean, for a little afternoon delight?"

"Could be."

"What do we do with this tasty tidbit?"

"Time to dust off your telescopic lens. Keep an eye on Marie's place."

"Sounds exciting."

"Go over today and scope it out. We'll touch base tomorrow and go from there."

Anne beamed. "Her place is tucked away in the woods. It'd be so easy for him to park and go in unnoticed. From the knoll across the road, I could see everything coming and going."

"Perfect."

"The garage is behind the house. I assume he'd park there and use the back door."

"We need a surveillance schedule."

"Surveillance? I love it. Just tell me what to do."

"Get there about 11:30 am. We'll regroup at the end of the week to see how it went."

***

Anne parked in a driveway overgrown with weeds about a quarter of a mile past Marie's and walked back. After several hours of kicking ants and swatting mosquitoes, she left.

The following morning she remembered to take her long-sleeved shirt and bug spray. Still, she quit midafternoon. Thursday was the same.

She returned with a thermos of ice water on Friday and squatted behind an apple tree. A little after noon, Anne watched a red pickup fly over the hill. When it came to a stop, Marie jumped out, picked up the mail and pulled into the garage. Anne caught it.

Steadying her camera against the tree, Anne took a sip of water and waited.

Steve's Caddy crested the hill.

CLICK, CLICK.

He pulled into the driveway and stepped out.

CLICK, CLICK.

Looking like a big-game hunter, Anne dragged her bags a few feet for a better view of the back door. When the heat got to her, she set her camera on a tripod and fell asleep in the shade of a large oak.

She heard a rustling by her feet. Opening one eye, she watched a black snake slither over her foot. She bit her lip as pee ran down her leg.

Feeling clammy and uncomfortable, and cursing herself for forgetting her watch, she saw the door opening. Steve stepped onto the porch, Marie in hot pursuit, her large breasts flopping.

She threw her arms around Steve's neck.

CLICK, CLICK.

Steve grabbed Marie around the waist and buried his face in her cleavage.

CLICK.

***

Anne drove across town in record time and called Karen. "I got them. I got Steve and Marie."

"Slow down, Anne."

"I took a shot when Marie got home, then when Steve arrived. Then I waited."

"And."

"Steve came out and Marie followed him onto the porch. I got a fantastic shot of Steve having dessert. He was knee-deep in cleavage."

"I can hardly wait to see them. Anything else?"

"Yes. While I was waiting a damn snake crawled over my foot. I wet my pants."

"Ha. Wait until Gerry hears about that."

"It's not for public knowledge."

***

Karen joined Anne at Gerry's conference table and slid the incriminating photos toward him, one at a time.

His eyes bugged. "Where did you get these?"

"I staked out Marie's place last week," Anne said. "Friday I hit the jackpot."

"You sure did. Is that it?"

Anne frowned at Karen. "Did you tell him?"

"I did not."

Gerry eyed Anne then Karen.

"She wet her pants," Karen announced.

"Karen. You said you wouldn't."

"Sorry, I couldn't resist."

Gerry laughed as Anne repeated her experience then turned to Karen. "Are you going to confront Marie?"

She shrugged. "I'm tempted, but ..."

"Why the hesitation? It's time to play hardball."

"I don't think I have enough proof."

"I think you do. Go for it."

Karen acknowledged that Gerry's instincts were usually spot-on. But she had reservations. What if Marie didn't cave like the others had?

***

"This is Marie Cabrera, how may I help you?"

"I'm Karen Holmes, the reporter from the *Gazette*. We had breakfast together at the Peabody."

"Oh, yes. You were on a shopping trip. How are you?"

"I'm fine. In fact, I'm involved in a special project. I need to speak with you right away."

"Sounds serious. What's it about?"

"President Schilling."

"I don't get involved with campus politics."

"It's about the two of you."

"Get out of here."

"I have pictures."

"I bet you do." Marie chuckled. "My association with President Schilling is limited to short phone calls."

"From what I've seen, you know him quite well."

"Ms. Holmes, I'm not wasting company time on some dumb pictures. If you want to talk, come out to the County Line Tavern Friday night. We'll have a little fun."

"I don't think you understand."

"I have a large mailing to get out today." The line went dead.

***

Karen called Sharon. "What are you doing Friday night?"

"Nothing, as usual."

"I need you to go with me to the County Line Tavern."

"Not again. What if Mr. Cagney is there?"

"I'll scout the place."

"He could show up."

"Come on. Stop working. I have to follow up on a lead."

"Okay. But if I see him, I'm out of there."

Two days later, Karen knocked on Sharon's door.

Hearing no response, she poked her head inside. "Sharon, are you here?"

She heard a faint reply. "I'm in the bedroom."

"You okay?"

"Not really. I have a terminal case of cramps."

"Anything I can do?"

Sharon forced a grin. "Do you have any chicken soup?"

"Sorry."

"I can't move. You'll have to go alone."

Cramps, shit! Karen got in her Camaro and headed for the tavern.

A guy in cowboy boots, with greasy hair, tipped his NASCAR cap when she walked in. "Evenin' ma'am."

Karen grinned and pushed her way through the throng. Making her way to the far side of the barn, she squeezed between two guys, bumping into the one.

"Pardon me," she said.

He gave her the eye. "You want something?"

"I'm looking for Marie Cabrera. Have you seen her?"

"You a friend of hers?"

"An acquaintance. I'm supposed to meet her."

He frowned. "You been here before?"

"Just once."

"I remember you," the other one said, then grabbed her arm. "Hey, Randy, strike up the band. We've got a live one here."

271

A man wearing several days' growth grabbed her arm and pulled her onto the dance floor. "Yahoo. Let's dance, little lady." The band broke into *The Stripper*. A large circle formed. People began to clap.

"You want to do it on your own? Or, do you need a little help?"

"Do what?" She pulled away. "What are you talking about?"

He grabbed her hands. "Do a little dance. Or, do you only dance for girls?"

"Let me go." Karen freed one arm, punched him in the chest. "What's wrong with you?"

"Feisty, aren't you?" He wrapped his arms around her. "There's nothing wrong with me. You're the one with the problem." He laughed and twirled her.

When he let go she staggered and fell against a blubbery hick who grabbed her ass. "You're in the wrong place if you're looking for girlies here." Lifting her off the floor, he spun her around. She held on to him to keep from falling. He kissed her cheek.

His peanut breath made her retch. "Uck! Who do you think you are?" She flailed her arms and kicked him in the shin. "Let me go. Let me go."

Cat calls drowned out her protests. He tightened his grip on her arms. She felt nauseated.

When he let go, she lost her balance and fell. A guy pulled her up and held her from behind. She felt someone loosen her belt and unzip her jeans.

"What are you doing?" she screamed. "Stop."

"Giving you a chance to show off," a guy said. He locked her feet with his own and slid her jeans below her knees.

"Are you crazy?" she hollered.

Someone jerked her sweatshirt over her head and held her hands inside. Everything went dark. She stood frozen in her underpants and bra; her hands holding her sweatshirt over her head. The cheers were deafening.

My God, no. Please God, no.

Someone snapped the waistband of her panties. "Shake it, baby. Shake it."

She felt her sweatshirt press against her right ear. "I'm letting your hands go now," someone said. "Hold your arms over your head and move your ass. If you don't everything will come off. Got it?"

She stood rooted to the floor.

He raised his voice. "Didja hear me?" She nodded her head. "Good. Now shake it." He slapped her on the butt.

The group chanted. "Shake it, baby, shake it." And the band played, *Shake it up, baby, twist and shout.*

Slowly, very slowly, Karen began to sway. A tear trickled down her cheek.

A roar came up from the crowd. She rotated her hips and heard whistling.

"Back off guys," someone said. "That's my friend."

A hush fell over the group.

The guy in the NASCAR cap straightened her sweatshirt. She pulled up her jeans and threw her arms around his waist. "A lady like you shouldn't be alone in a place like this. You okay?"

She had trouble catching her breath. "I guess … I'm so embarrassed."

"Hey, look at it this way; you'll never see any of these guys again."

"I thought I was going to die."

"I understand. What's your name?"

"Karen Holmes."

"I'm Bobby Simpson. What are you doing here?"

"I'm a reporter, on assignment."

"Assignment? You mean like Watergate?"

***

After her breathing had returned to normal, Karen spotted Marie at a table with two other women. She thanked Bobby and made her way to her table.

"Good to see you again," Karen said.

"Yeah. What do you want to talk about?"

"It's personal."

"Do you want us to leave?" one woman asked.

Marie paused. "I guess. It'll only take a couple of minutes."

Karen sat down. Marie gave her an icy stare. "So what's this all about?"

"I'm doing a story on President Schilling. I know you're having an affair with him."

"You gotta be shittin' me." Marie laughed.

"He's fooling around with other women."

"Other women? Steve Schilling? Ha."

"We have names and places. Photos of him with other women, and signed confessions."

"Confessions? What have you been snorting?"

"I've met with them. They've told me the details."

"Sure. And I can walk on water."

"Look. I'll strike a deal with you," Karen said. "You tell me about the affair and I'll remove everything from your file — your name, pictures — like it never happened."

"Pretty slick. I give you the goods and you nail him. What makes you think I'm involved?"

"I have pictures that were taken at your place."

"My place? What the hell are you talking about?"

Karen handed Marie a manila folder. "Here, take a look."

Marie flipped through the photos. She grinned. "Sure, I fucked him. I fucked him at the away football game too. What's the big deal? I've fucked lots of guys."

"It may not be a big deal for you but when it's the university president, it's a very big deal."

Marie chugged her beer. "What are you going to do? Get me fired? Shit, I'll file a harassment suit. The university will pay me big bucks."

Karen sat mute.

"Look." Marie leered. "I saw your little dance. Point out the guy you want. I'll fix you up for the night. All weekend, if you want."

"I'm not here for that. I'm only interested in the pictures."

"Pictures?" Marie held one up to Karen. "See that? You think that matters to me? Blow it up and hang it over the bar. Hell, they'll be standing in line."

Karen knew she'd been bested, and took a deep breath. "What about Don?"

Marie frowned, her eyes glazed. "Don who?"

"Don Cagney."

"What does he have to with this?"

"Don't be coy with me. I saw the two of you holding hands."

Marie squirmed. "Doesn't matter. You can't hurt me. Don and I are going to be married as soon as he divorces that bitch of his. One blow job and he won't remember a thing."

"I don't think so. Imagine a couple of stories in the *Gazette*. An editorial calling for Don's resignation. Another demanding the president's resignation. Your picture plastered all over. Love triangles sell like hot cakes. You won't have a chance."

"You can't do that."

"Oh, can't I? And how do you think Don will react? His board will be up in arms. He'll be fighting for his job. He won't be able to divorce his wife. You won't even be in the equation."

"You bitch," Marie shouted. "What do you want?"

"Your signature on this form. And the details. Where? How often?"

Marie smirked. "Shit. If I told you everything, it would blow your mind."

Karen shrugged. "It's your choice. Steve is going down. With or without your help. Do you want to go down too? End up with nothing? Or, do you want to marry Don and live in a big mansion? Sounds like a no-brainer to me."

"You're a gutsy broad, aren't you? You sure you don't want to fuck someone tonight?"

Karen shook her head.

"Give me the goddamn form. Got a pen?"

CHAPTER THIRTY

Rusty slipped out of the faculty senate office, sprinted to his office, and dialed Steve.

Carol answered. "It's Rusty," he said. He sounded breathless. "I need to talk to Steve."

"He left early. What's wrong?"

"I'm sworn to secrecy. But I can tell you, it's not good."

"Maybe you can catch him before he leaves for poker."

"Poker?" Rusty hung up, mopped his brow and dialed Steve's house.

He was ready to hang up when Steve answered. "What took you so long to answer?" Rusty barked.

"I was in the shower. What's up?"

"We have to talk. The shit's about ready to hit the fan."

"What happened?"

"The senate is preparing to vote on a resolution of no confidence."

"They can't do that."

"Hell, they can't. The executive committee just approved a draft statement, eight to one."

"So Bergmann's nose is out of joint again. Big deal. I'll talk to him next week."

"Damn it, Steve, you don't understand. This is serious. He's fired up the entire committee."

"I'll call him in the morning and set up a luncheon. Don't worry. I'll work it out."

"Are you listening to me? This is big trouble. The executive committee is behind him."

"He's always going off."

"He documented over a hundred phone calls."

"Smoke and mirrors. He can't prove a thing."

"This isn't a court of law. It's the faculty senate. They'll string you up by the balls."

"No way. You worry too much. I'll call you tomorrow. I gotta go. I'll be late for poker."

"Poker at 4:30?"

"I have to stop at the drugstore on the way."

"Poker doesn't start until 7 o'clock. Get your ass over to my place. Right now."

"Rusty, I …"

"You're going to Kate's, aren't you?" Rusty shouted.

"So? I was going to take her a box of chocolates. It's her birthday."

"That's bullshit. You were going to get laid."

"So what?"

"So what? You're self-destructing. People are watching. Bergmann has 26 pages. Every issue is itemized as a code-of-ethics violation."

"It's hearsay. He can't prove anything."

"Damn, Steve. I told you he doesn't have to prove it. The whole campus will support him."

"I have the votes."

"You don't have the votes. I just came from the executive committee. You lost."

Steve headed for the door. "I'll be at Kate's, then poker. We'll talk later."

"You can't slough this off. Ignore it and they will force you to resign."

"We'll talk."

"I'm calling Bill. Maybe he can talk some sense into you."

"I don't give a fuck who you call."

***

Bill glared at his protégé. "Sit down," he ordered.

Looking contrite, Steve mumbled. "It's not as bad as you think."

"Really? Rusty says it's a lot worse than you think."

Rusty nodded.

"They're on a witch hunt," Steve said.

"Stop right there. I don't want to hear another word. What planet are you living on? Your wife divorced you. Rumors are flying about your behavior — misbehavior. Many think you're guilty. Rusty believes the only way to avoid a vote of no-confidence is to push this into summer."

"He's overreacting."

"Shut up." Bill turned to Rusty. "How many votes can you turn?"

"Right now? None."

"We need the committee to table the vote. That'll allow time for tempers to cool. Any ideas?"

"I don't know, Bill." Rusty said. "You're talking about turning four votes."

"We need a hook to hang our hat on."

"Hmm, how about, 'don't rush to judgment.'"

"That's good enough for now. Let's run with it."

"Maybe we should call for a fact-finding committee. That'd take us into fall."

"I like that. Harold Porter and Virginia Larson would vote for that. They're good academics. Can you deliver the other two votes?"

Rusty hesitated. "Maybe Fredrick Borosch. And possibly, Theresa Hughes or Meg Falan."

"Let me know if you have a problem. Theresa and Meg have their own skeletons in the closets."

***

Rusty knocked on Dr. Borosch's door. "How are you doing, Frederick?"

"Not so good," he said in a thick German accent. "I've been thinking about the situation. I'm not sure I did the right thing. Dr. Schilling is the president. I'm only a professor."

"That's why I'm here. I'm worried that we might be rushing to judgment."

"That's what Meg Falan said."

"We're talking about a man's career."

Frederick nodded. "This is a university. We are professors, not a lynch mob."

"I agree. We need a motion to table the resolution. Would you support such a proposal?"

"I'll do more than that. I'll make the motion. And I'm sure I can get Meg to second it."

"Perfect." Rusty shook the professor's hand. "Frederick, I think it's best to keep this to ourselves."

"Of course. We don't need to antagonize the faculty senate."

***

Harold Porter and Bill sat catty-corner in Bill's sunroom. "Harold, thank you for stopping by. How long has it been since we talked?"

"Maybe five or six years."

"That long? I remember when you were a dean. We used to meet for coffee once a week. I miss those times."

"Me too."

Bill fingered the manila folder on his lap. "What ever happened to that graduate student? Edwards? What was her name?"

Harold's face flushed. "Heather."

"Yes, Heather."

"She's married, lives in Dallas."

"Did you ever tell Mary about her?"

"God, no, Bill. She would have divorced me."

"How long were the two of you an item?"

"A couple of years."

"As I recall, it was more like four."

"I tried to break it off. She pressed me to choose. I couldn't do that to Mary."

"Remember that week-long conference in San Diego? She tore up the dance floor."

"She was something, wasn't she?"

"The club photographer took your picture with her."

"Photographer?"

Bill leaned over and handed the folder to Harold. "I gave him 20 bucks for the photos," Bill said. "Maybe these will help refresh your memory."

Harold seemed to shrink. "Bill, we've been friends all of these years."

"Of course, Harold. No reason to worry. I'm thinking the senate may be rushing to judgment on Steve."

"Bill, he's guilty. You know it. Everyone knows it."

"There are just phone calls and rumors. I've yet to see any facts."

"It's obvious, Bill. I'm going to move the motion for a vote of no confidence."

"What's your phone number?"

Harold scowled. "You know it, Bill. You've called me a thousand times."

"Maybe I'll invite Mary over to see the pictures of you and Heather."

Harold jumped up. "Jesus Christ, Bill, you can't do that. She'll kill me."

"Slow down."

"I know you, Bill. What do you want?"

"A small favor. Table the motion of no confidence and call for a fact-finding committee."

"Table the motion? Bill, I can't do that. Not after I've been pushing for the vote."

"And, Judith Larson needs to second your motion."

"Judith? No one will ever convince her. She's as bullheaded as you are."

"I remember when the two of you were doing a lot more than talking."

"You bastard." Harold threw up his hands. "Okay, you win. You have your two votes."

***

Gerry flew in, nearly running over Karen. "Well, aren't you the early bird?" he said.

"I nailed Marie."

"You did?" He waved her into his office. "Let's hear it."

"I went to the County Line Tavern Friday night to meet Marie. At the last minute Sharon bailed, so I went alone."

"I don't think that was a good idea."

"You're telling me." Karen flushed. She bit her lip then covered her face. A tear trickled down her cheek. She sniffled then broke into tears.

Gerry handed her a tissue.

"I'm sorry."

"No need to apologize. What happened?"

"It was awful. I was terrified."

"Karen, it's just the two of us. You need to tell someone. You'll feel better."

"Okay." She swallowed. "I asked a guy if he'd seen Marie. Someone dragged me onto the dance floor and started to undress me." She blew her nose then told Gerry about Marie's confession.

Gerry shook his head. "Don Cagney? How'd you make that connection?"

"My friend Sharon — she's the PR director at First National — went with me to the tavern a few weeks ago. She recognized Don. He was playing kissy-face with Marie. Friday night, after Marie thwarted my attempts to break down her defenses, I played the trump card. She buckled."

"Good thinking. And some good luck, too."

"I guess."

"You've been pushing yourself very hard. Why don't you take some time off?"

"That sounds good. I haven't seen my parents for ages."

"Even better. While you're in New Orleans, I'd like you to make time for an interview."

"An interview?"

"The editor of the *The Times–Picayune* is an old classmate. We spoke last week. He's looking for an assistant editor. I told him about you. He's very interested. That is, if you are."

"Gee, I don't know. I like working here, Gerry."

"Karen. I'd like for you to stay in Ruston forever, but you're too talented to be stuck here."

"Thanks, Gerry. I'm very grateful for your mentoring. I've learned so much." She handed him two envelopes. "Here are my final reports."

"Wait. Why two?"

"I uncovered something else."

"Don't tell me Steve had a sixth woman."

"No. But it's something you need to know."

"Stop beating around the bush. What is it?"

"I'd rather you read the report. You've always said it's a reporter's job to uncover the facts. The editor has to decide what to do with them."

"Fair enough."

***

"We need to talk, right now." Gerry had fire in his eyes. He meant business.

Karen picked up her notepad and followed him into his office. She knew that look and tone. Heart pounding, she closed the door and sat down.

"Who's your source?"

"I can't tell you."

"Figures. Is the person trustworthy?"

"She is. Absolutely."

"She." Gerry's brow wrinkled. "Why did she confide in you after thirty years?"

"She thinks it will help solve our problem."

"How?"

"She believes there's a connection between Bill's behavior and Steve's actions."

"That's a leap. There must be something else."

"I don't think so. She kept saying, 'To understand Steve Schilling you must know Bill Thornton.'"

"What's that mean?"

"She thinks Bill has used his expertise in psychology to shape Steve's thinking, maybe even to control his behavior."

"Control? That's pretty heavy."

"My choice of word. Maybe influence is better."

"But how?"

"She said Bill and Steve talked a lot about Steve's childhood. My source thinks Bill projected his views and behavior onto Steve's thinking. In time Steve made them his own."

"Are you saying that Steve is Bill's puppet?"

"No. I asked her about that. She thinks Steve functions on his own. But Bill's thoughts had become so ingrained that Steve acted out Bill's views. By following Bill's lead, Steve became highly successful in his professional life."

"I agree with that," Gerry said.

"Over the years their leadership styles blended as if they were one."

"Steve became a clone of Bill," he confirmed.

"It seems that way."

Gerry pursed his lips. "Interesting."

"Things went awry in Steve's personal life. Bill was more discreet, kept his personal emotions within limits."

"That's for sure," Gerry agreed.

"But Steve's sex addiction overtook his personal life. Everything Bill had taught him fell by the wayside. Steve's obsession with success propelled his sex-driven ego even further out of control."

"I'll have to think about that. But I'll tell you one thing. If anyone is capable of such extreme psychological manipulation, it'd be Bill Thornton." Gerry scratched his head. "Your source had an affair with Bill, right?"

"Yes, for two or three years."

"Why did it end?"

"She learned Bill was having an affair with Sarah, his housekeeper. She gave him an ultimatum — it's me or Virginia. Bill couldn't decide."

Gerry chimed in. "So she ended their relationship."

"You got it. Some months later Sarah gave birth to Jimmy."

"How did you find that out?"

"My source felt certain that Jimmy was Bill's son. To verify it, I went to the athletic office and sorted through old football programs. I found Jimmy's picture, along with the date and place of his birth."

"Good thinking, Karen."

"I went to St. Louis, where Sarah had Jimmy, and made a copy of his birth certificate. On the official records it looked like she had crossed out something and printed Bill's name."

"So, Sarah listed Bill as the father. That makes sense."

"Sometime after that Virginia found out. She must have laid down the law. From what I dug up about Virginia, I think it's reasonable to assume she read Bill the riot act. She may have laid down rules for Bill: Treat Jimmy as your son, and Sarah as an employee. And if there's ever another incident, I'll divorce you and have you fired."

"So, that's why Jimmy always sat on Bill's lap and called him Mr. Bill. That would explain their closeness. I used to wonder ..."

"You got it."

"It all fits, except for one thing. At the end of her life, why did Virginia begin to treat Sarah differently?"

"Virginia knew she was dying. I think she forgave Bill. She probably went to the board of trustees and demanded that they issue Sarah a contract to take care of Bill until his death. If they refused, I think she would have blown the whistle on the affair. She was one strong woman."

"They were two strong women," Gerry said. "And you're one helluva reporter. I'm calling my friend in New Orleans. If he doesn't hire you, he's nuts."

CHAPTER THIRTY-ONE

"Steve Schilling has to go. The sooner the better."

"Why? Did he murder someone?"

"No, but he's having multiple affairs."

"Hold on, Gerry." Bill slid to the edge of his seat. "What are you saying?"

"Months ago Suzanne brought me prima facie evidence that Steve has been humping five women. Who knows, it could be six by now."

"Five affairs? That's unbelievable."

"I thought so too. I kept quiet until my top reporter investigated the charges. Sure enough, Suzanne was right."

"What evidence do you have?"

"The whole enchilada — dates, times, eyewitness reports, pictures — and signed confessions from the women." Gerry handed Bill a stack of manila envelopes.

"There's a file on each one."

"Jesus Christ, I need another drink." Bill filled his glass to the brim.

"I have to run the story. It's my professional responsibility."

Bill's spine straightened. "You can't do that. You're talking about the university. You'll destroy everything I've worked for."

"I'm sorry, Bill. I have to."

"But what about the university's image? We can't let one blip destroy it."

"A blip? This is a bombshell."

"Have you considered the fallout? We'll have recruitment problems. Fundraising will dry up. There might even be a state inquiry."

"I know how you feel Bill, but I can't ignore this."

Bill got up and paced. "Jesus, Gerry, we're talking about my life's work."

"I know. And I'm sorry about that. But I can't … I won't stick my head in the sand. I have an obligation to report the news, no matter what."

Bill turned to face Gerry. His tone was desperate. "Give me a couple of weeks."

"A couple of weeks? What good will that do? This has been going on for years."

Bill held up two fingers. "Two weeks. That's all I ask."

"You want me to sit on this for two weeks? You're kidding. All hell could break loose."

"Two weeks. Please. If you run it, the national media will be on us like flies on … *USA Today, The National Enquirer.* The town and the university would never recover."

Gerry's lips tightened. "What do you think you can do in two weeks?"

"Explore some options."

Gerry let go a deep sigh. "I'm going out on a limb, Bill. Don't screw with me. If this story breaks from another source, I'm printing it."

"Fair enough. I'll see you in two weeks."

As soon as Gerry was out the door, Bill sat down with the evidence. He had heard rumors, but had chosen to ignore them.

How could Steve be so dumb? Fucking Kate on a chaise lounge in broad daylight. I should have listened to Virginia. I should have picked someone else.

Nausea swept over him. He tossed the last report on the floor. *Retreat into action,* he'd once heard a motivational speaker say.

Pulling himself together, he took *The Chronicle of Higher Education* from the magazine rack and began combing ads for presidential positions. He took scissors from his desk drawer. With each snip he felt as though he was severing part of his life.

He called Eric Williams, an old friend and the chancellor of the North Carolina system. The two exchanged pleasantries, then Bill dove into his agenda. "I read your ad for Mountain State University. How's the search going?"

"The campus is moving slowly."

"Do you have many options?"

"Not really. I'd hoped to have someone onboard by fall but I can't get excited about the quality of the pool."

"What are you looking for?"

"We need a strong person with significant experience. Enrollment is down. The school has big-time financial problems. What can I say? The place is a mess."

"Maybe I can help."

"You have someone to recommend?"

"I do. My protégé has all the right stuff. He's articulate. Personable. Knows budgets and athletics. He's a crackerjack fundraiser. And he's ready for a fresh challenge."

"Why would he want to leave?"

"It's a sad story. But by no means a new one. His wife has created quite a stir. She has a drinking problem. And there are ... rumors. I advised him to end his marriage."

"That's too bad."

"I hate to see him go. Sometimes you don't have a choice. I'd like to help him start anew."

"Do you think he'd consider applying here?"

"I'm not sure. You know how faculty members react when a president applies elsewhere. No matter how much they love him, they can be fickle and say 'good riddance.' In cases like that, the president stands to lose all credibility."

"What if he knew it was a done deal?"

"Well, that would be a horse of a different color."

"Could you make it happen?"

"Maybe ... Yes, I think so."

"Good. Fax me his résumé. Here's my private number."

***

"Good morning, Carol, it's Bill. This is highly confidential. Can you talk?"

"Yes, I'm alone."

"Steve has to go."

"I can't say I'm surprised. What do you want me to do?"

"Fax his résumé to Eric Williams in the North Carolina chancellor's office. And bring me a copy."

"I can stop by during my lunch hour."

"Thanks Carol. And I need to meet with Steve."

She scanned her daytimer. "Wednesday afternoon is open. How about 3:30?"

"Perfect."

***

"I don't like what I'm hearing, Steve. What the hell happened?" Bill poured himself a second drink and took a gulp.

"It's not easy dealing with divorce. I'll never understand Suzanne, ending the marriage after all these years. She must be crazy."

"Suzanne? There's nothing wrong with her. You're the problem."

"I've told you, Bill, it's all hearsay."

"How could you let this happen? You didn't pay attention to one word I said. I'm so furious, I could spit tacks."

"Don't worry. No one knows."

Bill got in Steve's face. "I know. Others know," he barked. "Wake up. Pull your head out of your ass."

Steve poked Bill in the chest. "You can't talk to me that way."

Bill's face reddened. "I'll talk to you anyway I want." He shoved Steve onto the sofa. "You're nothing," Bill screamed. "I made you. If it wasn't for me, you'd still be teaching history. You lied to me. Over and over. And now you're about to destroy my university."

"Simmer down, Bill, it's not that bad."

"Not that bad?" Bill grabbed the envelopes from his desk and waved them in Steve's face. See these? Facts. Pictures. You're guilty as sin. And a pathetic excuse for a man."

"I can explain."

"Okay, smart guy, explain Kate Blanchard. And Sandra Whitehead. While you're at it, I want to hear about Christina Clark and Martha Brown. Maybe you can explain Marie Cabrera to me, too. Go on. I'm all ears."

Steve's voice was a whisper. "I didn't mean for things to turn out this way. I loved them all." He began to sob.

290

"Here we go again. If it weren't for the university, I'd let the media eat you alive."

Bill went to his desk and shuffled his notes.

Steve peered over his shoulder. "What's going on?"

Bill didn't look up. "I'm getting you a job, asshole."

"But I have a job."

"Not for long," Bill bellowed. "Here's an announcement for an opening at Mountain State University. And here's a draft of your application letter. You can fine tune it with Carol."

"But, why am I doing this?"

"Jesus Christ, Steve. Wake up. You don't have a future here. You're done. I've set the wheels in motion to find you a position elsewhere. Just do what I say for a change."

"I don't understand."

"It's simple. In two months you'll be interviewing. Until then, you'd better toe the line."

Steve gave Bill a blank look. "Okay," he whispered. "But what's my reason for leaving?"

"I told the chancellor that Suzanne had an alcohol problem and was fooling around."

"You can't say that."

"You're the last person to tell me what I can and can't say. Should I have told him you were having five affairs? Give me a break."

***

A smile crossed Bill's face as he walked into Gerry's office.

"You're in much better spirits than the last time we talked," Gerry said.

"For good reason. My plan is working out."

"What plan?"

"I can't say yet. It's going to take two or three months."

"Too bad. You have two days left on our agreement."

Bill raised his voice. "Gerry, please, trust me. I need a little more time for the pieces to come together."

"Bill, we agreed on two weeks. This is day twelve. I've drafted the editorial calling for Steve's resignation. And today I'm assigning the front-page story to Karen Holmes."

"You can't do that. We had an agreement."

"We did. Two weeks. Not two or three months."

"Steve will be gone by fall."

Gerry sighed. "How are you going to accomplish that?"

"I've worked it out with an old friend. He owes me."

"Don't give me the 'old friend' bullshit. I want specifics."

"I've sent Steve's résumé to the chancellor of the North Carolina system. He's signed off on it. The search will proceed normally — and Steve will be named president."

"Nice sham, Bill."

"It's not a sham. It's a win-win situation. It solves our problem and fixes theirs."

Gerry shook his head.

"C'mon Gerry. If you publish an editorial, it will touch off a crisis."

"I'll think about it."

Bill let out a sigh.

"There's something else. And I need to know the truth. No bullshit."

"Sure, anything."

Gerry handed Bill an envelope. "Read this."

Bill withdrew a two-page report and scanned it. The color drained from his face. "Where did this come from? Jesus, it was a one-time fling thirty years ago."

"One time? She's an attractive woman. She's been your housekeeper for many years. And, for all practical purposes, she has been living in your house since Virginia passed away."

"For God's sake, Gerry, that was Virginia's idea. Unbeknownst to me, she went to the board and set it up. Do you think Virginia would have done it if she thought something was still going on?"

"Okay, forget it. What about the second one? Who is 'the other woman?'"

"What's that have to do with anything?"

"You were screwing Carol, weren't you?"

"So what? It was ages ago. You didn't know her then. What does it matter?"

"It matters to me. I care for her, want to marry her. Since your romp she has had trust issues with men. I should say, distrust."

Bill stammered. "Okay. Okay. She was twenty-five and hot. I fell in love with her."

"You didn't fall in love." Gerry spoke through clenched teeth. "She was one more notch in your belt. You used her like you used the others."

"What are you talking about?"

"Don't play games with me. I heard about your woman in Pine Bluff, and the one in Little Rock. And that music teacher from Helena."

"Helena?"

"Yes, the woman who was on your advisory council."

Bill bristled. "There was nothing to that. We were platonic friends."

"Sure. And I'm the pope. You're no better than Steve. I have a file on you a mile long."

Bill looked stricken. "Gerry, I loved each of those women. I truly did."

"Love? You don't know the meaning of the word."

"Don't say that, Gerry."

Gerry shook his head. "Why Carol? Why couldn't you have kept your hands off her?"

"It wasn't like that."

"Please. Don't insult my intelligence. You tossed her aside like garbage. She's scarred for life thanks to you." Gerry shoved Bill against the wall. "If you weren't an old man, I'd beat the shit out of you."

CHAPTER THIRTY-TWO

Bill pressed the blinking red light. "You have one new message," came the robotic voice. "Bill, it's Eric Williams. Give me a call."

He dialed as quickly as his shaky finger would allow. "Eric, it's Bill. What's up?"

"Thank God. I was afraid I wouldn't reach you before the weekend. We have a situation."

"What happened?"

"Steve had a great interview. My staff wrapped up the final round of campus calls. I was ready to make an offer and ..."

"And?"

"This afternoon my vice-chancellor for finance came in with a game stopper. She had spoken with someone on your campus who directed her to Charles Bergmann, the chairman of the faculty senate."

"Where is this going?"

"Bergmann told her the senate had received more than a hundred calls about Steve's behavior. Bergmann prepared a resolution of no-confidence. That sure doesn't mesh with what you said. You told me Steve's wife was the problem. What the hell is going on?"

"I just heard about Bergmann, too," Bill fibbed. "He's been out to get Steve for years. Some old rivalry, I think. There's nothing to worry about."

"Easy for you to say. I can't ignore this. If word gets out, it could cost me my job."

"Calm down. It's all crap."

"Crap or not, I don't like the smell."

"Don't worry. I'll make some calls, let folks know Bergmann is not credible and apologize for giving your finance person an unreliable source."

295

"How can you do that?"

"Leave it to me. By Tuesday everyone will know that Bergmann had a personal vendetta against Steve."

"I don't know. I'm getting very nervous about the whole thing."

"No need. I can assure you, this will go no further."

***

I hope it's not a salesman, Bill thought as he answered the door. "Steve, I wasn't expecting you. Come in."

"I was so excited about the interview," Steve said breathlessly, "I wanted to tell you in person. I came straight from the airport."

"I heard it went well."

"How'd you hear that?"

"I talked to the chancellor."

"What'd he say?"

"You were the number one choice but ..."

"But what?"

"Someone talked to Bergmann."

"Shit. How'd they get to him?"

"It doesn't matter. I'll take care of it. But there's something else we have to talk about. Something I've ignored for far too long."

"What's that?"

"You can't go on like this, Steve. You're self-destructing."

"But I'm thrilled about getting a new job."

"Changing jobs and moving to a different location won't change who you are."

"But everything will be different."

"Maybe for a week or a month. Sooner or later you'll resume your old routine. And marrying Kate would be the worst thing you could do. You'll destroy her."

Steve sank into the sofa. "Sometimes I don't have a clue what you are talking about."

"You have to face reality. You have a sex addiction, don't you?"

Steve looked as though Bill were speaking in tongues. "Sex addiction? What the fuck?"

"Stop." Bill interrupted. "Stop, right there. You know perfectly well what I'm talking about. The newspaper investigation confirmed it. And I researched the therapist you met with last year. Dr. Jones is *damn good*. He told you that you have a problem, didn't he?"

Steve kept silent.

"Tell me the truth."

Steve broke eye contact with Bill and looked like he'd caught a blow to the gut.

"Steve, look at me. What … did … the … doctor … say?"

Steve's eyes glazed over. "I have a sex addiction."

"What else?"

"Nothing will change unless I'm willing to do something about it."

"That's what I figured."

Bill's shoulders dropped. "You're destroying yourself. You've lost your wife and your job, and you've hurt every woman you've been involved with. You can't ignore this. It's not normal."

Steve got up and lumbered to the window overlooking the rose garden. He thought about his mom and how his dad had abused her. He thought about the women he'd loved; the ones he'd hurt and the daughter he'd lost.

He swiped a tear. "I don't … I don't know if I can change."

"You may not be able to. But you won't know unless you try."

"What should I do?"

"That's your decision. I can't help you on this one."

Steve took a deep breath and sighed. "I'll try."

Bill gave Steve a hug. "Good. It's a start. You're a better man than I."

***

The Arkansas River glistened in the morning sun as Steve pulled off I-40 in Little Rock. A few minutes later he parked in front of the office in a strip mall. Dr. Jones was unlocking the door.

"I hope there's an extra coffee in that bag," Steve called out.

"Four double-chocolate donuts, too," he said, waving Steve in. "It's been a while. How have you been?"

"Busy."

"I read you're being considered for the president's slot at Mountain State in North Carolina."

"Yes. I should hear something next week."

"Good luck with that."

Steve followed the doctor through the small reception area into an office with a brown leather sofa and two matching chairs. The walls were a restful taupe and appeared freshly painted. The coffee table held travel magazines and a box of tissues.

"Have a seat. And help yourself."

Steve grabbed coffee and a donut and sat in one of the chairs opposite the psychologist.

"You sounded anxious on the phone. What's happening?"

"I've been thinking about what you said. You know, about making changes ..."

"It'll require commitment and effort on your part. I'm here to help. But you'll have to do the hard work."

"I can't go on like this. I've hurt so many people. And I've hurt myself. I have to change."

"You have to *want* to change. Remember when I told you it'd be a long, rocky road. Are you willing to make that kind of a commitment?"

"I feel like I don't have a choice. Yes. I don't want to screw up again."

"What will your schedule be like if you move?"

"That won't happen for another five or six weeks. I'll be in Ruston until then."

"Good. We can squeeze in a session every week, two if necessary. Where in North Carolina is the other university?"

"Near Ashville. But I'd rather not see a doctor there. Too close. Can you refer me to someone in Charlotte?"

"I can. A college classmate practices there." He flipped through his Rolodex. "Here he is. Dr. James Benderman. He's a fine therapist. You'll like him. I'll send him your file and give him a follow-up call."

"Thank you. I'd appreciate that."

Dr. Jones hesitated. "There's one more thing, Steve."

"Sure, fire away."

"Dealing with a sex addiction is far more complicated than most people realize. It would be helpful to have a close friend you can confide in. Someone you trust and feel safe with. Do you have someone like that?"

"No one in North Carolina. I have a couple of friends around here that I chat with once in a while."

"How about someone you speak with on a regular basis."

Steve hesitated. "There's Kate. I've known her since college."

"Is that the Kate you mentioned last year?" Steve nodded. "Have you been seeing her all this time?"

"Yes. If I wasn't so messed up, I'd ask her to marry me today."

"Does she date other men?"

"She has a few male friends, but nothing romantic."

"And do you feel close enough to discuss personal matters with her?"

"I do already — all the time."

Dr. Jones sipped his coffee. "Would you feel comfortable discussing your sex addiction?"

Steve stiffened. "You mean telling her about the other women?"

"You have to be honest about your problem. Transparent. Let her know that you need her support — all through this."

"That's a lot to ask of her."

"It is. But it's not only her, Steve. You'll be asking a lot of yourself, too."

"Whaddaya mean, Doc?"

"You have to be truthful."

"But I am."

Dr. Jones raised his hand. "There is no quick fix, Steve. It will be a long-term process. You have to be willing to evaluate your core beliefs. Neither Dr. Benderman nor I can do that. No therapist can. It's up to you to decide if you want to move forward."

"I have to. I want to do it. I need to do it."

"We haven't begun to scratch the surface."

"I'm willing to do whatever it takes."

"Okay, let's get started. You said your mother was abused by your dad."

"Bastard. I hate him."

"He still has a strong presence in your life. You said you pledged to be a better man than he was. And, you wanted to see your mother happy."

"Right."

"That's why the incident with Uncle Freddie was so important to you. Your mother was a symbol for all women."

Steve bit his lip and nodded. "Yes, I think I understand."

"There's more to it isn't there?"

Steve gave him a blank look. "Steve, answer the question. There's more to it, isn't there?"

Steve flushed. "Why do you ask?"

"Because there usually is. It can be very painful to uncover the truth. If you want to change, you'll have to do it. You've been hiding from the truth for so long, it's become your reality. I'll ask this only once. Did your father abuse your sister?"

Steve gulped. "I don't want to talk about that."

"You've been suppressing ugly memories for decades. That takes a lot of effort."

"I can't talk about it."

"You can, and you must."

Steve began to sob. Tears ran down his face. "She didn't want to. He made her. I hate him. I hate him."

"He did it more than once, didn't he?"

Steve nodded. "Every payday he came home drunk. He locked my little brother, mom and me in the tool shed. We could hear Sally screaming. 'No! Please stop! You're hurting me.' Then there would be silence. My mom held us tight whenever it happened. But she never tried to stop it. She'd say, 'I'm sorry boys. He'll kill me if I say anything.' The worst thing was, he made Sally put on her Sunday dress the next morning and come out and unlock the shed. I felt so sorry for her."

"That must have been frightening."

"It was awful. You have no idea. I still have nightmares."

"I know that must have been hard for you to talk about. But it's important that you share experiences like that. It's the only way you're going to get better. You've been carrying around a huge sack filled with ugly memories for year and years."

Steve blew his nose and regained his composure. "Phew. Doc, I never told anyone about my sister. I feel like a truck ran over me. I don't know how much of this I can take."

"Once you get started, you'll be surprised by the progress you'll make. One more thing. Did you have a girlfriend when you were a teenager? Someone very special?"

"Mary Lou. I loved her more than anything."

"Isn't that when you started smoking?"

"Yes. It must have been a coincidence. I started sneaking a cigarette or two. There was nothing significant about it."

The doctor gave Steve a quizzical look. "Maybe you were relying on cigarettes to help you cope with reality?"

"Could be, I guess."

"You said college seemed like a candy store." Steve grinned. "Making girls happy was very important to you. You wanted to be better than the other guys; better than your dad."

"That's right."

"Later in college you were serious with two or three women."

"Yes. There was Rhonda, Suzanne and Kate."

"Three girlfriends at the same time? Didn't you think that was unusual?"

"No. What's wrong with dating three girls at the same time?"

"Dating is one thing. But it was more than dating, wasn't it?"

"I guess."

"Steve, wasn't it more than dating?"

He looked sheepish. "Yes."

"How many of your friends had more than one girlfriend at a time?"

"None. I was the only one."

"Did you ever wonder about that?"

"No."

"Why do you think you had three girlfriends at the same time?"

"I don't know. I never thought about it. You're the expert. You tell me."

"It's not uncommon for sex addicts to have multiple relationships"

"Why is that?"

"Most addicts cannot establish intimate relationships. They view women as objects."

"But I loved them."

"You loved the sex. There's a difference. Many addicts draw energy from their passion. They see each woman as a unique challenge, a novel experience. It's like watching a woman undress for the first time."

"But we made love."

"You made love; that doesn't mean you loved."

"But ..."

Dr. Jones interrupted. "When you were with a woman, what was it like? What was your goal?"

"I wanted to make her happy, make her have more than one orgasm."

"And when you were with another woman?"

"It was the same. I tried to make her come two or three times. What's wrong with that?"

"Your goals were sex-focused. You haven't said a thing about the woman's endearing qualities or personality or how you felt about her. And when you married Suzanne, you continued your affair with Kate."

"That's right."

"Did your friends say anything?"

"Nah. They joked about it. They thought I was a stud."

"How did you treat Suzanne and Kate?"

"Like I thought they deserved to be treated. I loved them the same. Equally."

"And then you fell in love with another woman."

"Christina."

"You were having relations with three women and you had the same feelings for each one? Is that what you're saying?"

"Yes. I loved them."

"And then there was a fourth and a fifth?"

"Yes, I was in love with all of them."

"Steve, you made love to each of them. Didn't that bother you?"

"No, why should it? They were happy."

"Steve, they were sex objects to you. You equated sex with love. But you didn't have a loving relationship. Because you weren't able to be intimate. You weren't honest with them or yourself. Do you see the difference?"

"I'm beginning to …"

"Fast forward to the present. Suppose you get the job offer in North Carolina. What happens?"

"I'm in a tobacco state." He snickered. "I'll probably feel like I'm back in college."

"Exactly. If you don't stay strongly committed to changing, you'll behave like a college kid."

"No, I won't. I won't let that happen."

"What do you think lies ahead?"

"I don't have a clue."

"Here's my take. In the first few months on the job everything will be new and exciting. You won't have time to think about anything else. Like women. And finding the next sex partner."

"Probably so."

"By midterm you'll have your feet on the ground. You'll see an attractive woman. 'Not bad,' you'll say to yourself. Maybe she'll smile or you'll strike up a conversation. In the past, under those circumstances, what would you have done?"

"That's easy. I'd get a hard-on."

"You'd have those old feelings. Then what?"

"I'd fanaticize about her and masturbate."

"Then what?"

"I'd feel hooked. Like I have to see her."

"Right. You *need* her, like you used to need a cigarette. Months can pass. But the addiction is still there. It's lying in wait. If you give in, you'll pull out a cigarette and light up."

"No. I don't want to. How do I prevent that from happening?"

"That's the $64,000 question. If you give in, you'll be back to a pack a day."

"There must be a way to stop."

"Steve, there is no magic cure. Some people never stop."

"Why not?"

"It may be due to a lack of willpower. Or a lack of commitment. Some people think it will be easy. When they find out it isn't, they give up. Some sex addicts are like the smoker who says, 'I can quit anytime. All I have to do is skip my morning cup of coffee and stay away from bars.' The same applies to alcohol, drug and gambling addicts."

"I've heard that."

"Stopping an addiction takes much more than simply avoiding a situation. You have to change your behavior, be on guard constantly, watch everything you do. In your case, that means no flirting."

"I don't know, Doc."

"It's like reprogramming yourself. That's why it's so important to have a friend to talk to. What do you think?"

"I'll discuss it with Kate. I'm sure I can count on her."

"Let me know what happens. If she's willing, I'll arrange a time for the three of us to talk."

***

The Wurlitzer flashed psychedelic colors at Frank's Diner downtown. Carly Simon sang "You're So Vain." Townies recapped Ruston High School's victory over Blytheville. A group of university boosters talked about the chances of EAU beating the Razorbacks.

Some good ol' boys at a corner table shook their heads, pointed fingers and jumped on each other's remarks. Others buzzed about the headline in the *Daily Gazette:* SCHILLING NAMED N.C. PRESIDENT.

A geezer with a flattop smacked the paper down. "Can you believe that? We get a good president and he's up and gone."

"Yeah," a farmer in bib overalls said. "I liked him. He was a lot like Bill Thornton."

A plaid flannel shirt weighed in. "I heard some of the faculty were upset because he was getting a little on the side."

The gangly guy at the end of the table chimed in. "So what? Everyone up there is screwing someone."

The flannel shirt added his two cents. "From what I've heard it was more than a little. He'll have to make some big-time changes if he's going to last in North Carolina."

COMING SOON

COSTLY AFFAIR

CHAPTER ONE

Steve Schilling slammed on the brakes in front of Mercy Hospital and grabbed a parking ticket from the valet. At the information desk, he caught his breath. "What room is Elizabeth Webster in?"

A woman with tight blue curls and a sweet smile glanced at the printout on her desk then made eye contact with him. "She's in 732."

"Thanks." He ran for the elevator. After discharging passengers at floors two through six, the elevator stopped. He spotted Brittany Haywood, Elizabeth's administrative assistant, speaking with a nurse.

He ran to meet them outside Elizabeth's room.

"You can go in," Brittany said.

Steve cracked the door and peered in. A cocoon of tubes and wires enveloped the patient. A vital-signs monitor beeped. He tiptoed to the bed, kissed Elizabeth on the forehead and touched her raven hair, plastered to her scalp.

Her eyelids fluttered.

"How are you doing, sweetie?"

She gave him a half-smile. "Better now that you're here."

He pressed his fingers to her lips. "Sh, we can talk later."

Her eyes closed.

"They've done an MRI," Brittany whispered as she walked in. "The results will be available after lunch."

"Is her head still throbbing?"

"Less since the morphine kicked in." Brittany turned for the door. "I'm going to grab a sandwich and call Lizbeth's father with an update. Can I bring you something?"

Steve shook his head. "I can't eat."

He pulled a chair next to the bed and said a prayer, then leafed through a *Sports Illustrated.*

"Mr. Webster is on his way up," Brittany said when she returned.

Dr. Charles Woods, the chief of staff, and Elizabeth's father led a team of interns into the suite, painted a soothing pale green. In a firm voice, Dr. Woods asked, "How are you feeling, Elizabeth?"

"About the same," she said weakly. "Things are still fuzzy."

"That's to be expected. We have the results of the MRI."

Her eyes opened. She squeezed Steve's hand. "Go ahead, Dr. Woods."

"You have a tumor on your brain the size of a tennis ball." She gasped. Steve tightened his grip. "The good news is it's not malignant."

"Thank God. Are you sure?"

"I'm 99 percent certain. It's a meningioma — with a smooth surface and no tentacles." Elizabeth frowned. Dr. Woods continued. "Think of the meningioma as a hairnet holding your brain in place. Technically, the tumor is not attached to your brain. Do you want to see the MRI?"

She glanced at Steve. He nodded.

"Yes, I would."

The doctor held up the film and pointed to the light area over the left eye. "It may be blurry to you but this large mass is the tumor. It's pressing on your optic nerve, causing your blurred vision and creating pressure on your brain. That's the reason for the headaches."

"Can you remove it?"

"I can't, but there are specialists who can. I'll be conferring with them. For now, I want you to rest and try not to worry."

***

In his hotel room, Steve fell to his knees and clasped his hands as he had done countless times since he was a boy. "God, please take care of her," he sobbed. *I don't know what I'd do without her. She's my everything. I can't lose her.*

Unbuttoning his shirt, he stretched out on the king-size bed and recalled the first time they'd talked in a social setting — the Pacesetters Winter Ball in the Omni's Grand Ballroom. She was exquisite in a navy georgette cocktail dress with a deep V neckline. Hobnobbing at Charlotte's most prominent black-tie event, she took his breath away. He had wanted to undress her, unfasten her chignon — one hairpin at a time — and make love all night.

But she was much more than eye candy. She seemed to know everyone: the governor, North Carolina's senators, and East Coast media bigwigs. *What a turn-on.*

Ed Barkley, one of his top fundraising prospects, walked over, interrupting Steve's sexual fantasy. "What brings the president of Mountain State to a high-powered event like this?"

"I'm meeting influential people like you. Selling the university wherever I can."

"Sounds like you're buttering me up."

Steve flashed his megawatt smile. "Well, that goes with the territory. I'm organizing a presidential task force of community leaders."

"That sounds interesting. What's your intent?"

"We'll shape our plans on what surfaces at a series of focus groups this spring. May I count on you to attend?"

"I look forward to that. But you don't have to sell me on Mountain State. I met my wife there and our three kids are graduates."

"Alums like you will play an important role in shaping our future. Ideas from the community and campus reps will help us forge a strong partnership."

"Sounds good, Steve. You developed good practices at Arkansas. Your reputation as a strong leader is widely known and admired."

Steve blushed. "We had a good leadership team."

"C'mon. You went Division I, scheduled SEC schools and added a doctorate in education. Don't be modest. You built a new stadium, increased enrollment and got several million-dollar gifts."

"We had a good run. Now I'm focused on Mountain State."

"Are you approaching Lizbeth tonight?"

"Lizbeth?"

"Elizabeth Webster. She's Elizabeth in the office, but she's Lizbeth to friends."

"Thanks for the tip. And yes, I plan to pitch to her."

"Saving the best for last?" Ed grinned. "Her son graduated from Mountain State. He goes by his dad's name. Webster is her maiden name. She has a daughter in graduate school, too."

"You must know her well."

"Lizbeth and I serve on several boards. You're asking her for a biggie, right?"

"I need to learn more about her interests first."

Ed stepped closer to Steve. "Don't beat around the bush. She's a woman of action, not one to piddle around. If I were you, I'd ask for $10 million. But that's off the record."

"Ten million?"

"She can afford to do whatever she wants — and she usually does. She's big on technology, runs her corporate meetings from her office. And don't ignore basketball. She's a fanatic."

"I'll have to rethink …"

Ed cut him off. "Don't play guessing games with her. Be bold or you'll get nothing. Tell her you need a new basketball arena and you want her to pay for it."

"Ask her to foot the whole bill?" Steve's face flushed. "That could cost $15 million or more."

"She follows the Tarheels and the Blue Devils. If North Carolina or Duke is in the final four, she's there. Tell her you'll put her daddy's name on it."

"Are you sure?"

"Is my name Ed Barkley? Of course, I'm sure. You have any naming opportunities associated with the basketball arena?"

"There'll be two or three in the million-dollar range — the press box, loges, reception areas."

"Put Lizbeth's name on the press box. Who knows? Maybe she'll broadcast your basketball games. Think what that would do for recruitment in Charlotte."

"I'll think about it."

"Don't think too much. Hit it off with her and you can write your own ticket." Ed pointed to a tall, Spanish-looking guy. "See that guy?"

"Sure. You can't miss him."

"Two or three like him show up at every event — thirty-something, good-looking, and with all the right moves. He's going to hit on Lizbeth."

"Really?"

"You bet. Once in a while one of them strikes it rich with a hot socialite. He screws her until her daddy finds out. Before you know it he's back on the prowl, his pockets bulging with cash."

"I thought that only happened on TV."

"Think again. Here he comes."

Steve watched the gigolo stroll across the dance floor and stop reverentially behind Lizbeth. When she finished her conversation and turned to face him, he whispered in her ear.

She strolled over to the band leader. Moments later the band stuck up "El Choclo" ("Kiss of Fire," as popularized by several vocalists in the 1950s).

Lizbeth unpinned her hair and shook it. It cascaded over her shoulders. Steve's gaze turned to the large diamond-studded pendant hanging in her cleavage. Lizbeth wrapped her arms around her partner's back and pressed her breasts into his chest. He thrust his hips into hers. Her upper body arched gracefully as he guided her across the floor. Over her shoulder, she caught Steve's eye and winked.

"Did you see that?" Ed asked.

"See what?"

Ed slapped Steve on the back. "You saw it. She winked at you."

"I thought she was winking at you."

"Come on, Steve. You know her better than you've led me to believe."

"We've spoken a few times at the regional economic development forum. Last month I stopped by her place at Lake Lure to drop off a report."

"Lake Lure? You've been to her mountain home? Hell, I'd go for the whole enchilada."

***

When the crowd had thinned, Steve sauntered over to her table. After ending a conversation with the woman next to her, Lizbeth looked up. "I wondered how long it'd take you. I'd like you to meet my administrative assistant, Brittany Hayward."

"It's a pleasure to meet you." He reached for her hand. "I'm Steve Schilling."

"Yes. I know. You're taller than I expected."

"That'll be all, Brittany," Lizbeth said.

"Nice to meet you, Mr. President." She flipped her waist-length blonde hair over her shoulder and walked away.

He sat down in Brittany's seat. "Ed Barkley said you prefer to be called Lizbeth. Do you?"

"Yes, I do."

"You're a very popular woman. And a good dancer too."

"Did you notice?" She smirked. "That was for you."

"Me? I thought you winked at Ed."

"I don't think so."

"He thinks very highly of you."

"He's a difference maker. We serve together on several committees."

"So he said."

"Is that all he said?"

"No."

"What else?"

"That your son is a graduate of Mountain State, and that you're a basketball nut."

"And that you should ask me for a big donation, I bet."

"That too, but mostly we talked about you."

Lizbeth wore a quizzical expression. "So what do you know about Elizabeth Webster?"

"Not enough. Why don't you tell me more?"

She pursed her lips. "Do you always answer a question with a question?"

"Only when I'm interested in learning more."

"Smooth," she said, gazing into his eyes. "What would you like to know?"

Steve shrugged. "What do you like to do? Where do you like go? What do you do for fun?"

"Is this twenty questions?"

"Sort of."

"My age and weight are classified."

Steve morphed into a robot, arms flailing. "Warning! Warning! Critical data missing."

She laughed. "Okay. I'm the president and CEO of Webster International Media Group. I do what most Fortune 500 presidents do. And I love to shop. I'm divorced and have two grown children. The rest of the bio is on the website."

"I know. I've read it."

"Then why all the questions?"

"I'm interested in hearing what you have to say."

"Brittany said you're not like most men. What did she mean?"

"Beats me. I guess you'll have to find out." He winked. "Tell me about your kids."

"Richie is thirty-one. I'm grooming him to become our financial VP."

"And your daughter?"

"You are on top of things."

"I try."

"She's a lot like me." Lizbeth paused. "No, that's not right. She's like I wanted to be. She's very attractive and has had several small movie roles."

"She must be a knockout."

"She's beautiful, but she takes after Arnold's side."

"Arnold?"

"He's my ex. He runs our paper here in Charlotte."

"He works for you?"

Lizbeth nodded. "Some people think that's strange, but he's a damn good newspaperman. I just don't sleep with him."

Steve fell silent.

She cocked her head. "Aren't you going to ask who I do sleep with?"

"I thought that would be forward. And gauche."

"You're probably right. But I'll tell you anyway. I don't have a significant other. And I don't sleep around."

Steve tried a new tack. "What do you know about Steve Schilling?"

"A lot. I had Brittany run a search."

"Do you run a search on everyone?"

"Almost always on people I don't know. I want to know where I'm walking."

"Interesting." Steve rubbed his chin. "Where'd you pick up that phrase?"

"My daddy always said, 'You need to know the other person's agenda before you say a word.'"

"Makes sense."

"When I read Brittany's report, I said, 'This guy has had an impressive career.'"

"I've worked hard all of my life."

"You won extra points in the receiving line."

"What do you mean?"

"You were the only man who didn't sneak a peek."

He smiled. "You're talking about the diamond pendant, of course."

She gave him a sexy smile. "You looked me straight in the eye. I liked that."

"I peeked before."

"Aren't you the sly one?"

"Anything else you want to know?"

"I've read your resume and some stories in the *Ruston Daily Gazette*. I know you're recently divorced and you have a reservation at the Sheraton tonight."

"You know everything."

"Not quite. Want to dance?"

They fell into the rhythm of a familiar waltz. He liked her self-confident air — and the way her firm breasts pressed against him.

She snuggled closer, slid her hands under his tuxedo jacket to the small of his back.

He looked into her sparkling brown eyes. "Are you trying to turn me on?"

"Maybe," she whispered.

"May I talk about Mountain State for a few minutes?"

"I thought you'd never ask."

***

Brittany and Steve stood when Dr. Woods and Lizbeth's dad walked in. "I have wonderful news," the doctor said.

"What is it?" Lizbeth asked.

"Dr. Henry Brem at Johns Hopkins has agreed to review your case. He's the head of their meningioma center. It's ranked # 1 in the world."

"That's terrific."

"I overnighted a CD of your MRI. His team of surgeons evaluated it this morning. The panel meets regularly to determine who's best qualified for each case. I've had Dr. Brem's conference call transferred to your room. It should be coming any moment."

Dr. Woods picked up the ringing phone. "Yes, Dr. Brem. I'm putting you on speakerphone." He pressed the button.

"Lizbeth, this is Dr. Brem. Can you hear me?"

"Yes, please go ahead."

"I want to be very candid. The size of your tumor is a real concern. Left unchecked, it could be fatal. I'd like to put you on steroids immediately to shrink it. Do you understand?"

"Yes. Will the steroids produce any side effects?"

"Only short-term. We can talk about that before surgery. Since you're experiencing headaches and blurred vision, I'd like to schedule your surgery for next Tuesday. I've done hundreds of these procedures. Your tumor is one of the largest I've seen, but I don't anticipate any problems."

Lizbeth turned to Steve. "Can you be there?"

"Of course, dear."

"Tuesday is fine, Dr. Brem."

"I don't want you to fly," the surgeon said. "We can't risk air-pressure changes."

Lizbeth's dad spoke. "Earl will drive you and Brittany to Baltimore. Steve and I will fly up this weekend."

"That sounds ideal. We'll do your pre-op on Monday," Dr. Brem said. "I'll see you then."

CPSIA information can be obtained at www.ICGtesting.com
Printed in the USA
LVOW10s0340211113

362062LV00007B/66/P

9 781618 635594